THE
ORDER
OF THE
MAGI

AUTHORED BY
CONNOR PRITCHARD

ILLUSTRATED BY
CONOR BUCKLEY

EDITED BY
DAN SPENCER

ISBN: 0615681786

ISBN 13: 9780615681788

Library of Congress Control Number: 2012946703

I dedicate this book to my muse and little sister, Katelyn Mae Rose Pritchard.

Katy, I just erased dozens of sentences and drank two bottles of wine trying to think of the right words to thank you for giving me this idea.

All I could come up with is this list.

1) You inspire me.

2) You keep my ego in check.

3) I love you, Muppet. This is all yours.

CHAPTER I:
THE TWO OF HEARTS

ATLAS MOUNTAINS, MOROCCO

Rachel Alexander stepped out of her tent and swung her medical kit over her shoulder. The sun had just dipped below the Atlas Mountains, creating a jagged pattern of shadows in the valley below. She stopped to absorb the panoramic view. Of all the places she and her husband had traveled for humanitarian missions, Morocco was one of her favorites. She loved countries where two vastly different cultures had beat each other into submission and settled for a draw; in this case, it was a unique blend of Arab and African. She clicked with the rugged beauty of her temporary home, but it was the people who made her get out of bed. Rachel was born to be a doctor.

She allowed herself a final deep breath and then made her way through their mobile village, which consisted of twenty Bedouin-style tents and fifty-four inhabitants. As the sand parted beneath her boots, her mind shifted back to doctor mode and she began running through her mental checklist.

Rachel and her husband, David, ran a remote mountain school for orphan girls. They took in young women off the streets who had been abandoned or escaped the physical and sexual abuse of their male relatives. David and Rachel tried to find them before they were taken and sold into prostitution rings. Each new girl they rescued brought a heartbreaking backstory to camp. The majority of them had hepatitis A from drinking stool-contaminated water. Rachel had just traveled down to Marrakesh to pick up a new shipment of vaccines. As she made her way through camp, she kicked around creative ways to ease the girls' fear of syringes. Trust took a while to earn here.

At sixteen, Zahra was the oldest. She had been with them for two years. The other twenty-nine girls were under twelve. David and Rachel made weekly trips to the cities to find more. Some easily trusted the American man and the British woman, but most didn't. They had to set up camp in the secluded foothills of the Atlas Mountains because many of the Islamic madrasahs outlawed the educating of women. However, David and Rachel lived by two guidelines when operating in a third-world country: rule number one—never try to change things; rule number two—out of sight out of mind. Most tribal leaders didn't want Westerners breaking their laws right in front of them. The illusion of control was more important than actually having it.

Rachel reached the massive tent that they used as their classroom, common area, and mess hall. It was a Moroccan-style pavilion with high A-framed ceilings, and it was firmly tethered to the ground with two dozen roped stakes.

She heard her husband's warm voice through the canopy opening. "Who's ready for a bedtime story?"

The little girls responded with excitement, and Rachel knew she couldn't ruin their mood with the injections. *Tomorrow*, she thought, *David can help me think of a clever game to administer them.* She stopped outside the tent to greet Yousef, an elderly stick figure of a Berber. He was riding an exercise bike that was attached to a car battery powering a string of lights. David and Rachel's son, Isaac, had designed it for a class project. *Cheaper and quieter than a generator. Pretty smart for a seventeen-year-old*, she thought.

"How're the legs feeling tonight?" Rachel asked, slapping him on the back.

Yousef gave her a fearless smile revealing a tongue that looked like it was trying to break out of prison. "I feel as if I could win the Tour de France, Mrs. Rachel."

"All right, whistle if you need anything," Rachel said.

Yousef tried to whistle through his teeth and failed. Rachel chuckled. She was so much like her brother Jack—they both thoroughly enjoyed teasing people. The old man pumped harder, and the lights surged as Rachel entered.

She was greeted by a bright-green laptop in her face. "Say hello to Isaac, honey," David said. "He's giving a presentation on his bike battery tomorrow."

Zahra, an intense but beautiful Moroccan girl with green eyes, aimed the recording webcam at Rachel. Rachel said, "I would have put on some makeup if I knew I was going to be on camera." Everyone knew she didn't need it. She looked just as good brushing her teeth as she did in an evening gown at one of her husband's fundraisers.

David scooted into the frame and wrapped his arm around his wife. He was older than Rachel but still lean muscled and sporting well-groomed black and gray hair. "Isaac, buddy, the girls and I wanted to thank you for your invention." David spoke with a relaxed but highly confident voice that had become a staple of the new class of American

3

entrepreneurs. He was the kind of person who commanded authority but would roll up his sleeves and help you get the job done.

Rachel said, "Here it is in action." She pulled back the canvas flap to reveal Yousef and the bike in the foreground with the starry sky as the backdrop.

Yousef waved and smiled. "*Marhaba*, Sir Isaac."

Zahra focused the webcam back on David. "We're done with our schoolwork, and now, thanks to your bike, I can read the girls a bedtime story. Girls, tell Isaac what we're reading."

Zahra panned right, and twenty-plus Moroccan girls responded, "*The Wizard of Oz*." A smile even cracked through Zahra's hard face.

"Thanks again, honey," Rachel said. "Good luck in school, and we love you."

Zahra ended the recording and started converting the video to send to Isaac via e-mail.

Rachel leaned in toward her husband, "Are you sure you want to send that? Aren't we trying to keep a low profile?"

David pulled his wife close and gave her a reassuring kiss on the temple. "We'll be fine. Besides, I think something's up with Isaac. He's been distant the last few months. I thought that if he saw his invention in action, it would cheer him up a bit."

Right after Zahra sent the file, all the light except the glow from the laptop went out. The young girls shrieked and grabbed for each other. Rachel and David laughed when they heard Yousef trying to whistle.

"Calm down," David said with another laugh. "Yousef probably cramped up."

David stepped outside. Yousef was frozen, staring away from the tent.

He looked out and a jolt of panic shot from the nerve endings in his colon to the tips of his ears. Thirty Arab men on horseback surrounded their small outpost. They held torches that were being lit from horse to horse. The firelight illuminated their covered faces, and David could see they were armed with swords. He immediately thought they were the Islamic Maghreb. They had come to shut down the girls' school.

His gut reaction proved wrong when he saw one of the men pull off his keffiyeh and let it fall to his shoulders. *They had come for* him, *not the girls*. He knew these men. They were Corsairs, violent mercenaries from Turkey employed by an even more dangerous madman. They had found him—just like they had found the others.

A guttural Arabic voice came from a bearded man. "We have come for the American man and the British woman. Resist and you will be struck down."

Some of the workers poked their heads out of their tents, but most of them stayed inside. David watched the bearded man give hand signals to his soldiers. Every other rider dismounted in unison. The men on horseback grabbed the unmanned horses and spread out to maintain a perimeter. *These are highly trained assassins,* David thought. *I can take a few of them, but not all of them.* The men on foot unsheathed their *saifs*, which were long, curved swords, and held their torches high. They began to slice through the ropes holding up the Bedouin tents, which trapped the occupants under heavy canvas. They tossed the torches onto the collapsed fabric.

The herdsman, farmers, and workers kicked and clawed their way out of the smoky tents. Murad, a barrel-chested farmer, ran toward a Corsair cursing at him in Darija, the Moroccan dialect of Arabic.

Without hesitation, the Corsair sliced him open with his blade. Murad clutched his chest and writhed on the ground as the life drained out of him. The villagers who had crawled out of their tents tried to escape but ran right into the perimeter of men on horseback. The camp was in chaos as the Corsairs continued to smoke out the workers by cutting down their tents and lighting them on fire.

David looked to Yousef. "Guard this tent with your life. Do you understand me?"

Yousef nodded in fear.

David darted inside and pulled his wife close. "It's him."

Rachel had worked in hospitals so long she rarely panicked. She calmly asked, "What do we do?"

Zahra stepped closer to overhear.

David said, "We have to get word to Jack."

Zahra peeked outside and watched the men on horseback lighting the tents on fire. Their inhabitants scampered on all fours like animals. The Corsairs were slicing the men open and kicking the women into submission. Zahra had witnessed very ugly things her whole life but nothing this atrocious.

The girls in the tent covered their ears to hide from the cacophony. Zahra turned to David and Rachel and asked, "Who are these men? Why do they do this?"

"Everything will be fine," David said. "Stay here and protect the girls."

"They look for *you*," she said. "You cannot escape, but I can. What do you need done?"

David hesitated. "I'm not involving you in this."

Zahra grabbed David's forearm and dug her fingernails in to express her seriousness. "You saved my life. Let me help you."

"If anyone can sneak out, it's Zahra," Rachel said while looking at David.

David took a deep breath and looked back at his wife. "Stay here with the girls. Zahra, come with me."

David and Zahra crawled under the canvas tent and escaped just as Yousef was kicked in the stomach and knocked unconscious with the butt of a sword. A Turkish Corsair used the tip of his curved sword to push open the tent folds and step inside. The moon backlit his figure and made the shadow of his sword look larger than it was.

Rachel attempted to calm the girls by stepping in front of them. "Don't worry. Everything will be fine. Look down."

Then the Corsair violently grabbed Rachel by her hair, kicked her legs out from under her, and wrestled a black hood over her head. The girls screamed as he pulled her into the darkness. Only the drag marks from her heels remained.

Outside, David and Zahra sprinted toward his tent on the far side of camp. David yanked Zahra down behind a drum of water as two Corsairs flew by on horseback. They stopped a few meters away, and David overheard the men speaking in Arabic. Zahra leaned in and quietly translated to David. "They have Rachel."

"She's the only woman here that's as tough as you. She'll be all right," David said reassuringly as he pulled Zahra close to him. She had not been this close to a man since she escaped the fat slob who had bought her from her father. She hated all men, except David. He was good. He was the only man who had never tried to touch her. He had taught her how to read and write. Her head was right against David's chest, and she found it strange that his heart was beating slowly and steadily. *Why is he so calm?* The men on horseback galloped away, and David dragged her toward his tent. "Come on."

David pulled Zahra into his tent and retrieved a briefcase from under his bed. A sliver of moonlight allowed Zahra to see that it was no ordinary briefcase. David put his index finger on an electronic pad and the case clicked open. Inside the case were stacks of American bills, passports, an ornate wooden box, and a stone case. David turned on a portable lantern and then quickly opened the stone case. Zahra inched closer to get a better look at the object. It was a silver rod about a half meter long, covered in dozens of engraved symbols. It looked more like a machine than a work of art. Before Zahra could bend down, David quickly tucked the object into the back of his belt.

"Can you get across the water to Gibraltar?" David asked. He then handed her a thick roll of American one-hundred-dollar bills wrapped in a rubber band.

Zahra shoved the money into her knee-high slippers. "Mr. Alexander, before I met you, I had to steal my food. I know how to get places without being noticed."

David put his hand on her face. His gentle touch calmed her nerves. For a brief moment, he lost himself in her otherworldly green eyes. "What I am about to give you is what these men are after. It cannot fall into their hands. Do you understand me?"

Zahra nodded, and David handed her a dark wooden case. She ran her fingers over the engraving on the outside of the box. "What is this?"

"These are very old and very special. It's important that you get these to my son and Rachel's brother in Gibraltar. Find a trustworthy man who will take you across the strait. Walk into the first tavern that you find and ask for Jack O'Ryan. Can you do that?"

"What if I can't find him?" Zahra asked.

"Trust me," David said smiling. "Any pub will do."

Zahra knew how to take care of herself, but she was worried about them. "What's going to happen to you?"

Before David could respond, a Corsair stormed the tent. He saw David and pulled his sword. "American scum!"

"Go now, Zahra. Remember what I taught you." David kissed her on the forehead and turned to face the swordsman.

As Zahra scrambled underneath the tent, she looked back. The lantern inside illuminated their shadows on the wall. David pulled the silver object out from his belt and held it in front of his waist. He twisted his wrists in the opposite direction. Both ends of the rod shot out into a long metallic staff.

It is some kind of weapon, she thought.

David crouched into a fighting stance. "You should have brought your friends, Turk."

The Corsair lunged at David. He sidestepped the thrusting sword and used his staff to strike the enemy in the temple. The Turk's knees hit first, and then he collapsed. Zahra popped up from her backpedaling crab walk and ran for the edge of the camp.

She was about to reach the ridge of the mountain when two mounted riders appeared and cut her off. One of them jumped off his horse and closed in on her. Before Zahra could change directions, she heard something slice through the thin mountain air. A small metal wire coiled around the Corsair's neck and violently yanked him like a fish being pulled out of the water. It had been shot from the tip of David's staff. He detached the cord and let the Turk struggle for his last breath. Like a flash, David darted around her and landed a leaping staff strike on the second Corsair. Zahra watched his jaw almost unhinge from his face and then snap back. His consciousness disappeared from his eyes faster than David had moved. He slumped off the horse facefirst and smashed his cheek on a jagged rock.

"Remember *everything* I taught you," David said. Before she could respond, he had disappeared into the night. *Who, or what, was this man she thought she knew?*

Ptolemy Soter calmed his Arab stallion as it watched the violence unfold through its disc-shaped eyes. Women were being tied up, tents were burning, and the all the commotion had kicked up a pall of dust. Soter found himself eerily calm in violent situations. He attributed it to years of military service and the gradual drowning of all emotions except his cold motivating anger and the warm gratification of victory. He knew deep down that he was a sociopath of the highest level. But so were Napoleon, Alexander the Great, Genghis Khan, and anyone else who had imposed his will on the world. *Let them study me postmortem.* After *I've made my mark,* he thought.

Redbeard, a burly Turkish Corsair with an auburn-dyed beard, stopped his horse in front of Soter's. "We have the wife," Redbeard said, "but he killed two men, and there is a girl escaping down the mountain."

"I see." Soter always had the same reaction. He'd studied the great commanders; he knew not to react too soon or too brashly. He watched as one of Redbeard's Corsairs pulled Rachel toward him. He wasn't easily impressed by women, but he had researched Rachel's entire life and something about her intrigued him. She had fire, like him, even though she was a bit uncouth for a Brit. He dismounted and approached.

Rachel yelled, "I know who you are!"

"Good. That will save me time," said Soter. "Where is your husband?"

"Probably killing your men," Rachel said.

"Even better. More room on the flight home," Soter said with a cold grin.

A voice interrupted from the darkness. "What do you want from us, Soter?" David stepped out of the shadows. He held his magnificent bow staff behind his back.

Soter looked him over. "*Another* staff. I've amassed quite a collection lately." He looked to Redbeard. "How many exactly?"

"Two dead," Redbeard said. "One captured." David stared into the Turk's cold eyes.

"What do you want with us?" David asked.

"It's your *boy* that I'm looking for. You've hid him quite well," Soter said.

"Why Isaac?" David asked. "He has nothing to do with this."

"You would know the answer to that question if you spent less time trying to save the world and more time with your son," he answered. "Take him *alive*."

Ten Turkish Corsairs unsheathed their saifs and surrounded David. He twisted the middle of the rod, and a small, cone-shaped weight and chain dropped to the dirt just as one of the Corsairs attacked. David had turned his bow staff into a flail and wrapped the Corsair's leg. He pulled back, and the man's head whipped to the ground. David spun and wrapped the chain around a saif coming right at him. He then brought the back end of his bow staff over the top and knocked the Corsair out with a swift strike.

Redbeard began to dismount, but Soter stopped him with the calm wave of a hand. "Let him wear himself out."

David countered the Corsairs' attacks with his bow staff and quickly subdued four of the ten assailants. His weapon was designed to maim, not kill. One Corsair went down, gasping for air after David introduced his Adam's apple to the back of this throat. The remaining Corsairs regrouped and surrounded him.

"That's enough!" Soter yelled from horseback.

Redbeard put a curved knife to Rachel's throat as David looked over.

David pushed down on his staff. The ball and chain retracted. He twisted again, and the metallic rods folded back into the center piece. His weapon was like a medieval Swiss army knife. David dropped it and put his hands in the air. The remaining Corsairs tied him up and put a black hood over his head. One of the Corsairs picked up the staff. He pressed down, and a metal spike shot right through his hand. He screamed.

Soter watched him writhe on the ground. "All of their staffs are booby-trapped. Intricately weighted and balanced to be used by only one person." He pulled out a walkie-talkie. "Bring down the Augusta." Soter then turned back to Redbeard. "Kill the men. Leave the women, and then follow the girl. I have a feeling she might lead us right to our dear boy, Isaac."

Redbeard nodded. He pointed at three Corsairs, and they rode away on horseback.

A thundering Augusta helicopter emerged from the darkness and landed in the middle of the smoldering tents. Soter climbed in, and the Corsairs threw David and Rachel on board. Soter looked at the pilot, who wore night-vision goggles. "Take us to Thera."

CHAPTER 2:
THE TWO OF CLUBS

ROYAL NAVY BOARDING SCHOOL, GIBRALTAR

Isaac listened to his roommate, Gordie Mason, snoring and turned in his bunk. His brain quickly listed the disadvantages of being a seventeen-year-old insomniac:

- Classmates pegging him with vampire nicknames.
- Long, sleepless nights followed by uncontrollable fits of narcolepsy. The worst case having occurred on a movie date with

a local Spanish girl—she left, and he slept through three show-ings.

- A never-ending river of anxiety.

The only advantage was the cabinet full of prescriptions. They were his weapons of choice in his battle with sleep, and Isaac had the formula down to a science—early AM: One 60 mg Adderall and two Redbulls to wake up for morning classes; afternoon: two 10 mg Ritalin tablets to stay awake for afternoon classes, fencing, and rugby; late night: one 2 mg triscore Xanax to calm him down and one 20 mg Ambien to knock him out.

If Isaac didn't take his prescriptions, he would stay up all night and then have a bout of narcolepsy the next day, probably at the worst times possible. The regimen kept him on a normal schedule but had obvious side effects. First, Isaac had a perpetual cold that was noticeable from the dried snot on the cuffs of his favorite black hoodie, which he never washed. Second, his mind and body were constantly tense, as if he were the rope in a tug-of-war stalemate. It wasn't the healthiest way to live, but it was his only option.

Isaac was awake because he was dealing with a major crisis, and he was out of Ambien. He didn't have legal prescriptions, so he ordered them through his father's friend, Dr. Neville Ramanujan, and then had them forwarded to two different mailboxes before his uncle picked them up. Aside from being a philanthropist, Isaac's father was also a billion-aire, which made his son a potential target for kidnappers. From a very young age, Isaac had been trained on how to hide his identity.

Isaac hit his insomniac tipping point and realized that lying in bed was useless. He had something more troublesome on his mind, and he wanted to check on his latest shipment of meds.

Isaac sat up in his bed, powered up his iBook, and clicked on an open-source encrypted messenger program. The doctor was online using his screen name Aryabhata. Isaac logged in as Archimedes. Small chat icons of their respective historical figures appeared next to their dialogue.

Archimedes: Doc, u sleeping?

Aryabhata: I wish. My life has a tendency to unravel when
               I'm awake. Insomnia?

Archimedes: Ya, checking the ETA on the latest shipment of
               meds?

Aryabhata: Sent a week ago. It would be quicker if I could
               send them directly to you...

Archimedes: No can do. Strict orders to stay off the grid. You
               got time to look at some more sketches? Dreams
               have been intense lately. Starting to worry.

Aryabhata: Just tell me where you are. I can come visit you
               and give you an evaluation. I promise David
               won't find out.

Archimedes: Maybe, if it gets worse. I still need to get a sec-
               ond opinion.

Aryabhata: Send me your latest sketches, and we can discuss
               tomorrow.

Archimedes: Thanks, Doc. TTYL.

Isaac pulled his phone out, took photos of his latest sketches, and sent them through the built-in FTP site.

He jumped down off his bunk and looked at Gordie in envy. Isaac imagined he was probably dreaming about one of his two favorite things: damsels in distress or mashed potatoes. It was not a mistake that the two biggest loners bunked together. Gordie wanted to be left alone with his fantasy novels. Isaac wanted to be left alone with his inventions. Isaac threw on his black hoodie and opened up his medicine cabinet. All he had left was Percocet. He threw two in his pocket and sneaked out.

Isaac quietly crossed the courtyard, breaking up the blanket of ankle-high sea fog. Gibraltar had been a British naval stronghold since the War of Spanish Succession in the early 1700s. Now, the small peninsula was covered in British military bases and training academies like his secondary school. He enjoyed the strict academic regimen but would rather be in an environment that was more suited for a budding entrepreneur. For whatever reason, his father had placed him there and asked him to keep a low profile.

"Alexander!" A hushed yell shot through the night, and Isaac jumped.

Marty Keagan—the starting prop on the rugby team and all-around, pig-faced asshole—came out of the shadows. He was on night watch, a monthly requirement for all cadets.

"What, Keagan? I'm going to the library."

"You're so weird, Alexander. You stay up all night, and you sleep through class. You're not tough enough to be British, and you're too smart to be American. Are you a vampire?"

"Piss off. What do you want? I hacked the network last month so you guys would leave me alone. That was the deal."

It was true. Isaac had gotten around the academy's firewall so that his classmates could watch Internet porn. But Isaac wasn't like Nikola Tesla. He wasn't going to give his technology away for free. He had made a pact with three alpha males of his class, Keagan included: he'd hack the network, and they'd leave him the hell alone. Spit. Shake. Deal.

"I've already watched everything on youporn," Marty held out his hand. "Come on. I know you're holding."

Isaac saved his pain pills for this exact reason. Bribes. Pills were easier than booze to smuggle into the academy, and they didn't leave a noticeable stench like tobacco. Prescription pills ran the black market of the Royal Navy Academy.

"All I have are two Percocet," Isaac said as he placed them in Keagan's sweaty hoof.

"Don't get caught in there, or I'll find you on the pitch tomorrow," Marty said.

That was also true. Isaac's classmates couldn't just stomp him in plain sight, so they administered their punishments on the rugby field where it was applauded. Keagan then transferred the pain pills from hoof to snout, and Isaac sneaked into the library.

CHAPTER 2: THE TWO OF CLUBS

Isaac sat cross-legged in the psychology section of the empty library. It had taken two years, but he had navigated his enemies into a comfortable stalemate. However, there seemed to be a reoccurring pattern in Isaac's life. As soon as he slew one dragon, a bigger one showed up at his doorstep. Keagan and narcolepsy were like puppies and kittens compared to this fire-breather.

When Isaac would get bouts of narcolepsy during the day, intense visions accompanied them. Sometimes they would last five minutes, and sometimes they would last two hours. They were so vivid that he believed he was going crazy. His dreams felt more real than reality. When they increased in frequency, he sneaked off campus to visit a doctor. After hours of tests, the Spanish doctor diagnosed Isaac with prodromal schizophrenia. The prodrome phase occurs one to two years before the onset of full psychotic symptoms, namely hallucinations and paranoid delusions. Isaac had come to the painful conclusion that he had twenty-four months before he would need a steady diet of antipsychotics.

Over the previous six months, he had filled his journal with detailed sketches of his dreams and volumes of research on psychoactive disorders. That was the advice he was given by the only person he told about his disorder, Dr. Neville Ramanujan. Writing down his dreams was his only therapeutic release. He constantly worried about how he was going to tell his parents. However, Isaac had used his intelligence to beat everything else in his life, and he was going to find a way to beat schizophrenia—or at least to harness it. Isaac opened a half dozen psychology books on the floor. Then he opened his journal.

> Isaac Journal Entry #1
> Dear Myself,
> What's up, pussy? It's me again. Back to document our descent into crazy. Remember when we used to enjoy these dreams? Well, now they've put a ticking clock on our master plan. Granted, back in the day, they only happened every few months, but we

used to line the walls with our sketches. They looked like that computer game, Myst, that we played on Dad's laptop during the long flights to India. Now, if I don't take my meds, they occur daily. Daydreams, visions, hallucinations, I don't know what to label them, and I hate when I can't find something in my science books.

Anyways, as *you're* well aware, every dream starts and ends the same:

I wake up in a massive garden on an uninhabited island. When I was younger, I only wandered around the tropical plants and admired the snowcapped mountains in the distance. As I entered my teenage years, I became familiar with the reoccurring dream and taught myself how to enter a lucid state. To those of you reading my journal now (hopefully, I'm a famous inventor), a "lucid dream" simply means that your mind is fully aware that you're in a dream.

In the last two years, I have trained myself to enter this state of awareness. The bronze machines and terra-cotta walls feel real when I touch them. Now, I can closely examine intricate frescoes on the walls. When I wake up, I write down as much as I can remember.

I'm starting to get a decent map of the island. The central part is a huge temple surrounded by a round garden. When I climb to the top of the temple, I can see the island is made up of four concentric circles with round canals between them.

Sometimes, the dream feels like hours and I can walk to the outmost ring, and other times, it feels like minutes. I can tell my dream is about to end when I feel the earthquake. Seconds later, a massive tidal wave swallows the entire island. I drown and jolt awake. Usually, it happens when I've fallen asleep in class and is followed by insults from my fellow cadets.

Anyways, I'm just here to remind you, me and us (have to get comfortable talking to myself if we're going to go schizo soon) that we have two years to complete the three steps of our master plan.

2-Year Master Plan:
1) Graduate from the Royal Navy Boarding School, First Class Honors, and get accepted into James Martin Twenty-First Century School at Oxford.
2) Invent something that changes the world (for the better).
3) Meet a girl and lose my virginity.
No Problem. Remember, John Nash Jr. invented game theory when he was in the prodromal phase. So let's get to work. We can rest when we're schizo.

Sincerely,
Isaac Alexander
P.S. Wait a second, we've never even kissed a girl before. Maybe, we should start with that before we just jump right into the losing of our virginity.

Correction to 2-Year Master Plan:
3. Lose your virginity. Kiss a girl.

CHAPTER 3:

THE TWO OF DIAMONDS

PORT OF CASABLANCA, MOROCCO

"Little girl, it will cost you," said the stocky sailor as he eyed her. Zahra was too exhausted to care about the man's lechery. She'd been traveling all night.

"I have American dollars," Zahra said.

The sailor stood back, surprised that the young street girl had cash. "You little thief. Stealing from Westerners takes money out of *honest* men's pockets."

"Honest? What do you charge to shuttle Europeans across the strait? Then we can talk honest," Zahra said.

"Aggh. *Kawed!*" yelled the stocky sailor as he shooed her away from his boat.

Zahra looked around. Time was running out. The ferries to Tangier would not start for a few hours, and then she would have to catch another to Gibraltar.

As she walked down the pier, she thought about her journey.

She had felt her way down the mountainside by moonlight. It felt like days. Her hands were so cut and swollen she could barely make a fist. Her body was aching with exhaustion, and her empty stomach was making full sentences. She felt like she could fall asleep on the pier, but she had to keep going. She had come this far—hiked down a mountain, hitchhiked to Marrakech, and then taken a three-hour bus to Casablanca next to a disgusting Moroccan man who flossed his toes with his sock—she *had* to get to Gibraltar. The only people she cared about had just been kidnapped, and they had trusted *her* to save their son.

Zahra walked past another row of boats and a heard a voice. "Young one."

Zahra turned to see an elderly man pouring tea atop his boat.

"You will be hard pressed to find a captain at this hour," said the elderly man. Zahra studied him. He looked affable.

"Why is that?" Zahra asked.

"Most of them are still sleeping off hashish from last night. What is the nature of your trip?"

"I am looking for someone who will take my money and keep his mouth shut."

"Very well. Where are you going?"

"Gibraltar."

The elderly man took a sip of tea and stroked his white beard. "I will take you for three hundred American dollars," he said.

Zahra could feel the large roll of bills in her shoe. She had plenty of money but looked into the man's eyes for a final judgment call.

"How do I know I can trust you?" Zahra asked.

"I am too old to be intimate."

Everything in Zahra's gut told her to wait for another boat, but she knew that she had to get there as soon as possible. She pulled out the three hundred dollars and handed them to the man.

"When do we leave?" Zahra said.

"Right now. We will be in Gibraltar by nightfall," the elderly man said as he extended his hand to help her onto the boat. She purposely avoided it and pulled herself into the small cabin. As she stepped inside, she did not see the elderly man giving hand signals to the stocky sailor she had argued with earlier.

An hour later, the rickety boat was sailing up the coast of Morocco. "I will tell you when it warms up, young one," said the elderly man. "Stay inside and make some mint tea."

Zahra sat in the cabin and tried to adjust to the rhythmic dip of the waves. She had never been outside her country. It would be a waste to sit in the cabin the whole time.

The elderly man sang, and it calmed her down. She at least knew where he was on the boat. The eastern sun shone through the port light. Soon, she would go outside, but first, she reached into her linen pants. She had sewn in a secret pouch that rested right in front of her lady part. It was a precaution she had taken when living on the streets. Zahra pulled out the pine box and examined it. Like David's metal weapon, it was covered in intricate engravings. The most prominent was a large cross inside four concentric circles. She knew what a concentric circle was because David had taught her basic geometry, as well as English. Before she met them, her existence resembled that of a stray dog. In two years, they had expanded her life beyond what she thought was possible.

Zahra wasn't sure if she wanted to know the contents. She opened the latch but decided not to look yet. She placed it back in her pants and climbed out of the hatch.

"I told you to stay inside," said the elderly man. The stern tone caught Zahra off guard. She looked outside of the hatch and saw him. It was the stocky sailor she had argued with earlier. He was pulling his boat alongside of the elderly man's.

"I thought you said you were too *old*," Zahra said.

"It doesn't mean I can't watch," said elderly man in a threatening voice, all likeness to David had vanished.

Before Zahra could react, the elderly man closed the hatch. It swung down hard, smashing her fingers.

"Owwww!" Zahra screamed as she pulled back and fell down the ladder onto her back. The impact knocked the wind out of her, and she rolled onto her side to catch her breath.

"Stay put," the elderly man said as he fastened a lock on the hatch door.

Zahra's fingers throbbed. "You son of a whore! I should have never trusted you!"

As Zahra got up, the two fishing boats collided, and she fell to her knees. She was trapped. She had gone against her gut, and now she was stranded in the middle of the ocean as the bartering chip for a shady business deal. *Don't panic. You've been in worse situations.* Zahra looked around for a weapon but saw nothing except plastic plates and cups.

She overheard the stocky sailor board the ship, and they started to negotiate. "How much for her?" the stocky sailor asked.

"Did you see how beautiful she is?" said the elderly man. "She is not for sale. She is for rent."

Zahra was terrified, but she was not going to let anything happen. She was sixteen and had fought *hard* to remain a virgin. It was all she had left. Everything else had been taken from her. She was not going down without a fight. Zahra looked around and saw the teapots. *Good. Keep bartering, you pigs. I will have a surprise for you when you come down.*

Zahra fired up the stove and listened to the men discuss their deal.

"Three hundred dirham," said the stocky sailor.

"Aggh, Kawed," replied the elderly man. "I want double."

"Hear me out, old man. I pay three hundred dirham, and you keep your boat right here. I will go back and tell others to come to you."

I would rather jump off this boat and drown myself, Zahra thought. But she quickly recanted. She had to deliver David's message. In her heart, she knew that it was *very* important. Both teapots were barely steaming.

"Four hundred dirham and we have a deal," said the elderly man.

The stocky sailor was silent for moment. *Good. Keep talking.* Zahra looked at the teapots. They started to steam.

"Done," said the stocky sailor.

"But how do I know I can trust you to send others?" the elderly man asked.

"On my grandmother's grave," said the stocky sailor.

The pig had just made a pact on his dead grandmother that he would promise to tell his friends about raping a young girl. Zahra made a mental note never to trust another Moroccan man for the rest of her life. Both teapots came to a boil.

"One condition," said the elderly man.

"What?" the stocky sailor asked.

"I want to watch," said the elderly man.

"Won't bother me," said the stocky sailor. They laughed. It made Zahra's skin crawl.

She grabbed both pots off the stove. Zahra didn't have a plan. She was going to have to do what she had done her whole life: improvise.

"Young one, the more you resist, the harder this will be," elderly man warned, as he unfastened the lock and opened the hatch.

Zahra stood to the left of the ladder with her back against the wall. The bright sun cast a perfect shadow onto the cabin floor. She could see their silhouettes perfectly.

Both of the teapot handles burned her already mangled fingers. She wanted to drop them both, collapse, and start crying. *Stay strong. Five more seconds.*

The elderly man could not see into the dim cabin, so he put his shoulders inside the hatch. *Now.* Zahra spun and whipped her right arm upward.

"Take this!" she screamed.

The searing water wrapped around the elderly man's face. He screamed in pain, and his left leg slipped into the rung of the first ladder. He fell forward, and his tibia snapped like a dry branch. He tumbled onto the cabin floor in front of Zahra.

"Whoa," the stocky sailor said. Zahra watched his silhouette back away from the hatch.

The elderly man lay on the ground writhing in pain. "Help me, please! I can't see."

Zahra almost pitied the pathetic man. Almost. He was not going to crawl out of the cabin anytime soon.

"Back up, or I will do the same to you!" Zahra yelled.

She climbed out of the hatch. The stocky sailor moved to the other side of the deck and ducked his head under the boom.

Zahra held the other boiling teapot in her hand as they circled. "Get on your boat and leave me be," she demanded.

"Little girl, the longer you wait, the weaker your weapon gets," said the stocky sailor.

Zahra looked down at the teapot. He was right. The cool air was rendering her weapon ineffective. *Think quickly. Do something.*

Zahra tossed the pot into the ocean water and quickly pulled the money out of her slippers.

"This is almost ten thousand dollars." Zahra used two hands to spread the stack of hundreds. The stocky sailor's eyebrows rose.

"With this, you could retire and get fatter, you pig," Zahra said. "Which do you want more? My body or the money?"

The stocky sailor fell silent. They could both hear the elderly man moaning in pain. "I'll have both," said the stocky sailor with a grin. He got ready to pounce.

"Well, it's one or the other, *pig*," Zahra said. She crumpled a handful of the money in her hand and threw it overboard. The stack of hundreds caught the breeze, came apart, and landed atop the choppy waves.

"You crazy bitch!" screamed the stocky sailor. He eyed her up and then dove overboard to collect the money.

Zahra jumped onto his fishing boat, which was gasoline powered and untied the ropes. She got behind the large wheel. She had never driven a car, let alone a boat. Luckily, there were only three things in front of her: a key, a throttle, and a wheel.

Zahra turned the key and felt the engine rumble under her feet. Then she pushed down the throttle. The bow lifted, and the fishing boat accelerated. She looked back and watched the flailing arms of her attacker getting smaller. Zahra wondered what he was saying now. *Stupid pig.*

She opened a map that was wedged into the dashboard. It looked easy enough. Hug the coast of Morocco until it ended, take a left, and head straight at the Rock of Gibraltar. *Just beat the dark. Worry about docking this thing later.* The fishing boat skipped over the calm waters and headed north. Zahra watched the eastern sun peaking over the Atlas Mountains. She hoped that the girls in camp were all right.

One kilometer away, Redbeard watched Zahra through his binoculars. He stood on the deck of Soter's hundred-million-dollar Oculus yacht. It was designed to look like a killer whale and could slice through the high seas at twenty-five knots.

Redbeard was incapable of compassion, but he admired Zahra. She had the potential to be a great assassin—just like him. Through his binoculars, he watched the man in the water collecting the floating money. He turned to one of his Corsairs. "Bring me the harpoon."

CHAPTER 4:
THE TWO OF SPADES

ROYAL NAVY BOARDING SCHOOL, GIBRALTAR

Gordie Mason stood in front of the classroom shaking. Mr. Breen, a harsh but efficient science professor, sat with his fingers crossed over his protruding belly. "Get on with it, Mason."

Gordie pulled out his box. "For, uh...for my invention, I made... well, I guess I should explain the *why* before the *what*. Sometimes, I get hungry in between our meals."

The class snickered. Gordie was fat. Here, that meant he was weak. "Pipe down," Mr. Breen said. "Let him finish."

"I like to make a cup of noodles on my hotplate," Gordie said. The class snickered again.

"Christ, Mason," Mr. Breen said. "You're not helping yourself."

"I don't like to wait for the noodles to cool down, so I invented this." Gordie pulled out a pair of chopsticks that were attached to a battery-operated fan. The class went into a desk-slapping uproar.

Gordie demonstrated. He had made a cup out of cardboard and used strips of binder paper as fake noodles. "As you lift the noodles out of the cup, the fan blows the steam right off of them…so you don't have to."

Mr. Breen stopped the torment. "All right. All right. Good job, Mason. Sit down before it gets any worse. Mr. Alexander, you're up."

Mr. Breen looked to the back of the classroom. Isaac had his head on his desk. He was out cold, dripping snot onto his hoodie.

"Can someone please wake, Alexander?" Mr. Breen asked.

Nelson Shea, a stocky little ginger guy, kicked Isaac's desk, and the front legs rotated thirty degrees. Isaac jolted awake. He gasped and put his right hand over his chest like he had just come up for air. Isaac realized he was in a classroom and started to breathe again.

"You're flippin' loony, Alexander," Shea said loud enough for the whole class to hear.

Then he looked up to a familiar sight: a teacher with his arms crossed and a full class of turned heads. "Mr. Alexander, your project please," Mr. Breen said.

Isaac grabbed his iBook and walked to the front of the class, ignoring the muttered insults. He quickly plugged in his laptop and then pulled over his draped invention. "For my science project, I made a Pedal-a-watt."

Isaac removed the sheet to reveal his project. "It's essentially an old exercise bike attached to a battery and a small generator that produces enough electricity to power a string of lights."

Mr. Breen was the only one impressed. "This is brilliant, Isaac. How did you regulate the wattage?"

"Well, I blew out a few lightbulbs at first, but then I did some calculations and realized amps times volts equals watts. I just needed a few resistor diodes to protect photovoltaic modules from voltage spikes."

Isaac's classmates rolled their eyes. Mr. Breen knelt down to examine the generator. "How much did this cost?"

"Well, with used parts, these can be constructed for about one hundred pounds, but brand new, they would cost just shy of five hundred. It's not just for lights, either. The basic bike unit could also power water pumps, washing machines, printing presses, an amplifier for PA systems, and sewing machines."

Isaac handed his report over to Mr. Breen, who flipped through and examined the blueprints.

"My plan is to set up a donation center for old stationary bikes and elliptical machines. I can convert them and ship them with the accessories to third-world countries. Just one of these machines could completely change a village's economy."

Isaac reached down and pressed play on his laptop, which was connected to the projector.

Rachel appeared on the video from Morocco. Isaac's classmates came to life. Keagan said, "Alexander's mom's a MILF." The rest of the boys pretended to clear their throats but were saying, "MILF," to each other in cough-talk.

Isaac ignored them and turned to the screen. The quips about his mother drowned out when the webcam focused on Zahra. She was wildly beautiful—dark skin with striking green eyes. Isaac thought she looked like the Afghan girl from the famous *National Geographic* cover. He had seen pictures of Zahra but never a video.

Mr. Breen put his arm around Isaac and quietly said, "Just a few more years of torture and then they'll all be working for you." Mr. Breen patted Isaac on the back and turned to his students, "Shut up, animals.

You'll be glad to know that Mr. Alexander just set the curve with his project. You'll all be lucky if you get C's."

The entire class groaned. Isaac looked to his professor. "Thank you, Mr. Breen. Rugby practice will be splendid today."

Just as Isaac finished, Rachel said, "We miss you and love you." The class erupted.

CHAPTER 5:
THE THREE OF HEARTS

VICTORIA STADIUM, GIBRALTAR

"Ruck! Ruck! Ruck!" Somehow Coach Hoch's face got redder when he yelled. Two full sides of third- and fourth-year students ran around the beautifully manicured pitch for an intersquad scrimmage. Isaac and another thirty B-sides sat on the sideline in warm-ups.

Keagan and his forwards bowled over the defense just as the scrum half arrived. The advancing blue team was on the white team's twenty-two line.

"Kick! Kick! Kick!" The scrum-half heard Coach Hoch's play and spun the ball to the fly-half, Jarlath Peters. The perfectly thrown pass hit off Jarlath's hands. Knock-on.

"God bless it!" Coach Hoch blew his whistle, stopping play. "Mr. Peters, you couldn't catch syphilis in Thailand."

Coach Hoch turned to his sideline of players. "Alexander. Fly-half." The players on the blue team groaned. Isaac glanced up and pointed to his chest, as if to say, "*Who, me?*" He closed his journal and hid it under his cleat bag. Coach Hoch said, "No. Pope Fucking Alexander. Yes, you. Hop to it."

Isaac ripped off his windbreaker and jogged toward the coach. Coach Hoch put a hand to his shoulder and stopped him. "I know you're a smarty and you don't want to be here, but you're my only other kicker. So tough titty said the kitty when the milk went dry. Go hit a drop goal."

"Yes, sir," Isaac said and jogged out to join the ranks of blue team's second line.

"We are playing Uppingham next week, and they have some big, mongoloid Scotsmen. They're going to caber toss you little peckers unless we bring our kicking game. Drop goal from the scrum."

"Don't fall asleep," Keagan said.

Coach Hoch blew the whistle, and the blue scrum half rolled the ball into the scrum. Isaac looked up and could see Shea breaking off early from the white team's pack. It was clearly a penalty. Isaac watched as it came to a stop on the eight-man's cleat.

Here it comes. Don't worry about Shea. Nail your kick. The scrummy spun the ball, and Isaac reeled it in on the twenty-two line.

Isaac looked up. Simple physics. The field posts were twenty-two meters away, and he needed to drop the ball at 35 degrees for the best results. At that angle, his foot would avoid premature contact with the end of the ball and it would also allow a larger sweet spot for contact. Isaac focused on the ball as it dropped out of his hands and onto the ground. He kicked his leg back at the proper angle and then whipped it forward.

Instead of the rubber ball wrapping around his cleat, he felt his shoulder blades hit the ground with a thud. Isaac opened his eyes and stared at Shea's mug. He had decleated him, and his whole team cheered.

"That's for science class, you little shite," Shea said while stepping over Isaac in his rugby shorts. "Get used to those ginger balls."

"Alexander, get up. You're fine," Coach Hoch said. "Shea, that was a penalty. White team owes laps after practice." The white team shrugged.

Isaac rolled over and quickly popped up. He was not going to give Shea or any of the rest of his asshole teammates the satisfaction of staying down.

"Ready," Isaac said.

Shea looked over and grabbed his balls. "I can do this all day, Alexander."

"Good," Isaac said. "I'll give you twenty quid if you can do it again."

The challenge excited the entire team. Shea wasn't ready for it but accepted gladly.

"Cut the shite, Nancy boys!" yelled Coach Hoch. "From the scrum."

Coach blew the whistle, and the ball flew toward Isaac in seconds. So did Shea. He was so low to the ground that his knuckles grazed the top of the grass. Isaac caught the ball just as Nelson left his feet for a massive hit. At the last second, Isaac rotated his shoulders and kicked the ball right into Shea's face. His head snapped back, and the hollow smack made all the boys wince.

Isaac stepped to the side as Nelson slid two meters on his stomach. Coach Hoch was frozen. The blue and white teams were awestruck. Nelson came to a stop and lay motionless. No one knew whether it was accidental or on purpose. A loud voice broke the silence.

"Whoohoo!"

Everyone spun toward the bleachers. Uncle Jack sat in the stands drinking a Boddington's with his macaque monkey perched on his shoulder. He wore a tattered rugby jersey and sported an unkempt beard. Uncle Jack stood up and yelled, "Hey, Nelson. I fucked your older sister in the bathroom at the Prince of Wales pub in Twickenham. Her red cabbage patch came up to her belly button."

The ice was officially broken. Coach Hoch and the boys laughed. "Get up, Shea. You're fine," the Coach said. Shea staggered to his feet revealing a thick stream of blood on the V-neck of his jersey. He wouldn't even look at Isaac.

"Shea, hit the showers. White team, five laps. Blue team, one." Shea grabbed his bag and sulked toward the locker room.

Isaac watched Uncle Jack finish his tall can of beer and hand it to Horus, his Barbary macaque. Horus leaped onto the trash can, deposited it, and then sprinted back to his owner. The tailless apes were Gibraltar's unofficial animals. The local Spaniards called them Michael Jackson monkeys or *monos blancos*—the white-faced monkeys.

Isaac jogged in the back and could hear his teammates talking about his uncle. Jack was one of those polarizing characters whose exploits transcended into the realm of legends. It didn't matter if you loved him or hated him, you knew who he was, and there was a good chance he had slept with your sister.

Isaac finished his lap and approached his man-child, forty-year-old uncle and his bulbous-nosed, alcoholic rugby coach. Horus shrieked with excitement when he recognized Isaac. He climbed up his thick rugby jersey and perched on his shoulder.

"Grab your stuff, lad," Coach Hoch said. "Your uncle needs you."

"I'm not supposed to leave campus without a note," Isaac said as he wrestled with Horus.

"I'll take care of it," said Coach Hoch.

Uncle Jack was a navy rugby legend and was treated like royalty. In 1973, during the Inter-Services Army Navy game at Twickenham Stadium, Jack ripped the ball from the army inside center and ran one hundred meters for the win. The play came to be known as "the poach." It did wonders for young Jack's already overgrown ego.

"Come on, Little Lord Fauntleroy. I need help on the boat." Uncle Jack always used nicknames. He claimed that he started doing it when he was playing professional rugby in his twenties. It was too hard for him to remember all of his girlfriends' names.

"Where are we going?" Isaac asked. "I've got a ton of schoolwork."

"Taking out a boatload of tourists for a dive," Uncle Jack said.

"Take your time, lad," Coach Hoch said. "Let Nelson and the boys calm down a bit. You know they'll be waiting for you."

"Aggh, bollocks," Jack said. "You know what I do when I'm outnumbered?"

"What?" Coach Hoch asked, eagerly awaiting an Uncle Jack proverb that most likely related to drinking, fighting, and/or rugby. Isaac knew most of them by heart.

"Get naked," Jack said. "No one wants to fight a naked man."

Coach Hoch burst into laughter and slapped Uncle Jack on the back.

"You're a wild man, O'Ryan," Coach Hoch said.

Uncle Jack motioned for Isaac, and they walked off the field.

Coach Hoch turned and yelled, "Hey, Jack, did you really screw Nelson's sister?"

Uncle Jack turned and yelled back, "If you add enough detail, people will believe *anything*."

CHAPTER 6:
THE THREE OF CLUBS

THERA, GREECE

Sunlight engulfed David and Rachel as their hoods were pulled back. Rachel's eyes adjusted, and she saw Ptolemy Soter sitting in the cockpit of the Grand Augusta helicopter.

"Welcome home, David," he said.

"Where are we?" Rachel asked.

The Augusta circled the estate at a thousand meters. David looked out the helicopter window. He recognized the small, semicircle-shaped Mediterranean island.

"Thera," he said to his wife.

"Only a few of us can claim this as the birthplace of our ancestors," Soter added.

"And you just *killed* two of them," David shot back.

The sprawling marble compound was nestled into the side of a sheer limestone cliff. It looked like a museum.

The helicopter landed; they jumped out, and Soter guided them through a gardened courtyard decorated with Greek statues. "My family was on mainland Greece for hundreds of years," he explained.

Soter and the Corsairs led them through the front doors and down a beautiful marble hallway lined with Greek and Roman armor.

"We finally had enough money to buy the land at the turn of the twentieth century when my great-grandfather, Ptolemy Soter XII, became a famous archaeologist. The land sat undeveloped until the 1950s."

Soter slid open a massive glass door and stepped into a cobblestone courtyard that overlooked the ocean and surrounding islands. The setting sun dipped its toes into the water. "After World War II, my grandfather, Ptolemy Soter XIV, got a loan from the Greek government to buy seven T2 tankers. Mediterranean shipping lanes were a mess and run by fourteen inept families. Through a series of what some may call *ruthless* tactics, he monopolized the lanes, disposed of the system of nepotism, and created the Greek Merchant Navy. His fleet of seven turned into five thousand, and in ten years, the company was worth billions. He built this compound for our family and commissioned artists from all over the world."

Soter pointed to a beautiful rusted bronze fountain of Atlas holding up the globe. He was sprayed by statues of the seven planetary gods of Greece: Kronos, Zeus, Ares, Aphrodite, Hermes, Artemis, and Apollo.

"This sculpture of Atlas should be of particular significance to you, David," Soter said.

"Why is that?" David asked.

"Atlas was a primordial Titan and one of four brothers. Their father, Aether, was the god of space and stars, and his mother, Gaia, was the goddess of earth. When the Titans and Olympians went to war, Atlas and his brother, Menoetius, remained loyal to the Titans even though they knew they were growing weak. Their two other brothers, Prometheus and Epimetheus, believed the Olympian victory was inevitable, so they sided with them. After the Olympians won, Zeus banished Atlas to the western edge of the world and forced him to hold up the heavens for eternity."

David understood the metaphor. "So, in this analogy, I would be Atlas?"

"Correct," Soter said. "You are now faced with a choice. The Magi have become weak, and my victory is inevitable."

"You may have us on the run, but we are *far* from defeated," David said defiantly.

"Remain loyal and receive my punishment, or join me and earn a place in my consul. It's the same deal that I've offered the three other members of your order, and it is the same deal I will offer your son when he arrives."

"If you even lay a finger on our son—" Rachel said.

"Spare me the threats, Mrs. Alexander. Redbeard and his men are following the girl right now. Please, come. We have a lot to discuss."

Soter led them to a rustic wooden table near the edge of the cliff. Then he pulled the chair out for Rachel at the head of the table. For a man who was holding them hostage, he was quite polite. David sat down across from Soter. Rachel stared down at the spread of Mediterranean food. Their diet had been very sparse in Morocco, and her mouth watered.

Three of the Turkish Corsairs stepped back and watched from a distance.

"Please, help yourself. You must be hungry," Soter said as he swept his hand over the table of feta, olives, bread, and hummus.

Rachel was starving and knew it was the beginning of a long cross-examination. She didn't have the time or energy to help her husband establish dominance, so she served herself. "You two can cockfight. I'm going to eat," she said.

"What do you want from us?" David asked, getting right to the point.

Soter pulled out a walkie-talkie and placed it on the table. "First, the exact location of your son," he said. "My men are instructed to eliminate anyone who gets in their way. If you have someone guarding Isaac, they *will* be in danger."

"I would be more worried about your men," Rachel said as she bit off a piece of bread.

"Mrs. Alexander, my Turkish Corsairs are *highly* trained assassins, bred and raised from birth in the art of war," Soter assured her while pouring himself a glass of water. "They should be able to handle a seventeen-year-old boy."

Rachel said confidently around a mouthful of food, "I'm not talking about Isaac."

Soter stared at her. She carried herself like a Spartan wife—dutiful and fearless. He couldn't help but find her alluring.

David broke the long silence. "How did you find our members?" he asked.

"An internal source. Sir Lockyer was the easiest to find. He was teaching astrophysics at the University of Exeter. Your kind used to be warrior mystics trained in the deadly art of Kalaripayattu. Now, you're just weak academics. We snatched him up right in his own parking lot. Didn't even put up a fight."

"And where is he now?"

"In the ocean behind me," Soter said.

"And Dr. Rossi?"

"Yes, the son of the late Bruno Rossi. He was continuing his father's research on x-ray astronomy at the University of Padua. We broke into his laboratory, drugged him, and brought him here."

"And now?" David asked closing his eyes for a long moment to grieve his late colleague. Soter motioned over his shoulder to signify that the doctor had met the same fate as Lockyer. "Can you pass me that?" he added, pointing to the cherry tomato tapenade. Rachel handed it across the table. "This island has the best tomatoes in Greece. It's the volcanic soil," Soter said.

"You've taken two brilliant men away from their research," David said.

"No. I sat them down at this very table and gave them a simple choice. Join me and continue your life's work, or die."

"And who was the third?"

Soter motioned down at the fourth place table setting and said, "He chose to continue his research." He picked up his walkie-talkie, turned it to a different channel, and said, "Doctor, why don't you come join us?"

Two minutes later, one of David's best friends walked through the glass doors. Dr. Neville Ramanujan was a brilliant Indian mathematician and grandson of the great Srinivasa Ramanujan, a self-taught genius who died prematurely and left behind journals of theorems that were still being used in experimental mathematics. David jumped to his feet. The two Corsairs unsheathed their swords.

"How could you betray the order?" David yelled at Neville, who took off his lab coat and approached the table cautiously.

"He was going to kill my family," Neville said with his hands up. "Let me explain."

The Corsairs sat David down. Neville nodded to Rachel. "It is good to see you. I apologize for the circumstances."

Neville sat in the vacant chair.

"What have you done?" David said exhaling in defeat.

"Soter and his men grabbed me in Chennai," Neville said. "I was on my way to a lecture. He brought me here and sat me down. Lockyer and Rossi had previously refused his offer so they decided to raise the stakes. They showed me a live camera feed of my family's home in Tamil

Nadu. Then he told me Redbeard was going to butcher them if I said no. I have *four* young children."

Rachel turned to Soter. "You're an animal."

He smiled at her with an unblinking stare. *Even more attractive when she's angry,* he thought.

"What would you have done?" Neville asked his old friend.

David pondered it. He would not have been able to watch his wife and son die. "What did you tell him about Isaac?" David asked.

"When I came to visit you at the orphanage in Bihar, Isaac was with you on a break from school. He confided a secret with me that he was too afraid to tell you. Reoccurring dreams. It was the exact same issue that my grandfather had. To cope with it, he kept detailed journals, and I encouraged Isaac to do the same. I told him to scan his entries and e-mail them to me so I could help decipher them."

Rachel turned to Neville. "Why didn't you tell us about this?"

"He made me promise not to tell you," Neville said.

"What do Isaac's dreams have to do with any of this?" Rachel asked.

Soter folded his dinner napkin and placed it on the table. "I think it's time we show you," he said.

They were led down one of Soter's magnificent hallways. This one was not lined with ancient works of art. It was surrounded with rooms of servers and research labs. Neville slid a key card over on an electronic reader, and the door slid open, revealing a high-tech laboratory.

"This way," Neville said, ushering them inside.

Soter approached two identical rectangular structures that were encased in Plexiglas: one was rusted metallic green and the other, an exact bronze replica. The giant mechanisms looked like ancient grandfather clocks, and they both had seven concentric dials with handles on their front face. The original was rusted shut, but the replica's dials spun in different directions like the wheels of a safe. Dozens of wires ran from the bronze replica into a network of computers.

"This is the Antikythera Mechanism, or what our ancestors called *the Horologion*," Soter explained.

"Impossible," David said. "It was lost thousands of years ago."

Soter touched the casing. "In 1902, a group of Greek sailors were returning from Africa when they decided to wait out a storm on the island of Antikythera. They went diving off the coast and discovered a massive shipwreck containing bodies wearing Egyptian armor. With their limited equipment, the captain and the crew pulled up as much as they could—parts of statues, and most important, a corroded gear that had fallen off the original mechanism." Soter pointed to the corroded bronze original and continued, "They alerted the Greek Education Ministry, which was headed by my great-grandfather, Ptolemy Soter XIII. He organized a dive with the Hellenic Navy, and together, they excavated hundreds of artifacts. All but this one was reported and sent to museums. He kept this for himself."

Rachel stepped toward the casing. "And *what* exactly is it?"

"It's the world's first supercomputer," Neville said. "It's more powerful than any piece of modern machinery."

"My great-grandfather spent his whole life trying to find its purpose," Soter said. "He came up short, but left behind thousands of pages of research. After my grandfather built his shipping empire, he invested millions to carry on his father's research. In 1964, a team of scientists used advanced carbon dating and found out it was from the second millennium BCE. Ten years later, a team of our hired historians were able to piece together documents to determine its function."

Neville motioned for David and Rachel to step closer. The dapper Indian doctor pointed at the mechanism and said, "Each of the seven dials represents the position of one the seven planets of classical antiquity. All of which came to make up the seven days of our week: Sun-day, Moon-day, Saturn-day, and in the Latin, *Martis*, or Mars, for Tuesday, *Mercurii* is Wednesday, *Iovis* is Jupiter, or Thursday, and *Veneris*, or Venus, is Friday."

"We don't need a lesson in Latin," Rachel snapped. "Get to the point."

"Very well. At first, the team of researchers concluded that it was a mechanical calendar that was synchronized to the motions of the planets. They thought its purpose was to predict eclipses. However, Soter's grandfather believed their research was just scratching the surface, and it turns out he was right." Neville nodded.

"That's when I found Neville and brought him here," Soter said. "He was well versed in Bruno Rossi's research on x-ray astronomy and had the idea of x-raying the mechanism. It was a *huge* breakthrough."

Neville walked David and Rachel over to his computer and pulled up a 3-D replica.

"We used 3-D imaging to x-ray the mechanism," Neville said, "and we found that behind the seven dials were another sixty-five dials, representing everything from the solar Egyptian calendar to the zodiac cycle. We were able to translate the engravings off the inner dials and find out the machine's true purpose."

Soter took over. "When all seventy-two dials of this machine are synchronized, the machine can anticipate the behavior of the four natural elements...*nature itself.* In simple terms, it can predict natural disasters *before* they happen."

"That's impossible," Rachel said.

Neville opened a drawer and picked something up. "Think about it this way. The ancients believed that nature and the cosmos were like this Rubik's cube. It was a puzzle that could be solved. They spent hundreds of years comparing their astronomical observations with their observations of the natural elements. They essentially *cracked the code* and wrote an algorithm that synchronized nature and the universe. The machine can predict everything from eclipses to earthquakes simply by computing astronomical data."

Neville then turned to Rachel and said, "Pick a color."

"Green," she said.

Neville quickly twisted the Rubik's cube. "The ancients believed that nature was predetermined, and if one knew all the variables, it could be predicted. That's what the machine is supposed to do." He twisted one last time and held out the Rubik's cube. One side was all green.

Soter stepped forward. "The possibilities of the Antikythera Mechanism are very real. However, synchronizing all seventy-two dials is a tremendous task."

Neville pointed over to the spinning dials of the bronze replica. "I've created a computer program to try every combination, but at this rate, it could take hundreds of years."

David tried to process all of the new information. "And you think this has something to do with Isaac?"

Neville jumped into his chair and slid over to his computer. He opened a desktop folder, and a series of sketched images appeared on the wall-sized monitor. Rachel and David stared in awe at dozens of intricate sketches of the Antikythera Mechanism.

CHAPTER 7

THE THREE OF DIAMONDS

DOWNTOWN GIBRALTAR

Uncle Jack, Isaac, and Horus weaved through the crowded cobblestone streets of downtown Gibraltar. Sunburned tourists sipped iced tea, husbands bartered with street vendors, children snapped cell phone photos of Horus, and Jack made sure to nod to every moderately attractive female .

"I'm telling you, Isaac, you've got to work on your verbal sparring so you don't have to kick kids in the face to get them to leave you alone,"

Jack said. "Haven't you learned anything?" He moved through the crowd fluidly. Isaac had to sidestep tourists to keep up.

"Once again, you're putting yourself in *my* shoes and giving advice," Isaac said.

"That's it, you little emo," Uncle Jack said, as he turned around and got into an old-school boxing stance. "Let's brain box."

"Here?" Isaac asked.

Tourists stepped around them as Isaac reluctantly raised his fists. "Okay," Isaac said. "Wait. Ground rules first."

Jack circled Isaac in his upright stance. "Sure, nancy-pants."

"You can't insult me for being a weakling, and I won't insult you for being a dumb, tourist-swindling man-whore."

"Deal. Ready?" Jack asked, as they circled.

Isaac threw a fake jab, and Jack ducked. "I've already started."

"You little nutbag," Jack cried as he countered with a horrible impersonation of Queen Elizabeth's voice. "My name's Sir Isaac No-cock. My coin purse hasn't dropped yet, so I sit in the library all day and solve puzzles. I'm the best puzzle solver in all the land. Yay."

Isaac bobbed and weaved around Jack's half-speed punches. Isaac countered with a horrible attempt at a pirate voice. "Name's Jack O'Ryan, and just because I'm bigger than you, it doesn't mean I'm fat."

Isaac pinned Uncle Jack against the wall and went to town on his ribcage. Horus jumped on Isaac's shoulder and pulled his collar. Tourists shifted from second looks to stares.

"I play tough guy and sleep with a *lot* of women only because me Gypsy girlfriend broke me heart and left me with her smelly monkey," Isaac said as he reared back and let loose one solid kidney punch.

"Low blow," said Uncle Jack as he playfully fell to the ground. "Help me up."

They both laughed as Isaac reached his hand down. Jack grabbed his wrist and yanked him toward him. He wrapped his combat boots around his neck and twisted. Isaac fell to the concrete in an arm bar.

Uncle Jack sat up. "Quick, you little whey-faced namby-pamby. Uncle Jack's three rules of living."

"Come on, Jack, let me up," Isaac said, squirming.

"Recite them," Jack said as he tightened the arm bar and made Isaac grimace.

"Ow, ow, ow. Okay, number one. It's always better to ask for forgiveness than permission. Two. Screw 'em if they can't take a joke. And three. Do I have to say three? I hate that one."

Horus posed for a tourist photo, and Jack leaned back further.

"Okay, number three. Treat a lady like a whore, and treat a whore like a lady. Let me *up.*"

Jack popped up and then pulled Isaac to his feet. "Someday, the third one will make sense, Virgin Mary," he said as he rubbed Isaac's head. "Now, come on. Your *pirate* uncle's got to buy some fake treasure so he can swindle tourists for drinking money." Isaac rotated his shoulder and followed Jack into a Gibraltar secondhand gift shop.

An hour later, the sail's slackened on Jack's fifty-seven-foot Wellington Pilothouse as it slowed to a drift. The sailboat held fifteen British and Spanish tourists. Isaac looked toward the western horizon and saw the warm sun beginning its descent. "Hey, twathole. Quit daydreaming, and drop the mud hook."

Isaac released the anchor as the tourists snapped mantle photos for each other. Jack had already honed in on a Spanish mother-daughter combo. The stage was set. It was now time for the *Uncle Jack Show.* He stepped up and addressed the divers. "Ladies and Gentlemen, I am *actually* a pirate. Please hand over your wallets to my first mate, Horus."

Like clockwork, Horus climbed down and opened up a canvas bag. He shrieked and pulled on a tourist's pants. The tourists erupted in laughter and blinded Horus with a barrage of flashes.

"I'm kidding. My name is Jack O'Ryan, and I'm your captain. I'm a former Royal Marine, which means that I've done this a thousand times, and I'm also a former rugby player, which means we will be serving cocktails on the way home."

The tourists clapped in excitement.

"How many of you have been scuba diving before?" Jack asked.

Half of the tourists raised their hands. Jack held up a Neptune diving mask.

"Don't worry. These are state-of-the-art, full-face Neptune diving masks. You'll be fine as long as you don't forget to *breathe.*"

Uncle Jack pointed over his left shoulder to the Rock of Gibraltar. "Now, a little backstory about where you're diving. Ancient civilizations believed the Rock of Gibraltar was the end of the known world and one of the two Pillars of Hercules." Jack pointed over his right shoulder to a mountain in Morocco. "The other pillar being Jebul Musa in Morocco. The Egyptians, Phoenicians, Carthaginians, and Romans thought the rock was a sacred shrine. In order to secure a safe journey into unknown waters, they believed that they had to pay homage to the gods by placing jewels at the base of the rock. Ships that were loaded with Egyptian jewelry and Phoenician pottery were attacked by Barbary pirates right here."

The tourists were giddy with excitement. Isaac watched his uncle seal the deal.

Jack said, "Now, I'm not promising anything, but we're sitting atop a handful of shipwrecks. If you find anything, bring it to me, or the Spanish Archaeological Society will have my arse."

Isaac knew that there was no such thing as the Spanish Archaeological Society. He had gone home after one of Jack's dives and Googled it.

"Let's get everyone fitted downstairs," Jack said. "We're burning daylight."

The tourists shuffled into the cabin, and Jack approached Isaac. "Go astern and use your thinger-doodle to whip the you-know-what's into the water. Then go down and pour the crappy booze into the nice bottles."

Isaac nodded. "Copy that, Captain."

"Good. I'm going to tell that Spanish mother you fancy her daughter." Jack laughed and went under. Isaac shook his head. It was pointless to try to stop him.

Isaac sauntered to the back of the boat and made sure all the tourists were preoccupied. He opened up a box stacked with cheap jewelry, fake artifacts, and old pottery, which Jack had just purchased at the secondhand store for a grand total of forty-eight pounds. In the previous months, Isaac kept throwing his arm out winging the things into the ocean. It was right around the time when he was doing a report on Archimedes, so he decided to build a homemade catapult out of scrap wood, a shovel, and some old engine belts. It worked like a charm. Isaac pulled back the shovel, loaded a piece of pottery, and launched it fifteen meters into the ocean. Jack called it *chumming the waters*.

Twenty minutes later, Isaac watched the pear-shaped tourists waddle off the boat like penguins. It was time for Jack's big spectacle. He ripped off his shirt revealing a sleeve of tattoos on his left arm, hid a spare air canister in his rugby shorts, and climbed the mast. He still had a six-pack, but a steady diet of pale ales and kebabs had extended his abdominal muscles outward. Jack called down to all the divers. "Last one in buys first round!"

From the crow's nest, he leaped headfirst and landed a perfect dive from twenty meters up. The tourists rushed to the side of the boat and waited for him to come up—and waited. And waited. Two minutes passed, and they started to worry. The Spanish mother turned to Isaac and asked, "Can he hold his breath that long?"

Isaac shrugged and got up to join them. Suddenly, a hand emerged from the dark-blue water. Uncle Jack held a rusted bronze bracelet. He swam over to the pretty Spanish girl and handed it to her. She almost melted.

"Swim that way," Uncle Jack said pretending to catch his breath. The tourists jumped off the boat and started diving.

"You're starting to resemble a powder keg with legs," Isaac told his uncle as he climbed onto the empty boat.

"Overweight and outta shape, but it keeps my tattoos puffy," Uncle Jack said.

Uncle Jack got a tattoo every time he visited a new country. They stretched from his left deltoid to his left wrist. The two most prominent were his Royal Marine badge and a giant Romani wheel with name *Maia*. Jack propped his feet up, threw on a pair of aviator sunglasses, and cracked a beer. "Can't complain, Sir Isaac. Can't complain."

Isaac opened his journal and started to sketch Uncle Jack's tattoos. "Have you talked to her at all?" he asked.

Jack looked through the top of his sunglasses and noticed Isaac was staring at his tattoo. "Not since she left a year ago," Jack said.

"Any idea where she is?"

"Selling fake jewelry and telling fortunes on a street corner somewhere," Uncle Jack said.

"I liked her," Isaac said.

"Me, too. I've sampled every nationality of woman, but the one that got to me was a street-vending Gypsy," Jack said. "Go figure."

An ecstatic English tourist with celery-colored teeth climbed up and held a piece of pottery. "Mr. O'Ryan, look what I've found."

"Careful," Jack said as he jumped up and examined the pottery. "Looks Phoenician. What century do you think, Isaac?" He turned to the English tourist. "He's my history expert."

Isaac shook his head at Jack, took the pottery, and constructed a quick lie. "Yes, definitely Phoenician. Ninth century, BCE."

"Do you think it's of any value?" asked the English tourist.

Jack grabbed it from Isaac. "I'm sorry, sir. It's too risky. I have to report these to the archaeological society. I've been fined too many times."

Isaac observed a master in action. Jack had the tourist, hook, line, and sinker.

"Well, how much is the fine?" the English tourist asked.

"Sir, I *know* where this is headed, and I can*not* do it," Uncle Jack said.

"Three hundred pounds?" the English tourist persisted.

Jack shook his head in hesitation.

"Four hundred pounds?"

Jack shrugged his shoulders.

"Sir, if you tried to get this appraised, you would have to tell them *where* you found it," Jack said. "I could get arrested."

"Six hundred pounds and it stays on my mantle, solely for bragging rights," the English tourist said.

"Deal," Uncle Jack agreed. "But we have to do this quick before the others get back."

The English tourist ripped off his flippers and headed down into the cabin.

Jack turned to Isaac and mouthed the words, "Drinking money."

Isaac shook his head and finished the sketch in his journal.

THREE OF SPADES

COAST OF TANGIER, MOROCCO

As the boat rounded the northwestern tip of Morocco, it came into view—*Europe*. During her journey, Zahra had hugged the coast and used a map to identify landmarks. She had seen a flock of flamingos land in Merja Zerga's lagoon, massive jumbo jets had soared right over her, and now she stared at the sunlit skyline of Tangier. She remembered the analogy that David had used when he had pointed out her constellation, Aquarius. He explained that astronomers still had no accurate way to measure the distance of the stars from each other. The stars that make up a constellation appear to be of equal distance from Earth, when in fact they are dozens of light years apart. The same goes for a city's sky-line. All of the high-rise buildings look like they stretch down one long boulevard, when in fact they are blocks and blocks apart.

Zahra marveled at the pointed towers on top of golden-domed mosques and let her tired eyes rest on the warm glow reflecting off the pristine hotel windows. She blinked to wet her eyes and then snapped back to reality. Not only was she racing daylight, but she was running out of gas. Worst of all, she couldn't swim, an irony for someone born under the sign of Aquarius. The gas gauge was sitting below one-eighth, and Zahra had been fixated on the red dial for the last two hours. It seemed to be dropping quicker than before.

Ten kilometers past Tangier, the Strait of Gibraltar narrowed. Over her left shoulder, the tip of the sun disappeared. The last leg of Zahra's journey was going to be the most difficult. She knew that she was facing a major dilemma. The bottlenecked strait was jam-packed with tankers heading east and west and the last ferries of the day heading north and south. She could play it safe and stop in Morocco, or she could risk it and head for Europe.

Zahra remembered the time she had been caught stealing and the police chased her. She came to a crowded intersection, and her instincts told her she could make it across without being struck by a car. They were telling her the same thing now. Go for it.

Zahra spun the wheel left. Europe was less than twenty kilometers away. The swells picked up as the fishing boat ploughed through large wakes. The dashboard was covered with switches, but none of them turned on the lights. The boat rode dark, and the remaining shades of twilight were being submerged by the night sky.

Zahra looked behind her. Approaching were two high-speed cat-amaran ferries headed back from Morocco, probably full of tourists drinking champagne. The captain wouldn't even see the tiny boat until they were right on top of it.

In front of her, the situation worsened. To the northwest was a tanker headed into the Mediterranean. To her northeast was a tanker headed out to the Atlantic. She was boxed in; her only option was to thread the needle.

Zahra pushed the throttle all the way down and aimed the boat right in between the crossing tankers. She left the wheel and ripped open the boat's compartments. It was too dark to see so she relied on her sense of touch.

Zahra's right hand passed over fish entrails and other rotting substances that were equally repulsive to smell. Far in the corner, her hand brushed a piece of hard plastic. She squeezed her head and shoulders into the compartment, and her hand wrapped around the hard foam of the nylon life jacket. *Got it.*

Just as she tried to pull it out, the front of her boat hit a huge swell and a wave skimmed over the bow. Thwack. The cold water slapped Zahra in the chest. The boat tilted up, and she was flung backward. Her shoulders hit first, and the violent impact caused her head to whiplash right into the hard metal bars of a crab cage. The collision put her in the wobbly half state between consciousness and unconsciousness.

She struggled to her feet and looked over the bow. The swell had turned her boat left, and she was heading right into the path of the western tanker. Her knees gave out, and she fell onto her side. Zahra dry-heaved but only spit up a mouthful of warm bile. Her eyes watered.

Get up. Get up. Her brain gave commands that her body couldn't process. *You didn't come this far to give up.* Zahra struggled to her feet. The combination of the large waves and her concussion made her use both arms for balance. She dove into the compartment and pulled out the life vest. It was so bright she could see it in the moonlight. She quickly strapped it on.

The western tanker was only one hundred meters away and closing in. Zahra looked behind her. The ferries were a few hundred meters back, but slowing down to let the tankers pass. She had no choice. Seventy-five meters. She aimed right in front of the tanker and hoped her little fishing boat could sneak by. Fifty meters. She could not see one person on the tanker. Even if someone did spot her, it would be too late. *What happens if I go in? Will the ship chop me to pieces?* Zahra wiped her mind clean with a deep breath. *Don't think like that. You will get through this. You always do.*

Twenty-five meters. The fishing boat slowed down as it caught the massive wake from the starboard side of the ship, the engine grinding as it climbed. Ten meters. Zahra was not going to make it. She gripped the side railing and readied herself to jump overboard. Suddenly, the boat hit the crest of the wake and shot down. The small fishing vessel was now being propelled forward by the wake from the port side. It slipped past the wide part of the hull by only a few meters.

"Yes!" Zahra screamed. No one was there to hear her celebrate, but she didn't care. She looked over her left shoulder at the colossal machine. It was the biggest thing she had ever seen.

Zahra's smile was wiped from her face when she felt a rumble underneath her feet. A large cloud of smoke shot out of the engine and temporarily shielded the tanker's bright lights. The rumble stopped, and so did the engine. Her boat was out of gas.

It drifted to a stop. Zahra looked right. The eastern tanker was directly in her path and seventy-five meters out. *Damn it. Just one more minute, and I would have made it.*

Zahra didn't believe in God. She had seen too many men use him as an excuse for evil. But if he did exist, Zahra wished she could kick him in the testicles.

Fifty meters. Zahra was too exhausted to break down and cry. Every drop of liquid in her body had been sweated out. She didn't have a millimeter left to squeeze out a tear. The tanker's starboard lights radiated off the water, and Zahra noticed something floating twenty meters away. A water buoy. Twenty-five meters. *Now or never. What an introduction to my element,* she thought. Zahra fastened her linen pants and the straps on her life vest. *One. Two. Three.*

The frigid water froze her joints and collapsed her lungs. She bobbed up just as the tanker sliced through the fishing boat. The bow disappeared, and the back half sank quickly into the dark depths.

Don't panic. You're floating. The current from the tanker propelled her toward the buoy. She lifted her hands out of the water and used them like paddles. She only knew how to do it because David had shown her videos of him and Isaac surfing in India.

Zahra swam slowly, but she was in too much pain to move fast. Her body was covered in cuts from climbing down the mountain, and she could feel the salt water in each wound. They all throbbed together like a painful heartbeat. All that mattered was getting to the buoy.

The tanker had passed, and its lights faded, but a red light on the buoy flashed every three seconds. The red sea mark stood ten meters tall and rocked gently from side to side. They were placed in the narrow strait to keep ships in their lanes. Zahra reached out and felt its cold metal. She hugged the circular base and found a small ladder to climb up.

Her linen pants clung to her thin legs as she lifted herself out of the water. Zahra felt toward her lady part. *Thank you.* David's wooden box was still fastened tightly. She lifted her right foot onto the base of the buoy. *That's odd,* she thought. *Why is the base so soft?* Suddenly, a growl ripped through her eardrums. Zahra fell backward onto another soft surface, only this one moved. The red light on the top of the buoy flashed, and she realized she was sitting on top of a family of Mediterranean monk seals.

The one she stepped on raised its chest and opened its mouth, revealing large fangs. Although they were bottom feeders, seals were viciously territorial and the pod had an intruder. The large seal gnashed its teeth and tried to bite down on Zahra's leg. Darkness. The red buoy light went out. Her instincts kicked in, and she met its face with the flats of her feet. The whole pod of seals erupted in deafening barks. It was so loud she couldn't even hear herself think. Oddly enough, she had been in one similar situation before.

A group of local boys had followed her into an alley one time and tried to rape her. She had transformed into a banshee. She'd screamed, spit, kicked, punched, and even pissed in her pants. Zahra gave a repeat performance and avoided getting bit. The red light flashed, and she found enough space to scramble to her feet. She heard movement behind her and turned. The light went out.

A jet-black seal whipped its long neck and head-butted her upper thigh. Zahra was flung off the seamark like a rag doll. The frigid water was a relief compared to the teeth of the seals. She looked out to the horizon. *God damn it.* She had been turned around and had no idea which coast was Europe and which was Africa. She knew she was closer to Europe, but it was too dark to tell. What she wanted to do was unfasten her life vest and just peacefully sink to the bottom. But a familiar feeling told her to keep going. It was the same feeling that she'd had when her father sold her at the age of twelve. Her purchaser kept her locked in a room and constantly reminded her that on her thirteenth birthday she would be considered a woman. On that day, they could consummate their marriage.

Everything in her culture told her to accept those circumstances. She was lucky to have a husband to support her. It was impossible to resist hundreds of years of tradition. But deep inside, Zahra knew something else awaited her, something *better.* She couldn't pinpoint the feeling, but it became her motivating power. The night before her thirteenth birthday, she had climbed into bed and one of the legs of her metal cot snapped. She rolled into the center of the room and came to a stop right in the square of light that came through her only window. Zahra didn't believe in divine intervention. She believed in coincidences. She clubbed her fat husband in the morning and never looked back.

Just pick a direction, you idiot, or you'll freeze to death. Zahra started to swim toward one shore when she saw a bright reflection off the water. She used her hands to spin around.

CHAPTER 8: THREE OF SPADES

The massive Rock of Gibraltar lit up like a beacon so ships could navigate around Europa Point. The blue spotlights illuminated the white shale and crawled up the rock's thick base to its jetted peak. It was beautiful. But more important, it was *close.* It was only a few kilometers. Zahra was about to swim in the wrong direction. *Divine intervention or coincidence?* She had plenty of time to deliberate. Zahra headed toward her beacon.

From a distance, Redbeard watched through the long lenses of night-vision binoculars. Once again, he stood on Soter's Oculus yacht watching Zahra escape.

One of his Corsairs approached him. "Should I take the zodiac and pick her up?"

Redbeard turned to him. "I would not be who I am, if I had not suffered. She's too tough to die. She will also lead us straight to the boy."

CHAPTER 9

THE FOUR OF HEARTS

HERC'S TAVERN, GIBRALTAR

Herc's Tavern was bustling. Two Gypsy men played Spanish guitar, while bearded sailors wolfed down plates of *chili con carne.* The salty regulars settled into their elbow grooves. Isaac and Uncle Jack played nine-ball on the billiards table. The bartender set down a bowl of peanuts. Horus shrieked with delight and broke them apart.

"Those Gypos are decent, but no Maia," Uncle Jack said, as he motioned over to the guitarists.

"She had a great voice," Isaac said, as he nursed his pilsner. Uncle Jack approached his four-pint tipping-point when he went from friendly to *I'm bored, let's screw with someone.* Isaac could tell, because his eyes darted around the room looking for something to fight or fuck.

"Hey, bumhole. I've got your package upstairs. Don't forget it. Four ball, one-pocket," Uncle Jack said, as he lined up his shot.

"Thanks," Isaac said.

Jack sank the shot and rechalked his cue. "It sounds like a bloody African rain stick," Uncle Jack said. "I don't smoke a pipe, wear a queer hat, and solve mysteries, but I'm pretty sure I know what's inside." Uncle Jack made eye contact with Isaac as he lined up his next shot on the five ball.

"You know you can tell me anything," he said.

Isaac was on his second pint and felt loose. He debated whether or not to come clean about his schizophrenia but decided against it. "It's under control," he said.

Jack finessed the five ball into the side pocket.

Isaac only sought his uncle's counsel on the topics of drinking, fighting, and girls. Any other topic would end up back to an analogy of one of those three anyway.

"You've been wound tight the last few months," Uncle Jack said as he eyed the table for his next move.

"I'm fine," Isaac said.

"Family shite, school shite, or the insomnia shite?" Uncle Jack asked as he eyed the green six.

"I haven't got more than two or three hours of sleep in the last six months."

"You know what I do when I can't sleep?"

"I'm going to guess it involves a Spanish woman and some red wine."

Jack laughed. "Eat a bag of porpoise dicks." Jack banked in the six and stood up.

"Where would one acquire a bag of porpoise dicks?" Isaac asked sarcastically.

"Very funny, smart arse. Listen up. Lay flat in bed. Arms at your sides. Head back. Feet, shoulder-distance apart. Then flex *everything.*" Uncle Jack's whole body went rigid. From teeth to toes, he flexed as hard as he could. His face turned red, and his eyes bulged as he held his breath. Uncle Jack inhaled and said, "Hold this for one minute." Jack's body convulsed. His face went from bright red to dark purple.

Isaac shook his head and laughed. A minute passed. Jack let out a deep exhalation, and his body slackened.

"You'll melt into your bed like *wax.* Ten deep breaths and you're out."

"I'll stick with my pills," Isaac said. "I like to keep my eyeballs in their sockets."

Two leather-skinned fishermen walked up behind Uncle Jack. "Are you going to finish your game, or keep acting like a *stronzo?*"

Uncle Jack's eyes widened like those of a lion spotting a baby water buffalo on the Serengeti. He didn't know Italian, but he could swear in almost every language. He guessed by the French-sounding dialect that they were Corsican.

Jack winked at Isaac and then turned to face the two Corsicans. One had a brown beard and the other a black one.

"How about a friendly wager, Gentlemen?" Jack asked.

Brown Beard eyed him up and nodded.

"Eight-ball. Me and my nephew versus you and your boyfriend?"

"How much?" asked Black Beard.

"Enough so the loser doesn't want to stay and spend any more money," Jack said.

Brown Beard's intense eyes met Isaac's. He tried to get a read on the young boy. Isaac knew what to do. He looked away in apprehension. Brown Beard and Black Beard deliberated in Corsican. Then they pulled out wads of money and slammed them down on the table. "Three hundred euros. Take or leave?" Brown Beard said.

"We'll take it. And, after you lose, you have to leave," Jack said.

Brown Beard smirked. "Deal. Me and the boy lag."

Jack smiled. "Suit yourself."

Brown Beard lined up his lag shot and sent the cue ball to other side. It rolled to a stop ten centimeters from the head rail. Brown Beard was impressed with himself. He turned to Isaac and said, "*Vaffanculo!*"

Uncle Jack played up the theatrics. He rubbed Isaac's head and said, "Remember, it's *just* a game, lad."

Isaac spread his legs, crouched down, and lined up the cue ball. It didn't matter if these Corsicans had been pub champions for years, they didn't know the mechanics of the game like Isaac did. On the rugby pitch, he couldn't run or tackle, but he could kick one through the uprights. In the pub, he couldn't impress a girl or instill fear into one man, but the two fishermen had just stepped into his arena: physics. In this coliseum, Isaac was Spartacus. Newton's second law was his sword, and Hooke's law was his shield. The two Corsicans had challenged the wrong gladiator.

Isaac lined up his shot and replayed the formula in his head—force times mass equals acceleration. He calculated and shot. The cue ball bounced off the foot rail, coasted past the head spot, and stopped two centimeters from the rail.

"*Merda!*" screamed Brown Beard.

Isaac proceeded to clear the table.

"You cheated us," said Brown Beard as he tried to take his money off the table.

"Ah, ah, ah. Wait a minute," Jack said as he slammed down the pool stick right next to Brown Beard's dirty fingers. The music stopped. The twenty-five patrons in the bar heard the whack and turned in their squeaky stools. Their good friend, Uncle Jack, was about to provide the night's entertainment, and he *never* disappointed. The two Gypsy guitarists looked up and started to play a slow building duet that sounded like an Ennio Morricone song from a Spaghetti Western. A fistfight was inevitable. Isaac backed up.

Brown Beard turned to Black Beard. "We have been hustled. The boy is a *squalo.*"

"A bet is a bet," Uncle Jack said as he pulled their money off the table. He pulled out ten euros and stuffed the rest into his cargo pants. "I'll tell you what," he said as he held up the bill. The pub patrons leaned forward in anticipation. The next line would be an Uncle Jack original that would be recited over and over for the next few weeks. "Here's ten euros," Jack said as he crumpled the bill and threw it in Brown Beard's face. "Why don't you go outside, buy yourself a falafel, and then give your boyfriend a reach around?"

The bar cheered, and Brown Beard lunged. Jack stepped back and introduced him to a three-punch combo. The Gypsy guitarists picked up the pace. Black Beard wrapped up Jack, and the cyclone of tangled man bodies crashed into an empty table. The Gypsy guitarists hit full stride and had the patrons in a frenzy. They were pounding their fists to the music and yelling insults at the Corsicans. Horus ran out from under the bar, jumped on the rafter, and shrieked. The distraction gave Jack his window. He wrestled Brown Beard into a scissor-lock and then put Black Beard into a headlock.

"Say, Bonaparte?" Jack said, tightening his holds. Both Corsicans threw half-cocked body shots. "Someone bring me a pint," Uncle Jack finished playfully as he held his attackers at bay. The patrons continued to shout so no one heard the pub's door swing open except for Isaac.

Isaac noticed her eyes first. They were an absorbing green. Then he noticed she was soaking wet and on the verge of hypothermia. Her dark skin had taken on a light-blue tinge, and she shivered uncontrollably. Her wet linen clothes clung tightly to her petite breasts and thin legs. Isaac froze. *What was the beautiful girl from his parents' village doing here?*

Zahra stepped forward and crossed her arms. She desperately tried to stop her body from shaking. The whole bar was fixated on the fight. Zahra cleared her throat and channeled her last ounce of energy into a loud yell. "I'm looking for Jack O'Ryan."

The guitarists stopped. The patrons turned, and the wrestling ceased. Everyone stared at the soaking-wet Moroccan girl.

Minutes later, Jack carried Zahra's shivering body into his apartment, which was directly above Herc's tavern.

"Who is she?" Jack asked.

"She's from Mom and Dad's camp in Morocco," Isaac said. "I have no idea what she's doing here."

Zahra shook uncontrollably and mumbled to herself.

"She's got the *umbles*," Jack said.

"The what?" Isaac asked.

"The mumbles and the stumbles," Jack said. "She's moving into stage three of hypothermia. If we don't move fast, her organs could shut down."

"Should we put her in the shower?" Isaac asked.

"No. Hot water could give her a heart attack."

This was why Isaac always trusted Jack. One minute, he could be messing about in a pub, but if the situation called for it, he could snap right back into military mode.

"Go over and fill two canteens with hot water," Jack said. Isaac turned on the sink and rummaged through the cupboards for the canteens.

Jack placed Zahra on the bed and tried to pull her wet pants off. She was barely coherent but resisted. Jack gently cupped the back of her neck and said, "Listen, love. I am *not* trying to hurt you. If we don't get you out of these wet clothes, you could *die*. I know what I'm doing. Do you understand?"

Zahra nodded and then finally broke down. As Jack laid her down on the bed, she whimpered and tears rolled down the side of her face into her ear canals. Jack pulled off her wet pants and shirt. She was topless, lying on his bed in only her cotton underwear.

Jack reached under his frame and pulled out a sleeping bag. Isaac returned with the two canteens of hot water. He knew it was horrible to admire her naked body, but it was the most beautiful thing he had ever seen, even if it was blue.

Jack interrupted his gaze and yelled, "Isaac! Quit fucking about and strip down."

"What?" Isaac asked.

"Underoos! Now!" Jack yelled without a trace of humor.

His tone scared Isaac, and he stripped quickly. Jack opened the sleeping bag and placed Zahra inside. She was slipping out of consciousness.

"What are we doing?" Isaac asked.

"Saving her life," Jack said as he ripped off his shirt and pants. "Hand me the canteens."

Uncle Jack slid into the sleeping bag with Zahra, put the two warm canteens under her armpits, and zipped it up. "Get on the other side," he said.

Isaac crawled into the other side of the sleeping bag as Jack wrapped himself around Zahra's thin body.

"Wrap your arms and legs around her," Jack said.

Isaac slid into place. He could feel his penis settle between her buttocks. Every millimeter of her skin was freezing. Isaac wrapped his arms and legs around her body. He could feel her body sucking the warmth out of his like a sponge.

"Her blood is too cold to circulate," Uncle Jack said. "That why she's unconscious. Rub her skin to get it moving." On any other occasion, Isaac would have thought it was one of Jack's perverse schemes, but not this time. Isaac could sense the urgency in his voice. Isaac rubbed Zahra's upper thighs while Jack worked her upper body. It was, sadly, the most intimate thing he had ever done with a woman, and she wasn't even conscious.

Forty minutes later, Zahra regained consciousness.

"There she is," Jack said.

Zahra's eyes widened when she realized that she was naked inside a sleeping bag with two men. The banshee came out. She instinctively threw her knee into Jack's groin, and he exhaled a painful curse that came out as one long syllable. She brought down the back of her fist into Isaac's groin, and it split his bollocks like a Newton's cradle. Zahra kicked and screamed like a wild animal. Jack and Isaac scrambled out of the sleeping bag and backed up to the headboard.

"I think she's feeling better," Uncle Jack said. Isaac was terrified. He had never seen a girl become so violent so quickly. Zahra scurried to the other side of the bed and covered her naked body with the sleeping bag. She breathed heavily and tried to wrap her head around the last twenty-four hours.

"Calm down," Uncle Jack said. "That was the quickest way to warm you up. Grab one of the canteens in the bag. You need to drink some warm fluids."

"Where are my clothes?" Zahra asked.

"That's step two. First, Isaac and I are going to put our clothes on. You drink that water, and I will find you some of my ex-girlfriend's clothes."

Zahra nodded and then fumbled around the sleeping bag for the canteens. Isaac silently redressed while Jack jumped into his cargo pants and left the room.

Zahra sipped from the canteen and surveyed Jack's place. It was a small, two-room apartment filled with military artifacts from all over the world. Her gaze stopped on Isaac, who was too embarrassed to make eye contact with her. He was pale and still boyish looking apart from the small patch of chest hair on his sternum.

Isaac buttoned his Naval Academy shirt and broke the long silence. "Are you all right?"

Zahra nodded and finished the water. Jack returned holding a handful of clothes and wearing a jingling belly dancer's top. She spit out her water. His love handles bounced with every step. Isaac had never been more proud of his uncle. He always knew how to break up a tense situation. "My ex- was a belly dancer," Jack said as he turned in a full circle. "As you can see, most of her stuff is not suitable for a young lady."

"You look like a fool," Zahra said and smiled.

"Well, so do you. Here are some clothes," Jack said. "Isaac and I are going to go into the other room to make some food for you. Then, you need to tell us what happened."

She nodded, and Jack placed a pile of clothes on the bed with a pair of well-worn black leather knee-high paddock boots. Zahra's eyes lit up. They would be her first nice pair of shoes, and she felt like she had earned them.

Five minutes later, she came out in one of Maia's outfits: a long, flowing skirt; tight leggings; a colorful blouse; half-finger wool gloves; and a thin brown leather jacket.

"Brilliant," Jack said. "Just don't walk to close to tourists or they'll think you're a Gypsy pickpocket. Zahra tilted her head and squinted her eyes as she sat down. It was her go-to look when she did not understand an English reference.

Isaac nervously poured her a cup of Earl Grey tea while Jack arranged a cutting board of bread, cheese, and olives.

Zahra shoveled the bread into her mouth, starved. "Your parents have been kidnapped," she announced without hesitation..

"Who took them?" Jack asked.

"I do not know. They attacked our camp," she said.

Isaac's head tilted down toward the table, and his eyes started to dart back and forth. Zahra could see him imagining horrible scenarios. He looked disoriented, and he started to hyperventilate. It was the onset of an anxiety attack. Jack reached over the table, grabbed Isaac by the back of his neck, and snapped his fingers in front of his face.

"Calm down," Jack said. "You're parents have been in bad situations before."

"What if they're already dead?" Isaac asked.

"They're not dead," Jack said. "You know why, mate? They're loaded. Kidnappers don't kill rich people. They hold them hostage. We just have to find out who took them."

"David said that Isaac is in trouble," Zahra said.

"Me?" The mention of his name forced him out of his fog.

"He told me to give you this," Zahra said and swallowed a mouthful of olives. She reached into her jacket pocket and placed the box on the table.

Isaac unfastened the latch and opened the top. Inside, there was a neat stack of rectangular bronze objects with a concentric circle engraving. Some of the bronze had oxidized, creating growths of beautiful turquoise that acted as a protective coating. Isaac picked one up and held it to his face. The bronze made it quite heavy even though it was only about six by nine centimeters and no wider than a credit card.

"Bloody playing cards?" Jack asked, eyeing the opposite side of the object.

Isaac quickly flipped it over in his hand. All it had was two simple rusted etchings of spades. He pulled the remaining cards out of the box and spread them out in his hands. There were no numbers, but all fifty-two had different numbers of heart, club, diamond, and spade inscriptions. It was just like an ordinary deck of Bicycle cards. The royal cards had profile designs of regal-looking males and females, and the aces had one giant inscription of each suit. They looked like a hybrid between ancient Greek coins and playing cards.

"That mark on the back looks very familiar," Jack said.

Zahra was visibly disappointed. They were brilliant pieces of art, but she had just gone through hell-and-back to get them there.

Isaac turned the cards over again to examine the symbol and noticed it wasn't just an engraving. The concentric circles were made of intricate gears.

"These aren't just cards," Isaac said examining small divots in the side of one of the cards. "They're very intricately constructed."

"I'll be right back," Jack said. He left the room and started rummaging through a closet.

"Did my father say anything about them?" Isaac asked.

"No," Zahra said. "The men came in on horseback looking for him. Your father took me to his tent and told me to bring them to you. That is all I know."

"Maybe they're some kind of artifact worth a lot of money, but it also seems like they fit together somehow," Isaac speculated aloud.

"Before I snuck out, you're father and I were attacked," Zahra said. "He pulled out some kind of magic weapon and fought off three men."

Isaac looked up from the cards. Beautiful Moroccan girl in Gibraltar? Bronze playing cards? Kidnapped parents? Magic weapons? His head was spinning.

"Aha," Jack said as he reentered the room. In his hand was a leather necklace with a bronze cross exactly like the symbol on the cards. "Maia used to wear this all the time. I have no clue what it is, but I know who will."

"Who?" Isaac asked.

"There's an old Gypsy fortune-teller who lives above the botanical gardens."

Isaac turned to Zahra. "Are you all right to walk?"

Zahra stuffed the rest of the bread and cheese into her pockets. "Let's go."

CHAPTER 10:
THE FOUR OF CLUBS

MAIN STREET, GIBRALTAR

"Keep up, Isaac," Jack said.

Zahra had no problems keeping stride with Jack and Horus as they weaved around tipsy tourists. Isaac was a different story. Every other step, he had to say, "Excuse me." The group navigated their way to the end of Main Street. Jack failed to point out every single historical landmark. Instead, he pointed out his favorite kebab shops, the cheapest place to get a massage, and a park bench where he passed out once. Isaac had trouble reading Zahra. He couldn't tell if she loved or hated Jack. At least she and he had one thing in common, they were both quiet.

The group merged around the Queens Hotel—which Jack said was full of pasty-eating inbreds from Cornwall—and onto Red Sands Road. Jack nudged Horus with his foot, and the little monkey looked up at his owner. "Listen, you little bugger, we're going to cut through the botanical gardens. *No fighting.*"

Horus squealed back at Jack, and Zahra asked, "Why do you speak to him as if he can hear you?"

"Because he's the only one that listens to him," Isaac said. Quickly realizing that his sarcasm was lost in translation, he covered it by anxiously spouting off facts. "Did you know that there are two hundred and fifty wild macaques in Gibraltar, and they all belong to one of five troops?" The group entered the overhang of the lush gardens, and Isaac continued to ramble, "The macaques migrated from Morocco and all of their troops are matriarchal."

Zahra tilted her head.

"Matriarchal means that the women are in charge, and it's the males' jobs to raise the kids," Isaac said.

She pondered for a moment and said, "It all makes sense now. I come from a country where the monkeys are smarter than the people."

Isaac laughed as they strolled past a tipsy wedding party taking photos in a gazebo.

They entered a canopied bridge that was encased by tropical vines and thick wooden roots that looked like walls of boa constrictors. A pack of macaques were perched on top of the walkway and started to taunt Horus with high-pitched battle cries. Jack looked down. "Don't you do it, you little bastard." But Horus was too much like his owner. He climbed up the vines, leaped to a tree, and taunted the other monkeys right back.

"Damn. He'll find us later," Jack said. They came to a clearing and looked up to the massive white building nestled into the base of the mountain. "The Rock Hotel," he said. "This way. The Gypos have a place right next door."

The sign read, "*Fortunes by Madame Dragomir.*" Below the title was a painted photo of a woman in a long, flowing white robe, restraining a lion by his nose and jaw.

"That's the tarot card for strength," Jack said as he opened the iron gate. "Maia always left those lying around. It reminded me of our relationship and how she tamed this hairy beast." They stepped into a cobblestone courtyard lit by hanging paper lanterns. There were two Romani wagons filled with Gypsy gifts and a stone staircase that led to a small house above.

A tall, gaunt Gypsy unfolded from his chair. "My name is Gavril. May I help you?"

Jack sized him up and said, "We want to speak to the madam."

"She is done reading for the night," Gavril said, his tone dismissive.

Isaac saw Jack's fists tighten and stepped in. "We have something that would be of *great* interest to her."

Gavril stroked his conquistador beard and said, "Perhaps if you purchased a gift, I could see if the madam is still available."

Jack said, "Listen, you Gypo. We're not some pasty Brits here on holiday. Our family is in trouble, and she can help."

Gavril motioned over toward his wagon of trinkets. "There are some very nice bracelets for the girl." He smiled and revealed a gold-capped incisor.

Jack said, "This is a waste of time." As he reached the gate, Horus leaped up.

Gavril's eyes narrowed. "Horus?" The monkey recognized Gavril and climbed up his baggy clothing.

The tall Gypsy approached Jack. "Maia was a good friend," Gavril said.

"Hopefully not *too* good of a friend," Jack said taking a slight step forward.

Gavril laughed and said, "Go upstairs, Jack the Sailor. The madam will be in the back."

As the group climbed the long staircase, Jack playfully kicked Horus. "Good timing, you little bugger."

Madame Dragomir's room was filled with blood-red furniture and stained wooden antiques and the windows adorned with aubergine drapes. Slavic paintings and leather-bound books lined the walls. Incense and candle smoke were thick in the air.

"Hello?" Jack said as he closed the heavy wooden door.

Madame Dragomir parted the drapes in the back and spotted Horus.

"Horus?" The monkey leaped up and strutted across her table. The madam grabbed a bowl of peanuts off her shelf and put them in her lap. She was easily in her seventies, but there were signs of a faded beauty under her wrinkles.

"I do not know where she is." The madam motioned for the group to sit as she stroked the preoccupied monkey. "But I did read her cards and saw that a move was in her future."

"I'm not here to talk about Maia. Besides, she knows where to find me if she comes back."

"You should know two things, Jack the Sailor. One: there is something in a Gypsy's blood that calls to them. It puts them where they are supposed to be. If it was meant to be, fate will bring you together again." The madam leaned forward toward Isaac and Zahra. "Two: you shouldn't fall in love so easily."

"Hey, I heard that," Jack said. "I told you I'm not here to discuss my love life."

The madam's cat-like, hazel eyes moved from Jack to Isaac. "So, what are you here to discuss?"

"My mother and father were kidnapped in Morocco," Isaac said.

"I am sorry to hear that," said the madam, gently nudging Horus off her lap.

"Zahra was with them when their camp was attacked," Isaac said.

"And who is your father?" asked the madam.

"He's an American philanthropist. He invented the hundred-dollar laptop and does humanitarian missions all over the world with my mother, who's a doctor," Isaac said.

Zahra chimed in. "His father gave me something to get to Isaac. He told me to guard it with my life."

"And I suppose you want me to have a look at this item?" the madam asked.

Isaac reached into his backpack and pulled out the wooden box. The madam put on the reading glasses that hung around her neck and examined the engraved pine box. She unlocked the latch, pulled out the bronze cards, and spread them out in her hands.

"*Draga Dumnezeu!*" The old lady bolted upright so quickly that Isaac and Zahra flinched. "You have no idea how *important* these are!"

"What are they?" Isaac asked.

"Dear boy, I would not know where to begin," she said.

"How about the beginning?" Isaac suggested.

There was a long moment of silence as the Gypsy woman tried to figure out how to proceed.

"Get comfortable," the madam said as she spread the bronze playing cards into a perfectly shaped arch. Isaac, Zahra, and Jack settled back into their chairs.

"Most Westerners see playing cards as an object for games or gambling. Only Gypsies know that they have a much more *important* purpose," she said. "Think about cards for a moment. Their basic design has remained since ancient times, and they are engrained into almost every country's vernacular. I'm sure you can think of a few examples."

"Ace in the hole," Isaac said.

"Jack of all trades, like me," Jack said looking around for approval and getting none.

"There is a reason playing cards have a connection with us on a subconscious level. Their origin is shrouded in mystery. But what if I was to tell you that playing cards outdated any object or invention you could think of?"

"The cross," Isaac said.

"Much older," said the madam.

"Democracy? Invented by the Greeks in 500 BC," Isaac said.

"*Much* older."

Isaac turned to Uncle Jack for help. "Don't look at me. Before the British Empire, there was a bloke named Jesus, and before him, it was just a bunch of homos in togas."

"How about the alphabet?" Isaac said. "The Phoenicians invented it around 1100 BCE."

"*Much older,*" said the madam.

"Are you trying to tell me that poker was invented before the alphabet?" Jack asked.

"Playing cards were invented for something much more important than *poker*," she answered.

Isaac said, "Who were before the Phoenicians? The Egyptians? They invented hieroglyphs around 3000 BC."

"Now you're close, dear boy," the madam said. "Every great civilization claims to have invented playing cards: the Egyptians, Persians, Chinese, Mayans, and Europeans. Every one of those great empires had slightly different variations of playing cards, but all of their decks had four suits, twelve royal cards, thirteen cards per suit, and fifty-two cards in a deck."

Isaac, Jack, and Zahra quietly tried to process all of her information.

"Isaac, let me ask you a question. Did the Mayans and Egyptians ever have direct contact?"

"Nothing that was recorded," Isaac said.

"Exactly. Do you find it odd that two cultures from opposite ends of the earth developed the *same* invention?"

The group nodded, and the madam continued, "When we find a certain invention claimed by a large number of nations scattered across the globe, we must conclude that none of them were the *original* creators. They, in fact, received the invention from a civilization that preceded them by many years."

"Let me ask you a question," Jack said. "Is there an ending to this lesson? I've gotta find my goddamn sister."

In one quick motion, the madam whipped a peanut into Uncle Jack's unsuspecting face.

"Ow," Jack said as he rubbed his forehead. "What did you do that for?"

"If this group was a body, you would be the fist," the madam said and then asked, "Do you punch yourself when you're trying to think?"

"No," Jack said.

"Then be quiet and wait until there is something to punch," she said, motioning to Isaac. "Let the brain work."

Jack motioned for her to continue and then crossed his arms and sulked like a schoolgirl.

"This information is within *you*, Isaac. We just have to pull it out. Think about the numbers in cards as a pattern. Start with four."

While Isaac kicked around the possibilities, Zahra said, "There are four seasons."

"Beautiful *and* smart," said the madam.

Isaac's brain clicked. "It's numerology. Four suits for the four seasons. Twelve royal cards for twelve months of the year. Thirteen cards per suit must mean the thirteen new moons per year, and fifty-two is for the number of weeks in a year."

The madam said, "Then you take five plus two to get seven. Seven times fifty-two is?"

"Three hundred and sixty-four days a year."

"But it's three hundred and sixty-five days," Jack said tapping his index finger on the table.

The madam nodded at Horus, and the monkey chucked a peanut shell at Jack.

"Horus! You little eggs Benedict," Jack said.

"Actually, I learned about this in astronomy class. Ancient civilizations did not count December 31. It was considered a holiday, and they used it to factor in leap years."

"I knew you would get it, boy. The inventors of playing cards synchronized them to what you know as astrology and numerology. They spent thousands of years comparing the movement of the planets and stars with their observations of human behavior. Like you just did, they found a pattern, cracked the code, and embedded playing cards with the secrets of the stars."

"That's brilliant," Isaac said, running his hands over the bronze deck. "I would have never thought that the stars and planets could be part of some kind natural algebraic equation."

"Their inventors believed that the planets had a magnetic influence over human beings as they orbited around earth," said the madam. "The day of your birth determined your personality, your destiny, and how the planets would influence you for the *rest* of your life."

"Oh, come on. This is some crazy, kaka-laka bollocks," said Jack, covering his face as the madam reached for another peanut.

"There is another pattern developing here," she said, looking back to Isaac and Zahra. "You open your mouth, and I prove you wrong. Is it so crazy to believe the planets influence us? Just think about how the moon affects us. Zahra, have you become a woman yet?"

Zahra cocked her head to the side and said nothing.

"Have you menstruated?" asked the madam. "Are you able to bear children?"

Zahra was not comfortable responding with anything but a nod. Her cheeks were red.

"Women and their cycles are directly synchronized with the moon. The very word *menstruation* in Greek means *months of the moon*. It is so powerful that it pulls our tides to different ends of the earth and brings down vast continents, one grain at a time. Why is it so crazy to believe that planets, hundreds of times the size of our moon, have an effect on us?"

"All of my life I've clung to science, I think, because it gives me an easy way to identify and label anything that crosses my path, but this is something beyond my textbooks, and your argument is too logical to ignore. However, I'm still unsure about why my parents wanted *me* to know this."

"I said the same thing and got a peanut to the face," Jack said.

"Yes, but not as eloquently. We will start with *you*, Mr. Tough Sailor," said the madam. "One more question, and if my response does not astound you, then you can seek your answers elsewhere."

"Fine," Jack said as he rolled his eyes. Isaac calmed him down with a pat on the forearm.

"What is your day of birth?" the madam asked.

"April 10," Jack said in a disdainful tone.

The madam ran her hands down the bronze deck and pulled out a face card.

"You are the Jack of Diamonds," she said.

"How convenient," Jack said mockingly.

"It is a royal card, which tells me that you are dynamic and possess innate leadership qualities. You are able to quickly assess new situations and use them to your advantage."

"Nothing you couldn't have learned from Maia," Jack said.

"Your diamond suit tells me that you're innovative and enterprising," the madam continued. "You excel in commerce because you have an intuitive understanding of people's desires."

Jack was still unfazed. "Keep trying, lady. You're not going to find a kink in my armor," he said.

"It's chink, Jack. *Chink*," Isaac fired back.

"Like a Chinaman?" Jack asked laughing it off. "Don't think so, mate."

The madam's hazel eyes narrowed. Isaac could tell she was coiled and about to strike. "The Jack card tells me that you are immature and irresponsible."

"As are all people with good stories," Jack said.

"The combination of self-confidence and self-indulgence brings you to high-highs and disheartening lows," she added.

"And you also just described every alcoholic," Jack retorted. "Keep trying, love."

Madame Dragomir smiled. Time to go for the throat. "The Jack of Diamonds is plagued by two major conflicts throughout his life. The first is his battle with spirituality. Because the Jack of Diamonds is blessed with inherent business acumen, he gets trapped between what inspires him and what is financially lucrative. When he pursues success and recognition, his spiritual half becomes stagnant. His goal is to develop a healthy balance between his material world and his spiritual world."

Jack cleared his throat and shifted in his chair.

"Secondly, the Jack of Diamonds pursues freedom in all areas of his life but one: love. The Jack navigates through so much dishonesty in his business endeavors that he craves the opposite in his relationships. He seeks a partnership that is built on stability, loyalty, and honesty."

Jack looked down at his hands in his lap. For once, he was silent.

"Behind the fun-loving armor of the Jack, there is a lonely soul," the madam said. "It is hard for him to find a mate. It must be someone who allows him to remain a free spirit in the public eye while trusting him to remain devoted in their private lives."

"That's enough!" Jack yelled. "I told you that we're *not* here to discuss my love life."

"It is important for the Jack of Diamond's personal success and growth that everyone except his partner think he is single," she added.

Jack covered his eyes by stroking his forehead with his hand.

"Do I have your attention now, Jack the Sailor?" she asked.

Isaac said, "A team of psychologists couldn't have said it better."

Jack finally looked up. "I've already lived a full life, and she knows me inside out from my *birthday*? It's because Maia was up here blabbing."

"Isaac, I assume your parents wanted you to know something about yourself," the madam said. "When is your day of birth?"

"March 9," Isaac said.

"*Draga Dumenezeu!* That has *everything* to do with it." The madam ran her hand down the bronze deck. "Your card is the most feared and enigmatic card in the deck. You, my boy, are the Ace of Spades."

The madam pulled out the card that had only an engraving of one giant spade and placed it in front of Isaac.

"Many of histories' greatest and worst leaders were physical embodiments of this card."

"What's so different about the Ace of Spades?" Isaac asked.

The madam ripped off her thin scarf and held it up. "The Ace of Spades is considered to be the veil between our material world and the spiritual world. Let me ask you a question. Are you plagued by reoccurring dreams?"

He felt like he had just been punched in the gut. His head spun, and he gripped his chair for support.

"Oh, *dear* boy," the madam said. "You've never told anyone, have you?"

Isaac couldn't muster a response. Emotions flooded his body, and his eyes welled up. He did not want to show weakness in front of his uncle, so he burrowed into his hoodie.

"He's been taking serious medications for the last few months," Jack said. "Could that have anything to do with it?"

"Yes, of course. You see, the Ace of Spades—" The madam was cut off by a loud crash and scream from outside.

"Run!" Gavril yelled.

Uncle Jack jolted up, pulled back the curtains, and looked into the courtyard.

"What the hell?" Jack asked.

The Turkish Corsairs had cornered Gavril. He swung his long arms in defense, but Redbeard sneaked up behind him and twisted a knife into his kidney.

Zahra stood next to Jack. "It's the same men who took David and Rachel." Jack reached to unbolt the door. Zahra stopped him. "These men are *very* dangerous."

"So am I," Jack said.

Zahra refused to move her hand from the lock.

Madame Dragomir broke their deadlock. "Come this way. We can go out the back."

She quickly pulled a brown leather book from her shelf, while Isaac wiped his tears and threw the bronze cards into his backpack.

She led them out a back door and into another courtyard right as the Turkish Corsairs reached the front door. They heard several failed kicks and then the sound of shattering glass. Redbeard and his men were not far behind.

"Jack, do you know about Operation Tracer?" the madam asked as she led them out the courtyard into the steep cobblestoned streets at the base of the mountain.

"How do you think I get black-market shite in and out of this rock?"

"What is it?" Zahra asked quietly. Isaac was behind them, still trying to make sense of what had just happened.

"Gibraltar was used as a British naval base during World War II. They built a huge network of tunnels under the city so they could evacuate if the Germans attacked."

The group followed the madam through two narrow alleyways and into a courtyard that opened up to the base of the hill. She was nimble for an elderly woman.

Madame Dragomir led them up the rocky slope and stopped in a thicket of bushes.

"Quiet," she said pulling them down.

The three Corsairs stopped at the base of the hill to let their eyes adjust to the darkness. Zahra grabbed Isaac's arm when she heard them unsheathe their swords. They nodded to each other and then spread out over the hill.

The group crouched behind the bushes for cover.

"Time for the fist to get to work," the madam said as she looked at Jack. Then she quietly knocked on the ground. It wasn't dirt. It was metal. They stood on top of a large, hidden grate.

One of the Corsairs was stealthily ascending right toward them. Jack quietly slipped his fingers into the grate and lifted. The rusted metal grate slid open.

Jack looked at his monkey and whispered, "Boat. Go."

Horus tilted his head and then sprinted from the thicket. His tiny hands and feet crunched on top of the dry leaves. The Corsair picked up the sound and then ran toward it. Jack pulled the grate to the side releasing a damp odor from below. Madame Dragomir grabbed Jack by the arm and pulled him close. She leaned into him and whispered something that Isaac and Zahra couldn't hear. Jack looked right at her. "I know."

Jack then went, arse first, into the darkness.

Zahra followed. Madame Dragomir put her hand on Isaac and then showed him the book she'd grabbed in her room. "Go to visit this man. He will be able to answer all of your questions." The madam stuffed the book into Isaac's backpack. Then she reached into a small chest pouch that hung around her neck and pulled out a silver coin. She handed it to Isaac.

"What is this?" Isaac asked examining the Roman bust on one side and the goat with a fish tail on the other.

"It has been my family's good-luck charm for centuries," the madam said. "It will protect you."

Isaac pocketed the coin, started to lower himself down, and then stopped, "How did you know about my dreams?"

"They are not dreams, dear boy," said Madame Dragomir. "They are messages. You must learn how to decipher them. Now, go."

The old Gypsy closed the grate, and Isaac climbed down the ladder into complete darkness.

CHAPTER 11:
THE FOUR OF DIAMONDS

THE GREAT SIEGE TUNNELS OF
GIBRALTAR

Complete darkness. The air was so damp Isaac could taste it. He found the cold stone wall with his right hand and felt his way down the narrow tunnel. Thoughts bounced around his head like loose atoms. *What did she mean* messages? *Who the hell are these Arabs chasing us? Are my parents still alive?*

Uncle Jack's voice echoed from down the tunnel. "Keep coming."

Isaac felt the warmth of a body. A hand grabbed his. It was Zahra's. Her touch sent a shiver through his body. She gripped tight, letting him know she was also scared.

"Hold onto each other," Jack said as he led the group through the pitch-black tunnels. Isaac's hand perspired in Zahra's. *Funny,* he thought. *Girls scare me more than swords. We're being chased by assassins, and I'm worried about sweating.* Suddenly, the grate creaked open. The Corsairs had found the tunnel and climbed down.

"Pick up the pace, team," Jack said as he jogged. Zahra pulled Isaac faster.

"I know these tunnels like the back of my—" A loud collision prevented Uncle Jack from finishing his sentence. He had run right into a wall, and Zahra and Isaac stumbled over him.

"Bloody Hell!" Jack said.

Zahra looked up and saw a light at the end of the tunnel. "Look," she said. The tunnel had come to a split. They scrambled to their feet and sprinted toward the light.

"The tunnels are still full of equipment," Jack said. "Grab anything we can use as a weapon."

The group tore through the passageways, which were lined with small side-paneled lights. Isaac looked over his shoulder. Redbeard and his two Corsairs came out of the darkness, about one hundred meters behind them.

"They're coming!" Isaac yelled.

They sprinted toward a large fork in the tunnels. The schism split around a massive metal circle. "It's a water tank," Jack said, "for putting out fires."

They veered left, but Zahra stopped from a dead sprint. "Jack!" she yelled.

On the wall was a wooden door to an old mining shed. Without hesitation, Jack threw his foot into the door. The dried-up wood smashed open and revealed a closet of mining equipment. He reached for the dynamite. "Bloody arse, shite, damn it. I don't have a lighter." Jack grabbed a rusted pickax and turned to Isaac. "Grab the dynamite and run ahead. I have an idea."

Isaac ripped off his backpack, and Zahra stuffed it with the sticks. Jack stepped outside and looked down the tunnel. The Corsairs were fifty meters away. He looked up at the massive water container. It held at least 250,000 liters of water, enough to wreak havoc in a tight corridor. He aimed the pickaxe right for the center of the metal container. His first hit snapped the pointy edge in half.

"Twatcock!" Jack yelled. The Corsairs were twenty-five meters away, and Jack thought about trying to take them on with his mining tool. He flipped it around and swung. It dented the metal but didn't break it. Jack swung again. Redbeard pulled a throwing knife from his belt. He was almost within striking distance. Jack swung back with all his power and followed through. A meter-wide section of rusted container burst open like it had exploded. The force of the outpouring water ripped the pickax from Jack's hands. Redbeard released his throwing knife just as the waist-high flood of water tackled him. Jack ducked, and the knife ricocheted off the metal with a spark.

"Ya missed, wanker," Jack said as he turned and sprinted down the tunnel.

The hole in the container widened, and the water rushed down all three corridors. Redbeard and his men held onto the lighting wires, but the water rose from their waists to their chests in a matter of seconds. The force became too powerful. One by one, the three Corsairs let go and were swept down the tunnel.

Jack trudged through the knee-high water and reached Isaac and Zahra. They had climbed up a ladder to avoid the deluge, but it was already receding. It wouldn't be long before the Corsairs were back on their tail. The group ascended the ladder, and Isaac pushed open the grate above.

When Isaac poked his head out, he stared into an auditorium of stalactites and at least a hundred staring faces. They had come up into a packed tour of St. Michael's cave. The tourists were speechless. Were these three people part of the show? Jack was the last one out.

A voice from the crowd interrupted the awkward silence. "It's Captain Jack." They looked up and saw the Spanish girl and her mother waving enthusiastically. The crowd clapped and assumed it was all part of the tour.

Jack didn't miss a beat. "That's right, Ladies and Gentlemen. Next up, there will be some real-life Barbary pirates. Come down and get your pictures with them."

The large group of tourists stepped forward, and the Englishman from the boat approached Jack. "Hey there, Captain. Mum's the word on our little deal. Although...I was wondering if I could tell my wife."

"Sure," Jack said. "Give me your lighter, and we'll call it even." The Englishman reached into his trousers and handed it over. Jack shoved a confused tour guide out of the way. "All right, everyone, come closer," Jack said. "This will be your only chance to meet *real* pirates."

The tourists circled around the stage. Jack looked at Isaac and Zahra and said, "My boat. Now."

THE FOUR OF SPADES

GIBRALTAR STREETS

The group sprinted up Queensway Boulevard along the coast. Zahra easily strode past both of them in her new boots. Jack was full of pints, and Isaac was carrying a backpack full of dynamite. The pale ales sloshed around Jack's stomach and caused him to cramp up. Isaac saw his uncle do something both spectacular and disturbing. In a dead sprint, Jack crammed his index and middle finger down his throat and gagged himself. His entire body contracted and then ejected a jet stream of grayish-brown splatter. Isaac had to hurdle the vomit.

Without breaking stride, Jack turned to Isaac and said, "That's called a dockyard omelet."

Zahra was thirty meters ahead and stopped at the entrance of the Queensway marina. She looked down the long boulevard and pointed back. Jack and Isaac looked over their shoulders.

Redbeard and his Corsairs had confiscated a scooter from some unlucky tourist.

"Relentless," Jack said.

Redbeard drove, and the two other Corsairs sat sidesaddle in their soggy turbans and wet robes. Jack couldn't help but chuckle. Aside from the swords and the stone-cold faces, it looked like the beginning of a circus act.

"Flip your bag around and twist those wicks," Uncle Jack said.

They could hear the high-pitched whine of the scooter's engine. Isaac slid the bag to the front of his body and put his arms in the straps to secure it. Jack yelled ahead to Zahra, "End of the dock, my boat is called the *Sin Bin*." She cocked her head. "Just go. It's a rugby thing."

While running, Isaac unzipped his bag and twisted four of the wicks together.

"Ready!" he said.

Jack ripped the bag away, and it caught on Isaac's arm, which caused him to spin around. During his rotation, he caught a glimpse of Redbeard. In one motion, the three Corsairs threw the scooter to the side and hit the ground running. Jack lit the wicks right as they turned onto the wood slats of the dock.

Jack dropped the backpack full of lit dynamite twenty meters from the boat. Zahra waited onboard with Horus. The monkey had led the Corsairs away and then sprinted down to the boat.

Shit! Isaac came to a dead stop. He had forgotten his journal, the cards, and the madam's book.

"What are you doing?" Jack yelled.

"I'll be right there," Isaac said.

He sprinted back ten meters and opened the backpack. Everything went into slow motion as his adrenaline cranked his senses up to full alert. He could smell the wicks burning down. He felt his hand wrap around the leather book and wooden case. He saw the dock lights reflecting off the curvature of Redbeard's sword. Then he heard the rumble of the engine. There was only a quarter of the long wick left. He had to hurry.

Isaac dashed back, leaped off the dock, slid over Jack's hatch, and landed on the starboard side of the boat with everything clutched to his chest.

The Corsairs were only a few meters away when the bag exploded. The wood deck shattered into a million splinters. The blast sent the Corsairs cartwheeling into the placid harbor water. The shockwave ripped through the boat like an atomic boom. The fiery debris floated down and fizzled on top of the dark water. The only sound remaining was the boat engine.

Jack stood up triumphantly as his boat coasted away from the T-shaped dock. "Holy shite! That was sexy!"

Uncle Jack looked over the bow and saw Redbeard treading water. They met in a deadlock stare. It was the first time they were able to size each other up, but it was definitely not going to be the last. Jack yelled to Redbeard, "If you come after us again, I'm going to hang you with that turban!"

Redbeard pulled a large splinter out of his eyebrow, and a thick stream of blood ran into the water. Then he turned and swam back toward the smoldering dock.

Ten minutes later, the *Sin Bin* took a left out of the marina and headed toward the jettison that protected the harbor. It was too calm to sail, so Jack was relying on the gas engine that only went about six knots.

"Status report. Injuries?" Jack asked from the wheel.

Isaac and Zahra inspected each other and shook their heads.

"One of those bastards threw a knife at me," Jack said. "Who the hell throws *knives* these days? And what the *hell* are your mum and dad mixed up in?"

"Where are we going?" Zahra asked.

"I'm going to find a safe place to stash you two," Jack said, "and then I'm going to do some recon in Morocco."

"We have to go see this author," Isaac said. "Madame Dragomir told me that he could help."

"That old Gypo just filled your head with rubbish," Jack said. "Your mum and dad have been in captivity for two days, and if we don't get some intel soon, we'll never find them."

"The men who took them had a helicopter," Zahra said. "I don't think they were from Morocco."

The *Sin Bin* flipped around the jetty and headed south toward Africa.

"Doesn't matter," Jack said. "I need to find out who we're dealing with, and that's where I start."

Isaac sat down cross-legged and flipped to the end of the book to read about the author.

Zahra interrupted everyone when she pointed over Jack's shoulder. "What is that?" she asked. Soter's Oculus yacht was headed toward the jetty.

Uncle Jack looked back. "It's a bloody killer whale." He opened a container near the wheel and pulled out a pair of binoculars. Redbeard sat on the deck of the Oculus, staring right back at him. "Shite. Shite. Bloody *shite*," Jack said. "We can't outrun them."

The Oculus yacht cleared the jetty and kicked on its powerful engines. Their only advantages were that the marine fog was getting thicker and the ocean was getting choppier.

"We've got a kilo on them. We're going to have to lose them around Europa Point. That monstrosity won't be able to get that close to the coast."

"What do you want us to do?" Isaac asked.

"Go downstairs and suit up," Jack said. "We're going in."

Isaac took Zahra downstairs as Jack aimed the *Sin Bin* back toward the Gibraltar coastline. In the cabin, Isaac pulled out a wetsuit for Zahra.

"Squeeze into this," he said. While Isaac grabbed a waterproof bag, Zahra tried to fit into the suit in full clothes but couldn't.

"Turn around," she said as she stripped. Isaac put all of their belongings into a waterproof bag and then held up a Neptune diving mask.

"These are very easy to use. All you have to do is breathe," Isaac said as he fit the mask around her head.

Jack yelled from outside. "Hurry up! We're about to round the point!"

Isaac slipped on Zahra's water tank, clipped everything in place, and opened the valve. He held his thumb up to her mask to ask if she was getting air. Zahra nodded and took a deep breath. She was still too exhausted to be scared.

"Grab me a spare air!" Uncle Jack yelled.

Isaac threw on his air tank and grabbed the waterproof bag and the yellow canister of air.

The fog outside made for what sailors called *very* low visibility. You couldn't see anything past one hundred meters. Bright-yellow spotlights from the Oculus cut through the marine layer searching for their ship. Jack hugged the rocky coast, dangerously close. A wave splashed over the starboard side and knocked Zahra off her feet. Horus climbed up on Jack's shoulder to escape the choppy swells.

"I'm going to round the point and aim right at the shore," Jack said. "That's when you jump."

"What about Horus?" Isaac asked.

"Bugger's coming with me," he said. "He's got lungs like a goddamn merman."

Isaac lowered his mask and then helped Zahra slip into gloves and fins. The Oculus veered away from the shallow coast but kept its spotlights focused on their general position. The *Sin Bin* skirted around jagged rocks as an onslaught of rolling waves smashed into them and exploded upward into a falling spray.

"Zahra, you're going to be fine," Jack reassured her right as the *Sin Bin* scraped across foam-covered rock.

Isaac lifted his mask. "Where do we go?"

"They're not going to be able to follow us on the yacht. They're going to drop anchor right there," Jack said as he pointed to the spotlights on the Oculus. Before Isaac could turn around, someone shut off all the lights on the yacht. It was complete darkness again. "They're coming. They've probably got a zodiac. Swim to their boat and hold onto the anchor as tight as possible. Copy?"

Isaac swallowed his fear and handed his uncle the canister of spare air. Jack took off his clothes and redirected the boat. Then he took a rope out and tied a little harness around Horus's upper body. He put the other end of the rope in his teeth.

"What are you going to do?" Isaac asked.

"What I'm trained to do," he said as he strapped a large combat knife to his calf. "Jump off."

Isaac lowered his mask and grabbed Zahra's hand. He nodded to her, and they both jumped.

The first thing Isaac noticed was the silence. The cold black swallowed everything. Luckily, Europa Point had a powerful lighthouse to warn boats away from the rocks. Every few seconds, Isaac and Zahra were blessed with a wiping glow that let them know they were still together. The light also allowed Zahra to copy Isaac's slow and steady flipper kick. She gave him the thumbs-up as the light skimmed the water above them. He grabbed her hand again and pulled her beneath the current.

Jack was right. Isaac saw the motor of a small rubber boat approaching them. He pulled Zahra deeper and looked up right as the zodiac passed over them. If they kept heading straight, they would find the yacht. *But what if something happened to Jack?* Isaac decided not to worry. His uncle had seen worse than a few turbans and swords.

CHAPTER 12: THE FOUR OF SPADES

Zahra pointed ahead. The light whipped around and revealed the large keel of the yacht. They swam underneath the boat, found the anchor, and held on tightly.

Minutes passed, and Isaac's muscles ached. He couldn't even imagine what it was like for Zahra to jump back into the water after she'd almost died from hypothermia a few hours earlier. Both of them had their arms and legs wrapped around the anchor's chain. Every few seconds, the lighthouse flashed and illuminated Zahra's green eyes. She looked calm given the circumstances. *Who is this girl who traveled from the Atlas Mountains to save me? We haven't even had time to have a conversation that didn't involve an escape route.* Isaac promised himself that he would sack up and talk to her like a normal human as soon as they had the time.

Suddenly, something plunged into the water. It was too dark to see what it was. The lighthouse whipped around again and revealed a Corsair sinking with a diffused trail of blood above him. Jack was on board. Seconds later, another Corsair crashed into the water. The dark blood seeped through his white linens as he sank into the abyss.

A minute later, a third body fell right on top of them, only this Corsair was still alive. He was wrapped in a chain but had managed to free one arm. He grabbed Isaac's ankle and pulled him toward the depths. Isaac slid down the links of the large chain. The Corsair screamed in the water. Large air bubbles floated toward the surface and curved around Isaac's mask. Isaac's grip grew weaker as the Corsair's got stronger. He slipped down another few links. If the Corsair pulled Isaac free, he would sink with him. Zahra used the chain to lower herself down to the scuffle. She raised her knees to her chest and kicked her heels down into the Corsair's face. He released right as the anchor shot upward. Isaac and Zahra refastened their grips as they were pulled out of the water.

Jack hung over the side of the boat wearing a robe. The anchor came to a stop on the lowest deck, and he pulled them over the railing. They ripped off their masks.

"Jesus Christ, Uncle Jack, we were down there fighting and you're up here in a *robe?*"

Jack spun; his robe had a light-blue anchor and trident logo on the back. "Bad guys all gone. Besides, what's the point of a sexy adventure if you can't look good doing it?"

Isaac and Zahra dropped their tanks onto the deck.

"Come inside, you gotta see this thing," Jack said.

Zahra and Isaac were still in their dripping wetsuits when they stepped into the cockpit of the most luxurious yacht they had ever seen. Horus was soaking wet and shivering. He had burrowed himself into the couch to warm up.

Jack fired up the engine and pushed down on the throttle. "Watch this," he said.

Redbeard and his men quietly climbed over the rail of the *Sin Bin* with their knives in their mouths. The boat had crashed into shallow rocks about thirty meters from the coast. Redbeard pointed down to the cabin.

A loud horn interrupted the quiet and echoed through the fog. Redbeard recognized the Oculus's horn instantly. They'd been duped. To add insult to injury, Jack spelled out "EAT SHIT" in Morse code.

CHAPTER 13:
THE FIVE OF SPADES

THERA, GREECE

Soter sat with Neville in his private study. The high ceilings were lined with research binders, and the entire western wall was a tiled replica of the famous Alexander the Great mosaic. Laid out across his desk were bronze playing cards, identical to the deck David had given to Zahra.

"There were only five inventions that survived my ancestors' island," said Soter, "the Antikythera Mechanism and four bronze decks of cards."

Neville pulled out a jeweler's glass and carefully inspected the concentric gears on the top of the bronze cards.

"The Magi have another deck in Alexandria, but I've never actually seen them," Neville said.

"These have been handed down the Soter Dynasty for centuries," Soter said. "Look at the holes on the side."

Neville examined the divots closely through the magnifying glass. "They were built to be connected."

"Precisely," Soter said. "My ancestors created the Antikythera Mechanism to predict earth, wind, water and fire. But the purpose of these cards remains unknown."

"And you believe that if we x-ray these, we might be able to duplicate them?" Neville asked.

"Yes. But that's phase two of my plan. I've hired a team of historians to research the possible whereabouts of the last deck of cards, but we've been—" A knock at the door interrupted Soter. "Yes?"

A Corsair answered through the thick door in a heavy Turkish accent. "I have urgent news."

"Stand by," Soter said. He slid open a hidden panel on his desk that revealed an electronic pad. Neville was able to memorize the numbered code that Soter typed in by the unique sound of each digit—a trick he learned so he could memorize phone numbers during his missions with the Order.

Neville stepped closer to examine the wall. Each individual square centimeter tile was actually a tiny LED screen. There were thousands upon thousands of small screens making up the mosaic. Neville watched as the interlocking tiles pushed outward and then pulled apart to reveal a wall safe. "What is this?"

"It's an electronic mosaic," Soter said. "If you would like to remain living, you will keep the location of these cards to *yourself.*"

Neville nodded as Ptolemy Soter carefully placed the cards in the wall safe. He pressed a button inside. The mosaic closed, and the LED tiles reprogrammed. It turned into a replica of the famous zodiac wheel mosaic found in the Beit Alfa Synagogue in Israel. Neville ran his hands over it. The tiny screens looked and felt exactly like aged tiles.

"Enter," Soter yelled to the door.

One of Soter's Turkish Corsairs stepped inside. "Redbeard just reported back. The boy has escaped."

Soter ran his right fingers down the ridge of his jawline. "How? They were led right to him."

"They followed the girl to Gibraltar, but they escaped by boat. They had help."

"Who?" asked Soter.

"His uncle, the woman's brother," the Corsair said.

"The notorious *Uncle Jack*," Soter said.

Neville said, "British Navy. Royal Commando. Never met him, but I've heard the stories."

"When did this happen?" Soter asked.

"An hour ago," said the Corsair.

Soter looked at the Corsair with his piercing blue eyes. "You're telling me that one man and two kids fought off all of our men?"

The Corsair fidgeted. "Yes. They had a monkey, too."

"A monkey?" Soter asked.

"Yes. The uncle has a pet monkey, and they used it to escape," said the Corsair, who was starting to fear that being the bearer of bad news might cost him his life.

"Where is Redbeard?" Soter asked.

"Stuck in Gibraltar," the Corsair said looking away. "We sent your jet."

"Why did you send my jet when they have my yacht?" Soter had gone through the five W's and received worse and worse news each time.

The Corsair looked down at the floor. He had trouble relaying the last bit of information. "The boat they escaped on was yours."

Neville expected Soter to flip out, tip over his desk, and slit the Corsair's throat. He was surprised when he did the exact opposite. A small grin lifted the corner of his mouth, and he laughed. Neville had been there for months and had never seen him so genuinely amused.

He tucked each fist under the opposite bicep and leaned back. "To recap, they escaped capture on *my* hundred-million-dollar yacht, *and* we don't know their current whereabouts. Correct?"

The Corsair swore silently that he would drop on his knees in prayer if he walked out of this alive. "Yes. That is correct."

Soter stayed in an arm tuck and turned his back to formulate a plan. The Corsair let out a deep breath. Neville backed up toward the wall. He didn't want to be in arm's distance if Soter snapped.

Soter took a deep breath and said, "There are only ten Oculus yachts in the Mediterranean. They can't hide for long. Wire out a message to every major port that it has been stolen, and we're offering a hundred thousand euros for its capture. Send out photos of the three of them."

The Corsair nodded and started to leave, but Soter stopped him. "Wait. First, make sure to say in the message that the thieves must be taken *alive.* Second, bring Rachel down to the dock."

"Yes, sir," the Corsair said and quickly exited the study.

Soter cocked his head at Neville when he saw how far he had moved away. "I was bracing myself for a different reaction," Neville said.

Soter glared. "One of the principles my grandfather lived by was a quote from Napoleon Bonaparte. 'Nothing that happens is bad or worth despairing. Everything that seems bad contains the seed of the opposite, an opportunity, a turnaround.' I plan on restoring my family's power to its original status. Not tycoons. Not billionaires. Not kings. Emperors. I can't expect to do that without a few small setbacks."

Ten minutes later, Soter waited at the end of a long dock. The sheer limestone rock shot up forty meters to his compound. It was a perfect night. The waxing gibbous moon was just bright enough put a glimmer

on the calm water, but not light enough to drown out the constellations. Soter looked up and marveled at them. *An entire saga hovered above
them every night, packed with sex, violence, and betrayal, and this generation of spoiled
half-wits would rather stay inside and play video games. Maybe, they don't deserve me,*
he thought. *No matter. I will make them notice.*

His internal diatribe was interrupted when a different Corsair
marched Rachel down to the end of the pier.

"What do you want with me?" she yelled. The humid air made her
skin glisten.

Soter admired her long, lean body. She was still in the same outfit:
short khaki shorts, a button down, and hiking boots. He nodded to the
Corsair. "You may leave." The Corsair released his grip. Rachel watched
the armed Turk walk away. She thought about attacking him, but David
was still locked up.

"Please, step into my office," Soter said as he pointed down to a
small rowboat knocking against the pier.

"And if I say no?" Rachel asked.

"Back to your cell," Soter said. "But you might be interested in what
I am going to tell you."

"How do I know you're not going to hurt me?" Rachel asked.

"When I was four years old, I watched my drunken excuse of a
father beat my mother unconscious. I will *never* hurt a woman. And I
only hurt or kill men when I have an incentive to do so."

"Your brutes cut down innocent men at our school," Rachel said
through her teeth.

"Yes, they did. But it would not have happened if your husband had
given himself up immediately."

Soter stepped into the rowboat and politely held his hand out for
Rachel. She ignored it, dropped her hiking boot down, and stepped
inside. Soter grabbed both oars and rowed into the small dark waves.

"My grandfather used to take me out on these midnight rides when
I was a boy," he said.

"I'm a doctor, not a therapist," Rachel said. "I can't help with wounds that don't bleed."

"I have nothing to confess other than the fact he would point to a constellation and tell me all about its mythology." Soter pointed up at the celestial map above them. A nearly silent moment passed. Only the lapping waves made noise. Soter scooted closer to Rachel and pointed up to the Big Dipper. He was like an evil Adonis. She guessed he was in his mid-forties, but he had the physique of twenty-two-year-old athlete.

"Follow the curve of Ursa Major straight down and you will see Spica," Soter said. "It's the brightest star in your constellation, Virgo."

"How do you know my constellation?" Rachel backed away.

"I know a lot about you. You were born August 27, 1970. You grew up on Akrotiri Naval base on the island of Cyprus. Your father was a naval officer, who spent most of his years at sea. Your mother raised you and your brother. You excelled in school. Jack excelled in sports. You met David when he came to speak at Harvard about his new company."

The rowboat coasted away from the compound, and a band of sweat formed on Soter's brow. Rachel watched the top of his pectoral muscles flex in his unbuttoned dress shirt. He continued, "David was thirty-five, and you were a twenty-five-year-old medical student. Two years later, his company went public, he became a billionaire, you became a doctor, and you got married. You've been doing humanitarian missions ever since, which I don't plan on keeping you away from for too much longer. What you do is very good for the world."

"Then let us go," Rachel said.

The small boat was now two hundred meters away from the shore, and Soter stopped rowing. The large marble deck and the columns in his library were now visible from the water. They drifted to a stop. "It's not that simple," he said as he wiped sweat from his forehead into his blond hair.

"It is," Rachel said. "Leave our son alone, and you'll never hear from us again."

"Do you find it odd that there are only twelve hundred billionaires in the world, and both your husband and I are among them? How much do you know about his past? We have more in common than you think," Soter said.

"Just like me, he was a military brat raised in a foreign country. His father and grandfather were aerospace engineers in the US Air Force. He grew up on Ramstein Air Base in Germany, attended Cambridge to study history, and then volunteered in the poorest areas of the world for ten years before he started his company."

Soter let the steady sound of the waves return. "Your husband was not volunteering; he was training. He's been hiding something from you."

Rachel responded carefully, "And what's that?"

"Your husband and his ancestors have all been members of a secret society based in Egypt," Soter said.

Rachel nodded. "I know the little that he's allowed to tell me."

"They safeguard very powerful secrets. That's why I know about your husband and the other members of his order. The Soters have been hunting them down and killing them for hundreds of years."

"So, I shouldn't take it *personally* that you're trying to kidnap my family," Rachel said.

"No. This conflict goes back longer than you can even imagine," Soter said.

That's why David insisted on keeping Isaac hidden, Rachel told herself. *He wanted to protect him from this man.*

"Your husband's humanitarian missions are genuine in nature, but they're a front to keep himself hidden, too," Soter said. "I've become too powerful, and I wouldn't want my son to grow up in fear, either."

"Your son?" Rachel asked.

"Well...yes, that's what I came out here to talk to you about," Soter said. He met her gaze directly.

The expansive world of the ocean and stars immediately shrank. Rachel had let her guard down. She came to the realization that she was stuck on a rowboat with a delusional madman.

"What are you talking about?" Rachel asked.

Soter looked out over the ocean. "I'm forty-two years old and have not found a suitable woman to give me an heir."

Rachel quietly slid her hand down to the oar without Soter noticing. She started to pull it out as Soter continued, "You're smart, you're beautiful, and you're tough—like me."

Rachel had the oar out of the holder and gripped it in her hand. She whipped the paddle upward, but he ducked. The momentum spun Rachel around. Soter grabbed her by the waist and pulled her against him. She kicked and squirmed, so Soter put his other hand around her throat and pressed his tight body against hers.

"I would *never* hurt you, but I do have incentive to kill your husband," Soter said. "*He* is my enemy."

Rachel nodded and stopped resisting. She could feel Soter's rigid muscles flexing against every part of her body. If he wanted to snap her neck, he could.

"I don't want you as a wife. I want you to give me a child. If you agree to this, I will let your family go. If you and your boy refuse to help me, I will kill David in front of you."

Rachel started to tear up. She couldn't imagine the thought of watching her husband die.

Soter smelled Rachel's hair as he held her. "You've been in the mountains too long. You need a bath."

Soter flung Rachel into the ocean. She popped up, surprised to see him rowing away.

"Anafi is thirty kilometers east, or you can meet me back at the dock," Soter said. He rowed another ten times and then called back to her, "You were right about your brother, though. I underestimated him."

Rachel spit out a mouthful of seawater and allowed herself a smile. Jack and Isaac had gotten away. That bought them a little more time.

CHAPTER 14:
THE FIVE OF CLUBS

SOTER'S OCULUS YACHT

"Seriously, who owns a yacht with no alcohol?" Jack asked as he unfolded a nautical map of the Mediterranean.

"Bearded assassins who chase you with swords," Isaac said.

"Yeah, what kind of bloody psychopaths still use swords?" Jack asked as he clicked on a flashlight.

All the lights on the Oculus had been turned off, so they could not be spotted by helicopter. They both sat on the semicircle pilot deck of the yacht. Zahra was changing out of her wetsuit in the captain's quarters.

Jack ran his calloused finger down the coast of Morocco.

"There's no reason to go back," Isaac said.

"We need intel," Jack said as he eyed the port cities.

"They gave me the cards for a reason," Isaac said. "We need to find out why. If we go back to Morocco, it is just going to be villagers telling you what we already know—men that were not from Morocco came in on horseback, took my parents, and left by helicopter."

"Don't buy that kooky Gypo's crock of shite," Jack said.

"She gave us more facts than we wanted to believe."

"Give me one good reason why we should follow some Gypo's advice, and I'll consider," Jack said.

Isaac knew he had him now. He just had to base his next argument in logic. "It's safe to assume that the cards are both extremely mysterious and extremely valuable. Right?"

"Yes," Jack said as Zahra walked out of the captain's quarters in Maia's clothes.

"We don't know why people are after them, but we do know that the people chasing us are rich and powerful," Isaac said, sweeping his hand across the expensive yacht.

"Make your point, damn it," Jack said.

"Who is going to know more about the elite circle of powerful people who would want those cards?" Isaac asked. "An author who has dedicated his life to studying them or goat farmers?"

Jack shook the wheel in frustration. "Damn it. Blubbery white whale shit! I should have locked you both up and just headed there! All right, Mr. Deductive Reasoning, I concede. Where are we headed?"

Isaac flipped to the back cover of the madam's book, revealing a photograph of a white-haired professor in his mid-sixties with a conquistador beard. Isaac scanned the author's bio.

"His name is Professor John James Olney, and he lives on Madagascar," Isaac said.

"What? Absolutely not," Jack said. "Out of the question."

Zahra noticed Isaac smiling and ripped the book from his hands. "He lives on Malta," she said. Isaac laughed. He'd finally pulled one on his street-smart uncle.

"You little sodomite," Jack said as he put Isaac into a headlock.

"Look," Jack said as he released him and traced his finger across the Mediterranean. "Malta is a two-and-half-day journey. Judging by our gas levels, we'll have to stop once to fuel up."

They all stared at the north coast of Africa while Jack deliberated. "Tunis. Big port. Lots of traffic. We should be able to sneak in and out without drawing too much attention."

Jack heard no response. He looked up at his beleaguered shipmates and noticed the fatigue was finally starting to weigh them down. "Zahra, you've had a long night. Why don't you get some rest?"

"I sleep better under the stars," she said as she pulled one of the blankets out of the captain's quarters and headed to the front deck to lie on a bed-sized lounge chair.

Jack turned to Isaac. "Cabin Boy, go find me something good to eat and stiff to drink."

Isaac took Horus and used the flashlight to navigate the lower decks of the Oculus. Jack was right. There was not a single drop of alcohol on the boat. He rummaged through the refrigerator and put together a tray of grilled vegetables and flat breads with mint sauce. He tossed some scraps to Jack's hungry monkey.

Isaac set down the tray of food for Jack, who shoveled thick slices of eggplant into his mouth—a chomp and a swallow. Jack wrapped two pieces of flat bread around half of a tomato, dunked it into the sauce, and shoved the fistful of food into his mouth.

"Good job...hamph...to...day, buddy. The girl...is..." Isaac watched a stream of tomato juice shoot out of the corner of his mouth. He wondered how someone could be so admirable one moment and so repulsive the next. Jack inhaled and continued, "She...keeps looking... back...here. Go...outside."

Jack gave the thumbs-up as a lump of food passed down his esophagus. Isaac had promised himself that he would talk to Zahra as soon as had the chance. He racked his brain for an excuse, but Jack just pointed out to the deck.

"I hate you," Isaac said as he grabbed a large pear off the platter and walked out.

The front deck of the Oculus yacht was magnificent. The slated wood dropped down to two lower levels. The yacht coasted low to the water so the side paneling came up and over the deck. It looked like a giant planetarium.

"Did my dad ever help you find your constellation?" Isaac asked to alert Zahra that he was approaching. He pointed upward and walked toward the middle of the dark deck. "Mine is Pisces, and it should be right about—"

Zahra turned, and before she could say anything, Isaac fell through the deck. He had stepped directly into the Jacuzzi. He stumbled forward but caught his balance and quickly jumped out. His entire right leg was soaking wet. *Damn it. Good start, you idiot.*

Zahra laughed. "We have a saying from home. If you always have your head in the clouds, you might miss the cliff."

"I think that's a metaphor for my life," Isaac said. "I brought you a pear." He wiped it free of chlorinated water and sat down.

"Thank you," Zahra said, biting off a large piece. Isaac looked away so he wouldn't stare at her lips wrapping around the juicy fruit.

"My body is exhausted, but my brain is still running," she said.

Isaac was completely enamored with Zahra, and it was difficult to hide. Everything she said was simple yet intelligent. Her basic grasp of English forced her to be more direct. She didn't have the language to play manipulative games like other girls.

"Do you mind if I ask you how you got to Gibraltar?" Isaac asked.

"I climbed down the mountain, hitchhiked to Casablanca, stole a boat from two men who tried to rape me, swam to a buoy after the boat collided with a tanker, and was attacked by a group of seals," Zahra said, finishing her pear. "Then, I swam the rest."

"What? Are you kidding me? Jack would have stretched that into an hour-long story with fireworks shooting off in the background," Isaac said. "It's a miracle that you survived."

"All I *know* is survival," Zahra said. "Trust me; I have seen worse."

"Between you and Uncle Jack, I feel like the weak link," Isaac said.

Zahra cocked her head. "I do not understand."

Isaac took a deep breath. "Look, I'm not trying to downplay anything that's happened to you, but in a way, I'm almost jealous. I've been given everything—great parents, money, education—and I've traveled all over the world. I have it all, and I *hate* it all. You've had to struggle and fight every day of your life to stay alive, and it's made you strong. You deserve my life, and I deserve yours."

Zahra thought for a moment. "Your struggle is not with the outside world like mine. It is inside your head. They are different, but it doesn't mean that one is easier than the other."

A cold jet of air slipped over the front railing and lifted Zahra's black hair.

"How did you get so smart?" Isaac asked.

"I learned how to read and write from your parents, but everything else I learned by watching people. My father would lock my younger brothers in our room at sunset so he could go smoke and gamble. I always knew there was a bigger world out there, so I taught myself how to be invisible. For years, I would wait until my little brothers would fall asleep and then put on their clothes and sneak into town. I would hide on rooftops and listen to men play cards. I would watch through windows as people tried to make children, and I would sneak into dark alleys to watch men do bad things. Most important, I learned that you could tell a lot about a man by what he does at night. See?"

Zahra pointed up to the pilot's deck. Through the windows, they could see Jack lobbing up grapes for Horus to catch in his mouth. "You have a *good* family, Isaac."

She turned forward and curled up in her blanket.

Jack got Isaac's attention through the window, pointed at Zahra, and started romantically kissing the palm of his hand. Isaac shook his head in disagreement. He nodded. Isaac shook his head. The back-and-forth continued as Zahra closed her eyes and leaned a bit closer. Twenty more degrees and her head would be resting comfortably on Isaac's shoulder. Out over the horizon, a big swell was approaching the port side of the boat. Isaac's devious uncle turned the wheel and let the broadside catch the wave. It worked perfectly. The slight impact caused Zahra's head to fall right onto Isaac's shoulder. She stirred but remained pressed against his body. Isaac could see his uncle celebrating behind the pilot's window. He mouthed, "Go for it."

Isaac's palms started to sweat, his heart raced, and he carefully leaned down to pull Zahra's blanket over her legs. She opened her eyes, and they stared at each other. All Isaac could see was green. He could knock off phase three of the master plan right now. *If you do it, she could get mad, but if you don't do it, she'll think you're a pussy.* Then he remembered one of Uncle Jack's principles—*It's always better to ask for forgiveness than permission.* Isaac went for it. He closed his eyes, cupped her chin with his two fingers, and leaned in for the kill.

A throbbing pain shot from his cheek through his body.

Zahra looked at Isaac for a long moment and then said, "I thought you were different." She grabbed her blanket and went inside to sleep. She passed by Jack, who quickly opened a map and pretended to be checking coordinates. She locked herself in the captain's quarters and went to bed.

Five minutes later, Jack set the coordinates on the ship and sat down next to Isaac on the deck.

"That was your fault," Isaac said as he rubbed his cheek.

"No, that was the bloody Turks fault for not having booze onboard," Jack said. "One finger of whiskey and you would have been two fingers deep."

"Don't talk about her like that," Isaac said. "That was a mistake. She's had men treat her poorly her whole life, and I just threw myself into that mix."

Jack crossed his legs and put his arms behind his head. "You should try to get some sleep. You look worse than I do after a bender."

"I can't fall asleep without my pills," Isaac said.

"And I can't fall asleep without a drink," Jack said. "Looks like we're going to have to stay up and talk about our feelings and shite."

"I think Horus would be better help," Isaac said.

"Naw, listen. My lieutenant taught me this. Sometimes when it's a life-and-death situation, a man's gotta get the shite off his chest. There's a technique that doesn't make you feel like a pussy faggot."

"I'm too tired to brain box, Uncle Jack," Isaac said.

"No, this one is simple. Say whatever you need to say and just end every sentence with a made-up curse word. Watch, I'll show you. I'm scared to death of losing my sister, because I think she's the only woman that will ever love me, motherfungus."

Isaac was delirious but mustered a genuine laugh. Then he said, "I've never kissed a girl, and I'm afraid that I'm going to die a virgin, pecker-rag!"

Isaac thought the method was oddly therapeutic, because it turned your most repressed secrets into lines that sounded like they were from a Dr. Seuss book.

"Now, when are you going to tell me about your pill problem, nipplenugget?" Uncle Jack asked.

Isaac took a long, deep breath. "I've had the same reoccurring dreams my whole life, titfarm. I went to visit a doctor, and he diagnosed with me with prodromal schizophrenia, geezerjugs."

Isaac couldn't believe that his darkest secret had just rolled off his tongue with ease. It felt like a huge weight had been lifted off his shoulders. He immediately regretted not telling Jack earlier.

"And you think the cards, your dreams, and finding your mum and dad are all connected, bellydick?" Uncle Jack asked.

"Before I climbed down the tunnel, the Gypsy woman told me that they weren't dreams. They were messages…mullarkeyfarts," Isaac said as he almost forgot the obligatory curse.

"Well, we'll get you to Malta and see what the old man has to say about your nut-jackets. I'm going inside to lay down, muffkabob."

Uncle Jack patted Isaac on the back and got up.

"Thanks, Jack," Isaac said.

Jack walked away and gave a half-assed salute. "We'll find the Motherfungus."

Sometimes he wondered if his uncle screwed things up just so he had the chance to save the day, like a brilliant criminal who gets arrested just so he's presented with the challenge of escaping. Isaac took in a deep breath of ocean air. It was a good time to open up his journal.

Isaac's Journal Entry #2
First Night of Trip to Tunis

I'm sitting on the deck of a hundred-million-dollar yacht that we stole from Turkish pirates who kidnapped my parents. Yesterday, my day consisted of trig class and rugby practice. Today was backpacks full of dynamite and escape tunnels. How did it all seem so natural to Zahra and Jack? "Did you see when that throwing knife almost took out my jugular? (Yawn) Well, I'm going to go hit the sack, long day of avoiding death tomorrow." How do they do it?

My nerves are so fried that I don't think a whole bottle of Xanax could calm me down. Without my pills, I'm guaranteed to stay up all night, fall asleep tomorrow morning, and jolt awake with Zahra and Jack staring at me. Can't wait. She already thinks I'm crazy.

My body is calling for my old life back. My bag of pills that makes me feel whatever I want. My ergonomic desk chair. My iPod. Air, Daft Punk, Justice, Chemical Brothers, Royksopp, and the rest of the playlist that kept me awake in between classes. Hell, Keagan and Peters don't seem so bad in comparison to Turkish assassins. I wish I could go back, but I know I can't.

My brain wants answers. Who kidnapped my parents? Why did they send me a deck of bronze playing cards? What did Dad get mixed up in? Was there any truth in Madame Dragomir's speech about the cards? Are my dreams the first signs of schizophrenic hallucinations? Or are they coded messages? If so, what the hell do they mean?

All I can say is that I've already scoured the history books looking for something similar. No luck. The island is ancient, yet advanced, which leads me to the conclusion that it's a creation of my subconscious mind—a fictional-hybrid of my two favorite subjects, history and engineering.

The outer rings of the island are made of up exquisite terra-cotta palaces decorated with black, red, and white frescoes. The wall-sized paintings have exotic animals, advanced sailboats, nautical maps of the entire world, and depictions of a sport that looks like combination of bull fighting and gymnastics.

In the homes, there's running water fed by volcanic springs. Bronze pipes empty into tiled pools, and the volcanic soil in the gardens is so fertile that each home garden is lush with tropical fruit. The pomegranates are so fresh that sometimes I wake up with their bittersweet taste still in my mouth.

The innermost circle of the island is a columned citadel with an auditorium of marble seats that looks like the senate houses of ancient Rome. In the middle of this building is a giant bronze machine. It looks like a bronze grandfather clock. I've spent more time in front of this machine than anywhere else on the island. It *calls* to me. The strangest part is that it feels like something *I* created. The front has seven dials, and when I turn them, it comes to life. Hundreds upon hundreds of interlocked bronze dials start spinning in different directions. Like clockwork, as soon as I turn the machine on, a violent earthquake shakes the palace. It's followed by a massive tidal wave. Sometimes I wake up before the wave hits, and sometimes the water rushes in and I slowly drown. Those are the rough ones, because it always takes a second for my brain to tell my body that it's awake. Then I'll look up and see the faces of staring classmates.

Anyways, I hope Mom and Dad are all right. Here's my checklist for tomorrow.

Isaac's Checklist:

1. *Read Professor Olney's book: The Wisdom of the Ancients.*
2. *Apologize to Zahra.*

Isaac's Journal Entry #2 cont'd: Day 1 of 2 on trip to Tunis.

Damn it. I fell asleep trying to finish my checklist and woke up on the deck at 1:00 p.m. Zahra and Jack had built a tent for me out of bathrobes and towels so I didn't get sunburned. I was probably snoring with my mouth open while they built it. I jolted awake and ripped the towels away...I was drowning in my dream. When I turned around, they were both in the pilot's deck having a good laugh.

Jack showed us on the map how far we had traveled. To the north was Palma and then Barcelona. To our south was Algiers. He explained that he was staying away from the coast of North Africa because the Turks probably had eyes there. It was still another day and a half to round the horn of Africa and head into Tunis. Then another full day to Malta.

An hour after I woke up, Jack killed the engine. He'd used the yacht's sonar to find a large school of fish. While he stripped down to his skivvies, Zahra admired his muscled body. She got embarrassed when I caught her staring.

Jack came back up with a bluefin tuna that was the size of his giant Minotaur leg. He said, "If we're going to die, we're going to do it with full stomachs." Jack slid out the knife strapped to his calf. He gutted the fish with the accuracy of a sushi chef and served us tuna steaks with a mango salsa.

While Jack was eating, Zahra asked about his sleeve of tattoos. I know every embellished story behind each tat, but she pointed to the one that has been beaten to death. The tattoo just says 10-7. Zahra asked if it was someone's birthday, but it's actually the final score of his first Army versus Navy match at Twickenham stadium. Jack retold the fifteen-minute story about the play that made him famous. With no time left, he ripped the ball away in his own end zone and ran it one hundred meters for the win. Jack made sure not to leave out any details. Zahra probably understood every fourth word but was thoroughly entertained by Jack's theatrics.

After breakfast, Jack said, "You're enlisted crew on my ship, and you're not going to sit around and sunbathe all day. Take the binoculars and watch for any planes or helicopters approaching the aft. If these Turks have a yacht, they can afford air travel. If they come, I need to be able to head toward France." I think he sprinkled in the phrase "evasive maneuvers" too.

So, Zahra and I laid on the back of the Oculus, which looked like the mouth of the killer whale. We took turns on the binoculars, and she came up with bright idea to read Olney's book out loud. It was about the history of astrology and astronomy from the Babylonians to the Egyptians and the Greeks.

Shifts were a half hour apiece, and we got through three-quarters of the professor's book. We only had one false alarm (a passenger jet), but I did fall asleep twice on duty. I'm beginning to think my only chance at winning Zahra over is through pity. Like a little helpless pet that falls asleep in your arms and always comes running when you call. How could I ever compete with someone like Uncle Jack?

My only redeeming moment was making her laugh. Horus was lying in the sun grooming himself, and I said, "Beer me." Horus ran into the kitchen and came back with two water bottles. Zahra though it was the funniest thing she had ever seen.

I could have lain on that back deck forever. I told her about learning how to surf in Kerala, the southwestern province of India where my parents had their last school. She talked about my parents staying up late with her and teaching her how to read. Her first book was *Humphrey's First Christmas*, a story about the camels of the three wise men who rode to visit baby Jesus.

I tried to impress her with my stories of traveling—the opaque rivers and snowcapped mountains of New Zealand, the turquoise water and the wetsuit-like skin of the manta rays in the Great Barrier Reef, and the clouds so low in the African savannah that you felt like you could touch them. You know what impressed her the most? The shower she had taken that morning in the giant bathroom. She wouldn't stop talking about it. I kept trying to change the subject, because all I could picture was her naked body, but then I felt bad when she told me she hadn't had a hot shower in four years. I could smell the shampoo all day.

It took until the afternoon, but I finally worked up the courage to apologize. She brushed it off and said, "Just don't do it again, and we are friends." A win and a loss in one simple response. A loss because I've always been the friend. The one girls confide in and ask for advice about their boyfriends. A win because this beautiful Moroccan girl is warming up to me. She considers me a friend, and from the small pieces of backstory that I know, she hasn't had a lot of them in her life. *So don't screw this up.*

At sunset, Jack killed the boat to check on the engine and jumped off the back deck for a swim. I joined him, and Jack found out that Zahra couldn't swim. Not really. Somehow, in his simultaneously insulting and complimenting Uncle Jack-way, he convinced her that it was time to learn. She made us turn around as she stripped down into her underwear. It was weird. She's so tough, but when she got in the water, she looked like a little kid, excited and scared at the same time. Jack taught her how to kick, tread, and paddle. Then he took her on one of his infamous sea turtle rides. She held around his neck as he took her ten meters deep into a school of fish.

She came out of the water smiling. It was the most beautiful thing I've ever seen. This girl had never left the mountains of Morocco, and now she was swimming with schools of fish in the Mediterranean.

Jack convinced her that it was time to swim alone. I moved twenty meters away and Zahra furiously dog-paddled toward me. When she got there, she wrapped her arms and legs around me and held tight. I keep replaying the feeling of holding her over and over again in my head. It felt so *right*.

That night, Jack anchored off the coast of a small uninhabited island about seventy-five kilometers north of Tunisia. He dove down and came up with three lobsters—another delicacy that Zahra had never enjoyed. It's a shame that this short trip is coming to an end.

Day 2 of Trip to Tunis

Hi, my name is Isaac, and I am a bunghole. I stay up all night writing secrets in my journal and making weird sketches of catapults. I'm like Leonardo da Vinci meets Frodo Baggins.

I wish I wasn't part of the *weakest* generation of complainers to ever walk God's green earth. Not to mention, we all have fruity Beatles haircuts. Real men should keep it high and tight.

I wish my friends and I were more like Uncle Jack. That way, we could navigate without having to consult our smart phones every two minutes. We would also be able to talk to girls without having panic attacks. I should make a note to get my head out of my books and have my uncle teach me how to punch someone in the mouth.

Remember, there are only three books a man needs:

1. *The Power of One: When in Doubt, Ask Yourself WWPKD?*
2. *The Art of War: Know Your Enemy*
3. *Meditations by Marcus Aurelius: Life Is Tough; Deal with It*

Sincerely,
Sir Isaac Francis Hopplebottom Alexander III Archduke of Nutbag

Day 2 of Trip to Tunis

Well, looks like Uncle Jack got into my journal when I was sleeping, but I have to respect his creativity.

The strangest thing happened in my dream last night. The earthquake and tidal wave never came. I didn't wake up gasping for air. I woke up peacefully watching the sunset on the roof of the palace. What does this mean? If I take my Xanax and Ambien, I don't get the dreams. Every night I don't take them, I get the dreams and wake up thinking I'm drowning. This is the first time it hasn't happened.

Jack is calling to me from the pilot's deck. We've rounded the horn and are heading south to Tunis. I assume he wants to go over the plan.

CHAPTER 15:
THE FIVE OF DIAMONDS

GULF OF TUNIS

"Say good-bye to the Oculus," Uncle Jack said, looking down at the city of Tunis through binoculars.

"Why?" Isaac asked.

The engine idled five kilometers outside the port as they watched tankers come in and out of the harbor.

"The vessel traffic controllers will spot us, if they haven't already. This boat sticks out like a crooked dick-nose. We're taking the other zodiac in."

Zahra and Isaac nodded. Jack pointed toward a large ferry terminal. "See the ferries? They will have trips to Malta every hour." Jack checked the time on the Titan Chrono he wore on his left wrist.

"It's 1130 now. We rendezvous at the terminal at 1300. You two on food, water, and tickets. I'm on G and B," Jack said as he pulled a few thousand pounds out of his cargo pants.

"Where did you get the cash?" Isaac asked.

"I always keep my boat stacked, just in case," Jack said as he handed Isaac three hundred pounds.

Zahra grabbed it from Isaac's hand and said, "I am better at bartering." Jack agreed that haggling was not Isaac's strong suit.

As they made their way down to the back deck, Zahra asked, "What is G and B?"

Uncle Jack stopped on the back deck and mimed a Wild West showdown stance. He chugged an imaginary bottle of whiskey and threw it up in the air. He pulled his imaginary six-shooter and used the two-handed shooting technique to blow it out of the sky—sound effects included. Then, he went into slow motion and pulled his imaginary gun on Zahra. She shot a confused glance at Isaac, and he nodded. She awkwardly pulled a fake gun and said, "Bang!" Uncle Jack fell to the ground dramatically. He lay there for a long moment and then popped up, all business. "Cheers," Jack said. "Let's get wet."

Isaac turned to Zahra and said, "Guns and booze. He's watched too many Westerns."

"He is crazy, but I like him," she said.

Minutes later, Horus and the trio bounced over wakes on the zodiac. Jack steered the outboard motor while Isaac and Zahra ducked splashes of water. The African sun was so hot it dried the moisture and left salt streaks on their faces. Jack yelled to them over the loud motor. "No matter what, get on that ferry. If anything happens, I'll meet you in Malta."

"Where?" Isaac yelled.

"Where do you think?" Jack asked. Isaac hated using Jack's pirate-like vernacular because it felt unnatural to him, but it did save time.

"Got it. Find the ugliest sea-donkey in town and ask her where she drinks," Isaac yelled back to Jack.

"Today feels like a good day for an adventure, huh?" he asked, coasting toward the port.

Meanwhile, Aziz Gisgo, a Tunisian Port Authority officer, spotted the Oculus through his high-powered Barska binoculars. The portly bald man scanned the waters and found the zodiac. It was his lucky day. Inside was the British military man, a young British male, and a Moroccan girl, exactly like the all-points bulletin described. He could have picked up his radio, called the police, and had them arrested, but instead, he pulled out his cell phone. Calling the police was not going to bring him the bounty.

Gisgo dialed a local tavern that sold illegal whiskey and hashish. He knew the bartender and let his operation slide under the radar for a case of Johnnie Walker every month. There were always eight to ten Tunisian sailors in his bar that he could rely on for jobs like this. The bartender answered, and Gisgo said, "Akoyha, I have a proposal."

It took Jack thirty minutes to idle the zodiac down the thin channel into the bustling port in downtown Tunis. Isaac watched massive dock cranes unload storage bins off a reflective layer of polychromatic oil that floated on top of the murky water. The harbor was so contaminated with petrol that Isaac wondered if the water itself was flammable.

They parked the zodiac on a crowded pier. Jack said, "Take Horus. We have one hour and twenty minutes."

Isaac scooped up Horus and put him in a black military backpack that he had found on board the Oculus. "Stay down," Isaac said as he and Zahra walked toward the large outdoor bazaar.

Jack walked the other direction, looking for one shop in particular. Every city had one, and they were always a good gateway into the black market: a tattoo parlor. He knew from his time in third-world countries that it was one-stop shopping for anything illegal. Sailors get tattoos, and they love to drink. Gangsters get tattoos, and they know where to get weapons. Also, he had never been to Tunisia, and he had a tradition of getting a tattoo each time he visited a new place. Jack pulled up his sleeve and pointed to his arm. "Tatu? Tatu?" A luggage salesman understood and pointed him in the right direction.

Barca's Parlor was hidden between a crossing of two cobblestone side streets. It had an engraved, painted wooden sign of Hannibal Barca riding an elephant. Jack swung the door open, and a striking Tunisian girl with straightened black hair looked up from a gossip magazine. The parlor was empty.

Jack eyed the meat spilling out and over her form-fitting jeans. "Not what I expected, but you'll do."

The Tunisian girl eyed Jack up through her black-rimmed glasses. She had sleeves of nautical tattoos and two sparrows across her chest. "My name is Olfa. What do you need, sailor?"

"I'm Jack. Can I trust you?"

"Depends on what you pay me," Olfa said.

"*That's* what I wanted to hear," Jack said. "I need three things in an hour."

"Shoot." When she stood up to stretch, she inadvertently pushed out her chest, temporarily distracting Jack.

"A bottle of booze, a tat, and a gun," Jack said.

"I can do the first two for three hundred flat. The last one would take a few days."

"Deal. But why so expensive?" Jack asked as he pulled his cash out and placed it down.

Olfa counted the money while talking. "In Tunisia, we use expensive ink made of natural elements like copper and platinum. It will last about three years. Take off your shirt and sit down."

Jack ripped off his shirt and sat face-forward in the tattoo chair. Olfa came out a minute later with two glasses and a bottle of Johnnie

Walker Red. She poured them both two fingers. They knocked them back. Olfa straddled Jack a little closer than her normal customers.

"What are we doing?" Olfa asked.

The warm whiskey coated Jack's empty stomach and began to radiate through the rest of his body. He felt normal again.

"The Jack of Diamonds," Jack said tapping his left shoulder blade. "You've got an hour."

Isaac and Zahra made their way through the crowded bazaar. The sounds and smells were overwhelming. Each merchant presented an array of Arabic products—terraced tin cans of bright-red and yellow spices, boiling pots of dyed linens, and plastic bins containing the whole color spectrum of fruits and vegetables. Horus occasionally popped his head out to get a peek.

Isaac watched a snake charmer entertain a group of tourists as Zahra haggled with a merchant over a bag of dried fruits and nuts. She was good at stretching out their money, and the only thing Isaac insisted on buying was a street map of Malta. He was happy to walk around and take mental snapshots so he could sketch them later in his journal. Zahra approached Isaac and threw the food into his backpack. "We are being followed."

"Are you sure?" Isaac asked.

"I only open my mouth if I'm sure of something," Zahra said. "Walk with me."

Zahra pulled Isaac over to a stand with cheap sunglasses and said, "Try these on and look over my shoulder at the men at the entrance of the market."

Isaac did as he was told and subtly looked over. He saw three grizzled men wearing jeans and soccer jerseys. They stared right at them.

"What do they want?" Isaac asked.

"It doesn't matter," Zahra said. "Stay with me. I know what I'm doing."

Zahra approached a Tunisian merchant wearing a fez, who was talking to his neighbor.

"Estad. Estad. That man just stole something," Zahra said as she pointed to a Tunisian teenager.

The merchant patted Zahra on the head and ran after the boy. "Thief!" the merchant yelled as he ripped the backpack off him. The teenager spun around and called the old man a liar. The boy's friends backed him up as the merchant tried to wrestle his backpack away. A fistfight erupted, and fellow merchants ran out with thin sticks to defend their own.

Zahra looked up. The chaos blocked their view of their trackers. She reached out and grabbed Isaac's hand. They ran through a narrow gap between two souks and out into another street. Isaac was fast, but Zahra was faster. He gripped her hand tighter as they wove around tourists and locals.

"We have twenty minutes to get to the ferry terminal," he said.

They heard a loud finger whistle behind them. Isaac and Zahra looked back. It was the tracker wearing a Moroccan soccer jersey. He had spotted them across the open courtyard. He signaled, pointed to his partners, and took off after them at a sprint. Isaac felt poor Horus bouncing around in the backpack.

"This way," Zahra said as they cut down a narrow alleyway. It was a dead end. They turned around and found a narrow passageway to another street. Zahra slipped through sideways, shimmying down the corridor. Isaac stepped in, but the military backpack made him too wide.

"Hurry!" Zahra yelled.

Isaac stepped back out and rolled his shoulders out of the backpack; Horus was still trapped inside and shrieking. He put his left side in first and held the backpack in his right hand. It barely fit.

A scarred hand reached down the corridor and grabbed the strap on the backpack. He yanked backward, pulling Isaac out of the corridor. The Tunisian's eyes were as red as the national soccer jersey he was wearing, and Isaac could smell cigarette smoke.

"You come with me," the Tunisian said, in raspy voice. "I won't hurt."

Isaac still had one hand on the other strap and tried to yank it free. No luck. The leathery Tunisian was wiry but much stronger than he was. Zahra shimmied back.

"Where is your girlfriend?" the Tunisian asked as the circling tug-of-war continued.

Isaac saw Zahra sneaking out and violently swung right so the man would be facing away from the corridor. Then he sat his butt down and anchored in. Horus finally ripped the zippers open and jumped out. The Tunisian stumbled back in shock as the rest of the contents—the box of cards, bags of food, water bottles, the map, Isaac's journal, and Olney's book—spilled everywhere.

Zahra used the distraction to slip out. She grabbed a thick Coke bottle off the ground and shattered it over the back of the Tunisian's head.

"Damn it!" he yelled checking his head for cuts.

It would have knocked most men out. He turned his head to see Zahra fumbling through the trash for a stronger weapon. It was Isaac's chance. He normally didn't have split-second instincts like Uncle Jack, but it was now or never. He strode forward, thrust his foot back just like in rugby practice, and landed a powerful kick right to the Tunisian's groin. A powerful blast of fetid air shot out from the depths of the man's stomach, and Isaac was forced to backpedal away from the odor. The sailor toppled to the urine-stained concrete, cursing in pain. Isaac stuffed the cards, the book, and his journal into the backpack while Zahra scooped up Horus. They both took off running. The map of Malta and all of their supplies lay next to the groaning Tunisian.

Isaac and Zahra ran out of the alley and down two blocks before she pulled him into a clothing store. They used the rest of their money to buy traditional Arabic garb: a long white thawb and red-checkered keffiyeh for Isaac and a light-purple abaya and burka for Zahra. Lastly, they bought a stroller and threw Horus and the backpack inside. They had fifteen minutes to walk to the ferry terminal.

Olfa, with a cigarette in her mouth, taped the bandage over Jack's new playing-card tattoo. Jack checked his watch. "I got fifteen minutes to kill. Can you think of anything we can do?"

"Sorry, Jack," Olfa said. "That's not something I charge for."

"Good, because that's not something I pay for," Jack said.

"That necklace on your neck," she said. "Where did you get it?"

"Gypsy ex-girlfriend left it," Jack said as he lifted it up and examined the concentric cross.

"Did you know it's a map of the ancient city of Carthage?" Olfa said. "Tunis used to be Carthage. Look at the wall."

"No shite," Jack said as he found the map. The cross looked exactly like the concentric canal and port complex of the capital city of the Carthaginian Empire. Jack was just about to ask a question when the door of Barca's Parlor swung open. Standing outside were five tough-looking Tunisian sailors armed with pipes. Three were Middle Eastern and two were African.

Jack turned to Olfa. "Friends of yours?" he asked.

"Depends on who's asking," Olfa said.

The African ringleader—with short dreadlocks and yellow eyes—stepped forward. "Don't hurt him bad. They want him alive."

Jack turned to Olfa, calm as ever. "Can I take you out drinking sometime?"

"Sure, if you're buying," Olfa said.

"Now that's something I *do* pay for," Jack said reaching for the bottle of Johnnie Walker.

The five Tunisians stepped inside the small tattoo parlor. Jack opened the whiskey and took a swig.

"Empty your wallets, and I'll let you walk out of here with your faces intact," he said.

The Tunisian sailors laughed, and the African ringleader stepped forward. "They offered us two thousand apiece to bring you in alive."

"Minus whatever you break in here," Olfa said to the thugs.

The Tunisian sailors surrounded Jack in the small parlor.

Jack counted out with his finger. "One, two, three, four, five. Do they teach math in this shithole country?"

"That's ten thousand dollars," the African said.

"Good. I'm going to make you earn it," Jack said as he dropped the whiskey bottle like a rugby ball. Right before it hit the ground, he kicked it with his boot like a drop goal. Shards of glass and whiskey sprayed out in a meter-wide blast. Three of the sailors covered up, but two of them took shards to the face. Jack ran toward the back door of Olfa's parlor.

"Shite!" Jack yelled when he realized it was just a bathroom and a storage shed, not an exit. There was a small window, but it was covered with bars. He closed and bolted the door just as the Tunisians swung their pipes.

He put his back to the door and scanned the storage shelves for a weapon. Nothing.

The Tunisians yelled at each other in Arabic. The pipes stopped for a moment and then were quickly replaced with alternating kicks. The door wouldn't hold for long.

Jack spotted a large white tub. He kept his back to the door but pulled it over with his left boot. He unscrewed the black plastic top. It was an eight-liter jar of Neosporin.

The middle of the door shattered, but the lock held up. The Tunisians double-teamed their kicks. Jack quickly kicked off his boots and stripped to his underwear. He thrust both hands into the tub of Neosporin and rubbed it all over his body. His head, limbs, and torso were soon covered in the slippery ointment.

"We're going to tune you up!" one of the Tunisians yelled.

It was near impossible for Jack to pull his boots on and lace them up with the gel on his hands, but he managed to do it.

"Come on there, lads! We're just getting started," Jack said as he stuffed the wad of money in his cheek. He tightened the last strap and ran toward the back wall. Two of the Tunisian sailors shouldered through the door. They expected more impact and fell flat to the ground. Jack was already coming right at them. It took him four steps to get full speed. He rucked over the other three Tunisians, and they all flew to the ground. The sailors wrestled him on the tiled floor, but he was too slippery to grab.

They tried to get ahold of one Jack's limbs, but he easily pulled away. Jack ducked a pipe blow and squirmed free of the tangled mess of octopus arms. He hit the open door in a sprint.

Everyone on the streets stopped as the 220-pound, tattoo-covered man sprinted past them in his underwear. Five sailors with pipes chased him. Jack inhaled and puffed his cheeks. A group of security guards were talking at the entrance of an outdoor bazaar when they saw the commotion.

Jack headed straight for them, and the sailors behind him shouted. The security guards formed a wall to stop him, but Jack lowered his shoulder and bowled over three of them. They crashed to the ground. They tried to grab his legs, but their fingers slipped right off. Jack was like a freight train plowing through a parking lot.

He weaved through the crowded market masterfully. A young Tunisian boy watched as Jack raced toward him. At the last second, he held out his bottled water like a bystander at a marathon. Jack snagged it in stride and splashed it on his face. At the other end, the security guards parted like the Red Sea for Moses.

The last ferry horn blew. The boat was going to depart in one minute. Still in their disguises, Isaac and Zahra scanned the streets that converged into the busy ferry terminal. The last of the European tourists carried their bags of gifts on board.

"Come on. He'll meet us there," Isaac said.

"Do you think he is all right?" Zahra asked with concern in her voice.

"He'll find us," Isaac said. "I promise."

He wheeled the stroller around, and they handed their tickets to the ferryman. Zahra took out the third ticket.

"Our friend might be here shortly," Zahra said.

"How will I know who it is, little girl?" the ferryman asked.

"Trust me," she said. "You will notice him."

Isaac and Zahra made their way to the passenger seats. They were still too nervous to change out of their costumes, just in case someone had followed them on board. Isaac kept his head down because he was getting strange looks, being a white man in a kaffiyeh. He burrowed into the seat. The last ferry horn sounded, signaling the crew to cast off. When the horn died, it was replaced with the sound of stomping boots on hollow ground.

Jack came through the hallway and into the overcrowded passenger room. Everyone in the room stared at the man in nothing but boots and underwear. Jack buckled over and put his hands on his knees. He caught his breath, reached into his mouth, and pulled out a wet wad of bills.

"All right...who's...got...some clothes...to sell?" Jack asked.

Hours later, Redbeard and three Corsairs entered Aziz Gisgo's office in the Tunis Port Authority. Gisgo had with him three police officers holstering pistols.

"Hand it over," Redbeard said. His eyes were piercing black daggers. He was still simmering on a cold boil after being outsmarted in Gibraltar and had no patience with the greedy, little fat man.

"I have it," Gisgo said as he tapped his portly fingers on the breast pocket of his uniform. "But I think we should be compensated."

"Compensated? You made a mistake, and this is your last chance to fix it," Redbeard said.

"Twenty thousand—" Before Gisgo could get out the type of currency, Redbeard darted forward and punched him in the throat. His three Corsairs had blades on the police officers before they even blinked.

Gisgo's pear-shaped body teetered on the floor as he wheezed for breath. *This waste of a man is too fat to roll off his back,* Redbeard thought. *Like a turtle.*

Redbeard knelt down and pulled the map out of his breast pocket.

CHAPTER 16:
THE FIVE OF SPADES

VALLETTA, MALTA

The passenger ferry rounded the southern tip of the island, climbed back up the coast, and entered the Grand Harbor of Valletta. Uncle Jack's face was smeared against the window. After twenty minutes of bartering, he managed to buy a pair of khakis and a T-shirt off a middle-aged Italian man. He complained about the cologne stench, so he knocked back a few scotches and awarded himself a nap. From a distance, Isaac and Zahra looked like a happy young couple playing with their kid in a stroller. No one could see that their child was a macaque.

Isaac looked out the window and flipped the gypsy woman's coin in his fingers. The reflection of the domed cathedrals and palaces floated across the top of the calm water. The foghorn sounded. Uncle Jack jolted awake but realized he was still on the ferry and relaxed again.

"How long was I out?" he asked, checking his watch.

"A few hours," Isaac said as the passenger ferry gently collided with the rubber tires on the dock.

"Good, let's hit the ground running," Jack said as he counted the rest of his cash. "Do we have any idea where he lives?"

"No," Isaac said. "Somewhere in the city."

"We're low on funds, so first we buy light food and water and then a place to stay," Jack said as he stuffed the bills into his pants. "I'll find a tavern and ask around about this Olney bloke."

"If you get any information, will you *remember* it in the morning?" Isaac asked.

"Don't be a smart arse," Jack said.

The doors of the boat opened, and the passengers spilled onto the ramp. Uncle Jack made a clicking noise in the side of his mouth, and Horus leaped out of the stroller. He climbed up the seat and perched on Jack's shoulder.

Zahra and Isaac took off their Arab clothes and left them on the boat inside the stroller. As they stepped into the warm glow of the Valleta sky-line, a ferry operator yelled at Jack. "Hey! You can't have animals on board."

"He's not an animal; he's my best friend," he yelled back.

The streets of Valletta were beautiful—lively piazzas, massive cathe-drals, and limestone watchtowers. Jack, Horus, Isaac, and Zahra sifted through the crowded streets looking for a place to stay.

"Why do so many people live on this small island?" Zahra asked.

"It's had many owners, as you can see by the variety of style in architecture," Isaac said. "And it's been a very important stronghold all throughout history. It has Neolithic temples that predate Stonehenge, and it was the site of St. Paul's shipwreck. Later, it was captured by the Arabs, taken back, and rebuilt by crusading knights, only to be captured again by Napoleon, and then claimed by the British, who granted them independence."

"Why do the smallest places have the most history?" Zahra asked. Once again, she had outsmarted him—a long list of Wiki facts summed up with one intelligent observation.

The group spent the next two hours walking in circles. Isaac and Zahra stopped in gift shops and bookstores, but no one had ever heard of Professor Olney. Meanwhile, Jack found out that all the cheap lodging in town was booked. He informed his troupe that the hotels exceeded their budget. He didn't know how long they were to be on Malta and wanted to conserve the two thousand plus pounds they had left. The group suffered from hunger pangs, which led to bickering over the next course of action. Jack ordered them to stop at a food store just outside a town center. They laid out a cheap feast consisting of a loaf of bread, stuffed olives, goat cheese, and white beans with garlic on an outdoor metal table. Most important, Uncle Jack brought a jug of house wine to take the edge off. Jack and Isaac both laughed as they watched Zahra cough down her first sip of alcohol. The group inhaled the food and pointed out funny-looking tourists to each other.

Zahra saw a young woman in a large overcoat hobbling down the street. It was the beginning of fall, but it was too warm to be wearing a heavy coat. As she got closer, Zahra noticed the woman's face was deformed. Her limp was off, also. It didn't look like an injury; it looked like she was carrying something heavy. The woman leaned to her right and shuffled down the street carrying a canvas grocery bag.

"I need water," Zahra said, getting up. She followed the limping woman into the grocery store.

"*Buona Sera*, Cassie," said the Italian grocer.

Cassie raised her hands to greet the man but did not say anything. Zahra knew how to remain invisible. She watched through the aisles as the crippled woman placed groceries in her bag. Cassie then approached the grocer. She struggled to lift the canvas bag onto the counter and swung it too hard. The groceries spilled out and fell to the ground behind the counter.

"*Merda.* Every time," the grocer said, bending down to pick up the vegetables.

Suddenly, another set of hands shot out from the trench coat and started pulling in handfuls of chocolate bars. Zahra could spot another thief from a mile away. The spilled groceries were a distraction. Cassie's jacket hands helped reassemble the groceries and pay for them. Meanwhile, someone hid in the coat and stole gourmet chocolate bars. *Was it a child? The hands looked too big?* Suddenly, Cassie looked over her shoulder and caught Zahra staring. She ducked behind the aisle and waited for Cassie to pay the grocer and shuffle out.

Zahra ran back to the table where Isaac and Uncle Jack were fighting over the last of the bread.

"Give me the book!" she yelled.

Isaac shuffled through the bag and handed over Professor Olney's book. Zahra flipped to the author's bio and read. *"Professor Olney lives in Valletta on the island of Malta with his twins, Cassie and Polly."* Zahra looked up from the book. "Follow me."

The group trailed Cassie from a block away. She made her way slowly out of the packed cobblestone streets and along the picturesque Valletta Waterfront. Then, the young deformed woman took a sharp right and climbed a hill that overlooked the Argotti Botanical Gardens and the Valletta skyline. At the top of the hill was a long driveway with olive trees and moss-covered Greek statues. They hid at the bottom of the gate and watched Cassie open the front door with a key. The house was built like a Roman *domus.* Everything on the outside was fortified, while everything inside the walls faced an open-aired atrium.

"What now?" Isaac asked.

"We wait and see if he comes out," Jack said. But before Isaac could respond, Zahra headed up the long driveway with the book in hand.

She knocked loudly, and the sound emptied into a large chamber on the other side of the door. Jack, Horus, and Isaac arrived just behind her. There was a long silence and then the sound of shuffling feet on tile. The metal lock unfastened, and the entrance creaked open. There was still a chain lock holding the door. Cassie peeked through and handed them a card.

Isaac examined it. In three different languages, it read, "The professor does not take visitors, but you can leave fan mail at the door and he will respond to them in a timely fashion."

Cassie tried to close the door, but Isaac quickly put his hand in the gap.

"Wait. We need the professor's help."

Cassie stopped trying to close the door. Isaac could only see a sliver of her deformed eye and wondered what atrocity she had endured.

"Tell him that someone gave us these and said he could tell us what they were," Isaac said as he pulled the deck of bronze cards out of the backpack. Cassie took the box, examined it, and then closed the door.

"Hey!" Zahra yelled. "Don't steal those!"

Minutes passed. Isaac twice had to stop Jack from climbing the walls. The door opened, and a gray beard appeared through the crack in the door.

"Where did you get these?" the bearded man asked.

"My father," Isaac said.

"Where did he get them?"

"That's what I was hoping you could help us with," Isaac said.

"Who are you?" the man asked.

"My name is Isaac Alexander. This is my uncle Jack, his monkey Horus, and our friend Zahra, who brought us these from Morocco where my parents were kidnapped. We just want to ask you a few questions."

"Did anyone follow you here?" the man asked.

"No," Jack said.

"Did the cardinal send you?" the man asked.

"I have no idea what you're talking about," Isaac said.

The door quickly closed, and the chain was unlocked. It swung open into a beautiful stone atrium with a large fountain. Professor John James Olney's tall frame stepped toward Isaac and lifted him off the ground in a massive bear hug.

"Haha! I knew it! I knew it! It's real!" the professor said. Jack and Zahra were shocked at how quickly the professor had gone from hesitant to excited.

As the tall old man swung Isaac around, he noticed the professor didn't have a left hand. In its place was a prosthetic metal claw.

"I've been waiting *thirty years* for this," the professor said hugging him. The claw moved within inches of Isaac's widening eyes. Finally, he put Isaac down and greeted Jack with a hug. Jack looked around nervously and then decided to pat Olney on the back with one hand.

"Cheers, mate," Jack said.

"Tears of *joy*, Uncle Jack," Olney said as he wiped his joyful tears and leaned down to Zahra. "Your name means *princess* in Arabic, dear. I've been all over the world, and you are by far one of the most beautiful girls I have ever seen."

Zahra recoiled, definitely wary of the professor's overt friendliness.

He then held out his claw for Horus, who grabbed it reluctantly. "Hello, Horus, the Sun God," he said.

Professor Olney stood up and clapped his hand against his claw. The man was so tall and thin it looked like he had been drawn and quartered. He wore a dark-green tweed suit with a bow tie. He looked like a Monty Python caricature of a British history teacher.

"My name is Professor John James Olney, and I've been *waiting* for you. I see you've already met my twins, Cassie and Polly."

"Twins?" Isaac asked.

The deformed woman looked up at Olney, and he nodded in encouragement. Cassie unbuttoned the large overcoat and opened it. Underneath the coat, her sister, Polly, was wrapped around her body, hiding herself. Polly released her grip and turned toward the group, revealing an identical face. They were conjoined twins, joined at the hip. Each had her own set of hands. Jack and Isaac stepped back a moment in shock but covered it up so as not to embarrass the girls.

"Leave your bags here, and the twins will put them in your rooms," Olney said.

"Rooms?" Jack asked. "Let's start with some answers."

"Oh yes, there will be plenty of those, but I can't do it on an empty stomach," Olney said, leading the group down toward the atrium. "Cassie and Polly make the best vegetable paella in the Mediterranean."

"What about scotch?" Jack asked.

"Barrels of it," Olney said. He jumped up and clicked his heels like a leprechaun.

Jack turned to Isaac. "If we stay here, there's a good chance our heads will end up floating in jars of formaldehyde."

Isaac said out of the corner of his mouth, "I don't think he gets a lot of visitors."

"On your toes," Jack said, looking around.

Cassie and Polly trailed behind and grabbed Zahra's arm. Polly reached into her pocket and handed Zahra one of the candy bars. Then both twins simultaneously put their fingers over their lips to seal the secret. Zahra knew all about the thief's code and accepted the chocolate bribe.

CHAPTER 17:
THE SIX OF HEARTS

PROFESSOR OLNEY'S ATRIUM
VALLETTA, MALTA

"Much better," Olney said as he pushed his empty plate of paella away. The table was lined with fresh butcher paper and small dinner candles. Olney's Roman villa was magnificent. They sat in an atrium surrounded by large potted ferns. Above them was an open-air planetarium. The rooms surrounding the Roman-style peristylium held libraries of books, studies full of antiques, and guest rooms.

"How's the scotch, Jack?" Olney asked as Cassie and Polly cleared their plates.

"Making me feel normal." Jack tipped his glass to Olney. Together, they had almost finished an entire bottle. Zahra tossed scraps to Horus under the table.

"Now, correct me if I'm wrong, but you're Jack O'Ryan, the famous rugger, right?" Olney asked.

Isaac rolled his eyes and shook his head. An Uncle Jack ego-boost and scotch were a lethal combination.

"In my better days," Jack said, patting his full stomach.

"I was there, my boy," Olney said. "Pint in hand at Twickenham. I saw the poach with my *own two eyes*."

"Get straight outta town, mate," Jack said.

"I was teaching at Oxford and took the bus down to watch the game. You single-handedly beat Army. How come you didn't play for the red roses?"

"Duty called," Uncle Jack said. "Fifteen years in the Royal Marines."

"You know, I was a decent lock until I lost my hand," Olney said, holding up his hook.

"Yeah, I've been working up the liquid courage to ask you how that happened," Jack said.

"Siberia, 1985. Wooly mammoth excavation. Our camp was attacked by wolves. I had to fight them off with my protractor. Look," Olney said, holding out his wrist for Jack. "There's still a tooth in my arm."

Cassie and Polly had stopped clearing the table. Jack moved closer and ran his hands down the old man's wrist trying to find the tooth. Without warning, Olney barked as loud as he could. Jack jumped back. He'd been duped. Olney, Isaac, and Zahra erupted in laughter. Cassie and Polly snickered and then took the dirty dishes to the kitchen.

"I'm sorry, mate," Olney said. "I'm just playing. I blew it off in college messing about with an alchemy experiment."

Jack downed the rest of his scotch. "Game on, you ole bastard." Then he leaned over to Isaac and said, "This geezer ain't so bad, huh?"

Olney laughed, turned to Isaac, and placed the bronze deck of cards facedown on the table. "All right, my boy. You're eyes have been piercing daggers all night. You deserve some answers. So why don't you bring this old man up to speed?"

Isaac cleared his throat. "Well, my father is a famous inventor, David Alexander. He created laptops for kids in third-world countries. My mother, Rachel, is a doctor and goes with him all over India and Africa doing humanitarian missions. Their last school was in Morocco where they met Zahra."

"Continue," Olney said as Cassie and Polly brought out a silver demitasse tray of small Arabic coffee cups and served them after-dinner espressos.

"They had been in the Atlas Mountains for three years when they were attacked and kidnapped. My father gave Zahra that deck of cards. They also told her that I might be in danger. We visited a Gypsy woman who told us that playing cards hold a secret code. But before we could get more answers, we were attacked. The same men who kidnapped my parents followed Zahra from Morocco to Gibraltar. We escaped, but not before the Gypsy woman gave us *your* book."

"And we stole their yacht and got chased through Tunisia," Jack said with a smirk.

"This Gypsy woman, what else did she tell you about the cards?" Olney asked.

"She explained that my uncle was a Jack of Diamonds and I was an Ace of Spades," Isaac said.

"And you, Zahra?" the professor asked.

"I do not matter. Isaac does," Zahra said, directing the attention away from herself.

"Yes, Isaac Alexander, the *Laughing Defender of Men*," Olney said. "You're pretty serious though, wouldn't you agree?"

Isaac looked puzzled. "What?"

"In Hebrew, Isaac means '*of laughter*' and Alexander, in Greek, means '*defender of man.*' These cards, however, are no laughing matter, and neither is your birth card, the Ace of Spades."

"The Gypsy woman…she told me about my dreams." Isaac turned to Zahra and Jack and forced himself to continue. "I've had the same recurring dream since I was a boy. I wake up on an uninhabited island, explore the buildings, and then get swallowed by a massive tidal wave."

"And you have this dream every night?" Olney asked.

"Every night that I don't take medication," Isaac said. "I went to a doctor, and he told me I was in the early stages of schizophrenia."

"Do you have an idea of what this place looks like?" Olney asked.

"I wake up every morning and sketch what I can in my journal."

"May I have a look?" Olney asked as he put on his reading glasses. Isaac reluctantly unzipped his bag and handed over the leather-bound journal.

"You're only the *second* person to ever see these," Isaac said.

For a few minutes, Olney flipped through the journal. He traced his finger over each drawing and read some of Isaac's passages.

"Girls," Olney said as he motioned for the twins. Cassie and Polly shuffled over and leaned down. Professor Olney whispered something into Cassie's ear, and they walked out of the courtyard.

"First, my boy, I want you to join me in a *deep* inhale and exhale." Olney led and made Isaac follow.

"What's this for?" Isaac asked as he exhaled.

"You're not a schizophrenic," Olney said, "but I am preparing you for the truth…which is going to sound even crazier."

"And that is?"

"You're a *psychic*. More specifically, a clairvoyant. '*Clair*' is French for *clear*, and '*voyance*' means *vision*. You have the ability to see objects or events that cannot be perceived by the five senses. Your dreams are not hallucinations or conjured images of your subconscious. They are messages from your ancestors."

Isaac tried to process this revelation. He waited for the *aha* moment, but it never came. Cassie and Polly handed an old, leather-bound book to Professor Olney: *Timaues and Critias* by Plato.

"I've looked in every history book and have never found *anything* resembling my dreams," Isaac said.

"That's because your ancestors were erased from the history books," Olney said.

"Where are they from?" Isaac asked.

"All converging lines of civilization lead back to this island. I've devoted my whole life to researching it. Until I held this deck of cards, I never had proof that it existed."

"Proof of what?" Isaac asked.

"Isaac, you are a descendant from the long-lost civilization of Atlantis," the professor said.

Isaac wondered if the professor was playing another practical joke.

"What? Like unicorns and mermaids Atlantis?" Jack asked with a laugh.

"It's not fiction. It's a very true story. They were a highly advanced, Bronze Age civilization that existed for four thousand years. Roughly from 5500 BC to 1500 BC."

"Christ, first it's playing cards, and now it's underwater cities," Jack said, shaking his head.

"Isaac, have you ever come across Plato's books *Timaeus* and *Critias?*" Olney asked.

"I know Plato, but I've never read those," Isaac said.

"Are you certain?" Olney asked.

Isaac nodded, his eyes wide to show that he was sincere.

Olney opened the book to a marked page and held Isaac's journal next to it. Plato's map of Atlantis and Isaac's map of his island were exact replicas. They were both large crosses inside of concentric circles. Even the individual buildings were identical.

Isaac jumped up. "That's impossible. How did you...but..." The information was too much for him to handle.

"Holy shite," Jack said, pulling out the cross on his neck. "Is that what *this* is?"

Olney examined it. "The cross of Atlantis. It was their symbol and a map of their capital city."

"Okay, Professor, wait a minute," Jack said. "I'm not hopping on board the crazy train just yet."

"Brilliant! It took me decades to even find the station," Olney said. "Ask me anything."

"Where is the island?" Jack asked, his eyebrow quirked.

"Buried deep under water and lava rock on the Greek island of Thera," Olney said. "When the Greek writer, Solon, visited Egypt around 560 BC, he learned about an ancient trading empire that the Egyptians called *Keftiu*. His research inspired Plato's writings about Atlantis, but all of Solon's research documents were destroyed by the Christians when they burned down the Temple of Neith in AD 391."

"How is this all connected?" Isaac asked. "The cards? Atlantis? My parents? Every time we get one answer, three more questions pop up. I need someone to connect the dots."

"I'll do my best, but first you need to accept something," Olney said.

"What?" Isaac asked.

"I can tell by the small sampling of your writing that you're very left-brain oriented," Olney said. "You're hardwired to think scientifi-cally—to identify, to label, and to categorize. The answers you seek lie in uncharted waters. History's greatest minds, men like the man you were probably named after—"

"Isaac Newton?" Isaac asked.

The tall professor nodded and sipped his tea. "Yes, Mr. Newton. He learned how to bridge the gap between his left brain and his right brain. To him, science and spirituality were one and the same. You have to merge your conscious and subconscious minds to become whole and completely aware of yourself."

"Okay…*how* do I do that?" Isaac asked.

The professor laughed. "It's not like taking out the rubbish. It starts with patience and understanding."

Isaac nodded.

Olney cleared the books off the table, pulled a pencil out of his tweed jacket, and held it up for the group. "Now that I am caught up, it's *your* turn. Professor Olney, self-proclaimed alchemist-extraordinaire and master of all things esoteric, is going to give you a history lesson. Questions are encouraged. Ready?"

Zahra, Jack, and Isaac nodded, while Horus slept in Zahra's lap. Olney quickly sketched a map of the Mediterranean.

"Like I said, Atlantis was a highly advanced Bronze Age civilization that predated the Egyptians and the Babylonians. It existed from 5500 BC to roughly 1500 BC on the Greek isle of Thera." Olney sketched a rough map of the island of Atlantis in relation to mainland Greece. Isaac, Zahra, and Jack leaned in.

"Atlanteans—as they were called—made extraordinary advancements in the fields of astronomy, philosophy, mechanics, and health. They grew to a utopian state where mankind and nature lived in harmony. The kingdom of Atlantis was ruled by four kings—sound familiar?"

"Like a deck of cards?" Zahra asked.

"Brilliant, my little princess. Each king of Atlantis reigned over one season and one element: spring, summer, fall, winter; fire, earth, air, and water."

"So each suit stands for one season and one element?" Isaac asked.

"Precisely," Olney said, sketching out each playing card suit next to the alchemy symbol for each element. "Hearts represent spring and fire. Clubs represent summer and earth. Diamonds equal fall and air. The spades stand for winter and water. Good gods, I would give my other hand just to have *one* of your dreams."

Isaac laughed. The professor's enthusiasm was contagious. "Why?"

"Ha! Why?" Olney scoffed. "They were so in *tune* with human nature and the cosmos that they knew the day of your birth was like a placement exam for your career. Imagine the possibilities of a post-gender society that puts children into specialty schools according to where they are destined to excel?"

"Sounds like Nazi Germany," Jack said.

"Oh, shut it," Olney said to Jack. "Isaac, imagine if all you ever focused on your entire life was engineering? Would you not be able to accomplish something truly remarkable?"

"I guess. But wouldn't I be useless at everything else?" Isaac asked.

"Not useless. Interdependent. Let me explain. People born under hearts strive for human relationships. These people use their creativity and passion to create emotional connections. Your artists, painters, sculptors, performers, musicians, even health workers."

"My mother is a doctor, born August 27."

"Queen of hearts, my boy. Clubs are people like me—driven by understanding and information. We are your teachers, writers, philosophers, and all other professions that revolve around logic, communication, and the quest for knowledge."

"What about my suit? The Diamonds? Are we the dumb squaddies that had to protect all you eggheads?" Jack asked.

"Well, yes and no. The Atlanteans had a highly advanced navy, but the rest of the undeveloped world viewed them more as deities and trading partners than enemies. However, those born as diamonds are primarily concerned with understanding life through *values.* That is why they make excellent soldiers, merchants, politicians, and lawyers. Diamonds thrive when living by a code, whether it be warfare, politics, or commerce."

"Yes!" Jack screamed. "I finally got something right!"

"And mine?" Isaac asked.

"The spades are the least common. They are driven by the need to understand life through their work. Spades are usually innovators in one specific field—your scientists, engineers, architects, and mathematicians. Now, my point to all this is, when you only work in one specialty, you are dependent on others to fulfill obligations. Artists need teachers to inspire them; teachers need soldiers to protect them; soldiers need scientists to invent the tools to make that possible. And vice versa. Engineers need soldiers and merchants to use their inventions to explore the world and bring back information for teachers who inspire artists. And art, as we all know, makes life worth living."

While Olney was talking, he was sketching a rough diagram of the solar system. The professor looked up to three enthralled students.

"Right. Moving on. The people of Atlantis believed in a universal religion based around the laws of nature and the cosmos called the Religion of the Stars. Look above you right now."

Zahra, Jack, and Isaac looked up to the bright constellations above. The seven major stars of Orion's Belt flickered right above them.

"They believed that the stars and planets held a secret code that could determine, not only the actions of nature but the actions of all human beings. And guess what?"

"They cracked the code?" Isaac recalled from the Gypsy woman's brief lesson.

"Brilliant, my boy," Olney said. "I think I can see the fibril neurons in your *corpus callosum* chipping away at the Berlin Wall separating the two halves of your brain." Olney was out of breath by the end of the last sentence and inhaled.

Jack and Zahra shared a confused glance—too many big words for their liking. Olney pointed down to his completed diagram of the solar system and continued, "The people of Atlantis believed that the planets orbiting Earth were celestial bodies. Who can name the seven planets of the ancient world?"

"I believe they were Earth, Moon, Mercury, Venus, Sun, Mars, Jupiter, and Saturn," Isaac said.

"Now we're cooking," Olney said, his excitement building. "They believed that the orbiting planets had a magnetic influence on human beings."

"Like the moon. That is what the Gypsy woman said, too," Zahra added.

Olney sketched a rough diagram of the zodiac wheel that included each astrological sign.

"The people of Atlantis were the original inventors of the zodiac. Their religion was a synthesis of what we know now was astrology and numerology," Olney said. "Those two systems of belief predate any other known religion."

"So, why hide thousands of years of their research in playing cards?" Isaac asked.

"Excellent question," Olney said. "Somewhere around 1500 BC, their *entire* civilization was destroyed by a massive tidal wave."

"Just like in my dreams," Isaac said as he sat back in his chair, conjuring up vivid images of the flood.

Olney spread the cards out on the table. "These cards have been sought after by kings, conquistadors, emperors, and sultans. There are four known decks that survived Atlantis that are rumored to hold a very powerful secret when combined."

"So, what about David and Rachel?" Jack asked. "Why would they have these?"

"Well, it is rumored that there is a secret society that safeguards these cards. They've existed since the Egyptian empire, but their organization is shrouded in mystery. There's a possibility that your father is a member."

Zahra cleared her throat and spoke up. "When David gave me the cards, he pulled out some kind of weapon. It was silver and covered in engravings. It extended into a long—"

"Staff?" Olney cut her off.

"Yes," Zahra said.

"I'm afraid that we've only hit the tip of the iceberg," Olney said.

"So, what you're saying is that only the most powerful and intelligent people in the world know about these cards?" Jack asked.

"I'm afraid that we're not only up against the elite of the elite, but time itself," Olney said.

"You've lost me again," Jack said.

Olney pointed back to the zodiac wheel drawn on the table. "The people of Atlantis had an annual event called the Festival of the Bull. To them, the bull was the most sacred animal because their civilization existed under the age of—" Olney pointed his pencil to the horned sign on the zodiac.

"Taurus," Isaac said.

"Yes. Every 2,150 years, we enter a new age on the zodiac," Olney said, pointing to the zodiac sign above Taurus. "Every new astrological age sees the rise of great civilizations. The age of Taurus saw Atlantis and the Egyptian Empire. Now, what is this sign?"

"Hell, I know that one. That's me. Aries," Jack said. "I convinced my Gypsy ex-girlfriend to tattoo it on her bum."

"Well, thank you for that visual," Olney said and shook his head. "Think about the next great civilization, after Atlantis and after Egypt that is associated with the ram."

"Moses? Moses is always depicted with a ram's horn," Isaac said.

"Brilliant, boy. Moses led the Hebrews out of Egypt and ushered in the next astrological age—the Age of Aries. Here is where it gets *very* interesting," Olney said as he pointed back to his map of the Mediterranean. "Atlantis was destroyed in one day and one night by a combination of the four elements. A massive earthquake triggered the biggest volcanic eruption in ancient history. Geologists have concluded that the Thera eruption in the second millennium BCE was the second largest eruption in recorded history. It was several hundred times the size of a nuclear explosion! The shifting tectonic plates also caused the biggest tidal wave in recorded history. Colossal tsunamis swept from the eastern Mediterranean over the Greek isles and into the western Mediterranean, forever altering the landscape."

Olney drew north and south arrows over his dinner-table map from Atlantis to Egypt.

"The harsh winds carried a lethal volcanic ash all the way down to Egypt, suffocating any plant or animal within hundreds of kilometers. Now, Isaac, how does this all tie together? Think biblically."

"The plagues of Egypt!" Isaac said as he put his hands on his head. "The volcanic ash from Atlantis was what caused the days of darkness and the polluting of the rivers." Isaac's head spun as all of this accumulated knowledge started coming together.

"Spot on," Olney said. "There was so much water displacement in Egypt that it caused a severe drop in the Red Sea, and many *kooky* old historians like myself believe that's how Moses was able to cross."

"Maybe the crazy train isn't so crazy," Jack said.

"Welcome aboard," Olney said with a smile. "Now, look at the next astrological sign after Aries."

"That's me," Isaac said. "Pisces."

"And the universal symbol that represented Jesus," Olney said. "Two fish."

"So, Atlantis was under the age of Taurus. The Hebrews were under the age of Aries. And the Christians were under the age of Pisces," Isaac said. "Are we still in that now?"

Olney pointed to the zodiac wheel on the table. "Each astrological sign on the zodiac takes up thirty degrees on the wheel. However, constellations are not uniform in size, and many astronomers believe that the corresponding ages also vary in time. Aquarius is one of the largest constellations, taking up over 980 square degrees of the wheel. It's highly possible that the world has had an influx of crises and natural disasters because we are in the waning days of the Age of Pisces and the coming tide of Aquarius. Astronomers believe the transitional phase can last up to 280 years. Whoever is after these cards is most likely trying to unleash their secret so they can establish themselves as a leader of the New Age."

"If I find out you can turn water into wine and you've been holding out," Jack said jokingly.

The professor looked at Isaac, who wasn't even responding to his uncle's attempt at humor. He was just blankly staring at the table of sketches trying to figure out how he fit into this equation. Olney already knew that was how his brain worked.

"I've got an idea," Olney said. "It's risky, but it might help Isaac find some answers."

Jack looked at his nephew. Isaac glanced up and shrugged.

"What is it?" Jack asked.

"To my study," Olney said and stood, his old knees creaking.

The group walked down Olney's outdoor hallway, which was lined with marble statues of famous Greek gods. Olney opened a large wooden door, revealing a massive two-story study that was lined floor-to-ceiling with ancient texts. There was a large, bronze astral globe next to four brown leather chairs and a massive stone fireplace. The tables were filled with pages of mathematical equations, alchemic diagrams, and bottles of varying liquids.

"Welcome to my hermit shell," Olney said.

"I don't get you two," Zahra said as she pointed to Professor Olney first. "You love everything but hide here." Then she pointed to Jack. "He hates everything but travels everywhere."

Jack laughed. "She's got a point, Professor."

"There's a reason I've had to stay on this island," the professor said as he sifted through jars of bottled plants, "but that is a story for another time and place. Right now, our focus is on Isaac." Olney took five glass jars, which held various roots and plants, off the shelf. He placed them on the table and returned to grab more. Uncle Jack picked up one of the jars and examined the strange plant with a fearful eye.

Olney called to Cassie and Polly, who were waiting by the door, previously unnoticed. "Boil a pot of water."

Jack put down the jar. "And what, exactly, are you planning to do?"

Olney sorted through glass jars and mumbled to himself. Then he turned and said, "All of the answers already exist in young Isaac's brain. He just needs help bringing them to the surface."

Olney held up a dangerous-looking Victorian medical apparatus that made Isaac's stomach queasy.

"Pull it out?" Isaac asked.

Olney continued to look for one last jar. "Aha. Kava kava extract." He turned and held it up to the surprised group. "Yes, with young Isaac's permission, I am going to hypnotize him."

"Is he going to wake up with all of *his* limbs intact?" Uncle Jack asked.

Olney put his prosthetic claw behind his back and smiled. "Yes. I am going to make a mild sedative using some very safe herbal ingredients and retell him the story of Atlantis from start to finish." Olney grabbed Isaac's shoulder with his hand. "His subconscious mind will attach images to my words. Imagine it like a jigsaw puzzle in his head. Right now, all the pieces are scattered about. After this, it will be one, nice, crystal-clear image. The poor boy thinks he's a *schizophrenic*, for Christ sakes."

"Kind of like when I go out drinking and only remember flashes of the night," Jack said. "Once my mates tell me what I did, I can piece it together in my head. Isaac, do you feel comfortable doing this?"

Isaac looked around the room. It was his rabbit hole moment—climb down and find the truth or continue to hide in the dark.

"I have nothing to lose," Isaac said.

"Thatta boy. Now, I need the library cleared for the next few hours. Cassie and Polly can show you to your rooms." Olney picked up the teapot the girls had brought him and dropped ingredients in the water.

Isaac gave a reassuring look to Uncle Jack and then nodded to Zahra. He knew he was going to have to do this leg of the journey alone.

"I'll be fine," Isaac said.

"For some strange reason, I trust the kooky old geezer," Jack said to Zahra as they exited the large library. She wholeheartedly agreed.

Professor Olney poured a cup of boiling tea and handed it to Isaac. "Down to the last drop."

Isaac took the warm mug and sipped the piping-hot liquid. He coughed and forced it down. "It tastes like dirt," Isaac said.

"All the way down, lad," Olney said as he used his claw to lift the cup back up to Isaac's mouth.

It took three difficult swigs, but Isaac got it down. Olney put the mug to the side, grabbed Isaac by both of his shoulders, and looked him straight in the eye.

"*Everything* I have done with my life has led to this moment. You have validated me. I know you have your uncle to be your bodyguard, but consider me the ambassador of your mind. Being an Ace of Spades and a descendant of Atlantis makes you one of the most *important* people *alive*. Your subconscious memories are far more powerful than you can imagine. I know we just met, but I want you to know that am pledging my undying allegiance to you. Even if it costs me my other hand."

Isaac felt like the old professor was the grandfather he'd never had. He settled back into his chair and felt the outline of the metal divots on his back. He felt a rush of blood rise from his flushed cheeks to his drumming temples. The back of his shoulders and his neck seemed weightless as he rolled his head on its axis and sank deeper. A wave of euphoria swam through his veins up the back of his head and then spread to his frontal lobe. He felt like he had just put on a hooded sweatshirt made of painkillers.

"Am I floating?" Isaac asked as he gripped the arms of the chair for support.

"Relax. Relax." Olney's soothing voice took over. "Close your eyes."

Isaac closed his eyes as Olney slid an ottoman under his feet.

"Don't fight it," Olney said patting Isaac's forearm. "It's here to help you. Let it pump through your veins and calm you. Sink into the chair. Embrace what is coming."

Isaac let out a deep exhale. He was so relaxed that he had to remind himself to inhale through his nose.

"That's it. Deep breaths. Now, imagine the calm ocean waters. Free flowing. Fluid. Every particle of water meshed together in a slow... tidal...rhythm. Relax. Just think about the ebb and flow of the water... nothing else."

Isaac's face slackened. He felt like a tangled mess of cords that had just been unwound. His perpetual state of tension and anxiety felt like a distant memory.

"That's it. Calm ocean waters. Now, I am going to count down from ten. When you wake up, you will be on the island of Atlantis. Ten. Nine. Eight. Seven. Six. Five. Four. Three. Two. One..."

CHAPTER 18:
THE SIX OF CLUBS

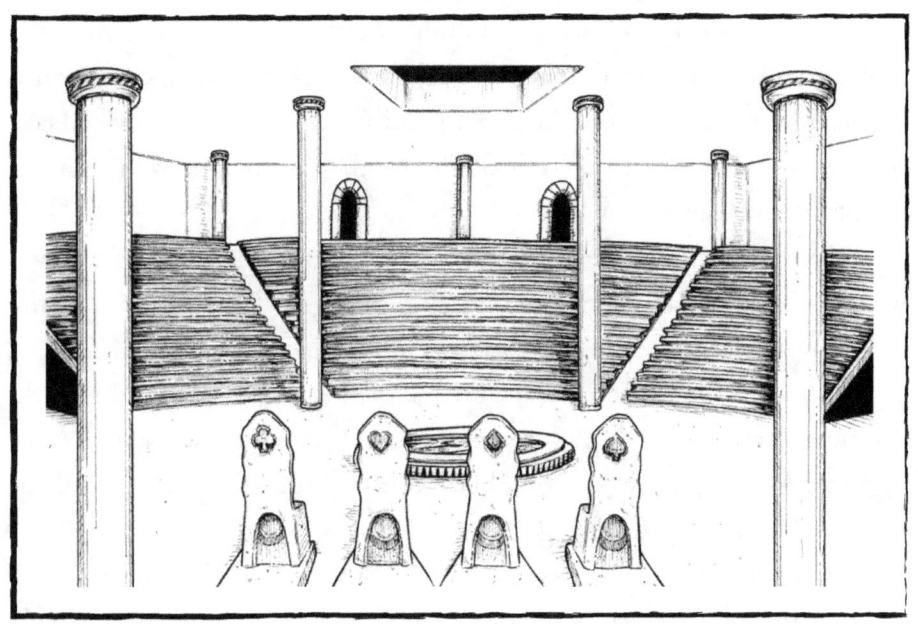

COURT OF NOBLES, ATLANTIS

Isaac heard an ethereal melody and opened his eyes. Above him was a giant, alabaster skylight and a rotating bronze zodiac wheel. He propped himself up on his elbows. He was lying on a plastered limestone floor inside of a massive rectangular megaron. Four Doric columns held up the ceiling, and each wall was lined with amphitheater seating. At the entrance, there was a teenage girl playing the lyre as dozens of nobles entered the great hall. The tunic-clad aristocrats looked too preoccupied to notice the mesmerizing, black-haired beauty in the white robe.

They climbed the stairs and filed into their seats. Young male servants handed them ice water in bullhorn rhytons. Isaac got to his feet and walked to the middle of the grand building.

"Where am I?" Isaac said to himself.

"Please be seated!" a voice called out. Isaac spun to his right. Four ornately dressed kings entered through a bronze archway and then sat atop gypsum thrones. Each crystalline seat had been carved into the shaped of one of the four suits—a heart, a club, a diamond, and a spade. The King of Clubs held his hand up to quiet the crowd. Isaac backed up. He was in the center of the room, and there were dozens of people staring directly at him.

"Sit down," the King of Clubs said. Isaac immediately sat down with his back to a large metal object. The King of Clubs addressed the crowd again. "Let us stay calm and decide the best course of action."

The grumbling senators sat down. Isaac felt cold metal on his back. He turned around and saw the ancient clock that he had visited every night in his dreams. Two men in black-and-red tunics walked directly at Isaac and passed right through him.

"Who are you?" Isaac asked the men, but they didn't answer.

The two men detached the bronze clock from the floor. Isaac slowly reached out and tried to touch one of their shoulders. His hand went straight through the man as if he were vapor.

"I'm dreaming," Isaac said to himself. Isaac put both hands over his mouth and yelled as loud as he could, "Hey!"

Nothing. The men continued to settle into their seats. Isaac took a deep breath. He was in his most comfortable state—invisibility. The two men pulled a bronze lever, and the ancient clock slid back toward the wall. It sat on top of interconnected bronze gears on the floor.

"All right, you're here for a reason. Pay attention," Isaac said to himself. He had been in this exact room hundreds of times, but now it had come alive.

The King of Clubs addressed the nervous crowd. "Senator Pontus, you have the floor."

Isaac looked over to the terraced marble seats. All of the senators wore either a red or black tunic with a white toga draped over it. Senator Pontus rose and addressed the anxious crowd. "My scholars and I have been double-checking the horologion day and night, and our results are conclusive. In one month, there will be a catastrophe, a violent combination of the four elements that will *destroy* our island."

A tense uproar shot through the crowd, and Senator Pontus raised his hand to continue.

"An earthquake followed by an eruption of our volcano and finally a completely destructive tidal wave," Senator Pontus said.

"We have gotten too close to the gods, and now they have sent nature to destroy us!" screamed an elderly man in a black tunic.

Senator Pontus turned to the four kings of Atlantis. "We have called this council for our kings to vote on the fate of our civilization."

The King of Hearts addressed the senator. "What are the options you are proposing?"

Senator Pontus said, "If we evacuate now, we can get everyone off the island."

An angry senator stood and yelled from the top of the auditorium. "Atlantis has existed for four thousand years. Our copper-mining expeditions have brought us to the four corners of the world, and our technology surpasses all other civilizations'. We must *preserve* our knowledge, or it will take the rest of the world thousands of years to catch up!" The senator's angry tirade was reinforced with verbal agreements from half of the nobles.

The King of Hearts raised his hand and silenced them. "And the second option?"

Senator Pontus stood up and said, "We accept what has been written in the stars."

A senator sitting on the bottom row stood up and said, "Other human civilizations have not evolved enough to adopt our way of life. The Egyptians were desert barbarians before we built their pyramids. We are gods, and no one is worthy of our knowledge. It should die with us!""

Yells of approval erupted from the other half of the senators. They were split down the middle.

The four kings of Atlantis turned to each other and deliberated quietly. Minutes passed, and hushed murmurs filled the great hall. The King of Clubs stood and addressed the auditorium. "The imminent disasters are clear signs from the gods that we have reached the end of our age," he said, pointing up to the zodiac wheel on the skylight.

The King of Clubs said, "We are leaving the Age of Taurus and must make way for a new age—the Age of Aries. We have based our whole way of life on reading the stars. Avoiding our own fate would be a clear violation of our religion. We will accept our destiny with open arms and view it as the end of our mortal age and the beginning of our afterlife. The gods are sending down the four elements to welcome us into their arms. As above, so below."

The senators were all moved by the king's speech and repeated his last line in unison. "As above, so below."

The King of Clubs sat down, and the King of Hearts stood. "We have also decided that this must remain a secret. We do not want our citizens to panic. The day before our destruction, we are going to invite everyone to the capital for a festival honoring the final days of Taurus."

Suddenly, everything in the giant megaron went out of focus, and Isaac lost all sense of depth perception. The sharply defined objects and contrasting colors flattened onto one plane and then bled into each other like an impressionist painting. Isaac felt disoriented and closed his eyes. When he opened them, there was an entirely different color palette in front of him. He was in a new location. The focus and contrast gradually returned, and he realized he was in the bedroom of a grand palace. The walls were lined with red, black, and white frescoes of a giant Atlantean naval fleet.

Isaac noticed a young male servant prepping the room and filling rhytons with wine from a large ceramic amphora. The servant bore a remarkable resemblance to Isaac.

They both heard footsteps outside. The young servant hid in a dark corner of the room. Isaac remained in the middle.

The King of Clubs swung open his door and rushed inside. A beautiful but distressed woman followed behind him. It was his wife, the Queen of Clubs, dressed in a red-and-black robe decorated with white peacock feathers. The gorgeous, olive-skinned woman was adorned with amber jewelry, and her rolling black hair was held up with intricately carved ivory tusks.

"You have to tell me what's happening," the queen said.

The King of Clubs walked to a table and picked up a rhyton of wine. He knocked back the entire contents of the glass in one gulp. "There is a tidal wave coming in one month that will destroy our island," he said, wiping his mouth.

Isaac looked at the servant. He hid in the shadows but could hear the conversation.

"What are we going to do?" the queen asked.

The King of Clubs turned to his queen and held her in his arms. "The other kings and I voted to keep it a secret, but I have a plan. We must keep *our* blood line alive."

"Where are we going to go?" the Queen of Clubs asked again.

"Egypt. I will steal the horologion, and my men will raid the warehouses. We will be welcomed as consuls to the pharaohs. As long as we have that machine, our family will remain in power."

The King and Queen of Clubs embraced passionately. Isaac noticed the walls going out of focus again.

When he came to, he was in a large, oval-shaped study. It was late at night, and a dozen senators spoke in hushed tones crowded around a marble table. Senator Pontus led in the servant boy who had witnessed the King of Clubs speaking to his wife.

The senator then addressed his peers. "It is true. The King of Clubs is plotting to escape. This presents us with a few courses of action. We can warn the other three kings, but then we run the risk of being executed for treason. It will be our word against a king's. We can confront the King of Clubs, but we will have to take on his armed guards. Or we can find a way to sneak all of our knowledge off the island in hopes that it is discovered by a *worthy* civilization."

The senators all raised their hands in unison and voted for the last option. "Very well," Senator Pontus said. "We have one month."

Isaac then heard something strange. All the sound around him became muted, and he heard only the ticking of the giant bronze clock above him. He looked up, and when the clock struck midnight, the minute and hour hands flew around the clock. When he looked down, the senators looked like they were in fast-forward. They rushed around the library opening documents, spreading them out on the table, and copying things down. They argued, slept in the corners of the room, and poured through hundreds of handwritten scrolls. Isaac realized he was watching a time-lapsed version of the entire month.

Isaac counted the sunsets and sunrises through the mirrored light wells that illuminated the room. The ceiling in the large, circular library was covered by a jewel-encrusted map of the constellations. He stepped over the marble table and watched the senators use crystal magnifying glasses as they carefully constructed the four decks of cards. There were layers upon layers of intricate bronze gears inside. Isaac watched the men piece the decks together for over thirty minutes. Then the movements of the clock's hands slowed down. The senators gradually returned to normal speed, and the sound faded back in.

Isaac could tell from the warm light that it was almost sunrise. The senators spread out the four decks of cards across the table. Senator Pontus and the twelve others who had helped make the bronze cards walked out of their library and across a lush garden. They entered the Court of Nobles, which contained sixteen young servants and twenty senators. The servants wore simple white tunics and formed a straight line in front of the senators.

Senator Pontus addressed the young men and women. "Our island is going to be destroyed, but not before *you* escape. You will each be given a deck of cards and a map that will lead you to a destination far, far away. Our plan is to spread these decks all over the globe in the hope that *someday* our secrets will be revealed."

The servant resembling Isaac stepped forward. "The kings' men are guarding the ports, sir. How are we supposed to get off the island?"

"We have written orders explaining that you are all fishermen going out to catch more food for the festival," Senator Pontus said. "You will not be able to use our naval ships, so your journeys will be made in our fishing vessels. It will be dangerous, but it must be done."

The young servants all nodded. The senators grouped them in pairs of four: two men, two women. Each group was given a deck of cards and a map. Senator Pontus then blessed them and said, "Today, we are tens of thousands. Tomorrow, we will only be *sixteen*. You are worthy ambassadors for our great civilization. Make us proud."

Suddenly, a group of armed guards rushed through the main entrance. Behind them was the King of Clubs. Senator Pontus turned to the servants. "Go to your ships!" The servants sprinted out the back entrance before the king and his centurions spotted them. The remaining senators crowded around the horologion.

The King of Clubs reached the center of the auditorium. He wore black and bronze armor and pulled a golden xiphos sword from the sheath on his belt. "Step aside, Senators," the King of Clubs ordered.

"We know what you're planning, and we can't let you get away with it," Senator Pontus said.

The senators were unarmed but clung together around the bronze machine.

"It is already done," the King of Clubs said. "The other three kings have been poisoned. Anyone who finds them will think it was suicide. Step aside, or I will send all of you to the gods."

The senators grabbed each other's tunics and pulled together. The King of Clubs nodded to his men. The unarmed senators stood no chance. The king's centurions hacked through them without mercy. The sound of slicing flesh and screams made Isaac queasy. He couldn't watch the massacre. He backed away as liters of blood poured into the bronze gears on the floor. It looked too real. He had seen enough. He turned and sprinted out of the building.

The city was packed with olive-skinned Atlanteans, but somehow, Isaac was able to spot the group of servants. He wove through flocks of black-haired denizens in the garden district that surrounded the Court of Nobles. Adults carried baskets full of fresh fruit, and young children's faces were decorated with zoomorphic designs in gold and turquoise paint. Isaac rushed past them but tried to soak in the peaceful images in order to clear his memory of the violent scene he had just witnessed. He realized they were on the innermost circle of Atlantis, which was made up of the four kings' palaces, lush portico gardens lined with dyed-red cypress trees, and all of the government buildings. Adolescent boys grappled on the lawns while their female counterparts braided saffron flowers into each other's hair.

The servants ascended the steps of a cross-shaped bridge that allowed its citizens to walk to all four rings of the capitol. Isaac had been there a thousand times and consulted his internal map. The servants made their way over the first bridge that looked out over the sky-blue canals filled with rich volcanic mineral water. The panoramic view from the crest of the bridge was surreal. The bright sky seamlessly blended with the sea, which made the small green utopia feel like it was encased inside a glass marble.

The bridges were lined with citizens who cheered on polished wood and bronze sailboats. All fifty-two white sails were covered with red-

and-black stitching of every card. Isaac took mental snapshots so he could sketch the regatta when he awoke.

They descended the steps and entered the second ring, which was much larger and overwhelmingly lively. There were a dozen glistening, naked women being coated in olive oil. They stood atop granite platforms that circled a shallow reflective pool. Clothing merchants pinned orange and cyan linens to their shiny bodies while cosmetic vendors brushed and scented their hair. Above them, polished bronze mirrors directed sunlight into the shallow pool so the women could admire themselves in the reflection of the still water.

Young alpha males, fresh from a boxing tournament and covered in bruises, unlaced bull-hide boxing gloves and stepped into a sunken public bath. They laughed and recapped their event as terra-cotta pipes pumped steaming volcanic spring water into the outdoor pool.

The rest of the circular boulevard was lined with shops and citizens drinking rhytons of wine and sharing lavish platters of figs, olives, and flavored almonds. While the group of servants stopped in front of a food merchant to stock up for their journey, Isaac used the time to explore the wide avenue. He knew he would never see Atlantis like this again.

The shops were selling everything from leather-bound papyrus books to ivory octopus flasks. At the end of the street, there was an open-air museum that resembled the design of the Temple of Hephaestus. The columned walls were lined with massive displays of amber-encased fossils—saber-toothed tigers, wooly rhinos, mastodons, human-sized dragonflies, and pterodactyls. The back of the museum had an outdoor deck that faced the large volcano in the center of the island. The deck was lined with bronze telescopes that had lenses made of ground crystals. Men, women, and children used the magnifying lenses to observe gaming preserves at the base of the mountain. They watched lions, elephants, pumas, and other exotic animals that their navy had collected from all over the world.

Isaac reconnected with the group of servants and followed them over the second bridge. A flotilla of bronze warships sailed underneath them in a tight formation. Along the beaches of the canal, families sat atop perfectly groomed black, red, and white sand. Isaac now understood why these were the island's primary colors. Years of volcanic activity had turned all the sand on the island into one of those three distinct pigments.

On the decks of the boats, armor-clad men lit the fuses of cannons. Isaac watched as the sight of the blast was followed seconds later by the echoing sound. There was an explosion of red fifty meters up, and colorful, powdered dye rained down on the beachfront crowd, decorating their white togas.

Isaac heard the roar from the next island before they were close. The bridge continued over a stadium like a freeway overpass. Isaac looked down and saw a terrace of thousands of spectators in open-air luxury boxes. In the dirt arena below, chiseled male and female athletes acted out a choreographed battle with flaming bow staffs. Their violent motions made it seem warlike, but their glistening bodies and rhythmic motions made it look sexual.

Suddenly, the athletes extinguished their staffs, and a stampede of muscular black bulls stormed through large bronze gates. The servants stopped on the bridge to watch, and so did Isaac.

The stampede ran right into the poised athletes, and they used their staffs to perform death-defying gymnastic feats. One athlete was about to be gored by the wild beast but grabbed the horns and used the momentum of the bull's head-butt to gracefully flip himself onto its back. Then he steered it past hundreds of screaming fans. Another trio of athletes flipped off a bull and landed in tight gymnastic formations. One female athlete used her staff to lift herself into an approaching herd. She ran down their backs, dove headfirst into the gravel, and popped up from a somersault. Isaac now knew why the Magi had chosen the staff as their weapon. It had originated as a ceremonial weapon honoring Taurus.

The servants decided to keep moving but stole glances every time the crowd went into an uproar. It was their last time on the island. It was clear that they wanted to soak up as much as they could before their long journeys.

They made their way through the cheering crowds and over the last bridge to the outermost ring of the city. It was by far the widest and lined with tin warehouses the size of airplane hangars. Each entrance had a wall-sized nautical map with a clearly marked region to signify its origin. The warehouses held industrial-sized quantities of copper from the Iberian Peninsula, cedar from the Levant, tin from the southwestern tip of England, and ivory from the southwestern tip of India.

It was the largest import and export operation he had ever seen. This was the real strength of his ancestors' civilization. They had controlled the seas and connected the developing world with diplomatic trade.

The servants came to a stop in front of four centurions who stood in front of limestone watchtowers guarding bronze gates.

One armor-clad soldier stepped forward and held up his hand. "Where do you think you're going, boy? We have orders that *no* one can leave the city."

Isaac watched as the servant reached into his parcel bag and pulled out a note. The centurion opened it and showed it to his fellow soldier. "It says they need more fish for the royal banquet. It is signed by Senator Pontus."

The second centurion said, "Check their bags."

The centurion opened the servant's bag and pulled out the contents. He opened up the wooden box containing the bronze deck of cards. Isaac saw that it was exactly like the one in his possession. The centurion examined the cards. "What are these, boy?" he asked.

The servant looked at his companions nervously. "For playing."

The centurion stared right at the boy and then handed the cards back. "Carry on."

The sixteen servants walked down the long bottom half of the cross, which was actually a canal leading in and out of the city. Along the water were rows and rows of docks. The servants found the four mid-sized wood and bronze fishing vessels that the senators had outfitted just for them. They gave teary good-bye hugs and said a quick prayer to Atlas. Then the groups untied their ships. Isaac was not sure whether he was supposed to go with them or stay on the island. At the last second, he jumped on board the boat with the boy who looked like him.

Isaac sat with the terrified servants for the next few hours. As they sailed east, the island of Atlantis became a distant speck on the horizon. From this perspective, Isaac could see a massive rock image of Atlas carved into the eastern side of the volcano. It was the size of the pyramids of Giza and must have taken decades to complete. While the four servants studied their nautical map, they missed the King of Clubs' warships escaping south toward Egypt.

The dim purples of twilight stretched across the sky when they heard the first rumble. They sat in the middle of the Atlantic Ocean, but the earthquake was so massive it felt like the whole world shook. The servants ran to the back of the fishing vessel and watched the volcanic mountain explode. A thick stream of smoke shot hundreds of meters into the sky. It was getting dark, but they could see vibrant orange rivers of lava pouring down the mountain above the capital.

"Gods be with our families," the servant who looked like Isaac said to himself.

They watched for the next hour as the glowing orange substance poured down the mountain. They were hundreds of kilometers away, and the curvature of the earth made only the tip of the volcano visible. Then, Atlantis disappeared on the horizon, and they could only see the massive cloud of smoke.

Suddenly, the servant boy noticed an ominous presence on the horizon. He rushed to the front of the boat. It was dark, but the stars right on the eastern horizon were disappearing. He looked closer.

"Ready the boat!" the servant yelled to his three companions. "The wave is coming!"

They all scrambled to the main deck and collapsed the main sail. Then the two male servants ran and rapidly turned large metal cranks. A perforated bronze roof extended from both sides of the boat and turned the fishing vessel into a covered diamond. Isaac thought it was genius. It was now a symmetrical shape that couldn't be capsized.

Once the roof was locked in place, the servants tied themselves to bronze rings anchored to the floorboards. Isaac knew he was dreaming, but he was still panicking. Even in his subconscious, tidal waves were terrifying. The massive swell towered over them and blocked out all the light from the moon and stars. The top of the wave crested, and the servants clung tightly together and prayed. The tiny ship was sucked into the base of the massive wave and pulled toward the summit. Isaac braced himself for impact as the rumbling monstrosity engulfed them.

Right as the boat was spit out from the top of the crest, Isaac heard an ominous voice cut through the night, like God. It was counting backward. "Three...two..." Isaac experienced the chilling sensation of weightlessness as the vessel plummeted down. "One."

CHAPTER 19:
THE SIX OF DIAMONDS

PROFESSOR OLNEY'S STUDY
VALLETTA, MALTA

Isaac screamed. He jolted awake and braced himself for the impact. "Calm down, boy," Olney said. "You're safe now."

Isaac had his head buried in the bend of his elbow. He peeked his eyes above his forearm, expecting to be underwater. His breathing returned to normal when he realized he was in the safety of Olney's library. The quiet crackling from the fireplace replaced the sound of his heavy breathing. Olney put his good hand on Isaac's shoulder.

"You're fine. Deep breaths," Olney said as he poured him another mug of tea.

"I'm not going back in," Isaac said holding up his hand.

"Don't worry," Olney said. "It's just a minor stimulant. It will bring your brain back to life."

Isaac took the warm mug in his hands and sipped.

"How long was I out?" Isaac asked.

"A little over three hours," Olney said. "It's almost one in the morning."

"Jack and Zahra?" Isaac asked.

"Comfortably snoring inside sheets of Egyptian cotton. One-thousand thread count."

"What just happened?"

"Your subconscious. When you're awake, your conscious mind acts as a gateway. I put you into a trance that allowed you direct access to your own subconscious. It was a lucid daydream."

"It was amazing. I've visited the island hundreds of times, but this was the first time that it came to life. How did you do it?"

"As I retold you the story of Atlantis, you were able to connect my conscious thoughts to images floating around your subconscious. Quite remarkable, huh?"

Isaac felt the caffeine in the tea pulsing through his arteries. He had a million questions to ask the professor. "The servants? Did they survive?"

"Indeed," Olney said, spreading a map of the world across a table. Isaac stood over his shoulder. "The Spades deck went to the ancient Babylonians, the Clubs deck to the emerging Indus Valley civilizations, the deck of Hearts went all the way to South America and was given to the dawning Mayan civilization, and the Diamonds deck kept moving all over the Mediterranean. Eventually, the protectors of that deck settled back in Egypt and became what we know today as Gypsies."

"Gypsies are from Egypt?" Isaac said. "I never put that together."

"They are from both Egypt and India but share the same ancestors. These servants became ambassadors and helped foster developing empires. That is how Chinese, Middle Eastern, Indian, and South American civilizations all developed the same zodiac wheel, even though they never had direct contact. All roads lead back to Atlantis." The professor circled his pencil around Central and South America. "According to Mayan and Aztec folklore, their great ancestors came from an island called '*Aztlan.*' That literally translates to '*the people from the water to the east.*' One of many fascinating pieces of evidence, my boy."

"What about the King of Clubs?" Isaac asked.

"He escaped the island with the horologion, his guards, and his family. They arrived on the shores of Egypt and were welcomed as gods. His family used the machine to counsel pharaohs and eventually took over. Not only did they rule Egypt for hundreds of years, but that family completely altered the course of history."

"There was a young servant boy who looked like me," Isaac said. "Could that be—"

"Of course," Olney said. "Your ancestors must have been on one of the boats that escaped."

"So why would my father keep that a secret? I don't understand."

"To protect you, or he was waiting until the timing was right," Olney said. "The Ace of Spades is the most powerful card in the deck. Many of history's greatest visionaries and worst tyrants have been born under your card. They, too, received coded messages in the form of dreams. Sometimes, those messages are interpreted for good, and other times, they are used for evil."

"Why me?" Isaac asked. "Is there a reason for all this?"

"The infamous '*why me*' question. I might need a cup of tea as well."

"Professor, if you're tired, we can continue in the morning. It's just that I'm an insomniac and don't get much sleep."

"Isaac, you've made this old man very happy," Olney said, sipping his tea. "We're going to stay up until you run out of questions. Just out of curiosity, what have you been taking to help yourself sleep?"

"Xanax and Ambien," Isaac said.

"Good God. Not anymore. Tomorrow you start a regimen of natural remedies—melatonin pills and valerian root. I'll have you hibernating like a polar bear in three days. Cheers."

Olney held his mug out, and they clinked glasses. Isaac took a big gulp and settled back into his chair.

"So, what do you think I should do about these dreams? Is there something I'm supposed to figure out?" Isaac asked.

"This brings us to the age-old debate of free will versus determinism. You see, the people of Atlantis believed our universe was like a giant grandfather clock."

"Like the horologion?"

"Exactly. They believed that if you knew all the variables of the universe, you could predict the fate of both nature and people. But the people of Atlantis also believed the gods granted them free will so they had the *option* to fulfill their destiny."

"Forgive me for sounding cynical, but those words—*fate, free will, destiny*—you sound like a fortuneteller."

"Think about it this way," Olney said. "Every person is born with a hand of cards. That is your fate. There are only so many ways you can play your hand. Some people are born holding a full house, and some people are born with off suit twos and sevens. The odds are stacked against them, but they still have a chance."

Isaac sat back in his chair and thought about it. "So, fate is the hand you've been dealt, and destiny is how you play it."

"Exactly," Olney said. "Our hand is still being revealed, but I can assure you, there are some tough decisions on the horizon."

Over the next few hours, Isaac and Professor Olney drank three pots of tea. They were too wired to sleep, and their conversation drifted through the various realms of science and back out into their own lives. Isaac learned Professor Olney's entire backstory.

His father, Harry Olney, was a wealthy chemist who held dozens of patents for a large London pharmaceutical company. His mother, Morrigan, was Harry's secretary and had him out of wedlock at the age of twenty-one. Harry quit his job, and they eloped and moved to a rural plot of land on the Isle of Man. Olney explained to Isaac that he was raised to be a perfect hybrid between his father's academic diligence and his mother's never-ending thirst for esoteric knowledge. Olney's parents pulled him and his two younger sisters out of secondary school, and they spent an entire year sailing around the world. He came back and double-majored at Oxford, earning both history and organic chemistry degrees. He got his masters in astronomy at London Imperial College and joined a few secret societies. It was during one of their alchemy experiments that Olney blew his hand off. The explosion also gave him mercury poisoning, which led to months of blood transfusions and rendered him impotent. Olney explained that, in a weird way, it saved his life. He put socializing behind him and focused on his studies. That led directly to a conversation about Cassie and Polly.

They were not his biological children. In the early eighties, Olney was part of an archaeological team that excavated wooly mammoths in Siberia. They were prepping in a small Siberian town when Olney wandered off to a local circus. Cassie and Polly were only four years old and on display like animals. Olney couldn't stomach their mistreatment, so he bought them from the circus owner and smuggled them back to Malta on private cargo planes. They had been with him ever since.

Isaac was also surprised to hear that Olney's wealth wasn't from writing his research books. The majority of it was handed down by his father, but a good portion came from writing Nebula-winning science fiction novels under the moniker Petrus Bonus. Olney told Isaac that one of his bestselling novels, *Moon Base Alpha*, had been made into a bad movie in the seventies. Isaac and Olney continued to swap stories into the early hours of the morning.

They never heard the Corsairs surrounding the house.

CHAPTER 20

THE SIX OF SPADES

VALLETTA, MALTA

Redbeard waited outside the front door of Olney's house and watched the sun coming up over the eastern horizon. This time, he had brought more than enough men—twelve Turkish Corsairs. He was not going to be embarrassed again. Redbeard patiently waited as one of his Corsairs scaled the wall, jumped down into the atrium, and opened the front door. Two other Corsairs held a large wooden chest. Their leather slippers didn't make a sound as all thirteen men moved in silence across the courtyard.

One Corsair stopped in front of a bedroom door and put his ear to the wood. He could hear Jack snoring on the other side. The two Corsairs holding the trunk placed it down and opened it. Redbeard walked over to the chest and pulled out a large glass jar. Inside was a jet-black African emperor scorpion over twenty centimeters long. Redbeard held the jar up to his face. The scorpion's torso was the size of his fist, and its stinger made a clinking noise as it jabbed against the glass. Redbeard looked into the chest. It held dozens of lethal scorpions, all encased in glass. He twisted the jar open and placed the opening at the base of the door. The scorpion's feet made faint clicking noises as it scuttled across the tiled floor. Redbeard held up three fingers to his Corsairs. They quickly opened and released three more scorpions. One by one, they all slid under the door.

They let four more scorpions go underneath the bedroom where Zahra slept. *She would have been a good assassin,* he thought, *but Soter gave me direct orders to eliminate* everyone *but Isaac.* Redbeard left three Corsairs at each door with their swords drawn. The rest of the men followed him across the atrium toward the faint vibration of music.

One Corsair knelt down and looked underneath the door of the library. He saw a fire to the left and two pairs of feet. He held up two fingers to tell Redbeard there were two men in the room. Redbeard circled the chest with his index finger, ordering them to release the remaining scorpions. The Corsairs quickly bent down and released a dozen scorpions underneath the library door. Redbeard then walked backed across the atrium to Jack's room and waited. He wanted to watch him die.

The first Scorpion in Jack's room climbed up the wooden frame of the canopy bed. Horus slept on top of the canopy with his head near the post. The clicking sound of the scorpion's legs was just enough to cause Horus to stir. He looked at the base of the door and noticed shadows. The hair on his back immediately straightened down his spine. He climbed down the bedpost quietly and spotted the first scorpion. Jack's right leg was out of the covers, and the large arachnid crawled up his calf and onto his inner thigh. Jack kicked his leg, thinking it was a mosquito. When the sensation climbed higher, he woke up. His eyes focused on the dark object. The large scorpion was about to crawl into his boxer shorts.

"Holy shite," Jack mouthed while trying to sneak his hand out from under the comforter without detection. The scorpion reared its stinger and was about to strike when Horus jumped down from the canopy. The monkey quickly grabbed the scorpion with his hand and splattered it against the wall with a crunch. Horus shrieked and held his hand in pain. The stinger had come down on his small hand.

"Horus!" Jack yelled. He spotted two more scorpions and scrambled toward the headrest. Jack backpedaled right next to the fourth scorpion that had crawled up the headrest. It lunged, and the stinger hit Jack's cheek.

"Damn it!" Jack yelled as he barrel-rolled out of bed and felt his face.

Horus brought his fist down on one scorpion, but the surface was overly padded, and it popped up in the air. The other scorpion stung Horus in the foot, and he shrieked. He grabbed the two scorpions and violently smashed them against the footboard. Unfortunately, both scorpions managed to sting him several times on the hands before being crushed to death.

"Hang on, Horus!" Jack yelled as he scanned the room for a weapon and settled on a large book.

Horus fell to his side. A large amount of venom was pumping through his small body. The remaining two scorpions approached him and slid under the white sheets. With repeated strikes, Jack violently smashed the book downward all around Horus. The outburst of energy heightened his heartbeat and caused the venom to spread faster. Jack's entire face became swollen like the Elephant Man's.

"Where did it get you, little buddy?" Jack said, ripping the sheets away. He had crushed the two remaining attackers, but his best friend was having trouble breathing. The venom spread to Jack's heart, and he fell to the floor with a loud slap. He looked up, and Redbeard stood over him.

"I win," Redbeard said.

Foam gurgled out of Jack's mouth. He tried to scream, but his body was paralyzed, and his throat was closing down like a vice grip. Redbeard knelt down and covered Jack's mouth. "Go to sleep," he said.

Jack's body convulsed, and the Turk watched him with a dark grin.

In the library, Olney set out breakfast biscuits to snack on. He played a Mozart concert on his old gramophone; neither he nor Isaac could hear the commotion on the other side of the atrium. Isaac and Olney had been up so long that they were both a little delirious. "So it was my second year at Oxford, and my roommate convinced me to split a bag of psilocybin mushrooms. We hiked way out into Wytham Woods and started to hallucinate. In the peak of our hysteria, we heard a band of wind flutes. We kept walking toward the sound, and it got louder and louder. We came out of a thicket and found ourselves in the center of a medieval village. We thought we had time-traveled, but it turned out that the Renaissance Faire was that weekend. It took us hours to figure out what happened."

Olney and Isaac laughed hysterically and never noticed the approaching threat. Isaac had tears in his eyes. "That's the funniest story I've ever heard."

An emperor scorpion had crawled up the leather and come to rest on the arm of Isaac's chair. Isaac slapped his hand down while he laughed and grazed one the scorpion's legs.

"What the hell?" he said, looking down. Camouflaged into the dark leather chair before he could identify it, the black emperor scorpion shot his stinger down on the top of Isaac's hand.

"Ow," he said, jumping out of his seat. "Scorpion!"

"Where?" Olney jumped out of his own seat and looked down at the chair. The emperor scorpion climbed down the back of the chair and out of sight.

"Bugger, that thing was the size of a rodent," Olney said. "Where did it get you?"

Isaac held out his hand, and Olney inspected his wound.

Suddenly, a scream pierced the night. "Isaac!" It was Zahra.

"They've found us," Isaac said.

"We've got to get you an antidote," Olney said as he quickly unfastened his belt and tied it around Isaac's arm. Then he lowered his hand below his heart so the venom wouldn't spread to his chest. Olney hadn't noticed that a large scorpion had crawled up his khakis. He felt a quick prick on his right side just above his belt. Olney looked down and another emperor scorpion ground its stinger into his oblique muscle. "Another one," Olney said. "It got me."

The old man panicked and tripped backward over his own feet. When he fell to the ground, two more scorpions stung him in the shoulder.

"They're everywhere! Run!" Olney yelled as he crushed one with his prosthetic claw.

Isaac looked down at the tile floor. A dozen scorpions came right at him. He scrambled backward and jumped onto the maps that covered the professor's table. Olney scrambled to his feet and jumped up as well.

"We need guacatonga plant," Olney yelled. "It's on my shelf!"

Isaac looked down at his hand. The top looked like half a grapefruit, and a numbing sensation was spreading up his body.

"What's happening to me?" Isaac asked.

"We need an antidote, or we're going to be paralyzed soon," Olney said.

They both looked down. The scorpions circled the table and crawled up the wooden legs.

Isaac felt a tingling sensation. He salivated uncontrollably.

The first of the scorpions came over the crest of the table, and Olney and Isaac stomped them. The large, predatory arthropods were tougher than they looked, and it took a few solid heels to eliminate them.

Isaac felt his heart rate climbing, and his hearing cut in and out. He looked over to Olney and could barely hear him yell, "I'm going for it." To avoid landing on the scorpions below, Olney backed up and leaped from the table to the leather chair. He was too heavy, and the chair tipped. Olney's head smacked onto the tile with a hollow thump, and he was unconscious.

Isaac knew he couldn't stay on the table. It was surrounded by scorpions the size of his feet. He leaped from the table and landed on the ground near Olney. He grabbed the professor underneath his arms and pulled him away from the bugs. Isaac felt dizzy and his knees buckled. He grabbed the professor's shirt with one hand and pulled him away.

Suddenly, the door swung open revealing Redbeard and his Corsairs. Isaac fell to his knees. He was losing consciousness. A foamy drool oozed down his chin. Redbeard calmly approached him, inserted a needle into his right arm, and injected him with a syringe of yellow liquid. The Turk then rifled through Isaac's pockets and pulled out the wooden box holding the bronze cards. He opened them while his Corsairs watched.

"Do *not* tell Soter that we found these," Redbeard said, and his men nodded.

One of the Corsairs threw a black hood over Isaac's face, while another quickly tied his hands and feet. They picked him up and carried him out of the room.

Seconds later, a small door at the end of the atrium creaked open. Four hands and two heads peered out into the courtyard. Cassie and Polly watched as Redbeard and his Corsairs carried Isaac out of the front door. The twins sneaked into the courtyard and opened Zahra's bedroom door. She lay in her underwear on the cold tile floor, and a small stream of foam drained out of the corner of her mouth. The twins knelt down next to her. Cassie's hands checked Zahra's eyelids while Polly's checked her pulse. She was in anaphylactic shock but still alive.

The twins checked Jack's room and found him and Horus in the same condition. They knew they didn't have much time, so they ran across the atrium as fast as their conjoined-body would allow. They entered the library and saw their adopted father lying on the ground surrounded by a dozen large scorpions.

The twins ran back to the courtyard and opened a storage shed. Inside was an industrial-sized shop vac. They wheeled it back into the library and plugged it in. Cassie held out the large vacuum pole, and Polly pointed out the creatures. *Thoomp!* The twins sucked up their first scorpion from a safe distance. *Thoomp! Thoomp! Thoomp!* The conjoined twins quickly cleared the library of all the scorpions.

Cassie and Polly looked at the stone mortars and pestles covering Olney's table. The only man who had ever cared about them was in danger. They had to hurry. He was barely conscious and mumbling to himself.

The twins moved together masterfully. Cassie boiled a cup of water while Polly chopped up the guacatonga plants. Their four hands moved in unison. They knew what the other was doing without looking or speaking. Cassie handed Polly a jar of plants, while Polly handed her sister a mortar of charcoal. They simultaneously added ingredients into the boiling water—ground-up plants, powders, and liquids.

Cassie then pulled four syringes off the shelf and handed them to her sister. Polly prepped the needles. Cassie grabbed a small liquid vile labeled *ephedrine*. She emptied the entire hundred-milliliter bottle into the water. Polly dipped the needle tips into the boiling liquid and with a syringe extracted the fluid.

The twins knelt down next to Olney. Cassie rolled up his sleeve, and Polly jammed the needle into his shoulder. Then the twins shuffled across the atrium with the shop vac. *Thoomp! Thoomp! Thoomp! Thoomp!* Cassie cleared the room while Polly injected Zahra, and then they did the same in Jack's room. His head had swollen beyond proportion, and his airways were completely cut off.

Polly was about to insert the needle into Jack's arm, but her sister grabbed her wrist and tapped her fingers on Jack's heart. Polly nodded and raised the needle above Jack's chest. She brought it down swiftly and injected the antivenom right into his heart. The adrenaline had an immediate effect as his eyes opened and he gasped for breath. Cassie and Polly struggled to hold the strong man down as he violently thrashed about. They finally subdued him and tilted his chin up to clear his airway. The antidote spread through his veins, and he began to breathe again. Cassie and Polly exhaled a sigh of relief.

They injected Horus as well, with a smaller dose, but the poor monkey had been stung too many times. Minutes passed, and the twins crisscrossed the atrium a dozen times to check on each person. Zahra was up first and helped them give the professor water.

"Where is Isaac?" Olney asked.

"They took him," Zahra said. "They followed us here."

"Jack?" Olney asked.

"Let's go check," Zahra said as she helped lift the tall professor off the floor.

Jack was in his boxers, kneeling on the cold tile floor. His back was to Zahra and Olney. When they approached him, they saw that he was holding Horus in his arms. The small monkey's eyes were half opened, and his chest was slowly moving up and down.

"He saved my life," Jack said.

Zahra put her hand on Jack's shoulder. It was the first time she had voluntarily touched a man. Tears started to stream down his face.

"You can make it," Jack said, his voice cracking.

Horus's eyes met Jack's and then closed. His arms fell to the side, and his body went limp. Jack pulled his beloved pet closer and cried. Zahra knelt down and wrapped her arms around Jack's neck.

CHAPTER 21:
THE SEVEN OF HEARTS

SOTER'S LIBRARY
THERA, GREECE

Isaac was glad to be out of the helicopter. He still felt the effects of the scorpion's venom, and he had trouble breathing through the hood over his face. Someone pushed his head down as he was dragged underneath the spinning blades. He felt the crunchy gravel transition into smooth marble, and then he was led down a long hallway. He heard a set of wooden doors open, and his hood was taken off.

Bright. Isaac squinted. The early afternoon sun poured through bay windows into the most beautiful library he had ever seen. It was three stories high with a black marble colonnade and was lined ceiling to floor with thousands of books. The architecture was a blend of Greek and Egyptian. In the middle of the room was a shallow rectangular fountain, and across from it sat a chiseled blond man in his forties.

"It's truly a pleasure to meet you, Isaac Alexander," Soter said. "Did you enjoy my yacht?"

Isaac didn't answer.

"I am *quite* impressed," Soter said, pouring a glass of blood-red hibiscus tea. "You managed to escape the most lethal assassins on the planet. Not an easy task."

Isaac said, "Where are Zahra and my uncle? What have you done with my mother and father?"

"I warned your parents that anyone who got in the way would get hurt," Soter said.

"Who are you?" Isaac asked.

"My name is Ptolemy Soter, and *I* kidnapped your parents," Soter said as he stood up and walked around the pool of water. Soter always dressed like he was about to go on safari—white linen bush shirts, pressed khaki cargo pants, and brown boots.

Isaac blinked. He was still adjusting to the brightness. "I want to see them," he said.

"In time. We have a lot to discuss first. I can assure you that they are both safe."

"Where are we?" Isaac asked, looking out the windows on the south end of the library. They sat on top of a cliff overlooking the ocean.

"You're standing inside an exact replica of the Grand Library of Alexandria," Soter said. "The original model was built in 323 BC by my great ancestor, Ptolemy Soter the First."

"And *where* exactly is this library located?" Isaac asked.

"A small volcanic island about two hundred kilometers away from mainland Greece named Thera. Beneath us lie hundreds of meters of lava rock and the ruins of our ancestors."

"The lost city of Atlantis?" Isaac asked.

"Not lost, just buried," Soter said. "That *crazy* professor taught you a few things. What else did you learn?"

Ptolemy Soter intimidated Isaac. His face looked like it was carved out of granite, as if his piercing blue eyes could stare through anyone or anything. "Withholding information is only going to delay a reunion with your parents," Soter said.

"He told me the story of Atlantis, but I don't understand how my family ties in," Isaac said.

"Your father is a member of a secret society called the Order of the Magi. Their headquarters is in Alexandria, Egypt, and they are made up of thirteen Jewish, Christian, and Islamic mystics."

"Magi? Like the three wise men from the Bible?"

"Yes," Soter said. "Melchoir, Caspar, and Balthasar were all members of the order. Let me backtrack to explain better. Only five boats escaped the destruction of Atlantis—four were fishing vessels that held servants carrying bronze decks of cards, and the fifth was a warship holding my ancestor, the King of Clubs."

"So, you're the descendant of a traitor," Isaac said.

Soter laughed. "I'm afraid we *both* are. All of those boats completely changed the course of human history. The Hearts boat used the Atlantic currents and copper shipping routes to make it all the way to Central America, where they taught the Mayan priests about astronomy. The survivors on the ship of Clubs sailed down the Sesostris Canal— which our ancestors designed for the Egyptians—into the Red Sea and then settled in the Indus Valley. They taught the emerging Vedic people about astrology, and the texts became the inspirations for Hinduism and Buddhism. The Diamonds ship crashed off the northern coast of Africa on their way around the Iberian Peninsula, and the survivors eventually migrated back to Egypt. They remained in hiding and eventually became a nomadic tribe of people called Gypsies. The Spades boat—holding your ancestors—docked in southern Turkey, and then they walked all over Babylonia and Assyria spreading their knowledge of astronomy. They eventually settled near Iran under the guidance of a Persian philosopher named Zoroaster. Together, they started Zoroastrianism, a new religion that combined Persian mythology with the astrological teachings of Atlantis. Then they initiated a secret society that trained young men to become mystic warrior-astronomers, which we now know as the Magi."

"Servants accomplished all of that?" Isaac asked.

"You have to understand Atlantis was the most advanced civilization in history," Soter said. "Servants from there would have been much more intelligent than our modern-day academics."

"What does the order do?" Isaac asked.

"The Magi view themselves as the bodyguards of living prophets," Soter said. "The people of Atlantis advanced beyond any other civilization for a *reason*. They knew that certain geometric positions of the planets and stars revealed the geographic birthplace of people who were destined to be great spiritual leaders or innovators. Then, they used their advanced navy to travel around the world and collect these young children. Essentially, Atlanteans cherry-picked the best of humanity for three thousand years. Imagine the possibilities of an isolated island utopia made up only of inventors, scientists, prophets, and philosophers."

"The Magi in the Bible—the three kings—didn't they follow a star to find Jesus?"

"It was actually a planetary conjunction of Saturn and Jupiter," Soter said, "and they were worried that the Romans were going to kill baby Jesus, so they brought him back to their headquarters in Egypt. Jesus spent most of his young adult life learning from the Magi."

"So, if this is all true, that means our families have been at odds for centuries? You've been tyrants, and we've been in hiding."

Soter admired the young boy. He would do well as one of his advisors. "That's why we can put a stop to this. It's *finally* time to join forces. Do you recognize that painting on the wall?"

Isaac examined the painting of a long-haired, bearded man who wore a cone-shaped basket on his head and held a scepter in one hand and a three-headed dog in the other.

"No," Isaac said.

"His name is Serapis. He is a Greco-Egyptian god created by my ancestors. The Greeks and Egyptians who lived under Alexander the Great despised each other. It was probably very similar to how Christians, Jews, and Muslims view one another today. My ancestors hired scholars to combine the Greek and Egyptian religions. They blended both sets of iconography, too. Look at Serapis. He looks Greek but is adorned with Egyptian accessories. The basket on his head, his robe, his scepter, and the serpent at his feet are all Egyptian."

"Did it work?" Isaac asked.

"Yes, because all converging lines of civilization lead back to Atlantis and all converging lines of religion lead back to astrology, which is the summation of all ancient psychological knowledge," Soter said. "Using this truth, scholars were able to find universal archetypes in all religions. They created a framework based on astrology that transcended time and united people. The Hellenistic religion lasted until the fall of the Roman Empire in AD 476. My ancestors were the last great architects of peace, and I plan to carry out a very similar plan."

"Sounds audacious. Even for a billionaire," Isaac said.

"It is not a coincidence that during all the transformative eras of human development—Greek and Roman antiquity, the Hellenistic Era, the Renaissance, the Elizabethan age, and the Scientific Revolution—that astrology and astronomy were held in the highest regard as a creation of the divine. A thousand years in between, the world went through the restrictive Dark and Middle Ages where astronomers were considered heretics."

"That's actually a very valid point," Isaac said.

"You see, there are two opposite paradigms embedded in all of human nature. One, that humans are continually evolving and two, we are heading toward our inevitable decline. We are at a crossroads right now, and you and I have the ability to prevent another dark age."

Isaac approached and examined the Serapis painting hanging at the northern end of the library. "Your family has been our enemy since the beginning of time," he said. "Why should I trust you?"

Soter pondered the question for a moment and then said, "Put yourself in my ancestor's shoes for a moment. You are the King of Clubs. Your civilization has created technology that is more powerful than anything ever invented, and your fellow kings decided to withhold the knowledge from the rest of the world. What would you have done?"

Isaac shrugged his shoulders. "I guess I would have tried to pass it on."

"Look at what's happening, Isaac. Our planet is being destroyed by pollution, natural resources are running out, and we have no alternatives. Deadly pandemics are spreading all over Asia and Africa, and organized religion has become more divisive than unifying. On top of all that, we are transitioning into a new astrological age, and it is causing catastrophic natural disasters—floods, earthquakes, tsunamis, hurricanes, and massive swings in global temperatures. These aren't the by-product of global warming. It's well documented that the elements go haywire every time we enter a new age. If we do not set the world on a proper course, there is a good chance our planet will phase us *out* in the next hundred years."

"We?" Isaac said.

"Yes. You're a very special young man. I am truly sorry that your parents hid that from you. We are both descendants of Atlantis, but I am a King of Clubs, not the Ace of Spades. You are the only living connection that we have to our ancestors' civilization. Hidden within your dreams…there is a secret code that has the power to change the world."

"How do you know so much about me?" Isaac asked.

"It will all be revealed soon," Soter said. "Let me ask you a strange question."

"Resisting seems meaningless at this point," Isaac said.

"Do you play billiards?" Soter asked as he motioned toward a canvassed billiard table in the middle of the library. "I guess you could say this is my only stress-relieving hobby, besides hand-to-hand combat."

"I play," Isaac said with a nod and a slight shrug.

Soter carefully pulled off the leather cover, revealing a beautiful black-felt-covered table. Each leg was a marble sculpture of one of the four kings of playing cards. The nine billiard balls were exact models of the nine planets of the solar system. Isaac examined the cue ball, which was an exact replica of the moon that even had a gradient dark side.

"It's brilliant," Isaac said running his hand over the carvings.

"Yes, I carved the legs myself," Soter said, placing the nine balls in a triangle formation. Then Ptolemy handed Isaac a stick. Isaac thought about attacking him, but his hand-to-hand combat reference told him it would be a bad idea.

"You can break," Soter said.

Isaac cleared the Mercury and Venus balls off the table but missed Earth.

Soter crouched down to shoot. "There is a primordial force that exists in our universe. Some call it *the soul,* some call it the *Holy Spirit,* and others have named it *the collective unconscious.* The point is there is an intelligent source recognized by nearly *all* of mankind." Soter sank the Earth ball into a side pocket. "Everything in our universe is governed by this force. The same law that governs a grain of sand governs the planet of Jupiter. People, too. We are no more responsible for our actions than planets or asteroids."

"What about free will?" Isaac said. "I refuse to believe there is an exact algorithm to human behavior."

"Humans are the same," Soter said right before sinking Mars into a corner pocket. "We are just sophisticated pieces of machinery."

"You're contradicting yourself. You just said that if we don't change the course of humanity, we'll become extinct. That *proves* that you believe in free will."

Soter stood up from aiming his shot. "Good counter, but the *we* part of my speech was just theatrics. Nothing occurs at random, but everything for a reason and by necessity. There is a reason my ancestors left Atlantis. History has progressed in the only manner possible. Yes, our actions are free, but they all work toward an inevitable end. No man has the ability to change the course of history." Soter finished and lined up his next shot.

"Again, you contradict yourself," Isaac said. "You stated earlier that the survivors of Atlantis changed the course of history."

Isaac's comment snapped Soter's stoic disposition and caused him to miss. He stood up and addressed Isaac without emotion in his voice. "They didn't change anything. It was their destiny. Inside all of us is an internal GPS system programmed with an end address. All we're doing is going through our lives, heading toward the destination set for us. It was my ancestor's destiny to preserve the knowledge of Atlantis, and it is my destiny is to be the leader of the Age of Aquarius. There is nothing you can do to stop me. Both of our paths have *already* been written."

"You're delusional," Isaac said. "What if I used my free will to snap this stick and stab you to death?"

"I want you to try. Please, I won't get mad."

Isaac swallowed his words. He had gotten cocky in his argument, and he was going to pay the price.

"If you can even graze me with that stick, I will let you and your parents go," Soter added.

"Do I have your word?" Isaac asked.

"On my grandfather's grave," he said.

Isaac swung the pool stick across the table trying to catch Soter off guard, but he easily dodged it. Isaac circled the table holding the pool stick like he was fencing. He lunged forward, but Soter sidestepped his attack and open-hand punched Isaac in the solar plexus. He fell to his knees, gasping for breath. Soter immediately grabbed him under his armpits and helped him up.

"Stand up and breathe," Soter said. Isaac made a note not to challenge him again.

Isaac struggled for air, and Soter looked him right in the eyes. "That was never going to work, because you're just a boy and I am a soldier. If you know all the variables in an equation, you can always predict the outcome. Let me show you."

Soter stepped toward the table and gathered the remaining billiards balls.

Isaac leaned on the billiards table and finally caught his breath. "That was stupid."

"Yes, it was," Soter said. "We both know you're not dangerous, so don't pretend to be."

"Yes, sir," Isaac said. It was a slip of the tongue programmed from too many years of military school.

Soter spent the next minute placing all nine balls in exact locations all over the table while Isaac rubbed his chest.

"What are you doing?" Isaac asked as Soter knelt down to inspect the exact location of each ball.

"An experiment. Imagine this billiards table is the universe. These balls represent everything from nature, to continents, to people. I represent the law of nature, because I know all the variables. I know the size of the table, I know the location of each ball, and I know how all of these will interact with each other upon contact. Therefore, if I know all the variables, I know the outcome of each ball."

"And what are they?" Isaac asked, examining the balls scattered all over the table.

"One, five, seven, and nine in the far corner pockets," Soter said. "Two, three, four, and eight in the near corner pockets, and the six ball in the left side of the middle pocket."

Isaac was a pool shark, but trying to predict the outcome of each ball was geometrically impossible.

"Watch," Soter said as he lined up on the moon. Soter took his time and then rifled a shot down the table. The cue ball collided with each ball and knocked them into their respective pockets. The eight ball slowly rolled off the edge of the pocket right next to Soter. It was the most amazing billiards shot Isaac had ever seen.

"I didn't think that was possible," Isaac said.

"You're wrong. There was no other way it could have happened," Soter responded. "Do you have anything in your pockets?"

Isaac plunged a hand into his cargo pants and pulled out the old Gypsy woman's coin.

"I have a Roman coin," Isaac said.

"Place it somewhere on the table," Soter said as he pulled the balls out of the pockets and placed them in the exact same locations as the last shot. Isaac approached the table and flipped the coin into the air. It landed on its side and rolled to a stop five centimeters away from head spot. Soter finished the exact placement of each ball and lined up the same shot.

"Now, watch what happens when one unknown variable is introduced," Soter said. He fired the exact shot down the table. The cue ball ricocheted off the edge, but this time, it skipped off the coin and flew clear off the table. The remaining balls collided with each other, but only one of them dropped into a pocket. The cue ball bounced across the tile floor and into a shelf of books. Not one ball was in the same location as it was with the last shot.

"You see what happens when you don't know the variables? Complete chaos," Soter said.

"How could one ever know *all* the possible variables of the universe?" Isaac said. "You would need a super computer beyond comprehension."

Soter grinned. "Good thing our ancestors already built one. All *you* need to do is turn it on."

CHAPTER 22:

THE SEVEN OF CLUBS

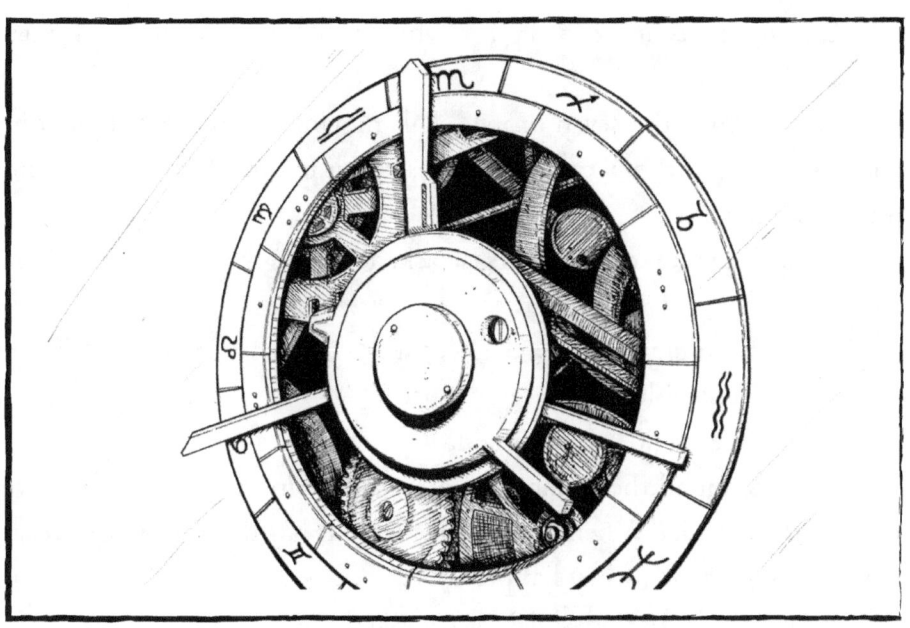

SOTER'S LABORATORY
THERA, GREECE

Soter typed an access code into an electronic keypad and pushed the door open. Inside was a state-of-the-art laboratory. The entire south wall was made up of a five-by-ten grid of computer monitors displaying a detailed terrain map of Earth. Isaac stepped further into the room and froze. Inside two Plexiglas cases were identical versions of the machines from his dreams.

"Impossible," Isaac said.

"This is the Antikythera Mechanism," Soter said. "Our ancestors called it the horologion."

Isaac moved closer to examine them.

"The rusted one is the original from Atlantis," Soter said. "It was excavated off the coast of the island of Antikythera, hence the name. The bronze one is an exact replica, which took us more than *fifty* years to make."

Isaac watched the seven bronze dials moving in different directions and then noticed the network of wires running out of the replica and into computers.

"How did you recreate it?" Isaac asked, placing his fingertips on the glass case.

"We x-rayed it and built a 3-D computer model," Soter said. "Then we carefully assembled it, piece by piece."

"What does it do?" Isaac asked.

"It takes out all the variables," Soter said, pointing to the interactive map of the world. "When it's synchronized, it has the ability to predict natural disasters *before* they happen."

"How can that be possible?" Isaac asked.

"Isaac, our ancestors had three thousand years of the brightest minds researching everything from organic chemistry to astronomy. They were able to synchronize the Antikythera Mechanism to the four elements. Tycho Brahe and Johannes Kepler tried to find a correlation between astronomy and weather patterns, but that is the closest anyone has come to understanding the power of this machine. Well, besides animals. Did you know that hundreds of flamingos flew toward higher ground hours before the 2004 Boxing Day Tsunami? Animals possess an inherent sixth sense, like you do."

"If it was so important to your family, how did it get lost?" Isaac asked.

"That crazy hedonist, Cleopatra," Soter said.

"What?" Isaac asked.

"She was the last successor of the Ptolemaic Dynasty," Soter said. "After she killed herself, her advisors feared that the machine was going to be confiscated by Octavian and his invading Roman forces. Augustus Caesar, as he became known, was a firm believer in astrology and even had his Capricorn sign put on all of his coins. He knew about the machine, so a small group of Greco-Egyptian scholars and soldiers tried to get it to Athens but shipwrecked off the coast of Antikythera. It was lost for almost two thousand years."

"And why do you think *I* can turn it on?" Isaac asked.

"Because you visit it every night in your dreams," a voice said from behind him.

Isaac spun around. Neville held up scanned copies of his journal.

"You've been helping him?" Isaac yelled.

"Isaac…they had my family," Neville said.

"That's how you know so much about me," Isaac said to Soter.

"Yes. I've been reading your journal entries for months. Unfortunately, you were smart enough to omit any and all clues regarding your whereabouts. All this violence could have been avoided," he said. "I'm sorry that you thought you were becoming a schizophrenic. Your parents should have told you that you're a clairvoyant."

Neville looked directly at Isaac and said, "If you cooperate, we can all go back to our lives."

"There is no going back," Isaac said. "My entire family has been kidnapped."

Neville stepped toward the bronze replica. "Isaac, you're the only one who has a chance to synchronize the Antikythera Mechanism. You are a descendant of Atlantis, and you were born an Ace of Spades. The divine can only manifest itself in our world as *thought forms* that come as visions or dreams."

"You have my journal," Isaac said. "Figure it out yourself and let us go."

"Think about all the lives you can save," Neville said.

"Imagine this scenario," Soter said, walking over to the wall-sized computer map and pointing to a small Caribbean island. "This machine tells us that there is going to be a massive shift in the Enriquillo-Plantian Garden fault near the southwestern part of Haiti. We immediately alert the media. Countries and corporations then donate money to sponsor relief ships. We use my tankers to carry thousands of storage bins full of temporary homes, fresh water, food, and medical supplies. The city of Port-au-Prince evacuates before the earthquake, and over 220,000 lives are saved."

"What if I can't turn it on?" Isaac asked. "Have you thought about that?"

"As I told you earlier, I have accounted for all the variables," Soter said. "However, I am giving you the chance to join me."

"How do I know that you won't exploit this for absolute power?" Isaac asked. "Am I the last line of defense against the next Hitler?"

"With your help, I want to *save* the world from itself," Soter said. "Civilizations decline when their people don't live in harmony with nature. My plan is to peacefully reestablish a new era—one that universally accepts astrology as the mother of all religions. It will guide the councils of presidents, the policy of all nations, and rule the actions of individuals both great and small. The stage is set. It's your destiny to be here. Our families have been enemies since 1500 BC, but you can end it. Your father has already chosen his path and joined the Magi, but they have become weak and outdated. This right here—" He pointed to the computer monitors. "—is the future. If you join me, I will guarantee you a spot as one of my top advisors. With this machine, we can change the world."

Isaac turned back to examine the seven bronze dials on the machine. He closed his eyes and tried to picture it in his dreams. He could see himself pulling the handles to exact degrees, but it felt more like intuition than a physical memory. His focus was broken when Neville approached him.

"Isaac, your father told me about your latest invention of attaching car batteries to exercise bikes," Neville said. "Picture what you could accomplish here. Direct distribution of your inventions."

Soter said, "Oxford would just slow you down. Here, you would have all the resources and financing you ask for. We can build you a separate lab and send your inventions out with disaster packages."

"What about the countries without natural disasters?" Isaac asked. "The ones that don't have the attention of the global news? Are you only going to ignore the rest of the third world?"

"You're absolutely right," Soter said. "We can't just focus on saving people. Part of my plan is to raise the standard of living for all humans. Consider yourself president of the *Isaac Alexander Nonprofit for Developing Countries.* I'll give you a hundred-million-dollar line of credit and a full staff."

"It's everything you could ever ask for, Isaac," Neville said. "A chance to help."

"I'll call my lawyers and have them start the paperwork today," Soter said. "In a few weeks, I will send out a press release saying that I specifically recruited you. Picture the look on your classmates' faces when they find out that one of the richest men in the world has invested in *you.*"

Isaac couldn't hide the fact that he would love to shove that into their faces. He wanted them all to know that he was special and they were ignorant assholes.

Soter continued his compelling argument. "Every major news network will want to interview the seventeen-year-old genius whose inventions are going to change the developing world. Maybe *then* you'll be able to get a date."

"I don't care about that," Isaac said with red cheeks.

"It was simply a humorous reference to your journal and nothing to be ashamed of," Soter said. "I know who you are, Isaac Alexander. You're an Ace of Spades. You're a practical visionary guided by the divine— a perfect hybrid of an idealistic humanitarian and diligent academic driven by the need to understand the secrets of our universe. You're not the next Newton, Edison, or da Vinci. You're the *first* Isaac Alexander. It's just a shame that your parents don't see what I see in you. I truly believe you can earn a spot among the greatest inventors of all time."

His argument was too convincing. It was everything he ever wanted. Isaac looked back at the seven dials of the Antikythera Mechanism and tried to imagine himself turning them.

"Give me a minute of silence," Isaac said.

He took a long mental image of the spinning dials and then tuned everything else out. He placed his hands on the Plexiglas and closed his eyes. He had been in front of the machine a thousand times. Isaac remembered what Olney told him about lucid dreaming and how to focus on seeing and controlling your hands first. He conjured up the images from his dreams and replayed them in his head until a crystal-clear picture emerged. He watched his left and right hands spinning each of the seven dials to exact degrees. As he finished, the outermost ring clicked into place and the hum of hundreds of gears brought the machine to life. Isaac opened his eyes and turned around confidently.

"If I choose to help you, I want both of my parents released," Isaac said.

"If you turn on the Antikythera, I will release your parents in six months," Soter said. "You will also have the option of leaving with them. You have my word." Soter held his hand out for Isaac to shake.

"Why six months?" Isaac asked, taking a step back.

"I have a detailed strategy in place to position myself as the architect of the new age. My grandfather and I have compiled years of research and have hired dozens of geologists, historians, psychologists, scientists, and economists to help us formulate a blueprint to foster diplomatic relations between conflicting countries. This cannot happen overnight, and unfortunately, I cannot release your father until the first few phases have been accomplished. He is too much of a liability."

"Can I read the document?" Isaac asked.

"In time," Soter said.

"I want to talk to my parents. Then I'll make my decision," Isaac said, finally stepping forward and shaking Soter's hand.

Soter picked up a walkie-talkie and spoke into it. "Bring them up," he said.

Isaac was confident that he knew the exact combination—but wasn't certain that he should turn it on.

CHAPTER 23

THE SEVEN OF DIAMONDS

VALLETTA, MALTA

Jack's shovel fought through the dry dirt outside of Olney's house. Zahra and Professor Olney watched him dig a very small grave. Cassie and Polly held Horus's limp body in a colorful Gypsy headscarf. They all stood under a single olive tree that overlooked the Mediterranean.

"Give him to me," Jack said.

Cassie and Polly handed Horus over. Jack pulled the silk headscarf over his little face and gently placed him in the grave. Jack used the back of his hand to wipe away his tears. Then he bowed his head, crossed his fingers, and cleared his throat. Cassie, Polly, Zahra, and Olney followed suit.

"Horus, you were a bastard. Not in the figurative sense, but in the literal. You were abandoned by your troop because your dad slept around on your mom. Maia found you on the street and raised you for eight years. Then she left, and it was just me and you, buddy." Jack's voice cracked. Olney stepped forward and put his hand on his shoulder for support.

"It'll be all right," Olney said, tightening his grip.

Jack cleared his phlegmy throat and spit on the ground. Zahra shuddered.

"You loved peanuts and marshmallows," Jack said tearing up again. "You knew how to get me beers, and you never judged me when I brought home double-baggers."

Olney and Zahra shared a confused look.

"You were a stubborn little shite, but you saved my life last night. Cheers, mate. It was an adventure, and you will *never* be forgotten." Jack grabbed the shovel off the ground and threw on the first batch of dirt.

Moments later, he had packed the grave tight. Zahra handed him a small wooden stake that had Horus's name carved in it vertically. Jack planted it in the ground and then stood up.

"How about a drink, Jack?" Olney said as he and Zahra walked back to the house.

"No," Jack said, causing them to turn around. "They took my sister, chased me out of my own city, kidnapped my nephew, and now they've killed my best friend. I'm not having a drink until I'm standing over that Turkish asshole's dead body." He knelt down and tightened the laces on his boots.

"What are we going to do?" Zahra asked.

"You're staying here," Jack said. "I'm going into murder-death-kill mode, and I can't do it dragging around an orphan and a one-armed man."

"Are you just going to walk into town and start interrogating people?" Olney asked.

"It's better than sitting here," Jack said. "And I'm sick of this sword shite. I need a gun. A big, bloody gun."

"You need us to help find out where they went," Olney said.

Jack loosened up his body and stretched his hamstrings. "I don't need any of you. Zahra, stay here with the professor."

"No!" Zahra yelled so loud that Olney jumped and Jack stopped stretching. "David and Rachel gave those cards to *me*. I hiked down a mountain, was almost raped by *two* men, and my boat was destroyed by a tanker. I was attacked by seals and then almost froze to death getting them to you. I have *earned* my spot in this group."

Professor Olney and Jack both were both speechless.

"I...I didn't know all of that happened," Jack stuttered. "I'm sorry."

"Remember what the Gypsy told us," Zahra said. "We need the *whole* body, not just the fist."

Jack turned to face the vast ocean.

Zahra said, "David and Rachel saved me, and I will do whatever it takes to save them."

"Zahra...I need to go to a dark place to get them back, and I don't want to bring you two," Jack said.

Olney stepped forward. "Everything we have done with our lives has led us to this moment, to this decision." He motioned toward Zahra. "I don't see an orphan. I see a beautiful but tough Five of Spades—a survivor who grew up in a restrictive country and taught herself how to be invisible. Fives are the most restless cards in the deck, and even if you left her behind, she would figure out a way to find you. She is a valuable spy who speaks our enemies' language." He stopped and motioned toward himself. "I don't see a one-armed man; I see a Seven of Clubs—a number guided by an inner voice that is associated with intuition and mysticism; a man who has dedicated his whole life to gathering information on the spiritual world is a useful guide into the unknown. And here—" Olney motioned toward Jack. "I don't see a drunk. I see the Jack of Diamonds—a man at a spiritual crossroads, a man who knows he has many talents but doesn't know he is the *master* of one. He is a protector."

"Yeah, look at the job I've done," Jack said, still facing away from Olney and Zahra.

"Right now, you're deciding with your ego and with fear," Olney said. "You're weighing the pros and cons and convincing yourself that Zahra and I would slow you down. But this decision belongs to your soul. Look within and realize that fate has brought the three of us together. I told Isaac and Zahra the meaning of their names, but I haven't told you yours."

"Does this soliloquy have an ending?" Jack asked.

"O'Ryan is diminutive of the great constellation, Orion's Belt," Olney said. "He was the greatest hunter to ever live and claimed he could kill any living animal. The gods accused him of hubris and created the scorpion to be his perfectly matched enemy. Orion's Belt rises in the west, and Scorpio rises in the east. When one ascends, the other disappears. They exist in a perpetual battle across the heavens. Isaac has a gift, and its purpose has not yet been revealed. Your destiny, Jack O'Ryan, is to kill the scorpion that *took* Isaac and protect his gift from getting into the wrong hands. Life is warfare, Jack. And Destiny is earned one tough decision at a time."

Jack took in a deep breath and addressed them with his back still turned away. "Goddamn it, old man, if I find out that was rehearsed, I'm going to punch you in the kidney." He wiped tears away.

"All from the heart," Olney said.

"You know, a few days ago, I didn't believe one iota of this crap," Jack said. "But you're right. There is a higher power at play. No other way to explain it."

"We have to do this together," Olney said.

Jack nodded in agreement and finally turned to them. "You know, I've ended a lot of lives. Most of them deserved it. But if doing this gets my—" Jack turned to Olney. "What did you call it?"

"Soul," Olney said with a grin.

"Yeah, if doing this puts my *soul* in good graces with the higher powers, then let's fucking do it," Jack said.

"Excellent. Minus the curse word," Olney said. "Zahra and I will go inside and start packing."

"I'm going to go for a run and clear my head," Jack said as he pointed to his eye. "I haven't had fluid come out these holes in a while. Just the other three."

Both Olney and Zahra shook their heads in disgust. Jack ripped off his shirt and tossed it to Cassie and Polly, revealing the new Jack of Diamonds tattoo on his back.

"It's about time I get back into shape," he said as he slapped his belly. "We've got a rescue mission to plan." Jack fired off a half-cocked salute to Zahra, Olney, and the twins. Then he turned around and started jogging down the hill.

CHAPTER 24:
THE SEVEN OF SPADES

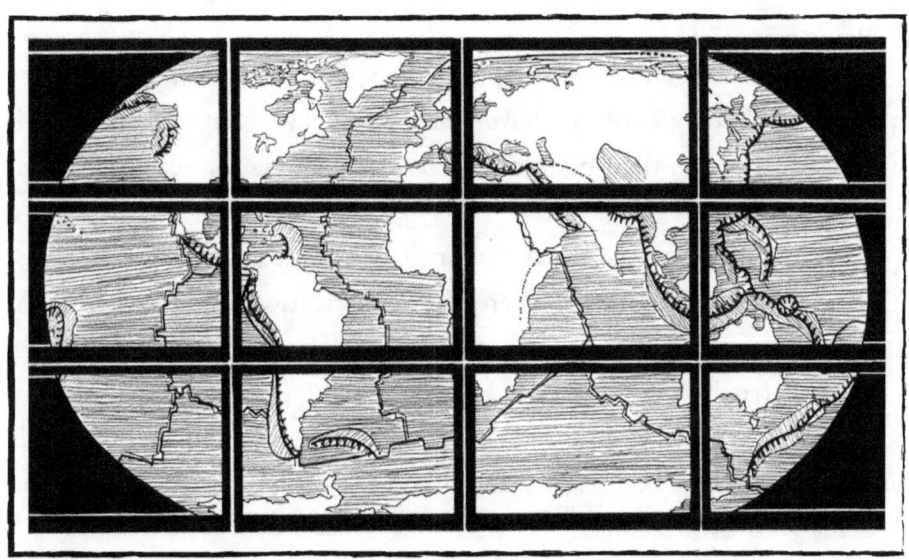

SOTER'S LABORATORY
THERA, GREECE

Isaac stood with Soter and Neville near the map on the computer screens as Redbeard pulled his parents inside. David and Rachel, both bound and gagged, were being held by a group of Corsairs.

"Isaac!" Rachel yelled through her gag as she kneed one of the Corsairs in the groin and broke free. Another Corsair pulled her back violently. David raised both of his tied hands, urging everyone in the room to stay calm.

"Your son has some questions," Soter said. "You have three minutes, and then it is decision time, Mr. Alexander." He checked his watch and pointed to the Corsairs, who untied David and Rachel's gags. "Go," Soter said.

David spit out his gag and responded quickly. "Isaac, whatever he has told you is a *lie*. This man is very dangerous, and you can*not* trust him."

Soter grinned and looked up from his watch. "Actually, David, it's quite possible for people we have just met to have a better understanding of who we are, than people who have known us for years. Isn't that right, Isaac?"

"Why didn't you tell me about any of this?" Isaac said. "The cards? Our family? My dreams? I've been taking medications because I thought I was going crazy."

David tried to walk toward Isaac, but the Corsairs held him tight. He shrugged them off and said, "Son, I didn't find out about our family until I was in my twenties. I wanted you to live a normal life. Let you become your own person."

Soter circled Isaac and whispered into his ear, "He doesn't think you're *strong* enough. Just like your classmates, he thinks you're *weak*." Then, he checked his watch and said, "Two and half minutes."

Soter was using his journal against him. Isaac's innermost fear was not living up to his father's legacy. He'd written about it countless times.

"I didn't know that your dreams were getting worse. We've been on the run for the last two years because *this* man—" David motioned to Soter, "has been hunting us down."

"You've lied to me my *whole life*," Isaac said.

"I haven't lied to you," David said. "I just haven't told you the truth."

Rachel looked at her husband. "There's no time, David. Just tell him."

"Two minutes," Soter said.

"Tell me what?" Isaac asked.

Rachel gave David a reassuring nod, and he cleared his throat. "The last stage of a Magi's initiation is a card reading with an oracle. The kingdom and crown cards dictate your life path and your legacy. I pulled the death card and the devil the card. The oracle prophesied that if my son followed in my footsteps, it would cause my death and lead our bloodline into an age of spiritual darkness. Isaac, you have to understand...I hid you to protect *you.*"

David choked on his last words and locked eyes with his son. Only the quiet hum of the computers could be heard. Isaac turned away from his father's stare. His world was spinning.

"What an interesting turn of events," Soter said excitedly. "David, *you* of all people, should know that a person often meets his destiny on the road he takes to avoid it. You indirectly ushered your son into his own fate. Astonishing." He put his hand over his mouth for a brief moment and then checked his watch. "Ninety seconds, by the way."

"Don't listen to him, Isaac," David said. "The greatest gift humanity has received is free will. Every moment of our lives presents us with an opportunity to change the outcome."

"Wrong," Soter said. "We are just sophisticated machinery. Fate rules the world, and everything stands firm by its laws."

"Isaac, think about your science classes," David said. "Quantum physics proves there is a microscopic randomness to the foundation of reality. There is no way of predicting what will definitely happen."

"Then why did you hide it from me," Isaac snapped, "if we always had the choice to change it?" He had found a loophole. There was a long pause.

Soter checked his watch again. "One minute," he said. "I can't tell you how much I'm enjoying this Shakespearean tragedy."

"*His* ancestor, Ptolemy the First, used Alexander the Great's life to politicize their empire, just like Augustine used Jesus's life to unify and expand the Roman Empire." David pointed to the Antikythera Mechanism. "That man is going to use that machine to establish *his* empire."

"But this machine can save thousands of lives. Why shouldn't I help him?" Isaac asked as he turned back to his father.

"The Magi are weak, Isaac," Soter said. "Their time has passed."

"Our ancestors cracked the codes of the universe," David said. "They defied the higher powers, and that is why they were destroyed. The Magi's job is to safeguard their secrets, not exploit them."

"For how long?" Soter yelled. "The Magi have watched the world rot from within and have done *nothing!*"

"It's not our role to change the world," David said. "We exist to protect it."

Isaac was torn. He loved his father, but he had lied to him his whole life. Soter was telling him the truth, but Isaac was certain that he couldn't be trusted.

"What have you told my son, Soter?" David asked.

"You've tried to hide him from the world," Soter said. "I want him to help me change it. More important, I've told him the *truth.*"

"The truth?" David yelled. "You've been hunting down and *killing* Magi. You don't think we have anything on you? Tell my son what you did to your father and the twenty-four men on board that shipping container."

"Gag him," Soter said.

David broke free, and the Corsairs struggled to put the gag back on.

"Isaac, he *murdered* his father and killed twenty-four men, so he could take over the family's company. *Do not help him.*"

Redbeard subdued David with a brutal punch to the kidney and then wrapped his scarf around his mouth. He rammed his knee into David's back to tighten his grip.

Soter checked his watch. "Time's up, Mr. Alexander. Turn on the Antikythera Mechanism, and I will release your parents." Soter's stoic charm had vanished, and his true nature was revealed.

"And if I don't?" Isaac asked.

"Suffer the consequences," Soter said.

Neville finally stepped forward and spoke quietly to Isaac, "It is better for everyone if you turn it on. His backup plan is far worse."

Isaac looked at his father, who stared right at him and shook his head. Then he looked at Soter and said, "One question. And I want the truth."

Soter nodded.

"Did you murder all of those people?" Isaac asked.

Soter's piercing blue eyes stared right through Isaac. "I will always tell you the truth. Yes, I did kill him. My father was a hedonist and a drunk. I watched him beat my mother within an inch of her life. He cared more about his mistresses than his family *or* his company. He was a disgrace to our dynasty."

"Then what happened?" Isaac asked.

"After I got out of the navy, he came to an agreement with my brother and me. If we worked two years as deckhands on our family's freighters, he would hand the company over to us. The crew thought my brother and I were lowly immigrants. They had no idea we were the heirs to the company. Unfortunately, my younger brother, Nicolai, was like my father. He loved to drink and gamble. The crew caught him cheating during a poker game. A fight erupted, and he was stabbed and killed. They tossed his body overboard and made a pact to tell their superiors that it was a drunken accident…but I found out."

"What did you do?" Isaac asked.

"I killed all twenty-four men and ran the ship into another tanker," Soter said.

"Why?" Isaac asked.

"I saw an opportunity for a clean slate," he said. "Yes, I mourned my brother, but it was better that he died young. He would eventually have turned into our father. I snuck back here and forced my father to sign a suicide note saying that he felt responsible for our deaths."

"And then you killed him?" Isaac asked.

"Yes, I shot him," Soter said. "Then I traveled back to Libya and pretended to be the only survivor from the shipwreck."

"The heir to a billion-dollar empire," Isaac said.

"That's my story. Now, how do you want to proceed with yours?"

Isaac was at the point of no return. He knew that his next decision would not only change his life, but possibly the lives of millions of people.

"Speak your mind, Isaac," Soter said.

Isaac debated on what he was going to say, and then he just came out with it. "I trust that you will always tell me the truth, but I can't trust you with that machine," he said.

Neville exhaled in disappointment. David nodded his head in agreement.

Soter got within inches of Isaac's face. "Playtime is over, boy. Change your mind, or there will be dire consequences."

"No," Isaac said. "You're delusional. You've used your money to create a house of cards. You're not the savior of the new age. You've just convinced yourself you are."

Soter violently grabbed Isaac by the throat, cutting off his air. "Watch this, boy!" Soter threw Isaac to the ground, and he slid backward. "Redbeard! Bring David here, and hold the boy!"

Redbeard brought David to the center of the room and kicked the back of his legs, sending him to his knees. Soter pulled a curved knife from Redbeard's belt. Isaac ran toward his father, but Redbeard crippled him with a vicious punch to the stomach. Rachel started kicking and convulsing, trying to get free. Three Corsairs had to force her down and put their knees on her back. Her face was pressed against the cold tiled floor, and she stared at her husband and her son. Redbeard held Isaac by his hair, forcing him to look right at his father.

Soter put the curved blade to David's throat. "Last words."

David bowed his head in prayer. "I have pledged an oath to protect the sacred science and knowledge of our ancestors from dark forces. I am an ordained initiate of the Order of the Magi."

Isaac noticed Neville mouthing the prayer as David continued, "We have sworn to protect the prophets of each astrological age so they can advance the collective consciousness of humanity. We are the workers of light and eternal enemies to all spiritual darkness."

"That's exactly what your friends said," Soter said as he pressed the blade harder.

David lifted his head and looked right at his son. "Promise me that you will not follow my path, Isaac. It will only lead to darkness," he said.

Isaac nodded with tears streaming down his face. Rachel closed her eyes and mouthed what looked like a prayer.

"I don't fear death, because I will *always* be with you," David said as he closed his eyes.

"The prophecy is complete," Soter said. He ran the blade through David's jugular. He dropped the knife to the floor and used both hands to point David's head right at Isaac.

"No!" Isaac yelled.

"Accept your fate, Isaac. This was *meant* to be," Soter said.

A flood of red poured over the bottom of the slit like an overflowing bathtub. Isaac closed his eyes and tried to turn away, but Redbeard held him firmly. David gasped for air as the blood ran down his neck like thick fingers. Soter released David's head, and he collapsed to the ground. Neville was crying, too. He buried his hands in his face. A thick pool of blood spilled across the sterile white floor. Rachel screamed into her gag. David's eyes closed, and he moved on to the afterlife.

Soter picked up the knife and walked across the room. He knelt down next to Isaac, gently placed two fingers around the base of the blade, slid upwards, and wiped it clean. "You had the choice to save your father," he said while he used his thumb to spread the blood into the tiny crevices of his fingertips. "His death is on *you*," Soter said as he wiped David's blood down Isaac's face. "Didn't I tell you that I have accounted for *all* the variables?" Soter said. "I have a way to get the information out of you, but I was giving you the chance to join me. Now, you and your mother will live out the rest of your days as my prisoners. And guess what?" Soter leaned in close to whisper into Isaac's ear. "Your mother is going to give me an heir, or I will kill you and make her watch."

Soter nodded to Redbeard, who put Isaac in a one-armed choke-hold. With his free hand, the Turkish assassin pulled a syringe out of a silver case and bit off the protective cover. The plastic cap bounced off the ground in front of him. *What is he doing?* he asked himself. *He can't kill me. He needs me. He can't kill me.*

Rachel emptied her lungs into her gag, and the outburst brought Isaac back to his senses. Redbeard's bicep tightened, and Isaac felt the needle enter his neck. The liquid spread through his bloodstream. His mother's screams faded out, and Isaac felt a warm sensation overtaking his head. *I'm dying,* he thought, *I'm dying. I'm dying.*

Redbeard released Isaac's limp frame. Isaac slapped down onto the cold tile floor. He was staring into the face of his dead father when everything went black.

CHAPTER 25

THE EIGHT OF HEARTS

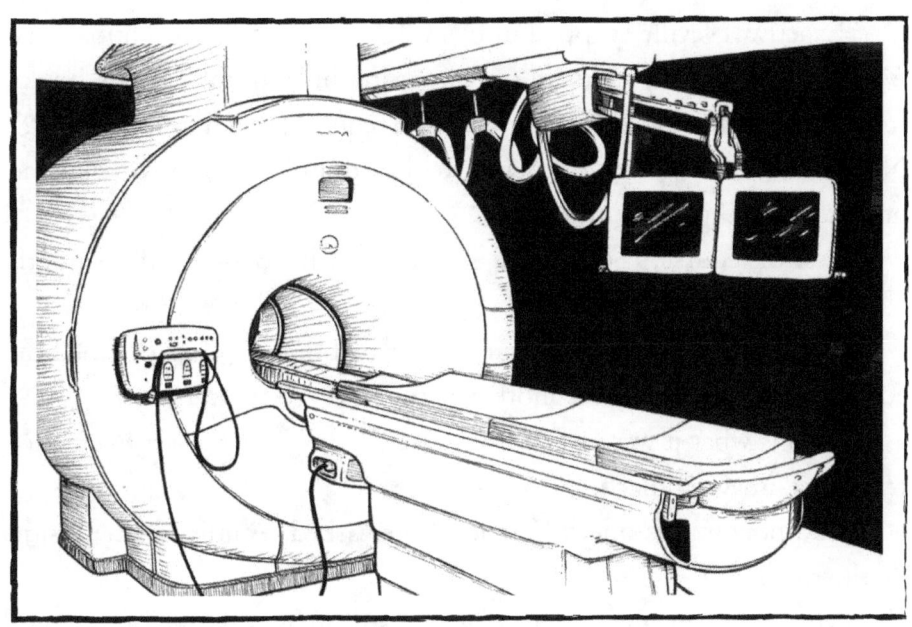

SOTER'S LABORATORY
THERA, GREECE

"Careful. He's not unconscious, just heavily sedated," Neville said as Redbeard and three Corsairs carried Isaac's body across the laboratory.

Soter followed with a perplexed look on his face. "You're sure this is going to work? You know I don't like variables."

"Eighty percent, to be exact," Neville said as they traversed the giant lab.

"That's better than normal odds," Soter said.

Isaac's eyelids were half open, and his limbs hung limp. He could see perfectly but was too drugged to establish who and where he was.

"Doing this to anyone else would enter the realm of science fiction, but we have one advantage with Mr. Alexander," Neville said.

"His dreams are set in a historical place," Soter said.

"Exactly." Neville stopped in front of a gigantic medical apparatus. "A place that we can virtually recreate using his journal and the books from your library. Do you remember that request for ten million euros?" Neville asked as he motioned for Redbeard and his men to lift Isaac onto a hospital gurney.

"Yes, of course," Soter said, running his hand down the smooth white machine.

They were in the far corner of Soter's laboratory, and the medical equipment was attached to another network of computers.

"This is what it was for," Neville said. "A state-of-the-art magnetic-resonance-imaging machine."

"And how is this one different?" Soter asked, examining the inside of the tube.

"Most MRI machines can only take still images of the brain every three to four seconds. This one can take video."

"Walk me through it," Soter said as Redbeard and his men strapped Isaac onto the gurney.

"We've already completed the first step of a three-part process," Neville said as he picked up a red, yellow, and blue brain scan and handed it to Soter. "Phase one was calibrating the brain decoding software. Every time the cerebrum gives an order, it sends an electric signal to the brain's cortex. If a subject kicks a soccer ball in his dreams or kicks one in real life, the brain signals are identical."

"I assume that's because the brain continues to operate but detaches from the body while sleeping?" Soter asked while snapping his fingers over Isaac's blank stare.

Neville nodded and said, "Precisely. Phase one took weeks of programming all the motions of the body. When someone lifts their right arm forty-five degrees, the computer knows exactly what that brain scan looks like."

"Each of the dials on the Antikythera Mechanism has thousands of degrees. We need it to be exact," Soter said, putting the brain scan down.

"Our margin of error will be severely diminished in phase two," Neville said. "Which is why we need to get Isaac into the machine while he is still sedated."

It took a few minutes for Redbeard and the Corsairs to strap Isaac securely into the patient tube of the MRI machine. Neville attached dozens of sticky electroencephalography sensors all over Isaac's head.

"These are EEG sensors that will measure his brain's electrical signals," Neville explained to Soter. He attached another device that locked Isaac's head in place. "This is the same apparatus that they use for Lasix surgery, to keep people's heads still and eyes open." Neville attached Isaac's eyelids to the small clamps.

"Why do his eyes have to be open?" Soter asked.

"I'll show you," Neville said as he motioned for everyone to back away. He pressed a button, and the patient tube slid into the MRI machine. A bright-blue light came on inside the tube. The machine looked like it belonged on a spaceship.

Isaac was heavily drugged but still conscious. He was struggling against the clamps a little and couldn't understand why his eyelids were being held open.

Neville felt awful doing this to someone he cared about, but he had come to a conclusion. The sooner he got the Antikythera turned on, the safer they *all* were. He couldn't watch any more of his friends die.

Neville motioned for Soter to join him at his computers. He sat down and opened up a desktop folder named "The Lost Island." A lifelike, three-dimensional recreation of Atlantis appeared on the computer screen. It resembled a video game.

"That's the Court of Nobles," Soter said. Neville moved the view closer to the three-dimensional model of the Antikythera Mechanism. It was an exact virtual replication of the original, which sat on the other side of the lab.

"We compiled all the information we could find on Atlantis from dozens of ancient texts in your library, Plato's books on Atlantis, and Isaac's journals," Neville said. "Then we made a 3-D model of the entire island." Neville zoomed out to an aerial view, and then he quickly zoomed in to the center of the city, focusing on the ground level of a lush garden. Lying among the tropical plants was Isaac's avatar.

"He looks real," Soter said as Neville rolled the point of view over digital-Isaac's face.

"So, as you can see, we've recreated the whole island, from the terracotta palaces to the pomegranates on the trees. The second phase is programming how Isaac's brain processes these images. Inside the MRI machine is a giant monitor. We are going to walk Isaac through the island, and the computer will synchronize the images to the corresponding brain scans."

"That's why he needs to be semiconscious," Soter said.

"Much like Google did when they took cars with video cameras around for their street view," Neville said as he clicked on a sidebar, "we are simply creating a three-dimensional map of Isaac's dreams."

The screen went into a first-person view inside the Court of Nobles. "The bad part is that we have to walk him through the entire island," Neville said as he double-clicked. "The good part is that the computer can process his brain scans at an incredibly high speed."

Inside the MRI machine, Isaac's eyes watched the moving images on the screen directly above him. On a second monitor, Neville watched the computer capture and process his multicolored brain scans.

"How long will this take?" Soter asked as he watched the second monitor.

"Roughly six hours to walk him all over Atlantis," Neville said.

"Then the computer will have the exact scans of both his images and his movements?" Soter asked.

"Yes. For phase three, we have to knock him out. Once his brain goes into REM, he should be synchronized with his computer duplicate."

"Isaac Alexander will be the first person in the history of the world to have his dreams recorded," Soter said.

"This technology won't really exist for decades," Neville said. "The only reason *this* might work is that we know where Isaac's dreams take place."

"Might?" Soter asked.

"That twenty percent still warrants a *might*, Mr. Soter," Neville said.

"Radio me before you start phase three," Soter said as he picked up a walkie-talkie and clipped it to his pants. "I have some business to attend to."

"Yes, sir," Neville said as he dragged a countdown timer to an open space on his monitor. "You have approximately six hours and four minutes."

Soter checked his watch and exited the laboratory.

Soter walked down a flight of stairs to a cellar. Two Turkish Corsairs stood guard. They saw Soter and opened the door. As he stepped inside, Soter said, "Only enter if you hear a commotion."

The Corsairs nodded and closed the door.

Soter entered the underground holding chamber. It was made up of high concrete walls and had a line of small rectangular windows just above ground level that let in light. Rachel was curled up on a cot, sobbing into her blanket.

"I hope you don't find these accommodations too meager," Soter said.

Rachel curled tighter into the fetal position. Her khaki shorts exposed her toned legs. Soter wanted to take her right then and there, but he wasn't a beast like his father. He knew that she would do what he asked of her to save her son's life. Soter looked around the room—four single-beds, a large couch, a tiny bathroom, a desk and two shelves full of fiction books. It was more welcoming than a jail cell, but not by much.

"I don't expect you to say anything, so just listen," Soter said.

Rachel pulled the blankets over her head. Looking at him made her ill.

"All he had to do was turn the machine on, and I would have let *all* of you go. That was our deal. Maybe he was so upset that his father had lied to him his whole life that he wanted to see him die." Soter expected a reaction but got none. He walked closer to the wall and looked out the small windows. It was twilight. "Or maybe he thinks I'm a delusional psychopath. It doesn't matter. What *does* matter is the deal I am going to give you." Soter walked toward the bookshelf and examined the titles.

Rachel's voice emerged from beneath the blanket. "What have you done with my son?"

"We have a way of getting the information out of him," Soter said. "He's fine and will be joining you this evening."

"Let us *go*." Rachel failed to sound threatening.

"That is up to you," Soter said as he walked away from the bookshelf and stood over her. "I've already demonstrated that I am a man of my word."

"If you lay a finger on him—" Rachel said.

"After I get what I want from your son, he's of no use to me. It's up to *you* what I do with him."

"What do you *want?*" Rachel asked, more adamant.

"I've already told you," Soter said. "I want an heir. If you don't give me one, I will kill your son."

"Why me? I hate you with every fiber of my being!" she said, trying not to sob.

"Exactly," Soter said. "I don't have time for love nonsense. It's easier for me to have a child with a woman who wants absolutely nothing to do with me."

Rachel whirled out of bed and attacked Soter. He quickly subdued her. "You animal! You kill my husband and then ask me for a *child!*"

Soter threw her onto the bed. The two Corsairs rushed into the room with their swords drawn, but Soter held up his hands to tell them it was under control.

He knelt down and whispered to Rachel, "The night that I announce myself to the world is the night you will have to make your decision. Give me an heir, and I will let you and your son go. If not, I will run the same knife through Isaac's throat and keep you here, in this cell, for the rest of your miserable life. A child for a child. I think that's fair."

Rachel nodded. "I'll do it. Just don't take him from me. He's all I have."

Soter lifted his hand to move a wisp of hair out of her face. Rachel pushed his hand away, turned over, and curled back into her blanket. He saw a handkerchief hanging out of her pocket and stole it without her noticing. Rachel was strong, but she had just been broken.

Hours later, Soter's walkie-talkie woke him from a nap on the couch in his study. Lying on his chest was a three-hundred-page report titled, *An Economic Strategy for World Peace.*

Soter cleared his throat and answered the beep. "Go."

Neville's voice crackled. "We're going to start phase three."

Soter placed his hand on the electronic reader, and the mosaic opened. He put the report inside, next to his bronze deck of cards. He opened a desk drawer and pulled out a freshly pressed, white safari shirt. He took off his wrinkled shirt and admired his own chiseled body. While he looked at himself, he pulled out Rachel's handkerchief and inhaled her scent.

Minutes later, Soter walked into the laboratory. Isaac was still strapped to the gurney, but Neville had him pulled outside the tube. His speech was slurred, and he feebly tugged at the restraints.

"Le' me outta here," Isaac mumbled.

"The sedative is wearing off," Neville said. "We have to move quickly."

Redbeard stepped forward, opened a silver case from his belt, and handed Neville another syringe.

"We can't use an anesthetic agent, because it will cut off the nervous signals to his brain," Neville said as he prepped the syringe. "We need a chemical that will induce natural sleep, so were going to use an injection of Flunitrazepam. This will also cut down his delta waves and get him into REM quicker."

"And REM is the stage of sleep where the most vivid dreams occur?" Soter asked.

"Yes, hold his head still," Neville said.

Isaac became more conscious and panicked when he realized his eyes were being held open.

"Please, let me up," Isaac said.

Soter could tell he was terrified. Tears bubbled up through Isaac's red eyes like water through a dry sponge.

"Please, don't kill me," he said with tears trickling down the sides of his face.

Neville moved quickly. He didn't want the boy to suffer any more than he had to. The doctor inserted the syringe into Isaac's neck and injected the Flunitrazepam. Then he carefully detached the apparatus holding his eyelids open and put his cold hands over Isaac's face, closing his eyes.

Isaac thought Neville was closing his eyes after a lethal injection. "I'm sorry. I'll do anything. *Please.* I don't want to die," he said, trying to sit up.

Neville continue to hold his eyes closed while Soter held his head down. "You're not going to die," Neville said, attempting a soothing voice. "You're just going back to sleep." It was a very primal moment.

The sedative took effect, and Isaac stopped resisting. He sank back onto the MRI table, and Soter released him.

"We'll see you in a few hours," Neville said as he pressed a button, which slid the patient's table back into the MRI tube.

Neville collapsed into his chair and kicked his head back. The long day had taken its toll, but he wasn't done yet. Soter could tell the doctor was having second thoughts.

"It's the homestretch, Mr. Ramanujan," Soter said, pulling up a computer chair next to his.

Neville sighed. "I feel bad for Isaac," he said.

"Don't," Soter said. "The first step to becoming a man is learning to live with the consequences of your actions."

Neville rewet his dry eyes with Rohto eye drops, let the burn pass through his retinas, and then opened an EKG monitor on his screen. Isaac's heartbeat was stable.

"It looks good," Neville said wiping moisture away from an eye. "He's out, but not too sedated."

"What now?" Soter asked.

"We wait two hours for him to enter REM sleep," Neville said as he reopened the computer version of Atlantis and zoomed down to the 3-D model of Isaac. "Then this little guy should tell us exactly what we need to know." Neville crossed his arms above his head and leaned back into his computer chair.

Soter followed suit and patiently crossed his fingers in his lap. His family had been waiting for hundreds of years. He could afford to wait two hours. The rhythmic beeping of the EKG became the only sound in the room as the two men stared at Isaac's computer version.

CHAPTER 26:
THE EIGHT OF CLUBS

PROFESSOR OLNEY'S ATRIUM
VALLETTA, MALTA

"What in the butt-fucking hell is all of this?" Jack asked as he kicked a huge pile of leather suitcases by Olney's front door.

The professor shivered. "Foul men swear, because they don't have the proper vocabulary to express themselves. *This* is my luggage."

Jack counted eleven leather suitcases and three wooden chests stacked in a pyramid.

"Well, excuse me, my Portuguese friend," Jack said, "but are you planning on hiring bloody Sherpas? We're not colonizing. This is a rescue mission."

Zahra sat down at the table. She waited to see if the knot could untie itself before she intervened.

"Two suitcases," Jack said.

"We don't even know where we're going," Professor Olney said.

"That's why we need to run and catch an ostrich," Jack said.

Professor Olney and Zahra looked at him like he had lost his marbles.

"It's an acronym," Jack said as he approached the table. He flipped over the butcher paper that Olney had used to give them a history lesson and wrote down RACAO vertically. "It's how we make decisions in the military," Jack said as he wrote down each step on the table. "R is for receiving orders. A is for analyzing the mission. C is for comparing plans. The second A is for approving the mission, and O is for getting orders. We have our mission, and the next step is to analyze our intel."

Professor Olney sat down at the table; Jack stood at the head of the makeshift war table.

"Zahra, what do we know about the guys who have been chasing us?" Jack asked.

"When I was escaping David's tent, I heard him call the man a Turk," Zahra said. "So we know that they are Turkish."

"Aha," the professor said. "He is an Ottoman Corsair." Jack motioned with his hand for the professor to continue. "From the sixteenth to nineteenth centuries, Turkish pirates ran North Africa, which was known as the Barbary Coast. They raided European towns and captured Christians to sell on the slave market. The most famous Corsair was Admiral Hayreddin Barbarossa. His name literally translates to *Redbeard*. It is believed that he retired in Constantinople to start a mercenary academy."

"So, it's possible that these mercenaries have been hired by someone very powerful," Jack asked.

"The blond man," Zahra said, remembering him looking out of the tent. "There was one white man with them. He had blond hair, and I could see the blue in his eyes from very far away."

"Good, we're focusing our sights," Jack said, turning to the professor. "All right, your turn. Think about the short list of powerful men with an interest in Atlantis who have enough money for a private army and a hundred-million-dollar Oculus yacht."

"Cassie, Polly, bring my laptop," Olney yelled to the twins, who were still cleaning the library.

"What the hell, Gandalf?" Jack said. "You're not smart enough to cough up a name?"

"My knowledge is not limitless," Olney said.

"Hypocrite," Jack said.

"How does that make me a hypocrite, you bootneck?"

"Hermit crab," Jack said, tapping Olney's metal hook with his pencil.

"Baloo," Olney said.

Zahra jumped up to expedite the laptop search while the academic and the soldier continued with juvenile name-calling.

"Merlin wannabe," Jack said.

"Philandering ignoramus."

"Bearded duck molester."

"Illegitimate son of a kelpy sea wench."

"Enough!" Zahra said as she slapped the laptop in front of Olney. "You are smart, and he is tough. We have work to do."

"Well played," Jack said, smiling and shaking the professor's hand.

"Back and forth like Wimbledon," Olney said opening his laptop. "*Merlin* is actually my password."

Both men laughed, and Jack slapped the Professor on the back. Zahra couldn't understand the shift. She liked to conserve her insults for when she really needed them.

Professor Olney and Jack spent the next fifteen minutes searching for owners of Oculus yachts. They narrowed the list down to twenty-two billionaires and twelve companies that had purchased boats from Schöpfer yachts. They went down that list, but none of the names jumped out at Olney. For the next half hour, they read news articles on each billionaire. They had only gotten through seven potentials when Olney and Jack grew frustrated with each other.

"None of these names ring your rusty bell?" Jack asked, frustrated. "Not *one* has bought artifacts at auctions or donated money to archaeological digs?"

"Intel is good research, and research is all about patience," the professor said as he leaned within a few centimeters of the screen to read the tiny print to himself.

Jack slammed his fist down on the table. "Stop reading with your mouth open, damn it! One of these men kidnapped my family, and you need to think a little quicker."

Zahra put her head down on the table. They couldn't go an hour without an argument.

"What do you want me to do?" Olney yelled. "Put on my Merlin hat and my wizard robe, look into my crystal ball, and find out where they are?"

Zahra's head popped up. One of Olney's words triggered something in her memory. She reached across the table and grabbed the pencil from Jack.

"No, ya old codger," Jack said. "Stop thinking in the past and start thinking in the present."

Zahra furiously sketched something onto the butcher paper tabletop.

"Ooohh, are you going to use the torture tactics you learned in the military to get it out of me?" Olney taunted. "What's the saying? Join the army. Travel to exotic distant lands, meet exciting and unusual people…then kill them?"

"Stop," Zahra said before Jack could muster a retort. They both looked over at her, and she pointed down to her rough sketch. It was an anchor on the bottom and a Grecian trident on top.

"This was on the back of the robe you were wearing on the boat," Zahra said to Jack.

"She's right," he said. "It was also on the towels we put on Isaac."

"Maybe it's a logo for one of the companies," Olney said.

They scanned each of the companies' websites. Soter Shipping was their ninth search. The website was in elegant white, and in the top-right corner was an Egyptian-blue logo of an anchor and a trident. Underneath was a motto in Greek.

"'*Great is the country that controls the sea.*' This has to be it." Olney clicked on the board members link. The web page opened up, and the man labeled as president/CEO was a handsome blond gentleman with piercing blue eyes.

"That is him," Zahra said. "He has eyes that you do not forget."

"Ptolemy Soter," Olney said. "Why didn't I connect those dots? This man claims he is a descendant of the Ptolemaic Dynasty." Olney clicked on another link. It was a black-and-white newspaper photo of a younger Ptolemy bandaged in a small hospital cot. The headline read, "*Twenty-Five-Year-Old Found in Shipwreck off North African Coast. Inherits 7.5 billion.*"

"Spot on, Zahra," Jack said, hugging her. She was not used to a man's touch, but she felt safe around her new companions.

Olney clicked on another article that was from an architectural magazine. It showed a bird's-eye view of Soter's compound. They marveled at the sprawling ancient-Greek-inspired estate that sat on top of sheer limestone cliffs.

"Where is it?" Jack asked.

"I don't need my crystal ball to know this one," Olney said. "It's on Thera, which is *above* the ancient ruins of Atlantis."

"Two bags, Captain Hook," Jack said holding up two hooked fingers. "We leave in one hour."

"And how do you plan on financing this operation?" Olney asked, crossing his arms in defiance.

Jacked had his palms flat on the table, and his head dropped below his shoulder blades. The old man had him by the bollocks.

"Three bags, but I'm not carrying one," Jack said.

"Ten bags," Olney said.

"Four bags and I'll stop calling you old," Jack said.

"Nine bags and I'll stop calling you stupid," Olney said.

Zahra knew where it was headed. She looked over to Cassie and Polly and mimed an eating motion. The twins smiled and beckoned for her to come to the kitchen. If Zahra was going to put up with these two, she was going to do it on a full stomach.

CHAPTER 27:
THE EIGHT OF DIAMONDS

SOTER'S LABORATORY
THERA, GREECE

Soter checked his watch—107 minutes had passed. Dr. Ramanujan tilted his head forward and nodded off. Soter glanced toward the monitors and noticed the brain scans changing—bright, pulsing red flashes. He shot his gaze over toward the computer screen. Isaac's computer version lay still, so there was no reason to wake the doctor. Soter was just about to look away when Isaac's avatar twitched.

"He moved," Soter blurted, causing Neville to jump and lose his glasses.

"Where?" Neville asked as he fumbled to put them back on. Isaac still lay motionless. Neville moved the view to an extreme close-up of Isaac's avatar. The eyes popped open, and both men jumped back.

Isaac's computer version looked around and lifted himself off the ground while Neville scrolled back to get a full-frame view.

"It's working," Soter said quietly.

"History in the making," Neville said.

"Could he become aware he's dreaming and hide from us?" Soter asked.

"Isaac can dream lucidly, but being that aware is a different level," Neville said as Isaac walked to a tree and plucked a pomegranate. They watched as the computer program wandered aimlessly through the gardens. Neville checked the brain scans. "We're not going to have him for long on this sleep cycle, ten minutes at most," Neville said right as Isaac's model collapsed to the ground.

"What just happened?" Soter asked.

"The first stage of REM sleep is always very short," Neville said. "To Isaac, it will be seamless, but we have to wait again."

"Damn it! How long?" Soter asked.

"I don't know," Neville said. "The important thing is that we're synched. We have three more cycles of REM, and they each get longer."

Soter couldn't sit down any longer. He walked to the open part of the lab and started an intense regimen of push-ups and sit-ups. Forty-two minutes passed before Isaac moved again.

"We're live," Neville said as Soter sat back down, beads of sweat running down his face.

Isaac's avatar moved with a purpose this time. He walked out of the garden and into an open-air courtyard. He walked straight over the bridged canals that circled the city.

"Come on, Isaac, walk inside," Soter said to himself.

Isaac walked down an aisle of terra-cotta columns and entered the Court of Nobles.

"Yes," Soter said in approval, slapping the doctor's back a little too hard. Neville followed right behind Isaac as he walked into the center of the room. He stopped in front of the Antikythera Mechanism.

Soter had been taught from a young age how to control his emotions, but he could feel his excitement and anticipation pumping through every artery. His great-grandfather had started the quest in 1901; it had taken over a century to complete. Isaac's right hand reached out and turned the first dial.

"Paper, damn it," Soter said, scouring the desk.

"It's all being recorded," Neville said.

"I don't trust it," Soter said, grabbing a pen and piece of paper.

Isaac's hand twisted the innermost sundial. Neville zoomed in close to get an accurate reading. Each of the dials had rotated 360 degrees.

"One hundred fourteen degrees," Neville said as Soter wrote it down.

Isaac's hand twisted the second dial.

"Two hundred seventy-four degrees," Neville reported.

Isaac continued to spin the rest of the dials as Neville read them. "Fifty-eight degrees, sixty-two degrees, forty degrees, three hundred twenty-two degrees, and eighty-eight degrees," Neville said. "I'm not seeing a pattern here."

"Plenty of time to figure that out later," Soter said. "Come with me."

He rushed across the lab and pulled out a key card. He swiped it over the electronic pad on the Plexiglas, and the light turned green. He turned the metal handle and swung open the airtight glass case.

"Is everything ready?" Soter asked, holding the piece of paper in his hands.

Neville double-checked all the wires running out the back of the Antikythera and into his computers.

"Good to go, Mr. Soter," Neville said.

Soter placed his hand on the cold bronze and turned the innermost dial to the exact degree. He did the same with the next five dials. The last dial was engraved with the symbol for Saturn—a cross with a sickle. Soter looked to Neville and turned the last dial to eighty-eight degrees. All seven dials sank into the machine, and a whir of bronze cogs came to life. Soter stepped back. "This is it. It's happening."

The seven dials were now synchronized to the motions of the planets. The central Sun dial rotated the slowest, while the next closest dials representing Mercury and Venus rotated quickly. The dials representing Earth, the Moon, Mars, Jupiter, and Saturn slowly clicked their way around the circle.

Neville slid into his computer chair and pulled up the three-dimensional blueprint on his screen. The seven dials on the face had unlocked hundreds of bronze cogs on the inside of the machine that all moved in different directions.

"Tell me what's happening," Soter said, unable to take his eyes off the machine.

"It's still synchronizing; we should have a reading soon," Neville said, opening up an encryption software file. Binary numbers rapidly scrolled up a black backdrop. "We're receiving data!" Neville yelled as he looked over to the wall-size map of the Earth.

Neville watched as a pop-up processing bar appeared on his monitor.

"Ten percent," the doctor said. "Mr. Soter, the map should be live in seconds."

Soter forced himself away from the hypnotizing bronze dials and approached the wall-sized Google Earth map. The interconnected screens towered over five meters tall and ten meters wide.

"Sixty-two percent," Neville said.

The blue glow from the oceans illuminated every crevice of Soter's chiseled face. He looked like a child eagerly awaiting his favorite film.

"Ninety percent, and we should be live in five, four, three, two, one," Neville said as the processing bar finished.

Suddenly, the computer monitors blinked and went dark for a split second while the information loaded. When it came back on, the terrain map glowed with hot spots.

"We're synched," Neville said as he zoomed in. The map had outlines of all the major fault lines and weather patterns developing at that very moment.

"Input this date: March 11, 2011," Soter said.

Neville opened up a program and typed. Soter spun around and watched as the seven bronze dials of the Antikythera rapidly spun counterclockwise to match their exact locations on that date. The interactive map began to rewind, and the weather patterns moved quickly over the hemispheres. When it stopped, a massive glowing red hot spot hovered over the island of Japan. Neville zoomed in and then walked over to the map to analyze the seismic data. They watched a reenactment of the Tohoku earthquake and tsunami off the coast.

"Mr. Soter, you've done it." Neville held out his hand.

"*We* have done it, Doctor," Soter said, accepting his handshake.

Neville knew he was working for a ruthless man, but he allowed himself a smile. He'd just earned a spot in twenty-first-century history books.

"Not only can we analyze natural disasters from the past, but we now have the option to go into the future," Neville said.

"Shall we find the location of the next catastrophe?" Soter asked with a clap.

Neville sat back down and moved the Antikythera dials forward day by day. Fifteen days had passed and there was nothing out of the ordinary besides massive rainstorms in Southeast Asia. Then a massive red glow appeared in Indonesia on the sixteenth day.

"Stop!" Soter yelled.

Neville zoomed into the red area on his computer screen. He stood up and analyzed the data on the interactive map.

"There it is," Neville said. "Earth's next disaster."

"Sumatra," Soter said. "It's on the Eurasian, Australian, and Pacific fault lines."

"It looks like the Eurasian tectonic plate is being forced under the Pacific plate. It's going to cause a massive, megathrust earthquake," Neville said as he stepped closer and put his finger on the glowing fault line. "Judging by this data, we're looking at about a nine point one."

"Then what?" Soter asked.

"The earthquake will trigger a massive tsunami. Just as big as the one in 2004. It should hit the city of Padang in sixteen days."

"How exact can we be?" Soter said. "Everything must be *precise* before I commence my operation. No variables."

Neville sat back down at his computer and moved forward and backward over the fault line. "The quake will hit at 4:17 p.m., and the tsunami will hit twelve minutes later, at 4:29 p.m.," he said.

"I don't like to be rushed, but this will have to do," Soter said.

Neville looked over statistics on his computer. "Close to a million people in that city. We can save a lot of lives."

"I have a lot to plan in these next two weeks," Soter said. "Get the boy up."

"Mr. Soter, we should let him wake naturally," Neville said.

"That was not a request," Soter said as he pulled his walkie-talkie off his belt. "Redbeard, come to the lab and escort the boy down to his mother."

Neville opened the patient tube on the MRI machine and detached Isaac from the gurney. He was still out cold. Soter slapped him several times in the face. Isaac stirred to life and opened his eyes.

Soter leaned over his face and said, "Congratulations, Mr. Alexander; you've just earned a place in history."

"What happened?" Isaac asked still hovering in a drug-induced stupor.

"You were the first person to have his dreams *recorded*," Soter said as Redbeard and his Corsairs entered the laboratory.

"What?" Isaac asked trying to use his anger to help him break through the murky sedative-induced fog.

"I told you that I had accounted for all the variables, even the one where you refused to help me," Soter said as he looked at Redbeard. "Take him down to the holding cell. I have work to do."

As Isaac was carried out of the laboratory, he saw that the Antikythera Mechanism was on and that it was synchronized to the wall-sized map. He didn't know how Soter and Neville had done it, but somehow, they had hacked into his brain.

CHAPTER 28

THE EIGHT OF SPADES

SOTER'S HOLDING CELL
THERA, GREECE

Redbeard opened the holding cell and tossed Isaac onto the concrete floor. His joints were numb with paresthesia. His wrists absorbed the impact, and pain shot up his arms and into his molars.

Rachel jumped up and ran to him. The Corsairs exited and locked the door.

"Isaac!" Rachel turned her son off his stomach and laid him in her lap. He had a small laceration on his forehead from the fall. Rachel reached for her handkerchief, but it wasn't there, so she cleaned her son's wound with her shirt.

"I remember them killing Dad…then I don't know what happened," Isaac said.

"They injected you with something," Rachel said, hugging him closer. "I'm just glad you're alive."

"Why did they kill him?" Isaac asked.

"Your father was the love of my life, but he had secrets that he couldn't even tell me," Rachel said.

"It was my fault," Isaac said as both of his eyes welled up. "I could have saved him."

"No, it *wasn't*," Rachel said. She stroked his hair and kissed his forehead. "It was *my* fault. I urged your father to tell you about the oracle, and Soter used it against us. Don't believe that prophecy crap for one minute."

Isaac lay in his mother's lap. It was the safest he had felt in days, but he knew that she was lying to him. The hard truth was that he did cause his father's death, whether he was directly or indirectly at fault.

Just like Soter had said, we do have an internal GPS, and no matter which route we take, it will always steer us back toward our predetermined destination.

"Uncle Jack will find us," Isaac said in an attempt to both change the subject and comfort his guilt-ridden mother. "I know he's still alive. I can feel it."

Rachel took a deep breath. "I made a deal with Soter."

"No!" Isaac yelled. He harnessed enough anger to help himself up. "You can't!"

Rachel covered her face with her hands and wiped tears away with the bottom of her palms. "I don't know what else to do," she said from her knees. "He is going to kill you if I don't."

Isaac stood. Anger pushed the remaining sedative out of his body. He clenched his fists into tight balls. *I will kill that man. I'll kill him before he touches my mother.* He looked at Rachel and softened a little. "That's not an option," Isaac said. "We're going to get out of here and stop him."

The holding cell door opened, and Neville walked in with his hands raised.

"What did you just do to me?" Isaac snapped.

Neville backed up as Isaac rushed to assault him. "Don't do this, Isaac. I don't want to hurt you," Neville pleaded with hands out in front of him.

Isaac's wrath came full force with a barrage of undisciplined punches. The nimble doctor grabbed his left wrist with his right hand and twisted it away from his body. The strain caused Isaac's knees to buckle, and he exposed his core for a counterstrike. Neville shoved the ridge of his left palm under Isaac's chin, applied pressure to the wrist hold, and then firmly but carefully backed him into the wall. Isaac was shocked and embarrassed that he had been incapacitated so quickly. His neck ligaments and arteries bulged out of his stretched throat.

"A simple procedure," Neville said, still securely holding the top of Isaac's head to the wall. "We knocked you out and analyzed your brain scans. Can I release you?"

"Yes. Sorry," Isaac said.

"I'm sorry David is gone," Neville said, releasing him and then straightening his shirt.

"What was that you just did to me?" Isaac asked while rubbing his wrist.

"Kalari. The oldest martial art in the world. All initiates, including your father, spend three years in India mastering the techniques," Neville responded.

The word *father* tore through Isaac like a serrated sword. Neville was hit with an upsurge of grief. He had considered David family.

"So now that machine is on, no one can stop him," Rachel said stepping toward them.

"Yes, I'm afraid he can only be *contained* at this point," Neville responded.

"You're responsible for *all* of this!" Rachel snapped.

"It's a temporary alliance. I didn't see any other options," Neville said.

"You and David swore an oath as members of the Order to safeguard the world from people like him," Rachel said.

"I'm just a scientist," Neville said with his head bowed. "I'm not a warrior like David was."

"There's still a chance for redemption, Neville," Rachel said. "Help us get out of here."

"He'll kill me," Neville said. "Then Redbeard will track down my family."

Isaac took a deep breath. "Then start by getting us Soter's plan. He keeps it in his private study."

"I can do that," Neville said. "I know the combination to his wall safe."

"We have to know his plan so we can stop him," Isaac said.

"Everything will go into motion in sixteen days," Neville said. "There's going to be a massive earthquake and tsunami off the coast of Sumatra. He's planning on predicting the earthquake to the global news network and then revealing himself after it happens. That would be your best time to try and escape."

"That gives us a little time," Rachel said.

"I'll do what I can until then," Neville said.

"Get me a change of clothes?" Rachel said. "I've been in these since Morocco."

He nodded and exited the holding cell. "I'll see what I can do."

The next morning, Rachel and Isaac awoke when two Corsairs entered their holding cell. One of them carried a breakfast of fresh fruit, grain oatmeal, and juices. The other carried a pile of new clothes. They placed them on the table and exited without a word. On the breakfast tray was a fresh bar of soap that Rachel held to her nose.

"I need a shower," she said as she took the soap and new clothes into the small bathroom. "I smell like one of Jack's girlfriends."

On top of Isaac's pile of clothes was his journal. He picked it up, and a packet of papers slipped out. He flipped through it. Neville had printed Soter's report, four pages per sheet, and then folded them inside Isaac's journal.

Isaac and Rachel spent most of the next day comforting one another. The shock of David's death had worn off, and their grief sank in. Isaac felt the need to channel his emotions into something productive. Otherwise, he thought he would go crazy.

"Tell me how you and Dad met."

Rachel sat up and sighed with a faraway look in her eyes. "Your dad spoke at a medical conference at Harvard while I was in med school. He was in the seed-capital stage of his hundred-dollar laptop idea. I had never seen anyone so business savvy and compassionate at the same time. He was tough, but human. He passed around a sheet for contact info. He planned to do a humanitarian mission once his company received funding. Med students would give free clinics while he handed out his laptops. I signed up and was on a flight to Peru a year later." She smiled.

"We spent a month in the floating villages outside the city of Iquitos. I was on two missions. The first was to help the people of Peru. The second was to win over your father. It took two weeks of eye contact and smiles before he finally asked me out. We became inseparable, and on our last night, we took a canoe out into the Amazon River and made love." She glanced at her son and blushed. "I'll spare you the details, but…well, we couldn't keep our balance, so the canoe tipped over and we got swept down the river. We got a boat ride back the next morning and were greeted by scrutinizing med students on the riverbanks. It was the best night of my life, followed by the worst morning." She laughed a little.

"It didn't matter, though. Everyone knew we were falling in love. We were married a month after I graduated. We've traveled together ever since."

Rachel swallowed, caught her composure, and then continued, "It wasn't until a year into our marriage that I found out your dad was more than a brilliant philanthropist. We were in Botswana taking a motor caravan of medical supplies to a remote village. A group of thieves armed with machetes blocked the road and attempted a smash-and-grab. David calmly opened up a hidden compartment in his briefcase, pulled a silver weapon out, and disabled all of them.

"After that, I forced him to come clean. He promised to tell me everything that I was allowed to know. He explained that his family was part of an ancient society, sort of like the secret service for spiritual leaders. They could trace their lineage back to the survivors of Atlantis. David's father, who was an aeronautical engineer for the US Air Force, had sat him down and told him about their history. He presented David with a choice. Either go on with his life, or follow the family legacy. David decided to become a member." Rachel was looking at Isaac but not really seeing him. She was seeing her life.

"He spent the next four years in Alexandria, Egypt, with tutors from the Order of the Magi. After he completed his studies, he was sent to Southwestern India for three years to learn kalari. Then it was a year of preparation for the initiation process—a solo journey through the Egyptian desert.

"David almost died in the desert, but he became the youngest member of the order at the age of thirty-one." She took a deep breath and sighed.

"He spent the next two years doing secret missions for the order and then was granted leeway to return to civilian life. That's when he started his business and used financial contacts through the order to fund it.

The only other information I know is that there were thirteen members of the order, and their headquarters were in Alexandria. David had to go there several times a year for meetings. I loved it. We stayed in the El-Salamlek Palace."

Rachel stared off into an imaginary distance, lost in memories of her beloved husband. Then she snapped back into the moment. "That's honestly all I know."

After a long, contemplative silence, Isaac reached out and squeezed his mother's hand.

Sleep eventually claimed them both, though Isaac awoke in the night, as usual. With nothing to do, he read Soter's report. His mother woke to find him poring over the documents.

"What does it say?" she asked.

"This isn't a blueprint for peace," Isaac said. "It's a detailed invasion manual. He has hired professionals to construct a plan from the broadest psychological strokes to the finest geological details. I hate him, but I admire his effort. He thought this through from top to bottom."

"Explain it to me," Rachel said. "Sounds like it might help me fall asleep."

Isaac summarized the report. "Phase one, Soter will build up his fleet and peacekeeping forces. After natural disasters, he'll award rebuilding contracts to the highest bidding defense companies. Then he'll use the money to enlist crews to his peacekeeping forces and buy more ships.

"Phase two, rebuild countries using ecofriendly and alternative-energy designs. After disasters ravage those countries, defense contractors will rebuild the cities using Soter's blueprints. The plans will include state-of-the-art public schools that will teach his doctrine of math, science, history, engineering, astronomy, and astrology. Graduates of his schools will take placement tests and be given jobs with his peacekeeping forces.

"Phase three, establish naval bases in unstable countries with large oil reserves. He names Algeria, Kazakhstan, Libya, Nigeria, and Venezuela.

"Phase four, incite civil unrest in those countries using espionage and undercover activities. Then he'll declare martial law and secure the oil deposits using his private military.

"Finally, in phase five, he'll institute astrology as the religion of the new era by financing Western and Middle-Eastern extremists, and escalating both superpowers into World War III. Soter plans on remaining neutral to both parties while secretly taking control of global ports and natural resource strongholds, like the United States did at the beginning of World War II. His plan is to let the Western and Middle-Eastern superpowers weaken each other and then step in and construct a peaceful treaty between both sides."

Isaac then read from the final page. "He also sank millions of dollars into stem-cell research. He plans on replacing his vital organs every ten years so that he can live to be 150 years old."

Rachel had been holding her hand over mouth as Isaac read to her. She finally dropped her hands and said, "He's mad."

"He has to be stopped."

Rachel produced a section of pipe that was hidden under the mattress. One edge had been filed to a dull point. She showed it to Isaac and said, "Leave that to me."

CHAPTER 29:
THE NINE OF HEARTS

INTERNATIONAL RED CROSS
HEADQUARTERS
GENEVA, SWITZERLAND

Head of Security Phillipe Broussard walked a metal briefcase down the hallways of the Red Cross chateau. He had already x-rayed and personally inspected the entire case, which was addressed to his boss, Simone Laplace. It was safe, but the contents of the case and the letter were the most perplexing thing he had come across in his thirty years of security work.

Broussard navigated his large frame through the frenetic hallways, walked past his boss's secretary, and entered her office. Laplace spoke on the phone. She was a beautiful, silver-haired Frenchwoman in her late fifties. She ended her phone call and hung up.

"What is so important that you barge in here?" Laplace asked, straightening her tight pencil skirt along her thin hips.

"This," Broussard said holding up the silver briefcase and then placing it on her desk. Laplace looked nervous, and he reassured her. "It cleared all security and is addressed to Simone Laplace, Head of the International Red Cross and Red Crescent."

Laplace clicked open the locks and swung the briefcase open. It was full of neatly stacked ten-thousand-dollar Eurobonds.

"How much money is this?" she asked, running her fingers over the bonds.

"Ten million euros," Broussard said.

Laplace was confused. She noticed a manila envelope tucked into the side of the briefcase. She opened it and read aloud, "Dear Mrs. Laplace, I have had my people research you, and I think you are the right person to contact. There is going to be a massive, 9.1, underwater earthquake off the coast of Sumatra in nine days. The quake will trigger a tsunami that will hit the Padang coast on September 14 at roughly 4:25 p.m. I have developed the ability to predict natural disasters, but for safety reasons, I cannot divulge my method yet. There are people after me right now trying to stop me. Please use this money to send aid to the country of Sumatra and evacuate people away from the coast. Once I predict this first disaster, it will be safe for me to reveal my identity. I have included a press release that you can send to the global news outlets. Sincerely, The King of Clubs."

She pulled out a Bicycle king of clubs playing card and held it up for Broussard, who took it with a handkerchief to have it checked for prints.

"Is that even possible?" Simone asked.

"Madame, I grew up with three black-and-white television channels," Broussard said. "Now I drive an electronic sports car that goes five hundred kilometers per charge. I have a titanium knee replacement, and my kids use iPads to do their homework with study buddies in China. The future has arrived."

Simone nodded and called out to her secretary. "Get me the BBC and CNN on a conference call." She turned back to Broussard. "Ten million euros is worth a phone call."

Soter's Labarotory
Thera, Greece

Soter watched as every major news outlet covered the story of the Sumatran tsunami prediction. Neville had moved the continuous coverage to the wall-sized monitors. Stations interviewed panels of analysts and pundits. Most of them bashed the anonymous donation as some kind of publicity stunt. Geologists from prestigious universities speculated over computer-generated fault lines. Published scientists explained that it was astronomically impossible to predict earthquakes. CNN aptly labeled the crisis, "Tsumatra?" Reuters, BBC, and CSNBC already had reporters in-country interviewing Sumatran citizens.

"The stage is set," Neville said.

"Indeed," Soter said. "The world will be watching."

The two men soaked in dribble from the arguing pundits for another minute. Soter marveled at the interconnectivity of the world. Technology had created a global consciousness. CNN had even brought in a New York University linguistics professor to decipher the words, syntax, and diction he had used in the letter.

Soter turned to Neville. "Nine days will come quick. The morning of the earthquake, I want you to call the BBC headquarters in Athens.

I want a news crew out here by six for my first interview. Redbeard will pick them up at the airport."

"Yes, sir," Neville said.

"Until then, keep analyzing the map. If the predicted time of the tsunami changes by more than one minute, I want an immediate update. I have to prepare my speech." Soter exited the library.

Half an hour later, Neville walked down the hallway toward the flight of stairs to the holding cell. He held a folded pile of clothes. He untied his tie, folded it neatly, and placed it into the center of the stack. Then the doctor walked down the stairs. The two Corsairs guarding the door stood up.

"No visitors," one Corsair said.

"Very well. Can you just give them a fresh change of clothes," Neville said.

The Corsairs unfolded all the clothes and searched every pocket and seam for anything suspicious. The tie fell out of the stack and to the concrete floor. Neville's jaw tightened, but he held his composure.

The Corsairs nodded to each other and unlocked the door.

When they heard the door open, Isaac hid Soter's report under his cot, and Rachel slid the filed pipe into her hiking boot. They were relieved when they saw arms and legs of empty clothes float into the room. Isaac got up and brought them to the table.

"You got some scrubs," Isaac said, holding up the green medical top and bottom.

"What else did he send?" Rachel asked.

Isaac sorted through the rest—black slacks, a white dress shirt, and a black tie. He searched all the pockets, but didn't find any messages.

"Why would he give you dress clothes?" Rachel asked.

"It's probably all he has," Isaac said. "It's what he wears under his lab coats."

Rachel surveyed all the clothes spread across the table. "That tie is wrinkled," she said. "The rest of the clothes aren't."

Isaac picked up the black tie and examined the small wrinkles. He laid it flat on the table and ran his hands down both ends. Nothing. He turned it over and inserted his fingers into the opening in the back.

"I feel something," he said. He came out with a small roll of paper. He carefully unfolded it as his mother leaned over his shoulder. It was hundreds of 0's and I's.

"What is it?"

"Binary code," Isaac said. "Any amateur hacker knows it. Give me a few minutes."

Six minutes later, he had translated Neville's message. He held it up for his mother to read quietly.

"Soter has a BBC news crew coming September 14, 6:00 p.m.," Rachel read. "Best chance to escape. More updates to follow."

CHAPTER 30:

THE NINE OF CLUBS

GREEK ISLES

"This still sounds like the beginning of a pirate joke, you know," Jack said. He stood at the helm of the Westwind 38 they had rented from a Maltese sailor. "A drunk, an orphan, and a one-armed man are on a boat..."

It was twilight, and the western glow provided just enough light for Olney to point out the approaching island of Thera. "The big one shaped like an inverted C is Thera," Olney said tracing the distant outline with his fingers. "The little one in the center is Nea Kameni. It's still an active volcano."

"Active?" Zahra asked.

"Oh, don't worry," Olney said. "It erupted in 1956, and won't again for a very long time. I wish we could have arrived during the day. We could have done some sightseeing."

"Shove it, Daddy Warbucks," Jack said. "It's called reconnaissance. We need to keep a low profile, so that means no sightseeing and no musical numbers with little Orphan Annie. Soter will have eyes everywhere."

"Aye, aye, Captain Jack," Olney said in a mocking voice. He elbowed Zahra, making her smile.

"You don't ever have to worry about me wanting to sing," she said.

The sailboat drifted into a small port outside the city of Thera's main harbor. Jack pulled into a dock manned by a middle-aged Greek man smoking a cigarette and listening to hard-hitting techno. The Greek man waved them in and pointed to an open slip. He wore white Pumas, skintight jeans, sunglasses on his head, and a tight polo shirt that accentuated his round beer belly.

"Look at this Eurotrash," Jack said quietly. "He's got the chest of a twelve-year-old girl."

The man flipped his cigarette into the ocean and caught their boat. Jack's teeth clenched when he heard him wheezing. The fat Greek man grabbed a rope to tie their boat to the dock.

"Slow down there, Adonis," Jack said over the blaring techno. "How much is the fee?"

"One hundred twenty Euros a night," the man said, followed by an asthmatic smoker's cough.

"Does that come with buxom Greek goddesses feeding me grapes?" Jack asked, distracted by the music.

"Yes. I find you super-fun-time party girls, but that costs extra," the man said, lighting another cigarette and bopping his head to the electronic beat. Jack couldn't hear himself think. He stepped off the boat and turned the radio dial down.

"It sounds like bloody robots raping each other."

The man was not happy that Jack had turned off his techno. He glared at him through the smoke that curled from his cigarette.

"Listen, I'll give you cash up front," Jack said, holding out the bills. "Eighty a night for five nights."

The man grabbed the money and counted it. "Deal," he said, turning his music back on.

"Use that to go buy a shirt from the men's department," Jack yelled over the radio.

The man ignored him. Zahra jumped off the boat and helped pull Olney onto the dock.

"What about your luggage, Ebenezer?" Jack asked.

Olney and Zahra walked down the pier, and he called back to Jack. "We made a deal. I buy and you fly. Pay someone to bring it up, Mr. Cratchit. Meet you at the top."

"Bloody geezer," Jack said as he rolled his eyes and looked up the island. A sheer-faced cliff climbed a hundred meters to the whitewashed village above. It was going to be a nightmare getting eight bags and two chests up the zigzagging trail. Jack looked at the Eurotrash texting on his phone.

"Hey, blowhole, how do I get up there with our bags?" Jack asked.

"Too late for taxi," the man said. "Get a donkey."

Jack did two trips from the boat to the base of the cliff, cursing the entire time. He found a young boy who had two donkeys. He paid him thirty euros, and they piled all eight bags and one chest on top of the decrepit animals. Jack had to carry the remaining chest by himself. He guessed it weighed over forty kilos. He could hear metal and glass jars clinking around and wondered what the kooky old man had him lugging.

It took twenty-five minutes to climb the mountain. Jack's biceps burned, and he stepped in donkey shit twice. He was dripping sweat, so he wrapped his shirt around his head. They had to stop three times to refasten a fallen suitcase. Jack's only solace was imagining the arthritic man hobbling up the steep trail.

At the top, he threw the chest down and doubled over. It was a semi-crowded street with outdoor cafés and tourist taverns. The donkey boy quickly unloaded his animals while Jack bent over to catch his breath.

"What took you so long?" Zahra asked.

Jack looked up. She sat on a bench with Professor Olney, and they both had gelato cups. Olney had been napping and jumped awake, almost dropping his empty cup.

"How the hell did you get up here so fast?" Jack asked, interlocking his hands over his head and still breathing hard.

"The gondola," Olney said, pointing to their right.

Jack looked. At the end of the street, he saw a gondola taking people up and down the face of the cliff.

"Eurotrash bastard!" Jack said. He looked over to take it out on donkey boy, but he was already halfway down the street making a get-away.

"Did you carry those all the way up?" Olney asked, trying not to laugh.

"I don't want to talk about it," Jack said putting his shirt back on. He looked across the street to the scooter rental shop. "We've got to move. Wait here."

Olney tried to sneak a scoop of Zahra's gelato, but she slapped his hand away.

Ten minutes later, Jack had two rented scooters with small trailers for their bags.

"There are not as many people on the other side of the island," Jack said holding up a piece of paper. "The kid inside gave me the name for a good local place to stay in Perissa."

"Known for its black-sand beaches," Olney said to Zahra.

Jack loaded the bags into the trailers and strapped them down. "Zahra, you come with me," Jack said as he handed them motorcycle helmets. "Professor, take the other scooter."

"Um, Jack?" Olney said, holding up his metal hook. "Might be a bit of a problem."

Fifteen minutes later, both scooters rode up and over the summit. The roads were empty, and the cool air hit Zahra's face through her open visor. She felt the vibration from the engine running through her body and tickling her inner thighs. She looked over at Professor Olney, who gave her a thumbs-up from the back of Jack's scooter.

"You're doing great!" Olney yelled.

Jack shook his head. Zahra had learned to drive a boat on her own, so Jack's rundown made the scooter fairly easy.

The professor wrapped his good arm around his reluctant scooter buddy and pointed his claw over the cliff. Zahra swung her head. The moon's reflection on the water looked like the yellow brick road. Zahra had done more and seen more in one week than she had in the sixteen years previously. She didn't know what lay ahead of them, but she took a moment to soak in the panoramic view.

Jack interrupted her gaze with a loud yell. "You can trot, little girl, but let's see if you can gallop." He pulled back the throttle, and the scooter zoomed forward on the dark road.

"Whoo-hoo!" Olney yelled.

Zahra loved that about Jack. He called her "little girl," but he never treated her like one. She'd made a promise to keep up, and he was going to hold her to it. Zahra loosened her fingers and then pulled back on her throttle.

They weaved down the eastern coast of the island and into Perissa. Jack pulled down an alley off the main street and turned off his scooter. The gray stone building had a yellow, carved sign that read, "The Sphinx."

"Stay with the bags, Galileo," Jack said as he motioned for Zahra to join him.

The lobby was simple but beautifully decorated with Egyptian pottery. Reds, yellows, and blacks accentuated the room, which contrasted with the white-and-blue combo synonymous with the Greek isles.

"Two rooms, no cards, no names, cash up front," Jack said as he peeled a fifty off his stack and handed it to the young Greek desk clerk. Then he handed her a few hundred euros for the rooms.

"Excellent, I think some of our suites just opened up," the Greek girl said, tucking the bill into her breast pocket.

Zahra watched as a group of tourists came down the stairs with cocktails and walked out to the crowded courtyard. She overheard two men talking about a singer.

The Greek girl handed them two keys and said, "I will have someone carry your bags up. If you want to eat or drink, our dinner show is starting right now."

Jack looked out the lobby windows to the courtyard as red lights came on and the small audience clapped. A low Egyptian horn filled the courtyard, followed by the high strings of a harp.

"We'll have some food sent up," Jack said, turning away. "I quit drinking, and we've had a long day."

He started to walk away when a low, seductive female voice floated off the stage. Jack stopped dead in his tracks. He turned around like he was in a trance. Zahra watched him walk wide-eyed back to the door of the courtyard. He opened it and stared onto the stage. Zahra sneaked up behind him to see what he was looking at.

In front of the musicians, there was a woman wearing a sheer hooded white Egyptian robe. Using both hands, she stretched out a flaming arrow on a massive wooden bow. She aimed it upward, toward the heavens, and then gracefully lowered the tip of the arrow to her lips. Silence fell over the audience. The flame lit her face and revealed the lines of her Eastern-European bone structure. The band's crescendo slowly built, and the woman rhythmically swayed with the tiptoeing horn. Without warning, she sprayed a fluid out of her mouth and a ball of fire erupted over the gasping audience. The singer grabbed the flaming arrow, dropped her robe, and slid right into a seductive belly-dancing routine.

The woman reminded Zahra of how Cleopatra was always described—not a striking beauty but surrounded by an unexplainable aura of seductive charm. Zahra tilted her head, like a snake charmer was hypnotizing her. Her voice was mesmerizing, and the way she moved her body was serpentine.

Zahra stared ahead but nudged Jack. "Who is it?"

Jack didn't blink. He couldn't take his eyes off the performer, who held the entire crowd in a fixed stare.

"It's my ex-girlfriend," he said.

CHAPTER 31:
THE NINE OF DIAMONDS

SOTER'S COMPOUND
THERA, GREECE

Redbeard rushed into the holding cell with two Corsairs. It was nine o'clock, and Isaac was reading *The Canterbury Tales* to his mother. Redbeard pointed to Rachel and said, "Come with me."

"You're not taking her," Isaac said as he stood and attempted his most intimidating stance. Redbeard and the Corsairs chuckled.

"Are you going to sulk me to death?" Redbeard asked. "He just wants to talk."

Isaac was sick of being belittled. He stood firm and clenched his fist.

Rachel got up from her cot. "This Turk is a killer, but he isn't a liar."

"Don't do this. *Please.*"

Rachel grabbed his face. "You have my word. Nothing will happen."

Isaac knew that it was impossible to argue. She was Jack's little sister, and they had liters of stubborn running through their veins.

"Be careful," Isaac said.

Rachel walked out of the holding cell with the Corsairs in step. They led her through Soter's elegant hallways, and she eyed the Greek armor on the walls. She wished that she had one of those swords and not just the sharpened pipe in her boot.

They made their way up a marble staircase and opened the door to Soter's private library. He sat at his desk writing his speech. Neville sat cross-legged with a traveling doctor's bag next to him. Rachel examined the electronic mosaic on his wall.

"The nine muses of Greek mythology," Soter said. "They're helping me write my speech."

"Are you including the part about being a mass murderer, or is that in the footnotes?" Rachel asked.

"Have you thought about our agreement?" Soter said. "I have."

"I'm not comfortable discussing it in front of your lackeys," Rachel said.

Rachel could feel the sharpened rod digging into the side of her foot. If she had any chance of killing him, she had to do it alone. She just hoped the others would have mercy on Isaac.

"This is just a business transaction. I don't hide anything from these men," Soter said.

"I will *never* forgive you for what you did," Rachel said, "but I want my son to get out of here alive."

"I can assume that your lack of a *no is yes*," Soter said. "Sit down."

Rachel sat in the chair across from him and wondered how quickly she could grab her metal spike and lunge across the desk. But then she remembered how fast Soter had been when she'd tried to hit him with the boat oar.

"I want your word that we will be released alive," Rachel said as Neville knelt beside her.

"I've already told you that I am a man of my word," Soter said. "Once I get my heir, you and your son are free to go. But if you threaten to expose me, you will be eliminated by one of these men," Soter motioned toward his Corsairs.

Neville rolled up Rachel's sleeve, rubbed an anesthetic wipe on her arm, and gave her an injection.

"What was that?" Rachel asked him.

"Urofollitropin," the doctor said, pulling out another syringe.

"Fertility drugs?" Rachel asked as Neville tied her arm off and drew a blood sample. "For someone that claims to be *one with nature*, this is quite contradictory."

"Just improving the odds," Soter said. "I've also done the math. From conception to birth, it is two hundred and sixty-six days. That puts the day of birth in the first week of June and makes it highly probable that he will be born under a royal card."

"What if it's a girl?" Rachel asked as Neville untied the wrap on her arm and examined the syringe.

"It won't be," Soter said. "I've accounted for that."

Rachel rubbed her arm. There was no telling what else Neville had just injected her with.

"One more condition," Rachel said, plotting her assassination. "These men can't be in the room."

"I wasn't planning on it," Soter looked to the Corsairs. "Take her back down. I have to finish my speech."

The two Corsairs grabbed Rachel underneath the arms and led her away.

Soter motioned for Redbeard to come closer. The Turk leaned over the desk, and Soter said, "The night of the tsunami, pump her full of opium and bring her up to my bedroom."

Neville overheard Soter's demand as he packed his medical bag.

"And what if the boy tries something?" Redbeard asked.

Soter smirked and said, "Cut one of his fingers off and watch him sob like a girl."

Redbeard nodded and exited.

CHAPTER 32:
THE NINE OF SPADES

THE SPHINX HOTEL
THERA, GREECE

Jack, Olney, and Zahra watched the rest of Maia's set from a candlelit table in the back of the courtyard. Her first song was a slow, flute-driven ballad, and the next three were percussion instrumentals. Maia slithered between the tables hypnotizing the married men with the fluid motion of her hips. Patrons clapped and took shots of ouzo as Maia tastefully dropped articles of clothing. She spotted Jack halfway through her set but never broke stride. The band finished with a long instrumental as Maia vibrated her hips in a rhythmic seizure. Her dark skin glistened with perspiration.

The song abruptly ended, and the lights went out. When the lights came back on, Maia was not on stage. The courtyard floodlights came on, and waiters appeared with the second course of their five-course feast.

"My God. I can see why she was hard to forget," Olney said. Jack shot him a death glare.

"Where did she go?" Zahra asked. She was just as mesmerized as the crowd. She had never seen a woman so beautifully sensual and in control of her body.

Jack was about to speak when a figure wearing a long hooded robe appeared to their right.

"How did you find me?" Maia asked, her face hidden inside the hood.

"Not on purpose," Jack said. "Trust me."

"You just happened to be on *this* island and walk into *this* hotel," Maia said. "You're trained to find people. Don't lie to me."

"You're right," Jack said. "The little girl is my demolitions expert, and the one-armed man is my sniper. We're looking for a con artist moonlighting as a belly dancer. Have you seen anyone that fits that description?"

"Who are you?" Maia asked Olney and Zahra.

Zahra and Olney shared a quick, nonverbal exchange and agreed to stay neutral. "Long story," Olney said. Zahra nodded.

"What do you want?" Maia said. "I can't have my ex-boyfriend punching people at my work."

"Who says I wanted to punch anyone?" Jack said.

"Lying doesn't suit you," Maia said. "How many of these people do you want to punch?"

Jack lowered his head. Zahra had never seen him look so flustered. She kind of enjoyed it.

"I don't want to punch anyone," Jack said.

"We dated for three *long* years," Maia said, crossing her arms. "Don't insult me."

Jack sighed and gave in. "Fine. Four people," he said while pointing to each man in the crowded courtyard. "The British dildo in the pink polo who made a sexual comment, the waiter with the pencil-thin moustache who came out to stare at you when he could have been on a break, the Eastern-European guy who tried to put euros in your skirt, and your barefoot horn player, just because I don't like his fat, fucking face."

"This is why I left," Maia said. "You're hardwired for violence. You search for it."

"I'm getting better," Jack said. "Remember when you made me quit punching people for Lent? I went the whole forty days."

Maia looked to Zahra and Olney. "I don't know who you two are, but you should run from him."

Jack lowered his head in defeat. Zahra could tell that he had no response.

"I have a second set in a few minutes," Maia said to Jack. "You need to *not* be here, or I'll get fired."

"Why did you leave me?" Jack asked, suddenly broken.

Maia shook her head and started walking away.

"Horus was killed," Zahra blurted.

Maia stopped in her tracks and turned to face them. "What happened?"

Zahra looked at Jack and Olney and realized she had to finish what she started. "Jack's sister has been kidnapped by a man who lives on this island. His men killed Horus and tried to kill us."

"Ptolemy Soter," Olney said.

Maia's face went white when she heard the name.

"Keep your voice down!" Maia looked around to make sure no one had heard. "Go upstairs, and wait for me," she said as she walked away.

An hour later, Professor Olney and Zahra were sprawled out on two separate double beds in their hotel room. Their open Venetian blinds welcomed a cool ocean breeze. They'd ordered room service—Greek salads, eggplant moussaka, and honey yogurt. They ate and listened to the muffled argument coming from Jack and Maia in the next room. They clearly heard loud, one-word insults but couldn't decipher full sentences.

Olney burped and tried to blow it out of the side of his mouth. Unfortunately, the smell was swept up by the breeze and blown right in Zahra's direction. She buried her face in her pillow.

"I'm sorry, love. Too many onions in my salad," Olney said, laughing. "An alchemist of all people should know the potency of lethal gases."

The arguing died down after a half hour, and it sounded like civil conversation vibrating through the thin walls. Olney was scraping up the last bits of his honey yogurt when they heard a loud crash come from next door. They both sat up in their beds.

"Are they fighting?" Zahra asked.

Olney turned and put his ear to the wall. Then he heard contents being swiped off a table and a shirt being ripped open. Olney realized what was about to happen. It definitely started with an "f" and ended with a "g," but it wasn't fighting. He scanned the room for something to switch on so Zahra wouldn't have to listen. The rooms didn't have a radio or a television, so he jumped out of bed.

"Up you go. How about a walk?" Olney suggested as he tried to mask the noise by singing the first song that popped into his head. *"Penny Lane is in my ears and in my eyes."*

"We need to break them up," Zahra said, cutting him off, still thinking it was a physical altercation.

Olney tried to usher her out the door while singing, *"Four of fish and finger pies."*

Zahra brushed the professor off, opened the door to the deck, and was about to climb over when she heard Maia laughing uncontrollably. Zahra realized what was happening and came back inside.

"They weren't fighting," she said.

"No, I'm afraid not," Olney said.

Maia fell to the ground she was laughing so hard. They could hear through the open deck as Jack tried to defend himself.

Five minutes later, Jack and Maia came into their room, all business.

"Maia knows where Soter lives," Jack said. "If I tried to get you two to stay here, would you listen to me?"

"No," Zahra and Olney said in unison.

"Let's go then," Jack said as they jumped up.

Zahra and Maia walked down the hallway together. Olney whispered to Jack. "It's all right, mate. It happens, even to men like you."

"Yeah, but this one was *devastating.*"

"I know," Olney said. "It's not easy when they laugh at you, either."

They made it to a staircase, and Olney stopped Jack. "You know, I have a Chinese root in one of my bags that will prevent this from happening," he said. "I've been happily impotent since the sixties, so I don't need it."

"What in the queen's testicles are you talking about, old man?" Jack asked.

"I heard what happened. You had a false start? Your horse left the gate early? Your rifle misfired? It's all right, I can help you." Olney elbowed him in the side. "With hips like that, I don't blame you."

Jack's eyebrows shot up when he figured it out. He roared with laughter. "You thought I...no way!" Jack said trying to curb his laughter. "We were *about* to, but then she ripped my shirt off and saw my tattoo." Jack rolled up his sleeve to reveal the Romani wheel tattoo with Maia's name. "I got it the day after she left me; she thought it was the dumbest thing I have ever done." He slapped the embarrassed professor on the back.

They continued down the flight of stairs. "Well, you could see how I could have arrived at that conclusion," Olney said as Jack continued laughing.

They came out into the alleyway where their scooters were parked. Zahra and Maia already sat together on one.

Jack looked upset. "Why don't you ride with me?" he asked Maia.

"I'll take my chances with Zahra," Maia said. "Besides, you two make a better couple. Follow us, and turn your headlights off when we get close."

Maia nodded to Zahra, who accelerated down the alley. They turned right and headed out of the town.

It was thirteen kilometers to Soter's compound on the southwestern peninsula of Thera. Both scooters merged onto the empty road. It was almost midnight, and everyone was either sleeping or drinking.

Maia leaned in close and comfortably nestled her chin into Zahra's shoulder. They rode for a moment in silence, their bodies vibrating together. Zahra couldn't explain it. She wasn't attracted to Maia. It was like magnetism. She was fascinated by her. Maia was strong and confident but also overtly feminine. Zahra had repressed every ounce of her sexuality in order to survive, but she felt like the woman she had just met was pulling it out of her.

"Jack told me what you had to do to get to Gibraltar," Maia said.

"I wouldn't be alive if it wasn't for David and Rachel," Zahra said.

"Jack will never compliment you to your face, but you always find out how much he cares about you through other people," Maia said in her soothing, velvet voice. "I know you just met him, but he cares deeply for you, just like he does for his sister."

It was reassuring to Zahra, but she was more concerned with impressing Maia.

"Don't feel the need to speak," Maia said with both of her arms wrapped around Zahra. "I know you haven't had a lot of strong women in your life, but that's going to change."

It was like Maia could read her thoughts. All of the horrible things that had happened to her—an abusive father, a fearful mother, escaping from her husband, living on the streets, and the last week of near-death experiences—seemed as distant as the stars above, just small specks on her blank canvas. She felt a calm sensation rush through her body. She knew that she could say or do anything and Maia would not judge her.

"Why did you leave him?" Zahra asked over the hum of the scooter's engine.

Maia leaned and talked into Zahra's ear. "Right man. Wrong time. I live my life by the cards. They put me where I need to be. Tonight wasn't an accident."

Zahra agreed. She saw a bright future ahead for all of them. Unfortunately, one of the most powerful men in the world stood in their way.

"He also snores like a bear," Maia said as they coasted down the dark road. Zahra smiled.

CHAPTER 33:
THE TEN OF HEARTS

THERA, GREECE

Jack, Maia, Olney, and Zahra hid their scooters and sneaked through five hundred meters of sagebrush. The waxing moon provided just enough light to prevent ankle injuries on the rocks.

Jack told them to army-crawl up to a large group of boulders. He was surprised when he didn't hear one gripe from Olney. They were 150 meters from Soter's compound. It was surrounded by a wall with an iron gate that opened into a garden.

"It looks like the National Archaeological Museum in Athens," Olney said.

"Shut your hole," Jack said as he took out a pair of binoculars. "Spells and fruity potions are your world, but rescue ops are mine."

"Yes, sir, General, sir," Olney said sarcastically.

Pairs of Turkish Corsairs guarded all the entry points. Jack counted twelve in the courtyard and wasn't sure how many were inside. The only thing that could be interpreted as good news was none of the Corsairs were armed with guns. Swords seemed to be their weapon of choice.

"Are they cloning those bearded turds?" Jack asked, looking through the binoculars.

Zahra climbed up and lay on the boulder to get a better view. It was still holding the warmth from the sun, and it felt good on her skin. She watched as the Corsairs patrolled the compound.

"Mmmmm," Jack moaned.

"What?" Maia asked quietly.

"Just imagining what I could do with a .50 caliber, semiauto, Barret M-82 with night optics." Jack made quiet shooting noises followed by entry-point sound effects.

"So violent," Maia said.

"Sorry, love, this situation calls for it." Jack looked down from his binoculars. "Get comfortable, gang. We're going to see how long the bad guys stay up."

An hour later, most of the Corsairs had entered the compound. Two of them stood guard at the gates, smoking cigarettes. Zahra lay next to Jack on the boulder. Her eyesight was amazing, and she pointed out movement all over. Jack thought she would have made an excellent sniper spotter.

"I can get in, you know," Zahra said.

"Can't risk it, Z," Jack said. "They think we're dead. The element of surprise is our only advantage."

"They will not see me," Zahra said.

"What do we gain by breaking in?" Jack asked.

"They think we are dead," Zahra said. "We need to tell them that we are coming, so they don't try to escape. We also need to know if they are still alive."

Jack knew she was right. A rescue operation with no one to rescue was a suicide mission. He'd been wrong on his last few decisions, but it felt insane to let a sixteen-year-old girl break into a compound guarded by assassins. Olney and Maia crawled up the boulder.

"What's going on?" Olney asked quietly.

"Zahra wants to break in," Jack said.

"Alone," Zahra said.

"Remember how you said fruity potions is my world and military operations is yours?" Olney asked. "Well, this is Zahra's. If she says she can sneak in, I believe her."

"Even if she gets caught, she can get word to Isaac and Rachel that we are coming for them," Maia said.

"How would you do it?" Jack asked.

"Olive tree on the far left side," Zahra said as Jack viewed it through the binoculars. "It's dark. I could jump down."

"Prove me wrong, little one," Jack said, surrendering.

"Hand me your scarf," Zahra said to Maia. Maia quickly passed the item to her.

Jack handed her his military watch, and she put it on. It was 1:31 a.m.

"If you're not back in one hour, I'm coming for you," Jack said.

"Fearless, that one," Olney said as Zahra scaled down the boulders.

From years of breaking into homes, Zahra knew how to be light on her feet. She strode across the parched earth as soundless as the nocturnal animals around her. Years of running in high mountain air had also built up her red blood cells. Her lungs could go for miles at sea level. Within a hundred meters of the wall, she crouched and quickly maneuvered from bush to bush.

Zahra reached the wall and ran up the base of the olive tree like a macaque. As she ascended, the lush garden courtyard came into view. At the gate to her left were two Corsairs rolling cigarettes. She took Maia's long scarf off her neck and tied it to a branch that hung over the other side of the wall. David had taught her how to tie a timber-hitch knot, because their camp had frequent windstorms that could blow the tents away. She pulled tight on the knot and used the scarf to repel down.

She landed on the balls of her feet and balanced herself with the tips of her fingers. The courtyard was much lighter, so she took a moment to scan for dark spots and security cameras. For thieves, getting in was the easy part, but getting out undetected was more important.

Zahra plotted her route and dashed across the courtyard. Statues, fountains, and purple gardens of iris helped hide her. She reached the wall of the compound and leaned against it. The front door to her right would be too dangerous, but she noticed small rectangular windows along the base of the building. She followed them up the eastern face of the compound looking for one that was cracked open.

Windows on the northern side of the compound faced the court-yard, so Zahra crawled through the dirt. She rounded the corner to the far western face of the compound and saw a soft light glowing through one of the windows. Her abs and inner thighs burned as she crawled through the flowerbeds.

Zahra peeked into the window and saw a pair of feet propped up in bed. She didn't have an angle good enough to see who it was.

Suddenly, a black journal was opened on the person's legs, and a hand started sketching a mechanical drawing. It was Isaac. *Thank God he never sleeps!*

Zahra crawled out further to make sure there were no Corsairs and then lightly knocked. Isaac didn't hear, so she knocked a little louder. He stopped drawing, spun in his bed, and whipped his head up toward the window. She almost laughed when she saw he was wearing slacks and a tie in his bed.

Isaac immediately put his index finger to his mouth, telling her to be quiet. Then he pointed to the door and used the same finger to make a unibrow. Zahra smiled and made a mental note to remind Jack that they had a new call sign for the Corsairs. Isaac walked toward the window and quietly woke Rachel. From her vantage point, Zahra couldn't see the cot under the window, so she assumed David was there.

Rachel almost cried when she saw Zahra's green eyes through the small window. She mouthed the word "Jack." Zahra nodded and pointed back toward their hiding spot. Rachel hugged her son.

Isaac held up his index finger, signaling Zahra to hold still. Then he piled a stack of fiction books onto a footstool. He ripped out a piece of paper from his journal and quietly opened the window. Isaac handed Zahra a pen and paper through the small crack.

She wrote, "We are coming to get you." Then she handed the note through the crack.

Isaac read it and wrote, "Soter has predicted that there will be a tsunami tomorrow at 4:25 p.m. in Sumatra. A news crew is coming into the airport at 5:00 p.m. Pull a Trojan Horse. Tell Jack, Soter killed my dad. We need to stop him."

Zahra read the note. She covered her eyes and cried when she found out David had been killed. She checked her watch and saw that she only had fifteen minutes to get back.

Back at the boulders, Maia and Jack watched for Zahra. Jack checked Olney's pocket watch while the professor used a moleskin notebook to sketch a detailed map of the compound.

"She's got four minutes," Jack said to Maia. "If she's not back, take Olney back and wait."

"No need," a voice said from behind them.

It startled Olney, and Jack quickly shot his thick hand over the professor's mouth. They turned around.

"Isaac and Rachel are both alive. David has been killed," Zahra said, handing Jack the note.

Jack removed his palm from Olney's face and read the note. "Moment of silence for a truly great man," he said as the group bowed their heads.

A moment passed and Jack said, "We grieve later. Revenge first. Isaac's plan is solid, but they already know what we look like."

"I have Romani brothers on the island," Maia said. "Soter's family is no friend to the Gypsies."

"Are you sure we can trust them?" Jack asked.

"As long as you don't mind them stealing a few things on the way out," Maia said.

"Not at all, but we've got a lot to plan," Jack said, getting up.

"I will go with Zahra," Maia said as she climbed down and grabbed Zahra's hand.

"Goddamn it!" Jack said.

"Good, I wanted to run some rescue plans by you," Olney said, walking after Jack.

"Shut it, old man. I just lost my brother-in-law," Jack said.

"But I made a map," Olney said, holding it up.

Jack snatched it from his hands without even looking, and the group walked back toward their scooters.

CHAPTER 34:

THE TEN OF CLUBS

SOTER'S LABORATORY
THERA, GREECE

Ptolemy Soter shut down the world.

The wall of monitors displayed over a dozen live broadcasts from Sumatra. His prediction was going to be one of the most ground-breaking scientific achievements of all time. He was a few hours away from a live television reveal that would crash Google's servers and send the world into an unparalleled frenzy.

It was one thing to watch the aftermath of Hurricane Katrina or the Haitian earthquake; it was something entirely different to watch it happen in real-time.

Soter watched screen shots—day traders in London sat motionless, students in China crowded around laptops watching live news feeds, Sumatrans evacuated the coasts, and Americans watched, in high definition, as their favorite adventure-seeking reporters hung out of helicopters. A poll popped up on the BBC stating that 84 percent of people thought that nothing would happen. But underneath the cynicism, he knew they were desperately hoping for a savior.

Soter took his eyes away for a split second and turned to Neville. "The news crew?"

"Your plane has landed in Athens. They will be boarding shortly," Neville said.

"And what did you tell them?" Soter asked.

"That we had information on the tsunami prediction but couldn't disclose all of the details until they were cleared by our security team," Neville said.

"Excellent. There can be no variables today," Soter said, checking his watch. The time was 4:13 p.m.—twelve minutes until the earthquake.

Soter watched the news helicopters over the hotels. Professional and amateur videographers lined the rooftops and balconies to document the event. Eight minutes remained. An aerial shot showed poor people pulling rickshaws and carrying their belongings away from the coast.

Six minutes. An NBC news helicopter dropped down and spotted two blond surfers paddling out. It zoomed in, and the surfers gave the hang-loose hand sign. Soter grinned. It was going to be the last wave of their useless lives, but he commended them for their bravery.

Two minutes. Soter bowed his head and breathed deeply. *This is your time,* he thought to himself. *Make your family proud.*

One minute.

"Bring up the map on half of the screens," Soter said to Neville.

The doctor quickly reprogrammed the monitors to a hybrid of live news and interactive map. The fault lines off the coast of Sumatra glowed red. A timer appeared in the top right of the map. Soter watched the red numbers count down. Everything in his life had led to this ticking clock. *Thirty seconds. Fifteen seconds. Ten seconds. Five. Four. Three. Two. One.*

Nothing.

A few seconds passed. Soter's skin crawled. The fault lines on the map continued to glow, but nothing happened. His stomach churned, and if he had eaten anything that day, he would have regurgitated it on the floor.

"What's happening?" Soter asked. Neville had never seen him so frightened.

The doctor examined the live seismic waves on his computer monitor, but there was no quake. Another minute passed, and the global news networks labeled it a hoax and publicity stunt. Soter felt his life spiraling down. There was nothing he could do pull it back up.

And that's when it hit.

Neville's seismic readings skyrocketed. He screamed, "It's huge!"

Soter watched the map as the two red fault lines went from a bright glow to a flashing red.

"Nine point four on the Richter!" Neville said, inches away from his monitor.

BBC reported it first, and then other networks followed seconds after. They cut between in-studio Richter scales and live shots. The quake shook the entire island.

Soter watched the screens as hotels caved in and stories collapsed into each other. Entire slum villages folded like they were made of cards. People who had dared to remain near the coast sprinted over each other toward safety. Crumbling buildings shot out clouds of dust. The quake lasted exactly seventy-two seconds and laid destruction to anything that was not built in the previous decade.

"No one will ever doubt me again," Soter said to himself, a smile curling his lips.

After ten minutes of earthquake carnage, the news cameras focused on the coastline. The ocean looked like it was being sucked into itself. Hundreds of meters of coastline appeared.

"The tsunami is coming," Neville said, eyeing his monitors. "It's big."

Soter watched the aerial view of the coastline as a cameraman tracked the receding water to his feet and then scrambled to the other side of the helicopter door to pick up the shot. When he panned upward and focused, a massive tidal wave headed right at them. It was traveling at three hundred miles an hour and gathered height as it hit the upward slope of the island's landmass.

Soter shifted his focus to the blue wave on the computer screen as it rippled out toward the Bay of Bengal, Southern Indonesia, and the northwestern coast of Australia. Then he whipped back to the live video coverage.

The tsunami was over ten stories tall. One cameraman on the ground got a shot of the crest forming as dozens of scared people rushed past him. The wave surged underneath the news helicopters; some of them had to climb at the last second. There were dozens of views to choose from as the helicopters filmed the back of the wave rip through the city.

It shredded through the coastal cafés and beach bars. It ripped buildings apart, swept up the debris, and then used it like battering rams. It uprooted palm trees and tossed cars like they were toys. The wave destroyed four high-rise hotels like sand castles. It wrapped around the crumbling buildings, fingering into the streets below.

There were hundreds of casualties, but most people had retreated inland. Soter had saved tens of thousands of lives. If the beachfront cafés, open-air markets, and hotels had been full of people, it would have been a catastrophe on par with the 2004 Indian Ocean tsunami.

"We just changed the world, Mr. Soter," Neville said in astonishment.

"It will never be the same again," Soter said.

As the water died down to a nonviolent level, the global news network reported tsunami warnings in Southern Indonesia and Sri Lanka. Then the networks went into split-screen mode. They showed live footage of people in Sumatra trapped on rooftops, while pundits recanted their doubts of the prediction.

The arguing newscasters became overwhelming, and Soter turned to Neville. "I've seen enough. The rest of it will just be opinionated lackeys trying to keep their jobs."

Neville brought the map back to full screen as the tsunami waves spread across Southeast Asia.

"We have the ability to broadcast from the island, correct?" Soter asked.

Neville nodded. "The news crew is bringing a satellite that I will patch into my computers. We can send the signal out to all the major networks."

Soter eyed the doctor and then took his walkie-talkie off his belt. "Redbeard, take a few of your men and pick up the news crew," he said into the microphone. "They should be arriving on my plane shortly."

"Right away," Redbeard's voice crackled over the speaker.

Soter turned to Neville. "I'll be in my study, rehearsing my speech."

He exited the laboratory, and Neville turned the news back on.

A CNN anchor stood in front of hundreds of thousands of dollars' worth of touch-screen monitors, addressing the millions watching. "Technology is evolving faster than humanity. Today marks the first time in history that someone has *successfully* predicted the exact date, time, and location of a natural disaster. This man or woman has developed technology that can save hundreds of thousands of lives each year. The world would like to know who you are, so we can thank you."

CNN cut to Sumatran villagers crying and hugging each other. They looked to the sky and dropped in prayer. An unknown savior had prevented a catastrophic tragedy. To them, it was a miracle, an act of the divine. Neville realized that Soter was about to become one of the most powerful men in the world, and it terrified him.

CHAPTER 35:
THE TEN OF DIAMONDS

THERA AIRPORT

Jack whistled casually as he walked into the employee locker room at the Thera airport. One of the employees even waved back to him. Clandestine services had one rule—act like you're *supposed* to be there. Jack waited for the man to get into the shower and then clipped open a few lockers with a pocket-sized bolt cutter. He rummaged through and pulled out reflective vests, caps, and noise-cancelling earmuffs. He smelled two blue jumpsuits and kept the clean one for himself.

Minutes later, Jack was dressed in a full runway uniform and handed the second blue jumper to Olney. They hid behind storage containers on the tarmac as the lanky professor put it on.

"Jupiter's red spot, this smells like aftershave and onions," the professor said, gagging from the foul odor.

"Buck up, saggy tits. Did you put the food and water inside?"

"Indeed," Olney said, donning on his reflective vest and cap. "Can you quit with the nicknames?"

"No can do. We have shared a life-and-death experience. You're like a brother, now." Jack pulled out a small pair of binoculars and scanned the horizon. The small island airport was dead, and the majority of the flights had arrived already. In the distance, Jack spotted a Gulfstream jet banking toward the runway and then saw the Soter shipping logo on the tail.

"They're landing," Jack said. "Get ready."

The professor picked up his orange runway cones. Jack walked to the large storage bin and knocked twice on the sidewall. An identical knock came back a few seconds later.

"How do I look?" Olney asked with his arms out.

"Too old," Jack said as he pulled a black bandana and aviators out of his pocket. He handed them to the professor, and he quickly put them on.

"That's better," Jack said as Olney took the earmuffs around his neck and added them to his costume.

The professor could barely hear a thing. Jack got up in his face. He spoke loudly and clearly so the old man could hear him. "It's very important that you remember to—" Jack purposely finished the rest of his sentence with inaudible gibberish and then nodded and said, "Okay?"

Olney turned and lifted the earmuffs off. "What? What did you say?" he asked.

Jack shoved him and said, "Go! Go! They're landing."

Olney jogged a few meters away, and Jack yelled to him. He turned, and Jack shouted another set of imperative directions in gibberish.

"What? I can't hear you!" Olney said, again lifting his earmuffs.

"Go!" Jack yelled, pointing to the landing jet. Olney hurried down the tarmac to greet the plane.

Jack climbed to the top of the storage bin and looked out toward the ocean. Soter's rescued yacht waited at the dock directly off the airport grounds. He could see Redbeard on deck.

Jack jumped down onto a small luggage truck. He looked around, used a knife to bust open the paneling, and quickly hotwired it.

Olney walked directly in front of the plane and led it away from the main terminal and from Redbeard and his men. Olney made a cross with his cones, and the jet rolled to a stop. The engines died down, and the latch door opened, shooting down a small staircase. A beautiful Greek reporter stepped off the plane and adjusted her gray skirt. She was accompanied by one cameraman and one audio technician, who took a few moments to unload their cases of gear.

"Bonjour, madame," Jack said, screeching to a halt in his luggage truck. "I will be escorting you today."

"Where are we going?" the reporter asked.

"Oh, don't worry; it's not far," Jack said as he stepped out, put her bag on the back, and helped her step into the open-air vehicle. Olney jumped into the front seat, still wearing the bandana over his face.

Jack helped the cameraman and audio tech load up four large cases of audiovisual equipment, and then everyone jumped on board.

While the little luggage truck zipped across the tarmac, Jack played tour guide. "Welcome to the island. Thera, in ancient Greek, means *hot lava explosion*."

The cameraman and audio tech looked at Jack like he was a moron. The female reporter touched up her makeup and paid no attention.

"Many *crazy* old-man historians think that buried deep under this island are the remnants of the lost civilization of *Atlantis*," Jack said, rambling while Olney shook his head. "Whaddya think?"

"How much further?" the reporter asked. "My makeup is running."

"Almost there," Jack said as he rounded the corner into a jungle of storage bins.

Maia waited outside a large storage bin dressed like a reporter. Three Gypsy men were with her. Marko and Beznik were dressed like cameramen, and Milosh was dressed in plainclothes. Marko was bone thin and had a Franz Josef beard. Beznik was husky with a bald head and had a silver-capped premolar. Milosh looked passably normal, apart from the random array of Gypsy tattoos. *Not the best undercover agents*, Jack thought, *but Maia had vouched for all of them.* Jack pulled up a ramp and into the large storage bin.

"What is going on?" the reporter asked.

"Wallets, keys, and credentials in my hat," Jack said, taking off his cap and turning around.

The news crew thought they were being robbed and quickly unloaded their pockets. Marko grabbed their laminated press credentials and placed their own passport photos over them.

"Gypsies do IDs better than anyone," Marko said in a thick Eastern-European accent as he ran the credentials through a handheld laminate machine.

"All right, you three, up against the wall," Jack said as the news crew backed up.

Beznik and Marko lifted down a large audio case and opened it.

"You can't lock us in here!" the reporter said.

Jack took off his airport uniform, and Milosh put it on. Jack walked toward the reporter and addressed her in his best Bond-voice. "Ma'am, my name is Hunter Attenborough. MI6. This is a top-secret operation of *national* security. We will call the airport and tell them where you are in one hour," Jack said it with such confidence that they all believed him. Then he hopped into the large case. "There's fruit and water in the corner. Cheers."

Marko and Beznik covered him with wires. They closed the case. Then the three Gypsy men picked it up and loaded it onto the back of the luggage truck. Marko handed them their freshly laminated credentials, and Milosh jumped into the driver's seat. The luggage cart sped down the ramp and out into the sunlight.

"Get comfortable," Professor Olney said as they waved to the shocked news crew and closed the doors.

Maia could see the vague image of two Corsairs in the distance. They were being blurred by the heat waves radiating off the chemical-coated asphalt. Maia hoped Jack had enough air to breathe. The Corsairs opened the chain-link fence. They waved for Milosh to drive through and pointed down the road to the yacht.

The small luggage truck passed through the airport fence and onto public property. It headed down a steep road and approached the beautiful Oculus yacht that had been recovered in Tunisia. Redbeard stepped in front and put his palm up.

"Passes," he said. Maia, Beznik, and Marko handed them their press credentials and tried not to look the Turk directly in his eyes. Redbeard examined them and then handed them back. He turned to four other Corsairs and said, "Load these cases."

The entire group walked down the dock. The two Corsairs carrying the case containing Jack had to rest because it was so heavy. Redbeard circled back and pointed to the case.

"What is in there?" he asked.

"It's our satellite and a lot of audio cords," Maia said, remembering her rehearsal with Jack earlier.

Redbeard knelt down to open the case. Marko's and Beznik's eyes widened, and they looked like they were about to take off running.

"I will show you," Maia said as she briskly walked back down the dock. She purposely clipped her high heel on one of the raised boards and tripped forward. Redbeard bolted up and grabbed her around the waist, right as Maia was about to fall into the water. The strong Turkish man pulled her back onto the dock and into his chest. She smelled wonderful. Maia played up the theatrics and wrapped herself around him seductively.

"You just saved my *life*," Maia said.

"It is just water," Redbeard said, still holding Maia. She looked up into his vacant eyes and could tell he was completely inept with women.

"You don't understand," Maia said flirtatiously. "This story is going to launch my career, and I didn't think to bring a change of clothes." She let herself blush.

Redbeard attempted a grin and released her. Marko and Beznik silently exhaled.

Forty minutes later, Olney and Zahra watched the Oculus yacht docking at the cliffs below Soter's compound. They hid behind a group of rocks two hundred meters away from the fence.

"Everything is going as planned," Olney said.

They watched from a distance as Maia and her fake news crew walked up the steps to the compound. Olney had a brown leather backpack with him, and he placed his good hand inside.

"I have a present for you, my Zahra," Olney said.

"What is it?" she asked.

"A long time ago, I was a grad student at the Imperial College of London studying astronomy and organic chemistry," Olney said, pulling out a leather pouch. "I made rent money working for a pyrotechnics company that planned New Year's Eve celebrations." He reached inside and pulled out a quarter-stick of dynamite about the length of his palm. "Each one of these is filled with a nonlethal chemical compound that will knock someone out."

Olney handed over the pouch. Zahra ran it through her belt. It sat comfortably on her right hip.

"How did you make these?" Zahra asked, putting her hand inside and feeling over a dozen tightly wrapped explosives.

"It's why I brought all those cases," Olney said, handing her the lighter. "It was my alchemy equipment. What's the point of sneaking up on people if you aren't prepared?"

Zahra nodded and turned back to watch the Corsairs unload the cases. They were just waiting for Jack's sign.

CHAPTER 36:
THE TEN OF SPADES

SOTER'S COMPOUND
THERA, GREECE

Redbeard and three Corsairs led Maia, Marko, and Beznik into the library. The Gypsies scanned the elegant room for items to plunder while Maia marveled at the architecture.

"This is one of the most beautiful rooms I've ever seen," she said.

"It's an exact replica of the Library of Alexandria," Redbeard said, stopping in the middle of the library. "Set up here. My boss wants the cameras to face the windows overlooking the ocean."

The Corsairs placed the cases down, and Marko and Beznik pretended to set up the gear.

Redbeard pointed to two of his men. "You two, come with me." Then he pointed to the last one. "You stay here and watch them."

The last Corsair nodded while Redbeard exited with the other two. The remaining Turk backed up and watched them with his hand on his sword. It was apparent that Marko and Beznik had no idea what they were doing with the equipment. Maia had to think fast.

She hiked up her skirt and shimmied down her lace underwear. The Corsair tried to not watch as she slid them down her tawny legs and dropped them in between her heels. She kicked them up to her hand and then purposely caught the Corsair staring right at her.

"Do you mind?" Maia asked. "Hot day. I have to put on another pair."

The Corsair nodded and turned his back. Maia pointed to Marko and Beznik and made a talking sound with her hand. They immediately started arguing in Greek about the equipment.

She knelt down and opened the case. Jack climbed out as Maia caught spindles of cables falling over the sides.

"Are you finished?" the Corsair asked. It was the last thing he ever said.

Jack coldcocked the Corsair right in the horseshoe divot that connected the back of his head to his neck. The violent strike turned him off like a light switch. His limp frame flew forward, and his nose cartilage made a sickening pop when it hit the tile. Jack grabbed the knife and sword from his belt and then pointed at Marko and Beznik. "Throw his body off the balcony."

The Gypsies dragged the Corsair by his loose linen pants toward the large windows that opened to a balcony overlooking the ocean.

Jack took out the map of Soter's compound that Olney had drawn. The library was on the southern part of the compound, and the cell with Isaac and Rachel was on the eastern. While they studied it, Marko and Beznik grabbed the Corsair by his arms and legs and tossed him over the cliff.

Right as the body was out of sight, Neville opened the only entrance to the library and was followed by five Turkish Corsairs. Jack hid between two bookshelves underneath the shadows of the overhang. Marko and Beznik were caught by surprise.

"What are they doing out there?" Neville asked.

"Quick smoke," Maia said casually.

Marko and Beznik came back inside and walked over to the gear.

"I'm Doctor Ramanujan, and I will be helping you set up. What kind of transmitter are you using? I need to run it through my computers so we can broadcast it back to Athens."

Marko and Beznik looked at each other and then down at the gear. Neville noticed the two men seemed very nervous. Marko knelt down and opened the case with the extendable satellite.

"It's a good one," Marko said. "It's right here."

"You have to forgive my guys," Maia said. "Most of our top crews are out covering the Sumatra story. These are recent hires, but they'll get the job done."

Neville knelt down and looked at the equipment in the hard-foam case.

"Are you going to broadcast in NTSC format?" Neville asked Maia.

"Yes, of course," Maia said.

"That was a trick question. All of Europe uses PAL format." Neville turned to the Corsairs. "They're imposters."

The Corsairs drew their blades.

Jack tightened the grip on his sword and took a step out of the shadows. He was outnumbered, but it had never stopped him before. Maia screamed in Romanian, *"Nu muta! Vom fi bine!"*

Jack knew enough Romanian to understand that she said, "Don't move. We will be fine."

The Corsairs and Neville assumed she was swearing at them in a foreign tongue. Jack took a step back into the shadows of the bookshelves.

Neville took out his walkie-talkie. "Mr. Soter, we have a breach."

"Who is it?" Soter asked over the radio.

"A fake news crew," Neville said.

"Throw them in the holding cell with the boy. We will interrogate them later," Soter said. "I promised a live interview at six. *Make that happen.*"

"Yes, sir," Neville said. "I will set up to broadcast on my computer."

The Corsairs held Maia, Marko, and Beznik at sword point and led them through the large wooden doors at the front of the library. Neville exited with them to head back to the laboratory. Jack waited for them all to exit and quietly followed behind.

CHAPTER 37:
THE JACK OF HEARTS

SOTER'S COMPOUND
THERA, GREECE

Redbeard walked down the hallways with two Corsairs behind him. His radio crackled, and Soter's voice came on. "There's been a breach. Bring Rachel up to my room immediately."

"Copy," Redbeard said into his walkie-talkie.

They ran through the hallway and down the steps to the holding cell. The two Corsairs guarding the door unlocked it.

Isaac jumped up. He didn't know if Jack had already attempted and failed a rescue.

Redbeard pointed at Rachel. "Come with me," he said.

"Not this time," Isaac said.

Redbeard lunged at him and punched him right in the throat. Isaac toppled to the ground.

"No!" Rachel screamed and rushed Redbeard. She kicked and punched him, but he just dodged the face shots. Isaac gasped for air on his hands and knees.

"Hold her down," Redbeard said to his men as he pulled a silver case out of his belt.

Isaac tried to get up, but there was no oxygen going to his muscles. He fell to his side.

The two Corsairs violently shoved Rachel to the ground and put their knees on her. Redbeard looked over to the boy and held up the syringe. "Opium," he said.

Isaac watched from his side as his mother was held down and injected with drugs. Her violent kicking and screaming gave way to a rush of euphoria. The two Corsairs picked her up. Isaac used everything in his power to force himself off the ground, but Redbeard moved swiftly across the room and kicked him in the ribs. He fell to his side and watched the bottom of his mother's feet being dragged out of the cell.

The two Corsairs carried Rachel up the marble steps and into Soter's master bedroom. The ceiling was dome-shaped with a painting of the zodiac above. Soter had just gotten out of the shower and wore only a towel. Lying on his bed was a brilliant, gray-striped Gucci suit with a light-blue shirt. Rachel was barely coherent. She moaned in pleasure.

"Put her on the bed and leave us," Soter said.

Redbeard and the Corsairs lay Rachel down. Her eyes were rolled up into her head, and she grabbed the blankets like one would during sex.

"You're *sure* that her brother is dead?" Soter asked Redbeard.

"I stood over him and watched him stop breathing," Redbeard said.

"Scan the property and make sure there is no one else," Soter said. "We'll deal with the others later, whoever they are."

Redbeard nodded and exited.

Soter sat on the bed and slid Rachel's medical top off. She was too drugged to even know her own name. She moaned and ran her hand down Soter's chest. He stood and took her hiking boots off. The sharpened spike fell out, and he picked it up.

"Were you planning on killing me with this?" he asked, grinning.

Rachel laughed and looked up at the zodiac wheel on the ceiling. "The ceiling is throbbing," she said, pulling her cheeks down with her palms.

"We are going to get you cleaned up. It's a big night for both of us," Soter said as he slid off her medical pants to reveal her simple undergarments.

Soter stood up and entered his walk-in closet. He came out holding a strapless, black formal gown.

"My mother was an Italian fashion model," he said, taking it off the hanger. "This was hers."

Rachel giggled and rolled her head in circles as Soter pulled the gown over her body. He zipped it up, and she ran her hands up and down the fabric. Soter took a step back to admire her in the gown. She looked gorgeous.

"It feels so *good* on my skin," Rachel said.

Soter ran his hands through her hair.

She opened her eyes and looked up at him. "Why are your eyes so blue?" she asked.

He stood up and took two ties out of his closet. He tied her wrists to the bedposts as she rubbed the bottom of her feet on his silk bedspread. She was too drugged to realize any danger. Soter took his time putting on his suit and then headed for the door.

"Where are you going?" Rachel asked, gripping the ties with her fingers.

Soter turned around in his slick gray suit and said, "To introduce myself to the world. Then, I'm coming back for you."

CHAPTER 38:
THE JACK OF CLUBS

SOTER'S COMPOUND
THERA, GREECE

Jack watched from a distance as Neville headed down one hall-way, and the Corsairs took Maia, Marko, and Beznik down a staircase. He waited a few minutes, and the Corsairs came back up. They exited through the front door and fanned out in the courtyard to search for more intruders. Jack hoped that Olney and Zahra were well hidden.

He sneaked down the hallway with the curved sword in his right hand and the knife blade in his left. The blade pointed down toward his wrist so he could punch and slash in the same motion. Jack crept up to the staircase and peeked down. Two sets of leather boots sat at the door. There was no time for a clever ploy or distraction. The situation called for a bullrush. Fortunately, the small hallway was too narrow for a sword fight. Jack was deadly with a knife.

He took a deep breath and sprinted down the stairs. He hurled the hilt of the curved sword like an overhand cricket toss. It whirled end over end, and the Corsair on the right tried to block it with his hands. The top-heavy blade sliced downward and detached both sets of thumbs and index fingers. He hit the ground before his appendages did.

Jack swiped the knife at the Corsair on the left, but he blocked the attack. The collision threw them into the wall, and Jack dropped his knife. The Corsair pulled his blade as they both scrambled to their feet. He lunged forward with his knife, but Jack caught his wrist and used his own momentum to spin him around. Jack used his left arm to put the Corsair in a chokehold while using his right hand to hold the knife at bay. They struggled for a moment, but the Corsair lost oxygen quickly. The one on the ground tried to pull his sword using his six remaining fingers. Jack looked over his right shoulder and violently donkey-kicked him with heel of his boot. His head slammed into the wall, and he was out cold. The Corsair in the chokehold went limp, and Jack dropped him to the floor.

"That was for Horus," Jack said.

The cell door opened. Jack held all of the Corsairs' swords and knives. Maia, Marko, Beznik, and Isaac jumped up.

"They injected Mom with opium and took her upstairs," Isaac said.

"They know we're here," Jack said, putting the weapons down on the table and unfolding Olney's map. "We need a plan."

They quickly gathered around the table. Isaac pointed to the upstairs.

"That's where Soter's room is," Isaac said. "We need to get her now. They've been pumping her full of fertility drugs. He wants her to have his heir."

"Is he up there now?" Jack asked.

"I don't know. He's scheduled to give an interview soon. If he gets on the air, we'll have no chance of stopping him."

"Shite," Jack said. "You and Maia go get Rachel. I'll go after Soter."

"No, let me," Isaac said.

"He's a dangerous man, Isaac," Maia said.

"You two get Mom out of here first. I'll stall Soter," Isaac said and turned to his uncle. "Once Mom is safe, come back for me."

"Are you sure you want to do this?" Jack asked.

Isaac grabbed a sword off the table and said, "He won't kill me. My gift is too valuable to him."

Isaac lied, but it was the only way to get his uncle to believe him.

"I'll be right there," he said, tugging on Isaac's tie. "What's with the tie, Einstein?"

"Neville sent me messages in it," Isaac said. He removed the tie and folded it into his pocket. Then he stuffed his journal in the front of his pants and put his shirt over it.

Maia looked at Marko and Beznik. "You two can help me carry Rachel." They both nodded.

Maia, Isaac, and Jack armed themselves with swords, and the two Gypsies took the knives. They climbed out of the staircase into the empty hallway. Marko and Beznik immediately dropped their weapons and took off running toward the front door.

"La Revedere, Maia," Marko said as he grabbed an expensive vase in full stride on his way out.

"Thick as thieves, huh?" Jack asked.

"Remind me to slap you later," Maia said as they sneaked down the hallway.

"The library is straight ahead," Isaac said. "Soter's bedroom is up that staircase."

Isaac looked nervous, so Jack grabbed him by the back of the neck. "I *will* come for you," he said. "No matter what."

Isaac nodded. "One more thing—before you come for me, go to the lab. Soter has two machines in there that we *have* to get out. No matter what."

"Roger," Jack said.

"It's called the Antikythera Mechanism," Isaac said. "Olney knows what it is."

"Got it," Jack said.

"Antikythera," Isaac repeated.

"Yeah, I said I got it," Jack said.

Isaac nodded and crept down the hallway.

Maia and Jack went up a staircase lined with ancient Greek and Roman armor. Maia stopped in her tracks when she saw a rusted green Corinthian helmet on a podium. Next to it was a leather muscle-sculpted cuirass and two leather wrist guards. Maia gently lifted the helmet from the stone shelf and turned to Jack.

"*No man, against my fate, sends me to Hades.* And as for fate, I'm sure no man escapes it, neither a good nor bad man, once he's born," Maia said as Jack knelt, and she placed the helmet onto his head.

"Gypsy prayer?" Jack asked.

"*The Iliad,*" she said grabbing the sculpted cuirass. "Now rise, my Hector, and send their bodies to the dogs."

"Will you marry me, if we get out of here alive?" Jack asked from his knee.

"Yes," she said and smiled.

Jack stood up with a look of invincibility, and Maia lifted the armor to his chest.

Isaac crept down the long hallway that led to the library. The two wooden doors were cracked open, and he could hear the faint sound of voices. His hands were sweating on the sword grip as he held it by his side. Isaac was a good fencer. All cadets were required to take classes, but he knew he wasn't strong enough to swing the curved blade at quick speeds. He reinforced every step forward by remembering snippets of Soter's plan. If he had the chance to kill Soter, he was going to do it— even if it cost his life. He was afraid to die, but his father's prophecy scared him even worse.

"How much longer?" Soter asked through the door.

Isaac could hear gear being set up and clicked into place.

"A few minutes, and then I just have to send out the signal from my computers," Neville said.

Isaac peeked through the slit. Neville had set up two simple lights, a video camera, and a small satellite. Soter turned to look out the windows to see the camera's point of view. Neville then hit a button, and the satellite extended upward. It made just enough noise. Isaac slipped through the door and hid in the dark shadows of the library's second-story overhang. The satellite stopped extending after four meters. Neville examined all of the connections one last time.

"We're good," Neville said. "I will radio you when the signal is ready." He briskly walked to the doors.

"Put in a call to the BBC and tell them I will be announcing my identity shortly," Soter said.

"Yes, sir. Use the keypad to lock the door after I exit," Neville said as he closed the doors behind him.

Soter walked toward the large doors and typed in a security code on the panel.

Isaac heard a large deadbolt slide into place. A feeling of desperation swept through him. Uncle Jack wouldn't be able to get through the door. It was just him and Soter locked in the room, and he had to kill him before the camera came on.

CHAPTER 39:
THE JACK OF DIAMONDS

SOTER'S COMPOUND
THERA, GREECE

"This way, Hector," Maia said. She eyed Jack's chest armor as they walked down the long hallway.

"Why doesn't anyone in Greece have abs like this anymore?" Jack said, rubbing the muscle-shaped armor.

The hallways had marbled floors with black carpets and were lined with busts of famous Greek philosophers. Ten doors were on either side of the staircase. Maia quietly opened the doors on the left while Jack opened the right-side doors. Inside were grand dining rooms, guest bedrooms, and rooms filled with antiques. They got to the last door and then heard something.

Jack removed his helmet and put his ear to the door. He could hear moaning coming from inside. He opened the door and rushed in with his sword drawn. He expected to find Soter and was surprised when he saw Rachel by herself. They rushed to her.

"Lay with me," she said, "and watch the ceiling move."

Jack looked at Maia and said, "She's goddamned drugged out of her mind. Is it life threatening?" He started untying her from the bed.

Maia examined Rachel's pupils. They were tiny. She felt her skin. It was cold and clammy. Maia then examined her arms and found a few small needle incisions.

"It's just opium," she said. "It should wear off in a few hours."

"That sick bastard drugged her up and was planning on having his way with her," Jack said, lightly slapping Rachel in the face. "Hey, muppet. It's me. Focus."

Rachel's rolling eyes slowly came to a stop, and she realized it was Jack.

"Jack, we're having a party," Rachel said, grinning.

"We're going to get you out of here," Jack said, lifting her up with Maia's help.

Rachel couldn't stand on her own two feet, so they stood on either side of her and walked her out. They made it down a quarter of the hallway when Redbeard and his men came sprinting up the stairs. Jack counted ten of them.

"How are you still alive?" Redbeard asked as they pulled their swords and inched down the hallway.

"When are you going to come play *without* your butt buddies?" Jack asked, handing Rachel to Maia.

"Put down your weapons, and we won't kill you," Redbeard said. "Right away."

"How many little unibrows do you have scurrying around?" Jack asked, putting on his helmet.

"Why do you want to know?" Redbeard asked, moving closer.

"I want to keep score," Jack said, tightening his left armband.

"There are fifteen of us and one of you," Redbeard said. "This will not be a game. It will be an execution."

"Did you count the two blokes guarding the door?" Jack asked. "They won't be partaking in this evening's festivities." Jack loosened up his arm by swinging his sword with both hands.

Redbeard shrugged. "Thirteen," he said.

"Twelve now," Jack said. He whipped out the knife and flipped it down the hallway. It struck one of the Corsairs in the collarbone, and he went down. The Corsairs charged, and Jack pushed Maia and Rachel into one of the adjacent rooms. He locked the door. It was good that Soter was security conscious. Jack could tell the strong door would hold them off for a while.

Maia dragged Rachel deeper into the guest bedroom and heaved her onto the bed. The Corsairs kicked and punched the door, but it wouldn't budge.

"What now?" Maia asked.

"In the Royal Marines, they train you how to attack when you're outnumbered," Jack said.

"What do they say?" Maia asked, panicking.

"One at a time," Jack said. "Pick one, kill one, and move on to the next." He knelt down, jammed his sword underneath the door, and quickly pulled back. The blade went through the inner arch of a Corsair's foot. Jack heard him fall to the ground. He repeatedly jabbed his sword under the door. He pulled it up. The blade dripped with dark blood.

"Eleven to one," Jack yelled through the door.

"Go get the axes from the walls," Redbeard ordered his men from the other side of the door.

"Jack!" Maia screamed, pointing to the balcony. Two Corsairs had climbed out another window and stepped down onto their balcony.

Jack sprinted toward them, screaming. He lowered his shoulder and burst through the glass-paned terrace door. The impact hurled the first Corsair backward. His hamstrings hit the marble railing on the deck, and he flipped over it.

Two hundred meters away, Olney and Zahra heard the windowpane break. They looked up and saw a Corsair fall directly onto a statue of Hypatia, breaking the arm that carried an astrolabe. The two Corsairs guarding the gate quickly opened it and ran inside.

"That's as good a sign as any," Professor Olney said. "Come on."

Back on the deck, Jack battled the second Corsair. He wasn't a swordsman like the Turks, so he used every cheap trick he could think of. He used a table as a defense, threw loose objects at him, and kept a safe distance.

"They're breaking the door down!" Maia yelled from inside as she heard two alternating axes hit the thick wood.

Jack circled and got an idea. He bent down and picked up the circular table by the base, tilted it toward the Corsair, and rushed him. It acted like a shield, and the impact knocked the Turk over the railing. His shoulders hit first, and then his head snapped back and cracked his skull on the hard gravel.

"You need a helmet, not a turban," Jack said, running back inside. There were two small holes in the middle of the door.

"Wait for both axes to get stuck in the door and then open it for one second," Jack whispered to Maia, readying his sword in his right hand. Maia watched as both axes came in and out of the door. They finally both got stuck in the wood.

"Now!" she said as she pulled the door open.

Jack's curved sword sliced upward from the floor and through two pairs of forearms like soft pears. The axes remained stuck, but the handless Corsairs fell to the ground. Maia immediately shut the door and locked it.

Jack had to point and count out how many Corsairs he had just offed. "That's seven to one!" he yelled through the door. "Put down your turbans, and I'll let you live!"

The axe attacks continued, but they aimed at the door handle.

"Get in the corner with Rachel," Jack directed.

Maia scooped her up and carried her into a walk-in closet.

Jack tightened the straps on his arms and readjusted his helmet. He was ready for all seven of them.

"Come on, Redbeard!" Jack yelled. "If you're a man, you'll be the first one through!"

Outside the room, the remaining seven Corsairs alternated kicks on the beaten-in door. Redbeard moved to the front of the pack. He had been challenged in front of his men. He would be the one to strike the deathblow.

Suddenly, a large pomegranate rolled down the hallway, right into the heel of the outermost Corsair. He turned around dumbfounded and looked down the hallway. There was no one in sight. He picked it up and turned it over in his hand. There was a wick popping out near the bottom. The Corsair tilted his head slightly as it exploded.

CHAPTER 40:
THE JACK OF SPADES

SOTER'S COMPOUND
THERA, GREECE

Olney covered Zahra on the marble staircase. The explosion rocked the hallway, shattering all the windows on the top floor. The splintered door blew Jack backward and knocked his helmet off. All of the Corsairs were hurled into walls, and their vertebrae shattered upon impact. A burning flame rolled down the hallway over Olney and Zahra, singeing their hair.

Zahra looked up at Olney. His ears rang from the explosion.

"I thought you said they were nonlethal?" she said.

"Jupiter's red spot," Olney said in shock. "That one may have had a little too much nitroglycerine."

The flame crawled across the white walls and caught the woven tapestries on fire. The professor and Zahra stood up and peeked down the smoking hallway. The tiny explosive had leveled all the walls in a six-meter radius. Zahra could only see the Corsairs' bodies scattered around the hallway.

"Jack!" Zahra yelled.

She watched the flames spread up to the ceiling. Whatever the professor had put in there was extremely flammable and was going to burn the entire floor down. Zahra and Olney sneaked down the hallway into the thick smoke.

They heard the crunching sound of wood. Jack and Maia carried Rachel out of the bedroom.

"What the hell did you two do?" Jack asked, covered in dust and coughing up smoke. One of the Corsairs was severely injured but crawled down the hall. Jack handed Rachel to Zahra.

"Wait here," he said, picking up a bust off a podium. "Who's this bloke, Professor?" Jack asked.

"That's Plato. Why?" Olney said.

"I hope he didn't preach nonviolence," Jack said as he carried the bust back into the cloud of smoldering remains.

Olney, Zahra, and Maia heard the marble bust come down on six different heads. Jack walked out of the smoke coughing and covered in soot.

"I only counted six," Jack said as he tossed down the bloodied Plato bust. "One of these cockroaches is still alive."

"What wrong with her?" Zahra asked, looking at Rachel.

"She's been drugged," Maia said.

"Maia, take Rachel down to the yacht," Jack ordered.

Zahra helped lift Rachel over Maia's shoulder. Rachel was still mumbling incoherently, and she smelled handfuls of Maia's hair.

Jack looked down the hallway. The flames spread into the bedrooms. The fire was too large to put out. "Downstairs," he said.

The group headed down the marble staircase. Maia carried Rachel over her shoulder and stepped into the courtyard.

"Meet me at the boat," she said with Rachel drooling on her shoulder.

"You two come with me," Jack said. "We're going to get the Antarctica machine."

"I'm sorry?" Olney asked.

"Isaac told me about some all-powerful machine from Antarctica," Jack said, stretching his injured side. "He made me promise to get it out of here."

"You mean the Antikythera," Olney said.

"Same thing to me, old man," Jack said as he led them down the hallway.

The hallway turned into a state-of-the-art walkway with rooms of computer servers on either side. They came to a metal door with a keypad on the right.

"How do you plan on getting in here?" Olney asked quietly.

"Kabcab," Jack said.

"What?" Olney said.

"Kill a body, check a body," Jack said, pulling out an electronic key card. "Took it off one of the unibrows upstairs." Jack swiped it across the electronic reader, and it turned green.

Inside the laboratory, Neville spun in his chair.

"What are you doing in here?" he asked.

"Turn that off," Jack said, eyeing Neville's computer screens.

"You must be the notorious Uncle Jack," Neville said as he turned on the security monitors and looked at the top floor of the compound burning down. "Damn it!" he said.

"Help us get the machines out of here, and we'll let you live," Jack said.

"Unfortunately, I've already thought this through," Neville said. "Soter is going to name me as his lead scientist, and this is the only way for me to protect my family. I'm sorry."

He typed in the last command on his computer and picked up his walkie-talkie. "Soter, you're live in three minutes."

A camera feed in Soter's grand library came on. Soter stood far in the distance watching the dark-blue twilight clouds rumble over the Mediterranean. The camera shot was too far away to see his face.

"What did you just do?" Olney asked.

"In three minutes, that signal will be broadcast to every single news station," Neville said. "He's going to change the world, and I will earn my place in the history books alongside him."

"Not if we have anything to do with it," Jack said. "Start unplugging, old man." He walked toward the Indian doctor.

Neville took of his lab coat and threw it off to the side. "I may look frail, but every member of the Magi spends years in the Indian jungles learning kalari."

"Is that so? Well, my martial art is called, 'I-don't-give-a-flying-donkey-dick-that-you're-a-black-belt," Jack said.

He circled Neville for a moment and then threw a punch. The doctor dodged it and kicked his heel straight up vertically. The bottom of his heel caught Jack under the chin and knocked him on his ass. Neville looked at the counter. He only had to stall them for two more minutes. He would be immortalized in scientific journals, and the publicity would prevent Soter and his Corsairs from harming his family. He no longer cared for his own life.

Olney and Zahra frantically unplugged the cords from the back of the Antikythera Mechanism.

"That machine is my crowning achievement," Neville said. "I've earned this."

Jack got up and spit out blood. He rushed the doctor, wrapped his legs up like a rugby tackle, and dump-trucked Neville into his own computer monitors. From his back, the doctor wrapped his left leg around the back of Jack's head while putting his right leg over his left. It created a triangle chokehold. Neville used his right hand to pull down and apply pressure. Jack's face turned bright red. Kalari was like yoga fighting.

"The constriction is cutting off your oxygen. You should start seeing black rings soon," Neville said, tightening his grip.

Jack picked the light Indian doctor up, held him above his head, and slammed him down onto the desk. The doctor held fast, and his grip tightened. Jack was seconds away from passing out. Neville looked up at the monitor. Thirty seconds.

Suddenly, the doctor screamed in pain and released. Jack stood up and saw that Zahra had jammed a fountain pen into his left hamstring. Jack picked up the heavy monitor and bashed Neville over the head, knocking him out.

There were fifteen seconds left.

"How do we turn off this signal?" Jack asked while randomly pressing buttons.

"Look for a power source," Olney said, busy with the Antikythera.

Zahra and Jack looked around but couldn't find the outlet. They both looked up at the monitor. Soter checked his watch and walked toward the camera. His face was still out of focus, but he drew close.

"Damn it!" Jack yelled as he watched the timer wind down to zero.

Soter was almost in recognizable range when the feed went dark.

CHAPTER 41:

THE QUEEN OF HEARTS

SOTER'S LIBRARY
THERA, GREECE

Isaac lifted the curved scimitar from the ground. He had used the sword to cut through the cables running from the news camera down to Neville's laboratory.

"What are you doing?" Soter asked as he checked his watch. He broke out in a cold sweat at the thought of missing his opportunity to reveal himself.

Isaac raised his sword and squared up to Soter. "I've been beaten, chased out of my home, poisoned, strapped to machines, and made to watch my father die in front of me. I have had enough. Only one of us is walking out of here alive."

Soter used the square fountain in the middle of the room as a buffer.

"Nice speech, but your threats are as empty as your dead father," Soter said, circling the fountain.

"Uncle Jack is here," Isaac said, circling.

"That door is reinforced with steel," Soter said. He sniffed the air. "It would take a battering ram to get in here. That means it's just me and you."

"You smell that?" Isaac said. "Your plan is coming down, just like your compound."

"Mr. Alexander, the world is waiting for me to address them," Soter said. "It doesn't matter where I do it. Your little charade weaves perfectly into my story; a peaceful billionaire develops the technology to change the world, and a secret society tries to kill him. I can expose and destroy the Magi with one interview."

"Neville gave me your report," Isaac said. "You're the one who's going to be exposed."

"Do you think it matters what you know? You're an insignificant speck from a line of slaves. I come from royalty! The world is crying for a new king! Three-quarters of the people live in poverty. Slaves from ancient civilizations are smarter than our brightest children today. We are destroying our planet and depleting its resources. Someone needs to raise the standards and enforce them with an iron fist."

"That person isn't you," Isaac said. "You're a false prophet. It wasn't destiny that led your family to the Antikythera! Your great-grandfather *stole* it."

"I offered you everything, but you secretly *wanted* to see your father killed," Soter said.

The last comment struck Isaac like a stomach punch. "I didn't kill him!" he screamed. "You did!"

"It was in your cards, Isaac. There was no escaping it. You hated him, just like I hated my father. He lied to you. He thought he was protecting you from your fate, but he led you right to it. Stop lying to yourself, and accept this truth."

"My father was a good man!" Isaac screamed.

"But he was weak. No one has ever accomplished anything great without hate in their hearts. Love is for complacent fools. Hate drives people like us to change the status quo. You passed on the greatest opportunity of your life, and now you will suffer the consequences. Any last questions before I kill you?"

Isaac raised his sword and pointed it at Soter's chest. They stood on opposite ends of the fountain.

"What happens when we get away with your machine?" Isaac said. "Then what? Your plan is ruined."

"How many times do I have to tell you that I have accounted for all the variables? I have backup schematics and plans in safety deposit boxes in five different countries. I knew the Magi would come for me once I announced myself to the world. Nothing can happen from this point forward that I haven't already thought of."

"You're wrong," Isaac said, tightening his grip on the sword. "You're not going to walk out of here."

Soter turned and sprinted up a spiral staircase. Isaac ran around the fountain and chased him, but he was too quick. Isaac backed up so he could see him on the second story.

Soter walked to the wall that held a wooden crest with two crossing xiphos swords. Both were sheathed in leather cases.

"Did they teach you fencing at the Royal Navy Academy?" Soter asked.

Isaac continued to back up and didn't answer. He looked to his left and could see small wisps of smoke creeping under the doors. The fire would spread to the library in minutes.

"In the interest of fairness, I will give you a fighting chance," Soter said as he tossed down one of the xiphos swords to Isaac. It rattled onto the tiled floor and slid to a stop.

Isaac tossed his large Arab sword to the side and picked up the Roman-style weapon. It was lighter.

Soter unsheathed his sword and walked back down the spiral staircase. He took off his suit jacket and tossed it on the ground.

"Enough talk," he said as he rolled up his dress sleeves. "It's time for a reunion with your father."

CHAPTER 42:
THE QUEEN OF CLUBS

SOTER'S COURTYARD
THERA, GREECE

Jack fastened the last of the computer cords to Neville's arms. He had tied him to an iron pipe against the wall. The doctor was still unconscious.

"Are you sure you want to leave him here?" Olney asked as he grabbed hard drives off Neville's desk and stuffed them into his brown leather backpack.

"Yes," Jack said. "He said he would die for his research. Now he can die with it."

They unlocked the wheels on the bottom of the Plexiglas cases and pushed both Antikythera Mechanisms out of the lab. The hallways were filled with smoke.

"Run straight and don't breathe in," Jack said as he entered the cloud.

Zahra and Olney pushed the rusted original while Jack followed with the bronze replica. They emerged into the lobby, which was slightly clearer because of the high ceilings, and took a right toward the front doors. Smoke curled out of the double doors and up the face of the building like a French inhale. Olney and Zahra coughed as they tried to fill their lungs with fresh air.

"We've got to get out of here before the roof comes down," Jack said, sprinting into the courtyard. He jumped inside a black Land Rover Defender and reversed it toward the front doors. When he looked up in his rearview mirror, he saw a shadowy figure emerge from the smoke.

"Behind you!" Jack screamed, but they couldn't hear his voice over the engine and the fire inside.

Redbeard pulled his knife from his belt and put it to Zahra's throat. Jack reversed the vehicle up the steps. Redbeard grabbed the girl by the hair and pulled her out of the way. His face was shredded from the explosion. Half of his beard had been burned off.

Jack jumped out of the driver's seat and approached them. Redbeard's face looked like it was melting. Zahra could smell the pungent odor of singed hair. "Load the truck, Olney," Jack said, out of the side of his mouth.

Zahra squirmed, but she didn't look scared. It wasn't the first time a knife had been held to her throat.

Jack put both hands up and approached cautiously. "This has nothing to do with the girl or the old man. This is about you and me. Let them go, and we'll settle this."

If it had been anyone else, Redbeard would have already slit her throat. But he admired Zahra. He released her, and she ran forward.

"I'm going to kill you and then get those machines back," Redbeard said.

"Take the truck down to the boat," Jack said.

"But—" Zahra said.

"Go. Now!" Jack yelled at her.

Zahra ran to the SUV and helped Olney lift the bronze replica into the trunk.

Jack was weaponless but circled Redbeard who held a knife. The fine gravel crunched under their feet as they stared directly at each other.

"How did you survive that blast?" Jack asked.

"I threw another man in front of me," Redbeard said out of the good side of his face.

Olney peeled out in the Land Rover as Zahra watched Jack through the window. The SUV sped down the terraced dirt road that zigzagged to the docks.

Suddenly, the southern face of the compound collapsed. Jack looked up for a split second, and Redbeard lunged.

Jack dodged the knife thrust and wrapped up Redbeard's right elbow with his left arm. The knife went behind Jack as the two men struggled for leverage. Redbeard repeatedly brought the knife up into Jack's left shoulder blade. His leather cuirass blocked most of the attacks, but some of them slid into his shoulder. Jack screamed and brought his right hand up to Redbeard's seared face. He squeezed the burned flesh as hard as he could, making a fist with the man's cheek muscles. The Turk screamed.

Their feet shuffled across the gravel as both tried to keep their balance. Jack's left shoulder poured blood, but he still had a fistful of Redbeard's face. Jack rotated his grip on the Turk's cheek and plunged his right thumb into Redbeard's left eye. The Turk's knees buckled. Jack lowered his hips and drove him toward the Hypatia statue like he was clearing a ruck. Redbeard was rushed backward and lost his balance. Jack stretched his hand over Redbeard's face, palming it like a rugby ball. He lifted his hips at the last second and lifted the Turk off the ground. Jack locked his elbow and slammed Redbeard's head into the square edge of the statue's base. The impact snapped Jack's radius bone, and he rolled off in pain. He held his broken wrist and jumped up quickly.

Redbeard's eyes rolled up. Blood oozed out of his mouth. The back of his head was severely dented around the right angle of the marble base.

"Jack of Diamonds beats the Four of Beards, bitch!" Jack said. He stepped over Redbeard and grabbed the knife in his good left hand. He plunged it into his stomach and gutted him for good measure.

"That's for drugging my sister," Jack said.

As he stood up over Redbeard's dead body, another section of the compound collapsed.

"Isaac," Jack mumbled to himself. He turned toward the flaming compound and disappeared into the smoke.

CHAPTER 43:
THE QUEEN OF DIAMONDS

SOTER'S LIBRARY
THERA, GREECE

Isaac parried Soter's lunge with a swiping sidestep. He was holding his own, but he could tell that Soter was only toying with him.

"Better than expected, but you still have no chance," Soter said, switching hands and stances.

Isaac lunged forward, and Soter sidestepped and nicked his bicep.

"Next are your wrist ligaments, so you can't hold that sword up," Soter said, circling from a safe distance. "Then your Achilles tendons, so you can't run. Lastly, I bring this blade across your throat just like I did to your father."

"Never," Isaac said as he lunged forward with a swinging combo. Soter easily blocked each attack and then lunged his xiphos at Isaac's abdomen. Soter's sword tip got stuck in something. He pulled it away and backed up. Isaac's journal had just saved his life.

Soter's retreat gave Isaac time to check his wound. Not only did he want to physically end Isaac's life, but he wanted to psychologically crush him, too.

"You know, I've been pumping your mother full of drugs," Soter said grinning. "I bedded her earlier today. Your half brother will do what you were too afraid to do."

"That's a lie!" Isaac screamed as he hurled his sword at Soter and rushed him. Soter blocked the spinning weapon but was caught off guard with Isaac's furious tackle. They both slid backward on the tile, and Soter dropped his sword. Isaac crawled over Soter's body and put his right arm into the arm bar that Jack had taught him. He put his calves over Soter's neck and pulled back.

"Good," Soter said. "Hand-to-hand combat. A much more intimate way to die."

Isaac pulled back tighter, and for the first time ever, he heard something from Soter's mouth that wasn't rehearsed or planned. It was a pained groan. Isaac looked to his right. The sword was out of reach. He couldn't kill Soter like this, but he could disable him. Isaac pulled back with everything he had, and Soter screamed.

"I am going to *thoroughly* enjoy killing you," Soter said, trying to mask the pain in his voice.

The fire had spread from the top floor to the library. The ancient texts, full of dry parchment, were spreading flames down the walls like kindling.

There was a loud banging on the door. "Isaac?" Jack yelled.

"Uncle Jack! I need help!"

"Not man enough to finish the job?" Soter asked.

Jack yelled from outside. "It's locked. I can't get in."

"Break it down," Isaac yelled back. "I can't move." He thought about releasing Soter and running for the door, but it was too risky. His muscles burned, but he had to hold Soter until Uncle Jack broke the door down.

Suddenly, Soter used all of his strength to sit up. Isaac held his arm bar but was now airborne. The strong Greek's arm was parallel to the ground while Isaac was wrapped around his upper body like a boa constrictor. He leaned forward and got onto one knee. Soter lifted himself to his feet.

"Hold on, Isaac!" Jack yelled from outside. He rammed the door as hard as he could.

"Hurry!" Isaac yelled, violently pulling back, trying to break Soter's arm. He was shocked at his threshold for pain.

"Too late, Isaac," Soter said as he stumbled toward the large book-shelf.

Soter twisted Isaac backward and swung him into the wooden shelf as hard as he could. The impact knocked him unconscious but also popped Soter's right shoulder out of its socket. They both collapsed to the ground amid a pile of ancient books.

CHAPTER 44:
THE QUEEN OF SPADES

SOTER'S COURTYARD
THERA, GREECE

Redbeard opened his eyes and spit up blood. He reached down with his right hand and pulled the knife out of his stomach. He fumbled with his belt and came back up with his silver case. Inside was a one-hundred-milliliter shot of amphetamine.

Redbeard spit out the cap and injected it into his arm. He unwrapped his turban and fastened it around his midsection to keep his intestines in. He bled profusely, but the speed pumped through his veins. He got up on one knee and then stood up. The back of his head had a V-shaped dent near his occipital lobe. His muscles pulsed, and the throbbing pain in his stomach and head started to subside. The drugs numbed his body. Step-by-step, he walked back into the flaming compound.

Redbeard heard a bang as he navigated through the inferno of fire and smoke. He applied pressure to his wound and walked down the hallway to the laboratory.

Neville was unconscious and tied to an iron pole against the wall. He shuffled toward him and knelt down. Redbeard slapped the doctor in the face. "Wake up," he said in his cold voice.

Neville's eyes circled his sockets and came to focus. "What? What's going on?" He hadn't been awake when the fire had started.

"I need the access code to Soter's safe," Redbeard said.

A large lighting panel fell to the ground and shattered. The roof was moments away from collapsing. Neither of them could breathe.

Neville eyed the knife on Redbeard's belts. "Cut me loose, and I'll give it to you," he said.

"Code first, then I cut you free," Redbeard said.

A storage closet erupted. The flames had ignited some of the chemicals.

"Cut me loose," Neville said. "I have to get my computers out of here."

Redbeard struggled to stand and started to leave.

"Wait, wait! I know it," Neville said.

"What is it?" Redbeard said.

"It's the day the Antikythera Mechanism was discovered by his great-grandfather," Neville said. "Thirteen, August, 1901."

"One three zero eight one nine zero one," Redbeard repeated.

"Yes, now cut me free," Neville pleaded.

"You're a coward!" Redbeard said. "How could you betray your own people?" He raised his knife and slit Neville's throat.

The doctor kicked and squirmed as his life emptied out through his neck. Redbeard walked to the closet and grabbed a gas mask.

The mask made it easier to breathe, but the heat was tremendous. He came to the main hallway. He could hear Jack's muffled screams, but he was too weak to take him. Their rivalry would have to be postponed. Redbeard slowly climbed the marble steps.

Luckily, Soter's private study was to the right and had not collapsed yet. It took every ounce of his strength to walk down the hallway. He opened the door and typed in the access code. The electronic mosaic opened, revealing the safe. Redbeard opened it. Inside was Soter's report and his bronze deck of cards from Atlantis. The flames were climbing up the walls and becoming unbearable. A massive bookshelf crashed to the ground.

Redbeard stuffed the bronze deck of cards into his belt. He climbed out the shattered window and leaped down into the fountain of Atlas as the building collapsed.

The cold water cooled his burning skin but only brought temporary relief from the pain. He sat up in the meter-high water and felt for his belt. The cards were still there. He reached down into his leather boot. Tied around his calf was a small transmitting device. Redbeard switched it on, and a red light blinked. He leaned back into the fountain, avoiding the heat from the burning building. Blood from his stomach stained the water red.

CHAPTER 45:
THE KING OF HEARTS

SOTER'S LIBRARY
THERA, GREECE

Isaac came to as Soter propped him up against the bookshelf. Soter looked like the Antichrist standing against the backdrop of a wall of fire. The entire western face of the library was ablaze. Fingers of fire crept onto the ceiling.

"What was the saying in the book of Exodus?" Soter said. "An eye for eye?"

He raised his right shoe and violently brought it down. The strike dislocated Isaac's shoulder. He screamed as his limp arm flopped to the ground.

"Or was it shoulder for shoulder?" Soter said as he turned around and walked toward his sword.

Isaac fell onto his good side. The pain was excruciating, but he got on all fours and snapped his shoulder back into its socket. He was trapped in a burning building with a man much stronger than he was. He began to accept his impending death.

"Look at what you did to my library!" Soter said, examining the wall of fire. "Thousands of books that can never be replaced."

Isaac watched his right arm quiver under his weight.

Then something under the bookshelf caught his eye. It was the cue ball that had bounced off the table during Soter's pool table demonstration. At that exact moment, Isaac realized that he was not supposed to die. The quarter on the table? The cue ball? The location of his fall? That was beyond coincidence. A higher power had presented him with an opportunity.

Isaac used his right hand to feel into this pocket. He still had Neville's tie.

Isaac grabbed the cue ball, which was designed to look like the moon. He sat up and pulled the tie out of his pocket. The ball fit perfectly into the back of the tie. He was creating a sling to bring down Goliath, just like the historic David had. The giant may have had the armor, the weapons, the training, and the courage to defeat anyone, but David believed that the divine was on his side. So did Isaac. He had the weapon that was going to bring down Soter. It was his destiny.

Soter knelt down to grab the sword and then turned to face Isaac.

"A valiant effort, boy, but your life ends here."

"Stop calling me *boy*," Isaac said, tightening the tie around his left hand. He knew Soter's right shoulder was dislocated and he wouldn't be able to block an attack.

Soter put the sword in his good left hand and walked toward him.

"What is that?" Soter asked, eyeing the tie. He couldn't tell it was weighted at the bottom.

"A variable you didn't account for," Isaac said.

"Impossible," Soter said as he lunged with the sword toward Isaac's chest.

Isaac sidestepped and swung his sling upward. Soter could not raise his torn right shoulder in time. Both weapons struck simultaneously. Soter's sword pierced through Isaac's right collarbone, and Isaac's cue ball concaved Soter's temple into his eye socket. Isaac fell back into the bookshelf, screaming. Soter stumbled sideways and lifted his hand to his shattered face.

Isaac dropped the tie, and the cue ball popped out. Soter's eyes widened when he saw the moon ball roll toward him. That tiny coin had become the variable that had disrupted his entire plan. He stumbled backward and fell into the large fountain.

Ptolemy Soter was dead.

Isaac sat down and felt a warm sensation oozing down his chest. He was losing a lot of blood. His temples pounded like drums. Everything slowed down. He could hear his heartbeat, louder than the fire. Dark circles swallowed the wall of flames, and he went unconscious.

CHAPTER 46:

THE KING OF CLUBS

SOTER'S COMPOUND
THERA, GREECE

Jack looked down the hallway to the grand lobby of Soter's compound. It was an impassible wall of flames. There was only way one way out, and it was through a reinforced door. On the other side was a delusional madman and his nephew.

"Come on, you *pussy*," Jack said, backing up as far down the flaming hallway as he could stand. He worked with about ten meters of space.

Jack's left sleeve of tattoos was drenched in blood from his stab wound, and his right wrist was broken.

He planted his foot and sprinted toward the door. He lowered his right shoulder directly at the handles and hit it at a breakneck speed. It barely budged. This was not going to be easy. Jack lay on the ground. He surely had a concussion from the impact. His knees buckled as he staggered to his feet.

"Just a big, bloody Samoan in a ruck," Jack said, wobbling back down the hallway. He hadn't heard Isaac for a few minutes and worried about what he might find on the other side. His right shoulder throbbed. Time was running out. The wall of flames would soon cut off his runway and his oxygen.

"Here we go," Jack said to himself, inhaling and exhaling quickly. He ran toward the door screaming like a wild man. He lowered his left shoulder and crashed into the center. The hinges shook, and it opened just enough to reveal two metal rods interlocking both doors.

"Damn it!" Jack said, as he slid down to the floor. "Isaac! Hold on, mate!" he screamed, trying to mask the pain in his voice. Both of his shoulders throbbed, and his face was cut up from the splintered wood. He sat with his back to the door watching the flames creep down the hallway. A lesser man would have given up, but everything important in his life was on the other side of that door. His nephew had been given something special. Jack wasn't going to pretend to understand the *whys* and the *whats*. That was not his role. He just knew that his newfound purpose was to protect Isaac at all costs.

He prayed for a sign—a weapon to fall off the wall or a break in the ceiling, but Jack had never asked for anyone's help. Why would the higher powers help him now? He was alone.

Jack clambered to his feet. He only had about eight meters of space left and flames were sucking the oxygen out of the hall. He got into a sprinter's stance, using his left fingers to prop up his upper body. Blood trickled over his tattoos and dripped onto the floor. This was it. His last chance.

Jack raised himself into a full stance, bowed his head, and closed his eyes. "God, Jesus, Allah, Yaweh, Zeus, Mother Earth, Santa Claus, I don't give a damn who's up there, but one of you is going to hear me. I know I'm a savage. I've killed and screwed my way through life, and for that, I ask your forgiveness. Do with me what you will, but I'm asking that you give me *strength*. You've given Isaac a gift. Help me save him so he can use it."

Jack focused his sights on the door. Heat burned the backs of his calves. He took in deep breaths, and everything slowed down. The burning and throbbing dissipated from his body like smoke from a cigarette. The loud crackling of flames was drowned out, and he felt a strange underwater sensation. All he could hear was his slow and steady breathing. Jack fixed his eyes on the door and took off.

A rush of fluidity ran through his body. His joints became numb, and his calves felt like they did when he was a twenty-year-old rugger. His legs started wide while he gained speed and then narrowed as his stride lengthened. It felt like he was being pulled toward the door. Jack closed his eyes and fully committed with a leap.

The collision was explosive. The wood holding the two metal locks shattered. Jack flew through the doors and slid to a stop on the library floor.

CHAPTER 47:
THE KING OF DIAMONDS

SOTER'S COMPOUND
THERA, GREECE

Olney kicked up a rooster tail of dust as he skidded around the dirt road in the black Land Rover. It was dark, and the sheer limestone cliff to their right would be a torturous finale to their escape. Zahra had only driven a few times, but she wished she were behind the wheel. Olney overcorrected, and they came within a meter of flying off the road. Zahra braced for a fall, but the car straightened.

"I got her! I got her!" Olney said, placing his hand and his hook at ten and two.

"Faster," Zahra said as she eyed the cloud of smoke high to their left.

The bright headlights on the Land Rover revealed the road widening at the bottom of the cliff. Olney pulled the wide SUV down the narrow dock and then did a five-point turn to put the trunk against the back railing of the Oculus.

"Rachel's onboard," Maia said, running out to the aft of the boat. "Where're Jack and Isaac?"

The professor pointed up. The steep cliff blocked the view of the compound, but they could see a cloud of smoke against the dark sky.

"The whole building is about to collapse," Olney said. "We need to pull the boat around to the southern face of the island."

"Then what?" Maia asked.

"There's a deck off the library," Olney said. "They're going to have to jump."

"Are you insane?" Maia said. "They could die from impact, or on the rocks."

Olney looked up and eyed the cliffs. "It's about forty meters. People can survive from much higher. It's their only chance."

"Let's move," Zahra said, getting into the backseat of the Land Rover. She sat on her butt and used both feet to push the replica Antikythera Mechanism over the tailgate. Olney and Maia couldn't lift the massive bronze machine but guided it down as softly as they could.

A loud crash came from above. Another section of the compound had collapsed. They all shared a look of concern and fear. They loaded the second machine.

"Careful," Olney said, guiding it down as best he could.

"No time," Zahra said, pushing it over the edge of the boat.

It came down with a crash and fell to its side. The Plexiglas case protected it.

"The ties," Maia said, running into the yacht.

Zahra jumped off the boat and scrambled down the dock to untie the boat.

"Go!" she yelled to Maia, jumping back on board. The engine fired up.

In the cockpit, Olney and Maia tried to assess the control panel. Zahra walked in and said, "Just go." She shoved Olney out of the way and pushed the throttle.

"What are you doing?" Olney asked.

The boat roared forward and collided with a fishing boat in front of them. Zahra held her hand down firmly on the throttle.

"Steer," she said to Maia, who fastened her grip on the wheel.

The Oculus ripped through the smaller boats, tossing them to the side like buoys. The yacht splintered through the T-shaped end of the dock. Maia turned it left toward the western-facing cliffs.

CHAPTER 48

THE KING OF SPADES

SOTER'S COMPOUND
THERA, GREECE

The wall of fire surrounded them like a capsule. Jack painfully lifted himself off the tiled floor and dashed toward Isaac. He got close and saw that both men were unconscious. Soter floated faceup in the fountain, his head caved in, and Isaac was slumped over in a pool blood.

Jack felt Isaac's pulse. It was faint, but he was still breathing. He sat him up and tapped him a few times in the face. Isaac didn't wake. Jack jammed his hand between Isaac's bollocks and squeezed. Isaac immediately jolted awake.

"Owwww!" he screamed. "What the hell?"

"Old navy trick. Better than smelling salts," Jack said, wrapping his hand around Isaac's neck before putting their foreheads together. "You did it. You *killed* that son of a bitch. Now, let's get the hell outta here."

Isaac noticed Jack favoring his right wrist and the stab wounds through his Jack of Diamonds tattoo on the back of his left shoulder.

"Are you all right?" Isaac asked.

"Shove it, boy wonder," Jack said. "That unibrow put up a good fight." He opened Isaac's shirt and inspected the wound.

A large wooden beam from the eastern side of the library fell from the ceiling and blocked the doorway.

"It's deep but missed your subclavian artery," Jack said. "You'll live."

"Mom?" Isaac asked.

"On the boat," Jack said as he wrapped Isaac up and got ready to lift him.

A loud foghorn cut through the roar of the flames. The first blast was seconds long.

"It's them," Jack said. "They're pulling the boat around."

Isaac was about to respond, but Jack put his hand over his mouth. The foghorn blasts had been split up into Morse code. It was Olney.

"J-U-M-P," Jack said, looking at the blocked doorway. "Can you walk?"

"Yes, but I'm pretty sure my shoulder is dislocated. I don't know if I can swim," Isaac said.

Jack grabbed the tie and quickly fastened a sling on Isaac's right arm.

"How did you kill him?" Jack asked.

"With the moon," Isaac said, pointing his head toward the cue ball on the ground.

"Up we go," Jack said, using his left arm to lift Isaac off the ground. "We're going to make sure." Jack grabbed the sword off the ground. He pulled Isaac over to the fountain.

The entire ceiling shifted. It was seconds away from collapsing. Jack switched his grip on the handle so the sword pointed down.

"This is for David, you scumbag arsehole," Jack said as he thrust the short sword right into Ptolemy's chest. The body didn't move.

"Hurry," Isaac said, watching a large crack form in the ceiling.

Jack dragged Isaac across the tiled floor and out onto the marble balcony overlooking the ocean. The southern face of Soter's compound hung over sheer cliffs. There was no way off to the left or right. They looked over the railing. Rocks jutted out randomly among the white foam as the waves crashed into the base of the cliff.

"Right there," Jack said, pointing to a small triangle of dark water.

"This looks pretty high," Isaac said.

Jack grabbed his nephew by the face. "After everything you've gone through, this will be easy. Don't think. Just jump."

Isaac gauged the vertical drop to be thirty to forty meters—over a hundred feet. A powerful spotlight from the Oculus yacht lit up the base of the cliff so they could see where they were going to jump.

"Don't use your arms to break the fall," Jack said. "Pencil dive. Then swim under the current toward the boat."

"Got it," Isaac said, kicking his leg over the railing and lifting himself up.

A severe case of vertigo hit him as he stared down at the rhythmic motion of the waves. Isaac's stomach was in a knot, and he felt warm prevomit flooding his mouth. Not only did they have to jump down, but they had to jump *out* to avoid the rocks. Isaac felt his feet involuntarily backing away.

"Look at me!" Jack yelled.

Isaac looked up at his uncle.

"You're *going* to survive, and we're going to laugh about this tomorrow," Jack said while reaching back to untie his cuirass. "We're both too goddamn handsome to die."

Before Isaac could look back down, the entire roof of the library caved in. The ceiling and all four walls collapsed into one massive heap of flaming wreckage. A torrent of dust and fire shot out of the balcony doors and knocked Isaac from the railing. Isaac turned toward Uncle Jack at the last second and was able to push off slightly with his left foot.

"Isaac!" Jack yelled, watching his nephew's widened eyes fall out of frame. Jack looked down, but the smoke blocked his view of the ocean. Jack couldn't see where he was jumping.

"Fuck it," he said as he ran down the railing sideways and leaped through the cloud of black smoke right where Isaac had fallen.

Jack felt the sensation of weightlessness. As he flew down, the white foam dissipated, taking away his depth perception. Jack flexed his body into a straight line and braced for impact.

His feet broke the plane, and his body shot in diagonally. The back of his head smacked into the water and sent a sharp tingle down to his toes. He quickly realized he was sinking. The leather cuirass was pulling him down, fast. He kicked his legs, but it only stalled his descent. He was going to have to get it off. He unfastened the ties on the side and then slid out of the armor. His wounded shoulder and broken wrist made it torturous to pull himself upward, but it was life or death. Jack surfaced and gasped for air.

Olney found him with the spotlight.

"Where's Isaac?" Jack yelled into the bright light.

"We didn't see where he landed," Olney yelled from about twenty meters away.

"Shite," Jack said turning himself in the water with his good arm. "Isaac!"

Olney skimmed the spotlight across the water looking for movement. The Oculus rocked back and forth. It was dangerously close to the jagged cliff.

The silence was broken when Jack heard hollow thuds on the boat followed by a splash. Zahra's jet-black hair popped up. She furiously paddled toward him.

"Isaac!" Zahra yelled from the bottom of her stomach.

Maia dove in, too. The three of them spread out and searched. Olney stayed on the boat with the spotlight.

Isaac sank toward the depths of the Mediterranean. He had fallen into the water sideways, and the impact had knocked him out. Small air bubbles trickled out of his nose as he descended. His mind was as dark as the black water below.

Suddenly, a sharp electric impulse shot through the synapses of his brain and his body twitched.

Isaac was awake, but he was also watching himself sink. He felt no panic or fear—no physical or emotional connection to his drowning body. He felt a deep, transcendent calm, and his mind expanded into a higher plane of awareness. Isaac was having an out-of-body experience. He understood everything that was happening.

Complexity seeks simplicity, he thought. *The divine is too complex to manifest itself in physical form. It knows no boundaries and exists in a limitless plane of sensation and space. My dreams have become the simple information vehicle that connects me to the divine. I am now a receptive clairvoyant, and I will use it wisely.*

His body convulsed again, and Isaac understood what was happening. The collective consciousness of his ancestors was downloading a new set of raw data to his subconscious so it could be transferred to his conscious awareness in the form of dreams. Only this time, it was not visions of the past. It was flashes of what was to come.

The revelations rushed through his brain in a barrage. As he sank deeper, they slowed to a recognizable pace. There were ten.

First, he saw himself among the stars falling toward a vast desert of sand dunes. He landed in the sand next to a giant Egyptian statue of a man holding his right hand in the sign of Benediction with two crossed keys at the base.

Second, he lay in a desert oasis, and beautiful women rubbed blood all over his naked body.

Third was an outline of a golden lion chained to a circle of palm trees in front of a full moon.

Fourth, the palm trees turned into flames as he stood at the base of a burning castle tower.

Fifth, dozens of screaming bodies leaped from the windows and landed around him.

Sixth, one of the men landed in a palm tree suspended upside down by his leg.

Seventh, a black-and-white horse pulled an empty chariot right over a sand dune and crashed on top of him.

Eighth, he looked up from the ground and saw a faint glow in the distance.

Ninth, a bearded man in a cloak held a lantern on a cliff high above him. The man pointed up to the constellation of Orion's Belt as it pulled the other constellations toward it like a black hole. Together, they slowly formed into a figure eight lying on its side.

And tenth, he watched himself sinking. He was having an out-of-body experience.

Suddenly, out of the darkness, an ominous presence emerged and surrounded him. The moon broke through the clouds and revealed a glimmering movement of silver wrapping around his body in a figure eight. The presence had stopped his descent but did not lift him toward the surface.

CHAPTER 49

THE ACE OF HEARTS

THE AEGEAN SEA
THERA, GREECE

"Isaac!" Zahra screamed. Tears streamed down her face and into the dark Aegean. Maia and Zahra were treading water when Jack came up for air.

"I can't find him!" Jack yelled, trying to catch his breath.

Maia, Zahra, and Jack were spread out in a large triangle around the area where Isaac had fallen.

Hopelessness hit them. Isaac had been underwater for over a minute. There was a good chance he had already drowned. Jack panicked. He started to hyperventilate.

From the boat, Olney heard the swirling sound of water. He swung the spotlight toward the noise, and the light revealed a giant whirlpool forming.

"Over there!" the professor yelled, pointing toward the light.

Jack looked to his right. Five meters away, the ocean surface swirled rapidly. He felt the strong current sucking him toward it like a riptide. Jack took a deep breath and used every remaining ounce of his energy to swim closer.

Olney watched from the deck as a glimmering figure-eight symbol emerged on the surface of the water. He wiped his glasses and moved closer. It was an enormous school of fish.

"Dear God," Olney said in shock.

Isaac was slowly lifted to the surface at the nexus point of the figure eight.

Jack arrived at the whirlpool. He stopped for a brief second as the school of fish wrapped around his body and continued in their path. Then he saw Isaac's body emerge.

"I got him!" Jack yelled.

He swam toward Isaac, who was still unconscious. Jack used his left arm to wrap up his chest, but the current was too strong to swim out of. Jack kicked as hard as he could, but they both spun in the whirlpool's current.

"Throw me a line!" Jack yelled to Olney.

Olney couldn't move. There were thousands upon thousands of fish circling without stopping

"The symbol of infinity," Olney said to himself.

Without warning, the whirlpool died and the water calmed.

Jack dunked his head under. The fish had disappeared. He had to get Isaac on board and get the water out of his lungs. He frantically swam the boy back to the boat.

"Stay with me," Jack said, trying to keep Isaac above water.

Maia and Zahra beat him to the yacht. Jack's body cramped, but he made it back. The girls pulled Isaac onto the small loading deck on the back of the boat.

"CPR," Jack said from the water, still trying to catch his breath.

Zahra didn't even think. She just reacted. Rachel had taught her CPR, because a lot of the girls had allergic reactions to the medications.

"Compressions," Zahra said to Maia as she tilted Isaac's head back. She wrapped her mouth around Isaac's freezing blue lips and exhaled.

Jack hoisted himself onto the deck, too out of breath to help.

"Thirty compressions, two breaths," Jack gasped from his back while he coughed up water.

Zahra plugged Isaac's nose tighter and breathed into his lungs for the second time. The only sound was the waves lapping against the boat and Maia counting the compressions to herself.

"Again," she said to Zahra, instructing her to start another cycle.

"Come on. Come on, boy," Olney said as tears leaked down his face, tracing lines through the soot the remnants of the fire had left.

Zahra took in a deep breath and blew it into Isaac's lungs. She sat up and inhaled for the second time. She titled Isaac's head back and delivered all of her air. Isaac's body convulsed. His eyes shot open, and he realized that Zahra's mouth was wrapped around his. His first kiss saved his life.

Maia turned him to the side as he coughed up water and caught his breath. Olney was the only one with enough energy to celebrate. He jumped into the air.

"Your mother's inside," Maia said as she rolled Isaac onto his back. "She's going to be fine."

His eyes refocused. A brilliant, clear sky full of constellations came into view followed by something more beautiful—a green-eyed Moroccan girl leaning over him. Zahra was crying but smiling, too. Isaac hoped that was a sign of good things to come.

CHAPTER 50

THE ACE OF CLUBS

THERA, GREECE

At dawn, a black EC-145 helicopter arrived from the northwest and circled the smoking rubble of Soter's compound. Only the white columns remained, but even they were now covered in soot.

Inside the helicopter sat a young, handsome Turkish prince dressed in a white robe and turban. He was with four Turkish Corsairs, who were analyzing Redbeard's tracking signal on a digital screen.

"Prince Osman, the signal is coming from the middle of the build-ing," a Corsair said.

The prince looked out over the remains. His jawline was slender, his skin was smooth like a child's, and even though he had a wispy beard, he looked much younger than thirty-five.

"Land there," Prince Osman said in his delicate voice while pointing his thin finger toward a patch of gravel.

The helicopter touched, down breaking up the smoke with its powerful rotors. The Corsairs jumped out and opened the door for their prince. They knew better than to offer their hand to help him down. Above all else, the prince hated being touched.

Osman jumped down onto the gravel, while holding his white turban under the blades. Three Cosairs escorted the prince, who followed another Corsair with a digital map. They walked toward the smoking debris.

"It's in the center," the Corsair said, climbing through a safe passage of rubble. The group arrived at the fountain in the center of Soter's atrium. Beams and large columns of stones had collapsed around the fountain like a teepee. The Corsairs lifted the burned beams and rubble off the fountain.

Prince Osman watched as his bodyguards removed the wreckage and revealed a rusted bronze sculpture of Atlas. Redbeard wore a gas mask and lay in a pool of red water underneath the statue of the Greek Titan. Atlas held up the debris. Two of the Corsairs pulled him out of the water. One took off his gas mask and felt his pulse.

"He's alive," he said, examining his tightly bandaged stomach wound, dented head, and burned face.

"Wake him," Prince Osman said.

The two Corsairs lightly tapped Redbeard in the face until he woke up. His skin was pale. He had lost a good amount of blood, but he was able to open his eyes.

"Do you have the cards?" Prince Osman asked.

Redbeard couldn't move. He whispered, "Belt."

His fellow Corsair reached down into his belt and pulled out a leather pouch. The Corsair stood and handed it to the prince. Osman opened the pouch and pulled out not one, but *two* original decks of cards from Atlantis.

"Get him on the helicopter," the prince said, grinning. "We have to get him back to Istanbul immediately."

The Corsairs bent down to pick Redbeard up, but he stopped them and whispered something.

A Corsair repeated to the prince, "My prince, he says he does not deserve to live. He let them escape."

Prince Osman gracefully strode toward Redbeard and knelt down next to him.

"Turn around," the prince said to his bodyguards. They did. The young prince stared at a central point on Redbeard's chest with his enigmatic brown eyes. Vibrating rings of black clouds surrounded Redbeard's body.

"You are one of the greatest assassins alive. You have worked for me since I was a child," Prince Osman said quietly. "Yet you fear me. Why?"

"Because I know what you can do," Redbeard whispered.

Prince Osman watched as the pulsating black rings around Redbeard's body got darker. Redbeard looked around but could not see what the prince was seeing.

"Yes, I have a gift," Prince Osman said. "I can read people. But there is no reason to fear me, soldier."

"I failed you," Redbeard mouthed, no sound escaping his burned lips.

"The Antikythera Mechanism was never the objective," Osman said. "I sent you to find the cards. When the four decks are combined, they unlock a secret *far* more powerful than merely predicting the weather. Now we have two, and I have tracked down the location of the third. I need *you* to get it for me. These Western dogs have had their day. With these cards, we can bring the Ottoman Empire back to the height of its power. Will you help me, soldier?"

Redbeard nodded. The prince watched the energy field around him change from black, to gray, to pale red.

"Insha'Allah," Prince Osman said, standing up and watching the color around Redbeard change to a darker red. "This is just the beginning."

"Yes, my prince," Redbeard mouthed.

The Corsairs pulled out a temporary stretcher and carried Redbeard toward the helicopter.

CHAPTER 51:
THE ACE OF DIAMONDS

VALLETTA, MALTA

Cassie and Polly were outside picking vegetables from their garden when they heard cars coming up their dirt road. The twins stood up and saw two black SUVs escorting a Mercedes Benz with red and white flags on the hood of the car.

Their father had drilled them on what to do if he was gone when the bad man showed up. The twins ran back into their bedroom and opened a hidden compartment behind a wall-sized mirror where they brushed each other's hair each night.

Cassie and Polly got inside, pulled the wall shut, and looked through the double-sided mirror. The twins were safe from harm but terrified. They didn't know who was coming into their home. They only knew that this man and his men were their father's biggest fear and the reason he had been stuck on Malta for a very long time.

Outside the compound, the caravan came to an abrupt stop in front of the house. The Mercedes had two small red flags with white Maltese crosses on the hood—each cross with four symmetrical beams, each point ending with two sharp edges. Eight military-type men jumped out of the SUVs wearing earpieces and holding machine guns. They were all dressed in black suits with bright-red ties that also had white Maltese crosses.

One of the soldiers opened the Mercedes door. A seventy-year-old man stepped out wearing a bright-red Cossack, a large wooden cross, and a red liturgical biretta.

"Cardinal Cromley," the soldier said with a slight inclination of his upper body.

The other seven soldiers bowed their heads. Cardinal Cromley raised his hand and blessed them.

Minutes later, the soldiers had kicked the front door down and spread around the house. Cassie and Polly couldn't see anything, but they could hear the house being ransacked.

"It's just a small bronze deck of cards, but we know it was here," Cardinal Cromley said, pacing through the atrium.

The soldiers tore down bookshelves, ripped up floorboards, and trashed Olney's library. Cardinal Cromley walked toward Cassie and Polly's bedroom.

The twins watched through the double-sided mirror as the cardinal entered the room and closed the door behind him. He sniffed the air. The cardinal examined the room and then sat on their bed. He pulled the blankets up to his wrinkled face and took in their scent.

Polly grew nervous and almost whimpered. Cassie had to put her hand over her sister's mouth to quiet her.

The Cardinal walked to the wall-sized mirror and studied his face. He tilted his head left to right examining his perfectly white smile. Then he lifted both of his hands to his mouth and pulled out his upper and lower row of dentures.

Polly almost screamed when she saw what was underneath, but Cassie held her sister tight. The cardinal smiled into the mirror again. He looked demonic. His real teeth had been filed down into sharp points, and his gums were rotted black. It was the most horrific face the twins had ever seen.

There was a knock at the door. "Cardinal Cromley?" a soldier asked from outside.

The cardinal kept his back to the door, and hid his dentures in front of him. "Enter," the cardinal said.

"No sign of the cards," the soldier said, holding his machine gun across his chest.

"Olney's girls are probably in town," the cardinal said. "Conjoined twins on a tiny island shouldn't be too hard to track down. Give me a moment, and we will continue our search downtown."

The soldier closed the door. Cardinal Cromley stared back into the mirror, smiling and pushing saliva through his feral teeth.

On the other side, Cassie and Polly were staring at the short man, face-to-face. Polly locked eyes with the cardinal and was transfixed. She felt the energy draining out of her body, but she couldn't look away. Her eyelids fell down. She was becoming increasingly lethargic. Cassie struggled to hold her up.

Cardinal Cromley had finished attaching both sets of dentures when he felt a familiar sensation. His joints tingled, and his blood started to circulate faster. He felt a flush in his cheeks. The cardinal rolled his fingers into tight fists and squeezed. He was gaining strength from something. That was when Polly fell to the ground and took her sister with her. Cardinal Cromley smirked and reached forward to open the hidden compartment.

CHAPTER 52:
THE ACE OF SPADES

SOTER'S OCULUS YACHT
SOUTHEAST OF CRETE

Isaac's Journal Entry

We passed Crete a few hours ago, and we're heading to the Magis' headquarters in Alexandria. Mom's orders. She's fine. She woke up this morning with a vicious hangover. We let her recover for a few hours, and then Uncle Jack started imitating her on opium. We're all deliriously tired and sad, but it helped lighten the mood. Mom didn't remember anything, so Uncle Jack recapped our escape and made sure to beef up the action. It's safe to assume that from this day forward, the number of Corsairs will increase exponentially.

Mom treated our wounds and made a splint for Jack's broken wrist. He's still complaining about the lack of booze on the yacht and tried to get us to stop in Crete for a tradition he called "mission-accomplished cocktails," but we outvoted him. Now he's up on the captain's deck arguing with Maia about their supposed wedding. With my father gone, I guess Uncle Jack and Professor Olney are now my protectors. I have a soldier to watch over my body and a scholar to watch over my brain. After this, I know that those two will never agree on anything...except my well-being. For that, I'm grateful.

Olney pulled me aside earlier this morning and explained to me in detail what happened while I was underwater. A month ago, I would have tried to find an explanation to justify it. Those days are over, and I now have to accept who and *what* I am. I spent the first seventeen years of my life curled in the fetal position, avoiding the obvious signs and hiding from the world as it came crashing down on me. It took my father's life, but it also forced me to get up. My eyes are open now, and I'm on my feet. The weather has cleared, and there's a path in front of me that leads to an understanding of *why* all this is happening. I will no longer fight this force. I'll have faith that it's guiding me. My dark, overwhelming fear has been replaced with a clear sense of purpose. Somehow and in some way, I'm connected to the universe. For the first time in years, I actually feel good.

I told the professor about my new set of visions. He explained that I had passed a milestone on my life path and was now being given a new set of instructions. Fate has reshuffled my deck and dealt me a whole new hand. But with the professor here, I don't have to keep this round close to the chest. I can play them faceup.

As for Zahra, we've gone back to our awkward shells, but something inside both of us has changed. We're together for a reason, even if we don't know our role in these unfolding events. I *do* know that I have until tomorrow night to try and steal a kiss from her. A mutual one. I'm trying to decide how to play it. Let her approach the quiet, wounded hero? Or just grab her and kiss her like a swashbuckling pirate? Don't worry. I won't do either. I'll find a way to screw it up.

As for my father, I can't even finish a sentence without feeling responsible for his death. If I had known earlier what I was... would this have happened? Or was this outcome inevitable? It presents me with an extremely difficult decision. The only way of uncovering the truth about my prophecy is by joining the Magi. However, this is *exactly* what the oracle warned my father not to let happen. Again, I must have faith in free will, because at this point, I'm *all in*. Egypt and the Order of the Magi await.

As above, so below,

Isaac Alexander, the Ace of Spades

THE SECRET OF THE PLAYING CARDS

These explanations are courtesy of the teacher, author, and master astrologer Robert Lee Camp. For more information or personal card readings, visit his website: www.7thunders.com.

Playing card designs by Alex Beltechi and Ionut Covaci: www.alex-beltechi.com

The Hearts

King of Hearts: The Father Card

Birthdays: June 30, Cancer; July 28, Leo; August 16, Virgo; September 24, Libra; October 22, Libra; November 20, Scorpio; December 18, Sagittarius

Standing at the top of the suit of love, the King of Hearts recognizes that love is the highest power of all. These people make devoted parents, but not always the best spouses. Their devotion to their children and profession often displaces the love they would give their spouse. They do love everyone, forever, it's true, but sometimes, the wrong associations bring problems. These people can be overbearing, as all Kings can, but this is only the case when they have been betrayed by those they hold closest to their hearts. From past lives, they bring with them the knowledge of mastery of their emotions and of their family life. Consider yourself blessed if they consider you to be one of their "family." There are inevitable losses of loved ones in their lives, but they know the truth and can let go though they still feel the pain. Many of them are mentally gifted and sometimes psychic. Much knowledge just flows to them, and they use this to rise up to the top in their careers.

Queen of Hearts: The Mother Card

Birthdays: July 29, Leo; August 27, Virgo; September 25, Libra; October 23, Scorpio; November 21, Scorpio; December 19, Sagittarius.

As the "double Neptune" card, the Queen of Hearts has its share of idealism. All of these people possess a certain charm and magnetism that attracts others. They are the "mothers of love" and share this love with all they come in contact with. They either get married and devote themselves to family or get involved in some professional career. These people are very sweet, attractive, sociable, and loving. They can be successful artists and all have an appreciation for art and beauty. Many are aware of and make use of their abundance of psychic ability. As long as their idealism is guided by truth, they can live the life of love and nurturing that is their birthright. When operating on the lower levels, they can be too self-indulgent, lazy, frivolous, and into the "good life." There are many escapists and alcoholics among the Queen of Hearts as well. Once they set their sights, however, there is no limit to how high they can climb in their work and career.

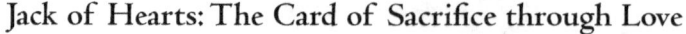

Jack of Hearts: The Card of Sacrifice through Love

Birthdays: July 30, Leo; August 28, Virgo; September 26, Libra; October 24, Scorpio; November 22, Scorpio/Sagittarius; December 20, Sagittarius

As one of the three fixed cards, the Jacks of Hearts feel strongly about their version of love. They are surrounded by the Christ spirit of sacrifice through love. Even though they are Jacks, which are sometimes immature and crafty, they are influenced by the wisdom of the Christ spirit, which gives them higher guidance and higher motives in general. They must watch, however, that their martyrdom does not get out of hand. They can also become escapists and misguided, but this is the exception. Love is their power and birthright. They have come to love others and to show them the way by their example. They often make sacrifices in their life and their personal fulfillment may be given up for some higher cause or philosophy. As born leaders, they must be successful in their own profession. They all carry the spirit of higher love within them, and all people they associate with are in some way uplifted by their presence. They find their greatest fulfillment on a spiritual path.

Ten of Hearts: The Social Success Card

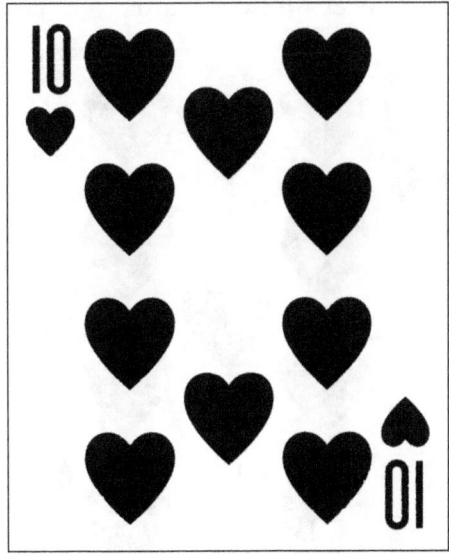

Birthdays: July 31, Leo; August 29. Virgo; September 27, Libra; October 25, Scorpio; November 23, Sagittarius; December 21, Sagittarius/Capricorn

Like the Ace of Hearts, these people have much ambition in their life and could stray off the path of truth as a result. However, they have already experienced the truth and have the knowing that is their birthright to guide them at each step on the way. They are creative and usually artistic. They are leaders, not followers. They love children and groups of people they may regard as their children. They are innovators and can make a great contribution in their chosen field as long as they exercise clarity in their judgment. Their motives can either be humanitarian or selfish, and this usually has a lot to do with their ultimate destination. They are independent and often impulsive, but this is usually kept in balance by their wisdom. They can make a unique mark on the world through the application of their inherent gifts. They are usually gentle and wise people—at least the wisdom is there. Their wisdom is their protector and guiding light.

Nine of Hearts: The Giver of Love Card

Birthdays: August 30, Virgo; September 28, Libra; October 26, Scorpio; November 24, Sagittarius; December 22, Capricorn/Sagittarius

This is a card of great fulfillment, great loss, or both. This card, and its Karma Card, the Seven of Diamonds, are both spiritual numbers, and the fulfillment that comes is rarely personal until all personal desires are set aside and in their proper place. This is the double Saturn card—these people cannot deviate from what is true and "right" without swift, and sometimes bitter, rebuke. All nines have come to settle affairs and debts from the past, to pay what they owe and move on. For the Nine of Hearts, there will be some completions or endings of key relationships that mark their completion of certain "soul chapters." If these endings are resisted, they will turn to disappointment and loss. Their life path is full of spiritual lessons. Those who heed the call and adhere to higher values will have seemingly blessed lives, while those who give into their fears and escapist tendencies will suffer greatly. They are givers, endowed with great minds and hearts to share with the world.

Eight of Hearts: The Emotional Power Card

Birthdays August 31, Virgo; September 29, Libra; October 27, Scorpio; November 25, Sagittarius; December 23, Capricorn.

The Eight of Hearts has "power in love," and all eights have to exercise discrimination and responsibility in its use. Both Karma Cards of the Eight of Hearts are sevens. This tells us that they will see almost immediate results when they misuse their power with others. With wisdom and spiritual awareness, they can rise to great heights in sharing their love and healing power with others. Operating out of their fear, they find those who are the dominators of those they love and seek to manipulate others through guilt and withholding of affection and acknowledgment. These people have high ideals about love and relationships; sometimes these ideals are too high to ever be met. They have great minds and make excellent teachers, or they can excel in any occupation where a good mind will make a difference. They have to work hard for the money they make, but it can be made and they need not worry about it. With all the power at their command, there is little they cannot do, as long as it is not motivated by fear.

Seven of Hearts: The Spiritual Love Card

Birthdays: September 30, Libra; October 28, Scorpio; November 26, Sagittarius; December 24, Capricorn

The Sevens of Hearts have a quest for the truth about love and relationships. They are old souls who have come here to reach the highest in these areas "or else." With two nines in their Life Path, they have come to complete a grand cycle in their soul's work and to let go of many things so that they may progress to the next level. These people must learn to let go of all personal attachments and give to others without expectation of return or reward. On the low side, these people can be preoccupied with many suspicions and jealousies, which is but a reflection of their own nature. On the high side, they find those who make great personal sacrifices for others and who give much to the world. All must find some way to give to the world to attain peace and satisfaction. This usually manifests as teaching or consulting. Anyone born as a seven or nine must learn to give and let go or suffer great pain and disappointment. The Sevens of Hearts are the givers of knowledge and love and can reach the highest.

Six of Hearts: The Peacemaker's Card

Birthdays: October 29, Scorpio; November 27, Sagittarius; December 25, Capricorn

This is a card of harmony and stability in love and family. The Six of Hearts people are aware of the "law of love" and apply themselves to maintain stability in relationships. This stability can make for a satisfying life or one of monotony and boredom. It all depends upon how it is handled by the individual. They are somewhat fixed and dislike changes. Sometimes this can keep them in a relationship longer than necessary as they sort out their intentions and motives. They are usually successful and can apply their great mental power to most any area with success, in spite of occasional fears about not having enough. They are here to settle karmic love debts and to forgive and forget, and they can rise to the heights of spiritual awareness by their actions. They never get away with injuries to others and are well aware of that. As the card for Christmas, their lives are intended to be those of plenty and giving. It is here that they find happiness.

Five of Hearts: The Emotionally Restless Card

Birthdays: October 30, Scorpio; November 28, Sagittarius; December 26, Capricorn.

All fives need to settle down, and the Five of Hearts is no exception. Their unsettledness also extends to finances because of the Four of Diamonds underlying. The Fives of Hearts want to experience all that love and money have to offer but often fail to find it because they never concentrate on one person or job long enough to get the rewards of sustained effort. Is it any surprise that the basic meaning of this card is "change in affections" and "divorce"? These people invariably meet many people and have many "friends," but few ever get close to them. They have the ability to make as much money as they want, if they would apply the power of their Four of Diamonds and stick to one thing. But that involves losing out on all the other possibilities of life and only few make that sacrifice. Their lives are enhanced by the study of spiritual knowledge in any form. It provides answers and blessings. They can become great teachers. They usually find more satisfaction in relationships that are noncommitted and open.

Four of Hearts: The Family Card

Birthdays: October 31, Scorpio; November 29, Sagittarius; December 27, Capricorn.

Here we have the first four in the deck, the first to seek stability and foundation. The Four of Hearts seeks this in relationships. These people have high ideals about love and family, and when these ideals are not reached, the pain can be so great that they need some form of escape to soothe themselves. If their ideals are combined with truth and objectivity, these people can have wonderful lives of fulfillment in family and other love areas. Many are healers and protectors, and others come to them for love and support in times of need. They all have a need for self-expression and do well with groups and organizations as teachers and event organizers. Some have great scientific minds as well. They are very good with money and have no one but themselves to blame if their lives are not happy and productive. They must maintain good health habits as this card, more than others, never gets away with indulgence, either physical or emotional. Satisfaction comes in giving.

Three of Hearts: The Indecision in Love Card

Birthdays: November 30, Sagittarius; December 28, Capricorn.

The Three of Hearts is the first card in the Mundane Spread of cards and represents the departure of Man and Woman from the Garden of Eden. In search of what and who they love, they can often become confused and dissatisfied, even when they find the perfect love standing in front of them. Of the threes, all of whom demand the freedom to explore possibilities, the Three of Hearts can become the most confused and bewildered mentally and emotionally. Either they are very fickle in love or the one they love is fickle. They are quite psychic and hard workers and have success whenever they apply themselves. They need a certain amount of change or travel in their vocation to be happy. They are very charming and attractive people and have no trouble attracting others to love. The challenge comes once they find someone. They are here to learn to make decisions about love and money and to learn the value of higher knowledge. Once they do, they find great fulfillment in giving love and truth.

Two of Hearts: The Love Affair Card

Birthdays: December 29, Capricorn

As one of the semifixed cards, the Twos of Hearts are certain about their direction and will accept it from no one else. They have marvelous minds and a natural, insatiable curiosity that leads to great mental development. However, they never stray far from the basic meaning of their card, that of the "lovers." They need other people and have very high, sometimes unrealistic, ideals about love and marriage. They would always prefer to be with someone rather than be alone and will wait as long as necessary for the right person to come along. They usually end up associating with others of means and power and prefer this kind of company. Financial fears crop up from time to time and must be handled carefully so that they do not affect their health and well-being. A study of metaphysics will always bring more positive guidance and fulfillment. Many have natural psychic ability that can be used for fun or profit. As Capricorns, all have a tendency to be too practical and hard. Lighten up, Two of Hearts!

Ace of Hearts: The Search for Love Card

Birthdays: December 30, Capricorn

The meaning of the Ace of Hearts, the first card in the deck, is the "desire for love." However, the desire for money is also present because of their Ace of Diamonds Karma Card. People with this birth card have strong spiritual inclinations, but they are often "tempted" off the path by indecision and their hidden desires. More than other cards, they can have the best success by turning this indecision into creativity, and many become accomplished writers. In any case, they need some variety in the work that they do. All are Capricorns, so their work is important along with a desire to achieve something of importance in this life. Much difficulty in later life is avoided when they turn their interests toward metaphysics. They should avoid a tendency toward fickleness and pro-miscuity if they are ever to find the peace of mind and heart they are seeking. Giving brings them the highest rewards.

THE CLUBS

King of Clubs: The King of Knowledge and Master of Distinctions

Birthdays: January 27, Aquarius; February 25, Pisces; March 23, Aries; April 21, Aries / Taurus; May 19, Taurus; June 17, Gemini; July 15, Cancer; August 13, Leo; September 11, Virgo; October 9, Libra; November 7, Scorpio; December 5, Sagittarius

Sitting atop the suit of knowledge, the Kings of Clubs have everything needed to be an authority in any area they choose. These people have a direct line to knowledge accumulated from many past lives. Rarely do they live their lives by any doctrine or philosophy other than their own. The well that feeds their minds is inexhaustible and from a high source. These are the people who live by their own truth. They can be found in all types of professions, usually in positions of responsibility, always respected in whatever capacity they are engaged. They have many opportunities for marriage. Relationships and partnerships are important to them. However, they also need a certain amount of personal freedom, and for many, this is more important than a marriage. They seem to do their best work with a partner, and most Kings of Clubs are destined to be in partnership. This is the most psychic card in the deck—so much so that their intuitive approach to life is second nature.

Queen of Clubs: The Mother of Intuition Card

Birthdays: January 28, Aquarius; February 26, Pisces; March 24, Aries; April 22, Taurus; May 20, Taurus; June 18, Gemini; July 16, Cancer; August 14, Leo; September 12, Virgo; October 10, Libra; November 8, Scorpio; December 6, Sagittarius

All Queens are service oriented and receptive in nature. The mental nature of clubs inclines the Queen of Clubs to deal in the publishing trade, secretarial work, or in the more aware ones, psychic work. Being Queens, they are always aware of their place in the royal court and resist anyone trying to mold them in any way. Their Karma card, the Three of Hearts, as well as the Five of Clubs in their Venus position, tells us that indecision about love and friendship makes it hard for them to find lasting happiness in these areas. Their mental gifts are abundant (Ten of Spades in Mercury), and whether or not they realize it, they are always receiving knowledge from the "other side." Their Ace of Spades in Jupiter promises many rewards if and when they follow spiritual or psychic lines of work or pursuits. They have a deep heritage of knowledge from past lives that is always available. The Queen of Clubs is also known as the "Mother Mary" card, and many of them have one or more "children" for whom they must make sacrifices in their life.

Jack of Clubs: The Mentally Creative Card

Birthdays: January 29, Aquarius; February 27, Pisces; March 25, Aries; April 23, Taurus; May 21, Taurus/Gemini; June 19, Gemini; July 17, Cancer; August 15, Leo; September 13, Virgo; October 11, Libra; November 9, Scorpio; December 7, Sagittarius

Creative or dishonest? Which is which? As we can imagine, those who are the most creative can also be the most dishonest and vice versa. Here is a card of mental and financial creativity, and these people are no lazy bones. Their brilliant minds are far ahead of the common person and society. They are the people of the Aquarian Age. As members of the royal family, they dislike pettiness and tend to be somewhat impatient with the failings of others. They need respect and a position that allows their brilliant minds free reign to create and explore. They are never at a loss for ideas, some of which will bring them huge financial returns. On the negative side, the Jack of Clubs can be irresponsible and in some cases, dishonest. They can see things from so many levels that nothing is really "wrong"; it is just another way of looking at things. They don't get away with much in that regard though. Saturn's swift chastisement always reminds them of the boundaries that keep them balanced and fair in their dealings.

Ten of Clubs: The Teacher Card

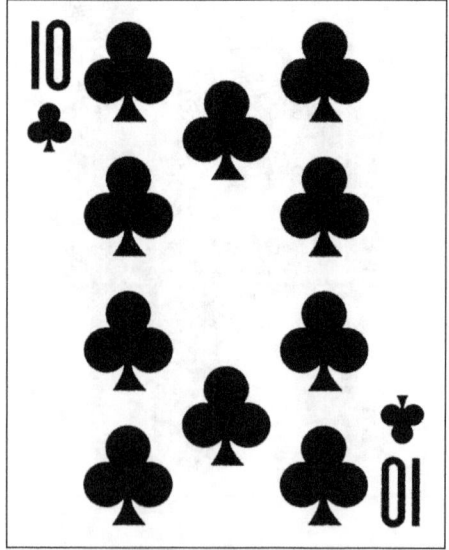

Birthdays: January 30, Aquarius; February 28, Pisces; March 26, Aries; April 24, Taurus; May 22, Gemini; June 20, Gemini; July 18, Cancer; August 16, Leo; September 14, Virgo; October 12, Libra; November 10, Scorpio; December 8, Sagittarius

The Tens of Clubs have come full circle in their quest for knowledge. They have a powerful mind and a consuming desire for more knowledge as well. In this life, they must learn to regain the control over their mind, which has developed somewhat of a life of its own. The best path back to self-mastery is to direct the mind into right motives and higher principles. Their Three of Hearts in Mars makes for emotional restlessness, which can be a strain on relationships. The strong desire for spiritual wisdom and study of spiritual philosophies will bring contact with many uplifting groups and will increase enjoyment of life. The Tens of Clubs have good luck in work and labor relations and could do very well in the real-estate business. Their Three of Diamonds Pluto Card signifies that in this life, they will be doing much experimenting as they work toward finding out what really satisfies them. They often spend a lot of time deciding what is their life's work. Once they decide, they can rise to the heights. Choosing things that allow for freedom and travel gives them the best results.

Nine of Clubs: The Card of Universal Knowledge and the Giver of Knowledge

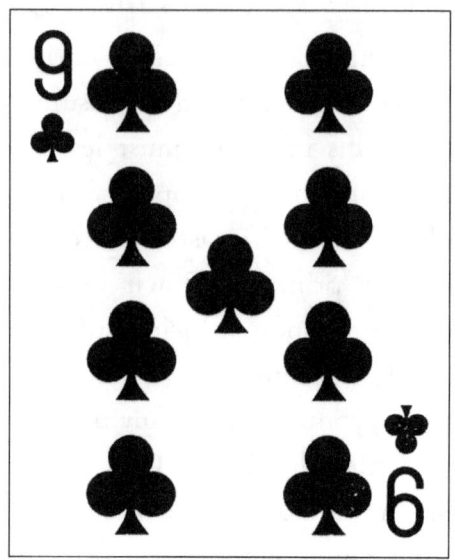

Birthdays: January 31, Aquarius; February 29, Pisces; March 27, Aries; April 25, Taurus; May 23, Gemini; June 21, Cancer; July 19, Cancer; August 17, Leo; September 15, Virgo; October 13, Libra; November 11, Scorpio; December 9, Sagittarius

Though this is a card of expanded consciousness, it is also a card of negative thinking. These people must let go of many negative mental patterns accumulated from past lives if they are to access the inherent power in this card. There are many who do and who have reached the very heights of recognition. This is a card of sexual enjoyment and pleasure seeking. If this is allowed to dominate, much time and energy is wasted that would otherwise elevate them to great accomplishment. The Nine of Clubs is here to end a major cycle in their soul's development, a completion that should see them giving their wealth of knowledge to the world. There are some debts to be paid, especially to the Six of Diamonds and Queen of Hearts, but once these debts are paid, they can proceed with their cosmic task of enlightening the world. Financially, they are always assisted by diamond men, and they do well in their own business if they don't let it spoil their spiritual values. They cannot be totally materialistic or mercenary.

Eight of Clubs: The Card of Mental Power

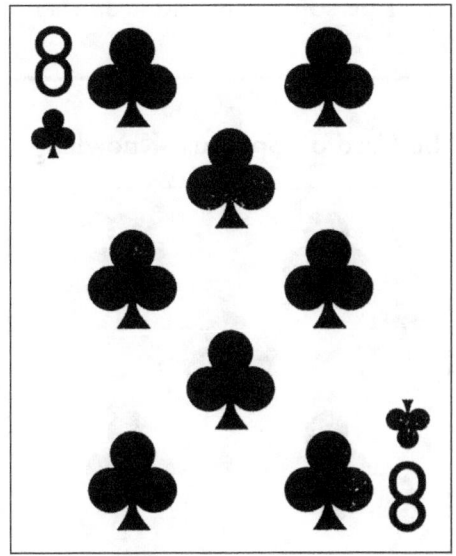

Birthdays: March 28, Aries; April 26, Taurus; May 24, Gemini; June 22, Gemini/Cancer; July 20, Cancer; August 18, Leo; September 16, Virgo; October 14, Libra; November 12, Scorpio; December 10, Sagittarius

The Eight of Clubs is one of the three "fixed" cards. With their strong mental power, they are not easily swayed by others' views and opinions. Many successful attorneys, chemical engineers, and rocket scientists are Eights of Clubs; however, their power can be applied to any of the mental fields with great success. Their life path is one of the most successful in the deck. They can have almost anything they set their mind to achieving, and most attain wealth and prominence, but they must make sure their life is kept in balance, as mental peace is essential. They have much psychic power and can be great healers. All of their gifts can be applied to attain great success, and they only need to become aware of their true goals to have a life of success and accomplishment. However, being so fixed has its own drawbacks, mainly that it is difficult for them to deal with changes. Working with a Jack of Hearts or King of Spades will bring far-reaching success. For best results, they should let their work come before their personal lives and keep them separate.

Seven of Clubs: The Card of Spiritual Knowledge

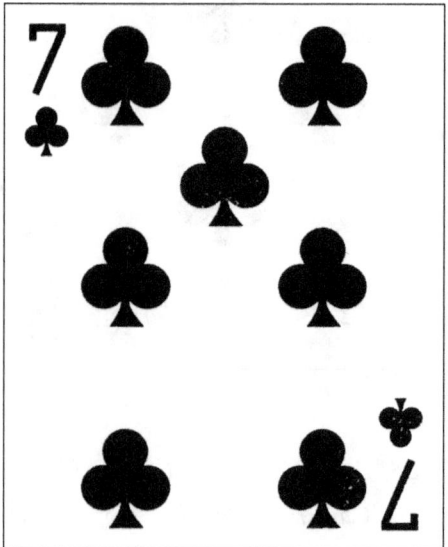

Birthdays: March 29, Aries; April 27, Taurus; May 25, Gemini; June 23, Cancer; July 21, Cancer; August 19, Leo; September 17, Virgo; October 15, Libra; November 13, Scorpio; December 11, Sagittarius

All sevens are highly spiritual cards, but it is up to the individual to manifest this spirituality and to turn negativity into accomplishment. The Seven of Clubs' challenge rests in the negative aspects of the mind, which are worry, doubt, and pessimism. They have much inherent inspiration and insight, but when they don't follow it, Saturn's influence brings much despair and sometimes depression. They have power to overcome their problems and to attain the fame and recognition they secretly desire, but they must apply themselves diligently. They are likely to have large sums of money at different times in their life, but often they spend it as fast as they get it. All their difficulties in life can be traced directly to their thoughts. So people of the Seven of Clubs, more than any other card, have a great responsibility to maintain positive, healing thoughts. Any contact with spiritual thought or ideals is sure to have a positive effect on them and is highly recommended.

Six of Clubs: The Card of Higher Purpose

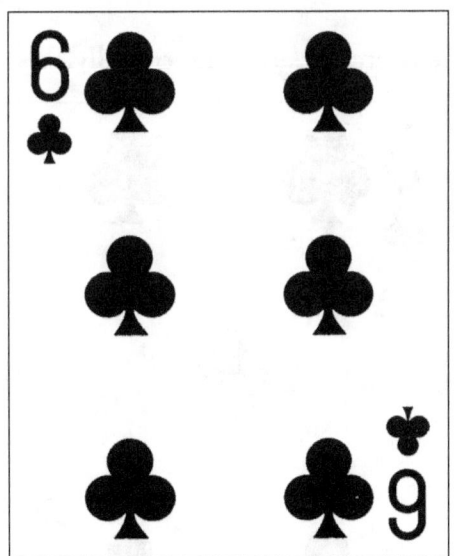

Birthdays: March 30, Aries; April 28, Taurus; May 26, Gemini; June 24, Cancer; July 22, Cancer; August 20, Leo; September 18, Virgo; October 16, Libra; November 14, Scorpio; December 12, Sagittarius

This card is also known as the psychic card, and it is surprising to see how few of the people of these birth dates are aware of their gift. The Six of Clubs means responsibility to truth. These people must learn to find a system of truth that they can believe in and live their life by. Once attained, there is no limit to how much good these people can do in the world. Those who have not yet found their path can be the biggest worriers and procrastinators of all the cards in the deck. They have a responsibility to maintain inner balance and peaceful communications with those in their lives. They often attain financial affluence and have inherent protection over their lives. Love is important to them. The women make good wives and mothers while the men are often dominated by a woman. Once they tap into their hidden reserves and their natural intuition is recognized, they find their lives guided and protected from the highest sources possible.

Five of Clubs: The Mentally and Emotionally Restless Card

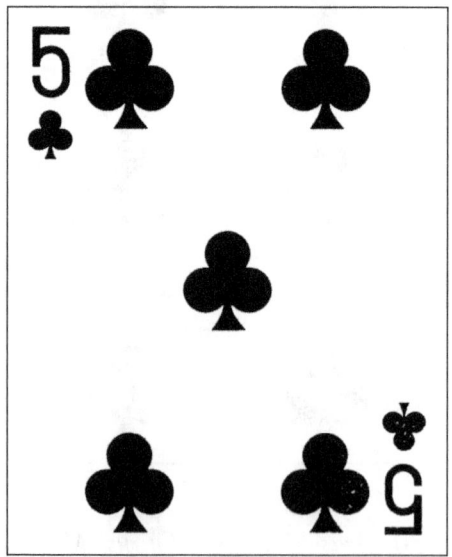

Birthdays: March 31, Aries; April 29, Taurus; May 27, Gemini; June 25, Cancer; July 23, Cancer/Leo; August 21, Leo; September 19, Virgo; October 17, Libra; November 15, Scorpio; December 13, Sagittarius

The Five of Clubs means changes and restlessness of the mind, and we find these people to have a lot of curiosity and restlessness in their lives. Their Five of Hearts Karma Card tells us that they also have many changes in their romantic life as well, and for this reason, they are not usually well suited for marriage. They have the Ace of Spades in Venus, and that speaks of secret love affairs and indecision about which to choose. Their Seven of Diamonds in Jupiter is a millionaire's card, and many of them have lots of money, though they often spend it as fast as they get it. Speculation and gambling should be avoided. Their natural curiosity brings them much knowledge, but they often do not apply it or stick to one train of thought. This tends to make them skeptics, not even getting satisfaction from their own self-created belief structures. An interest in spiritual studies brings more satisfaction in their later years and provides answers that bring more peace to their lives. A spiritual teacher is helpful in this regard.

Four of Clubs: The Card of Mental Satisfaction

Birthdays: April 30, Taurus; May 28, Gemini; June 26, Cancer; July 24, Leo; August 22, Leo/Virgo; September 20, Virgo; October 18, Libra; November 16, Scorpio; December 14, Sagittarius

Though this is a card of stability, their Five of Clubs Karma Card also indicates a hidden restlessness that can manifest in several ways. These people are progressive and can utilize this to create new ideas in their chosen line of work, rather than let the restlessness keep them from achieving any success. These people know what they know and are not likely to change their minds on your behalf unless they see the value of change for themselves. "Stubborn" may describe it better in many cases. They are fond of argument, since they usually win, and usually do well in legal matters. They have a good constitution and are not afraid of hard work. This is a successful card. They are good at sales work and enjoy talking about what they believe in. They are popular and do well in groups. As long as they don't let their love of debate get out of hand, they will keep a fine reputation in their work. They also want a successful love life, and this is their major life challenge.

Three of Clubs: The Writer's Card

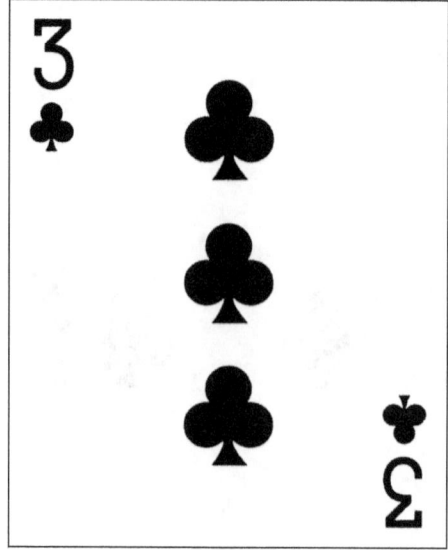

Birthdays: May 29, Gemini; June 27, Cancer; July 25, Leo; August 23, Virgo; September 21, Virgo; October 19, Libra; November 17, Scorpio; December 15, Sagittarius

The creativity in this card can manifest in many ways. On the high side, these people can be highly successful writers, teachers, or performers. On the low side, they can worry, spend their time on frivolous activities, and never reach their full potential. Success in life always depends upon the individuals and how they use their God-given gifts and abilities. The Three of Clubs is gifted, but their fear of poverty may entice them into using their creativity in questionable ways. If this happens, they seldom get away with it. They make great salespeople and propagandists, but they are ineffective until they decide upon one philosophy and stand behind it. They are sure to have emotional losses, many of which are destined. If they see them as "completions" that lead them to a higher level, they avoid disappointment. If they use their inheritance of spiritual knowledge, much success can be realized.

Two of Clubs: The Card of Conversation

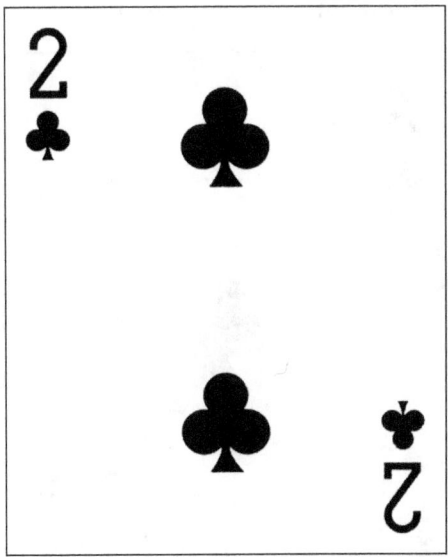

Birthdays: May 30, Gemini; June 28, Cancer; July 26, Leo; August 24, Virgo; September 22, Virgo; October 20, Libra; November 18, Scorpio; December 16, Sagittarius

Among the people of this card, you will note a wide variety. Many are fearful of everything, especially being alone, and will do everything in their power to make sure they are surrounded by people who admire them. All are sociable and enjoy good, stimulating conversations. Then there are those who are reclusive and appear to need no one. In truth, they are just as afraid and always have one special person to whom they attach themselves. The Ace of Spades Karma Card can mean an inner fear of death or change, and this explains much of their behavior. However, these people are well endowed with many natural abilities and gifts. They can be exceptional in business and with people, preferring to work in partnership rather than alone. There is much protection surrounding this card, and they all have much to be grateful for. If they simply recognize the abundance in their lives, they will help to dispel their underlying fear that can do so much damage.

Ace of Clubs: The Desire for Knowledge Card

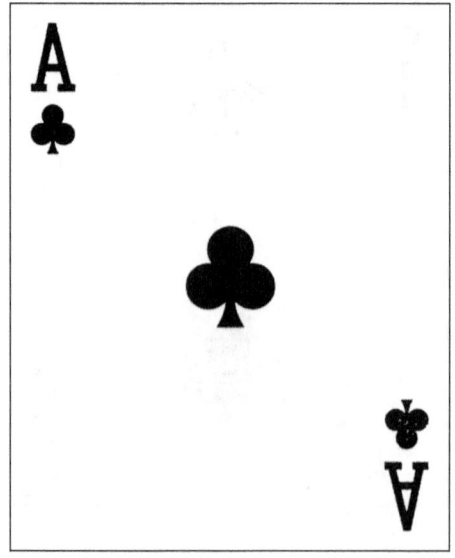

Birthdays: May 31, Gemini; June 29, Cancer; July 27, Leo; August 25, Virgo; September 23, Libra; October 21, Scorpio; November 19, Scorpio; December 17, Sagittarius

The desire for knowledge, accompanied by the desire for love, are the main ruling influences for this card. Combine these together, and you have a person who is a student of love, as much as one who would find his or her ideal mate. This card is known for promiscuity, but this is only true until they find the person of their dreams. They would rather be with anyone than be alone but will not give themselves fully until the right person comes along. Like all Aces, they are impatient and restless. Their curiosity leads them to be avid students with immense libraries. They are very smart and can use their brains and creativity to generate ample funds. They can make money in things associated with the arts or groups of women. Their later years will not be satisfactory unless they turn to spirituality for guidance. They are the divine discontent card and need travel and changes in life and their work to satisfy both their desire for knowledge and their inner restlessness.

THE DIAMONDS

King of Diamonds: The Business Owner

Birthdays: January 14, Capricorn; February 12, Aquarius; March 10, Pisces; April 8, Aries; May 6, Taurus; June 4, Gemini; July 2, Cancer

The King of Diamonds is the master of values. In this regard, these people can do very well in any business pursuit, applying the inherited knowledge to their business with much success. These people always do better as heads of their own business. They can be very mercenary when it comes to money and business, but they don't have to be. This is the only "one-eyed" king in the deck, which means that they tend to see everything from their own point of view exclusive of others. This can make them very stubborn and one-sided in their viewpoints. However, all of them know what is of real value, and if they follow their knowing instead of their fears, they can be the most respectable people in the business world. They must always guard against using their power to get things to go their way. They have good marriage karma in general and usually marry someone who is intelligent and able to contribute to their goals. They are very creative and can make huge amounts of money by using this gift. The Kings of Diamonds are powerful people who can do much good in the world and can be examples of those who are "in the world but not of it."

Queen of Diamonds: The Philanthropist Card

Birthdays: January 15, Capricorn; February 13, Aquarius; March 11, Pisces; April 9, Aries; May 7, Taurus; June 5, Gemini; July 3, Cancer; August 1, Leo.

Like some other cards in the deck, the Queen of Diamonds has much indecision about values (Three of Diamonds Karma Card). Although they are in the royal suit of money, they are often worried about money and have some difficulty in managing it. Queens of Diamonds are known to be charming and enjoy the finer things in life. Often, they spend beyond their budget, and this adds to their financial worries. Their Three of Diamonds Karma Card speaks of indecision about what they want that has them constantly seeking new adventures and sometimes relationships as well. Many of the world's greatest givers are Queens of Diamonds, though personal relationships are usually difficult because of the indecision about what they want and their changeable nature. If they adopt a spiritual path in life and realize that they have a mission, they can achieve the heights of spiritual realization and self-mastery (Queen of Spades in Neptune). This realization will also dispel all of the problems that they have with money and love.

Jack of Diamonds: The Financially Creative Card

Birthdays: January 16, Capricorn; February 14, Aquarius; March 12, Pisces; April 10, Aries; May 8, Taurus; June 6, Gemini; July 4, Cancer; August 2, Leo

This is the salesman's card. These people are sharp, clever, and always able to make a good living using their wit and charm. They are very independent and creative and operate as much on their instincts as they do on their quick minds. They can always get along and do well in life by virtue of their inherited financial expertise. Few heed the call of their highest ideals and become the king that stands close to them. Their natural psychic ability can lead them to direct spiritual realization, but all Jacks are fixed in their minds and often this prevents them from exploring that which is one of their greatest gifts. All Jacks can be immature and crafty, due to their vast creativity, and they usually mean well even when they are not able to come through on their promises. They love to be social, and they are the best salespeople in the zodiac. They must find a career that gives them an outlet for their creativity and recognition of their superior talents. The United States is a Jack of Diamonds (July 4).

Ten of Diamonds: The Blessed Card

Birthdays: January 17, Capricorn; February 15, Aquarius; March 13, Pisces; April 11, Aries; May 9, Taurus; June 7, Gemini; July 5, Cancer; August 3, Leo; September 1, Virgo

This card sits in the very center of the Grand Solar Spread of cards, protected on all sides by Jupiter's blessings. It is *the* card of material opulence. With so many blessings, you might expect them to be generous souls, but that is not always the case. Many of them simply direct these blessings to the acquisition of more money, and some of them even become ruthless in this regard. Others, however, pay heed to their Queen of Clubs Karma Card, the Mother Mary card, and devote their talents and resources to helping the world. In this way, they use their natural intuition and fulfill a desire for devotion and service. With their creativity and intelligence, they are always successful in whatever they undertake. Usually, this power is directed toward business and gain. Many of them inherit or marry into wealth. If they develop their spiritual awareness, their later years will be filled with expansion of their minds and souls instead of doubt and indecision.

Nine of Diamonds: The Card of Universal Values and the Giver's Card

Birthdays: January 18, Capricorn; February 16, Aquarius; March 14, Pisces; April 12, Aries; May 10, Taurus; June 8, Gemini; July 6, Cancer; August 4, Leo; September 2, Virgo

Nine of Diamonds people are here to let go and complete a major chapter in their evolution. This entails a lot of giving to others. If they have not heeded the call to give and let go of others, money, relationships, and love, their life can be filled with disappointment and remorse. Those on the positive side are philanthropic and generous, happy and productive. All have the opportunity to experience firsthand, the heightened consciousness that comes from living a "universal" life. Despite losses from time to time, these people can do very well in business, especially when it involves selling or other creative enterprises. If they keep money in proper perspective, they may even attain affluence. A disregard for the higher laws will inevitably result in misfortune and misery. They should be careful while driving and in taking other chances. They can be reckless. Marriage is usually karmic and often long lasting. The men should always beware of female Clubs cards.

Eight of Diamonds: The Sun Card

Birthdays: January 19, Capricorn; February 17, Aquarius; March 15, Pisces; April 13, Aries; May 11, Taurus; June 9, Gemini; July 7, Cancer; August 5, Leo; September 3, Virgo; October 1, Libra

As the sun card, the Eight of Diamonds has the opportunity to rise to great heights in this life. Regardless of whether they make the move for great fame, they are always respected and looked up to in their work. They love to "shine." These people are powerful and can be dominating. Their eight power and position in the Crown Line gives them an independent and sometimes "pushy" nature. In any case, they know what everything is worth and can drive a hard bargain. They can achieve anything through hard work and the application of their inherent intuition. When they learn to redirect their power inward to themselves and stop trying to change the world, they can attain the lasting peace of inner power and self-mastery, the key words of their Queen of Spades Karma Card. In love, they tend toward fickleness. The Eights of Diamonds' independent, changeable nature may resist marriage. They must learn to give others freedom of expression without trying to change them. They also need to learn to accept themselves as they are.

Seven of Diamonds: The Millionaire's Card

Birthdays: January 20, Capricorn; February 18, Aquarius; March 16, Pisces; April 14, Aries; May 12, Taurus; June 10, Gemini; July 8, Cancer; August 6, Leo; September 4, Virgo; October 2, Libra

By suit, the Seven of Diamonds is always connected with finances. As a spiritual number, they must maintain a nonattached attitude about money or there will be continuous problems in this area. Once they put money in its proper place, however, they often attain or inherit great wealth. Regardless, many of their life lessons will come through this avenue. The other avenue is their close relationships. Family, lovers, and friends are all very important to the Seven of Diamonds person. They have close ties, for better or worse, with their family and share in their trials. They are usually restless, making frequent changes in either occupation or location. Their love life usually entails sacrifice and disappointment until they learn to let others go and be as they are. In their spiritual studies, they find inner satisfaction and validation for their own intuition. Once on the path, everything in their life is put into proper perspective, and they can excel in any chosen field.

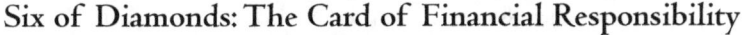

Six of Diamonds: The Card of Financial Responsibility

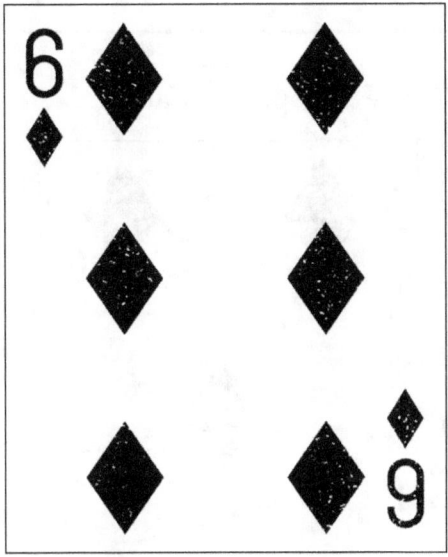

Birthdays: January 21, Capricorn/Aquarius; February 19, Aquarius/Pisces; March 17, Pisces; April 15, Aries; May 13, Taurus; June 11, Gemini; July 9, Cancer; August 7, Leo; September 5, Virgo; October 3, Libra; November 1, Scorpio

The number six implies responsibility, and diamonds relate to finances. Six of Diamonds people are keenly aware of debts and their repayment. Like all sixes, they receive exactly what they put out. They may fall into slumps as a result of their inertia, so they need to remember to prod themselves into action. Once they get going, they can attain most anything they desire. There is protection in work and action. On a deeper level, the Six of Diamonds is here to settle karmic debts from past lives. Finances can go from one extreme to the other in this process. If they accept what they inwardly know, they will always be happy whatever the circumstances in their life. If they have discovered their special mission in life, they will not worry about how much money they have. These people make great teachers. They are givers and can be entrusted with great responsibility. What they have to give is a clear knowledge of values and discrimination.

Five of Diamonds: The Salesperson Card

Birthdays: January 22, Aquarius; February 20, Pisces; March 18, Pisces; April 16, Aries; May 14, Taurus; June 12, Gemini; July 10, Cancer; August 8, Leo; September 6, Virgo; October 4, Libra; November 2, Scorpio

This card has its share of challenges and its share of gifts. Like all fives, they dislike routine and abhor anything that pretends to limit their freedom. They can be perpetual wanderers, never settling down for anything long enough to make it pay off. This includes their work and relationships. All fives have an inner restlessness, but they truly want to accomplish something of value and stability in their lives. They are inherently spiritual and know what is of true value. The challenge comes in practicing what they know. They come into this life with a certain amount of karma, which often takes considerable hard work to discharge. If they are lazy, there will be many problems. They must practice what they know and do what it takes to get the job done without shirking responsibility. They make great salespeople, and they have tried many things in life and know how to relate to anyone on their own level. Their inner truth is their guiding light.

Four of Diamonds: The Card of Solid Values

Birthdays: January 23, Aquarius; February 21, Pisces; March 19, Pisces; April 17, Aries; May 15, Taurus; June 13, Gemini; July 11, Cancer; August 9, Leo; September 7, Virgo; October 5, Libra; November 3, Scorpio; December 1, Sagittarius

The Four of Diamonds is a card of protection in finances; however, that protection is only accessed through hard work. This card, above most others, must put forth the effort to reap the rewards, but the rewards are surely there. To achieve this, they often have to come to terms with their own inner restlessness (Five of Spades Karma Card) and dissatisfaction. They never receive anything without paying some price for it. Often the work they must do involves their marriage or their closest relationships. These people are very sociable, meet many people, and usually have many friends. They have high ideals concerning love and often these ideals can cause confusion in real-life romantic situations. There are difficulties to be dealt with in their life and they must watch a tendency to get into a rut and get stuck there. However, all they need to do to have more happiness is to work. Once they get into action, everything smooths out, and their fears are laid to rest.

Three of Diamonds: The Undecided Values Card

Birthdays: January 24, Aquarius; February 22, Pisces; March 20, Pisces; April 18, Aries; May 16, Taurus; June 14, Gemini; July 12, Cancer; August 10, Leo; September 8, Virgo; October 6, Libra; November 4, Scorpio; December 2, Sagittarius

The Three of Diamonds is considered one of the more difficult of the life paths of all the cards, especially when the Three of Diamonds is a woman. Indecision in values, along with past-life karma (Six of Hearts Karma Card), in relationships causes many challenges in the affectional life. A natural interest in metaphysics should be cultivated if they are to know more peace in their lives and overcome the many hurdles and temptations. They always know what is right and wrong, though sometimes they try to ignore what they know. They have more satisfaction in business where they can travel or do various different things. There is usually someone younger for whom they must make sacrifices, often one of their children. With three nines in their Life Path, their later life can be disappointing, *unless* they have developed their spiritual side, which will give them peace and solace and wisdom. These people are here to try many "things" on for size and then to settle on the truth. They are very creative. Some of them discover a divine mission and follow a lofty path where their innate creativity serves a higher purpose and they find peace and contentment.

Two of Diamonds: The Wheeler Dealer Card

Birthdays: January 25, Capricorn; February 23, Pisces; March 21, Aries; April 19, Aries; May 17, Taurus; June 15, Gemini; July 13, Cancer; August 11, Leo; September 9, Virgo; October 7, Libra; November 5, Scorpio; December 3, Sagittarius

The Two of Diamonds has an innate intuition that, if followed, will always lead them to success in all their dealings. Inherent in this intuition is a high set of values and often a "mission" in life, a mission that always involves partners and "others." There is a certain amount of ambition, usually for money, that keeps them motivated. This is good because they can get into ruts at times—especially in their closest relationships. If they tap into their inner guidance, they will find a path awaiting them that is fascinating and rewarding. They do best by establishing themselves in one business and sticking with it. They should be careful that their social obligations do not tax their health and well-being. They usually make large sums of money in real estate in their later years and maintain good health throughout their lives. These people love to mix and mingle and to do "deals" with others. Once they have discovered their special mission, they find more success.

Ace of Diamonds: The Card of Desire for Money and Love

THE DIAMONDS

Birthdays: January 26, Aquarius; February 24, Pisces; March 22, Aries; April 20, Aries/Taurus; May 18, Taurus; June 16, Gemini; July 14, Cancer; August 12, Leo; September 10, Virgo; October 8, Libra; November 6, Scorpio; December 4, Sagittarius

The inherent passion in this card can be expressed in a variety of ways, but it always seems difficult for them to have both money and love at the same time. Perhaps this is because there is not enough energy to acquire as much as they want of both. In any case, we find these people striving to attain one or both most of the time. They are often loners in spite of their desire for love contact. They can be impatient and mercenary, or they can be the greatest givers. These people are creative and capable of working two jobs at once. They meet new people every day, and much of their good fortune comes from these meetings. Romantically, they are often indecisive, or they attract others who have difficulty making decisions. They like to be away from their loved ones for periods of time. All of them are inclined to be psychic. If money or power does not take top priority in their values, they can have lives of great satisfaction and accomplishment.

THE SPADES

King of Spades: The Master Card

Birthday: January 1, Capricorn

The people of this card are masters of anything they decide to do. Unless the men decide to stay as Jacks, they always rise to the top of their chosen profession. The King of Spades is the last, most wise and powerful card in the deck. These people have a high regard for wisdom, a love of learning, and are willing to do whatever it takes to achieve success and recognition. They are capable of managing the largest organizations. They have indecision about love and close relationships, and often, they forego marriage for a single life. They are always enterprising and ambitious, rarely lazy or of a lower persuasion. Even though they don't all reach a high place, all of them have the wisdom and rarely do they sink down to lowly acts. With all their abilities, they are often discontent. This can be channeled as progressiveness or dissatisfaction. When they go within, to the spiritual realms, they are able to penetrate the deepest secrets with ease. These are the masters.

The Queen of Spades: The Card of Self-Mastery

Birthdays: January 2, Capricorn

These people of such power and authority are surprisingly not always found in positions of authority. They can end up in menial positions where they bitterly complain about their position in life and never amount to much else. However, this is the card of self-mastery that sits in the very crowning position in the divine plan. If these people recognize their powerful gifts and take responsibility in their life, they can rise to any heights they desire. Among them, we find some who are the most caustic and hard-driven and others who are the true mothers of the world and compassionately share and teach their wisdom. They should avoid mixing love and money, and there is always trouble when legal matters arise. They love to spend money, and they hate getting the short end in legal affairs, but they usually do. They do best when they realize their place in the royal family and access the inner wisdom that is their birthright. They are exalted in the eyes of God.

Jack of Spades: The Spiritual Initiate or the Thief Card

Birthdays: January 3, Capricorn; February 1, Aquarius

Through an excess of mental power and creativity, the Jack of Spades can either become a visionary or a thief. This card also represents the spiritual initiate. Among these people, we find those who have either or both qualities present. There is no doubt about their creative power, and their ability to do anything with their minds. The question is whether or not they direct this energy with wisdom and patience or whether they are lured by the "easy wins" they can extract out of many situations and move toward the low side of their card. They sit in a powerful place, and this power can either take them to the highest or tempt them to the lowest. These people always do well with the public and can become successful artists or actors. They often inherit money even though they can make enough on their own. They are usually ambitious, and it is their basic value system, usually a result of their childhood, that is most responsible for their direction and success.

Ten of Spades: The Workaholic Card

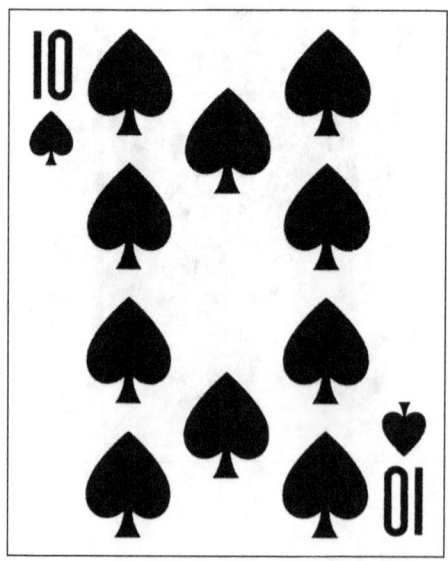

Birthdays: January 4, Capricorn; February 2, Aquarius

Ten of Spades people can be very materialistic and workaholic types, and when they are, their home life always suffers and they suffer with it. Home, family, and personal relationships are very important to them and so is their work. It all depends upon the individual as to what their main focus in life is. There are many spiritual influences present that can make these people the masters of their destiny and lead them to great heights in helping others, but there is also the pull toward material accomplishment that can blind them to their possibilities and limit their growth. As spades, they have the opportunity to transcend the material through spiritual awareness. There can be indecision about love and problems in marriage revolving around a fear of poverty. If they misuse the power given to them, they can cause many difficulties in their personal lives. And yet, these people are capable of great, unattached spiritual love and can have everything they want if they look to their higher sides for direction and guidance.

Nine of Spades: The Universal Giver Card

Birthdays: January 5, Capricorn; February 3, Aquarius; March 1, Pisces

This is the strongest of the universal nines with the strongest call toward letting go and completions in life. Among these people, you will find those whose lives are filled with losses, and others whose lives are filled with giving and fulfillment. These people can never completely ignore their inherent spirituality or psychic side. Those who acknowledge this important part of themselves are guided to a life of universal giving. In this regard, some of them can make the greatest contributions to the world. Many are successful artists, teachers, or performers. The King of Hearts Karma and Venus card gives them strong emotional and love power and wisdom that can bring much success to them as well as guide them through some of the endings they are sure to encounter. Many are artistically talented. The broader the scope of their work and the more they focus on giving to larger groups, the more their inherent power shines and they rise to prominence on their mission of love.

Eight of Spades: The Power through Work Card

Birthdays: January 6, Capricorn; February 4, Aquarius; March 2, Pisces

As the "eight of eights," the power card of power cards, the Eight of Spades has the heaviest burden and obligation to use his or her power for good. Spades take us into the spiritual realms though many spade people cannot unrivet their attention from material gain and mastery. Success is almost easy for them, as long as they are willing to work for it—many of these people are workaholics. They know that they possess great power. The test comes in how they choose to use it. When they work from a lower sense of values, or when operating from their "fear pattern," they can use this power to destroy themselves. They need to be admired and will work hard for it. They make good providers and will often try to marry those of means also. Divorce is often lucrative for them. They can handle obstacles, which often serve as a measure of their true abilities. They have a profound healing power and if directed, can transform the lives of those they come in contact with.

Seven of Spades: The Card of Faith

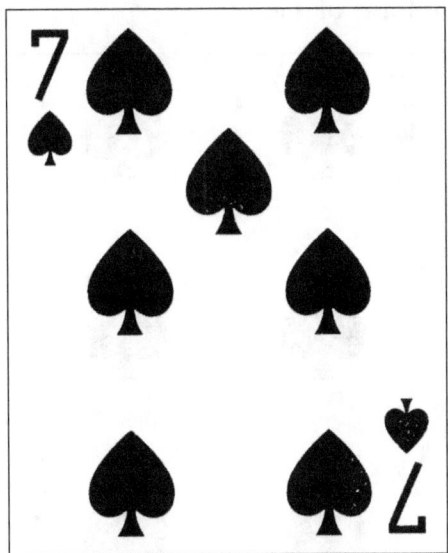

Birthdays: January 7, Capricorn; February 5, Aquarius; March 3, Pisces; April 1, Aries

This card is regarded as one of the most spiritual in the deck, and these people can have great success in their life as long as they do not disregard the wisdom that is intended to guide them through life. These people are here to learn to *trust* and keep going in spite of circumstances. Their main challenges will come in the areas of work and health. The underlying King of Diamonds mandates that they must live the higher values they know if they are to have the blessings and power that is inherently available to them. Being the Seven of Spades puts them on the line. They must think, speak, and act from a higher perspective or suffer innumerable ills. They are protected by a high, spiritual force, but even this is not as powerful as their own actions and attitudes. They must live what they know and follow their intuitive guidance. Many marry into money or receive support from associations. They can always do well if they work hard and maintain honesty. Nothing can stop them but themselves.

Six of Spades: The Card of Fate

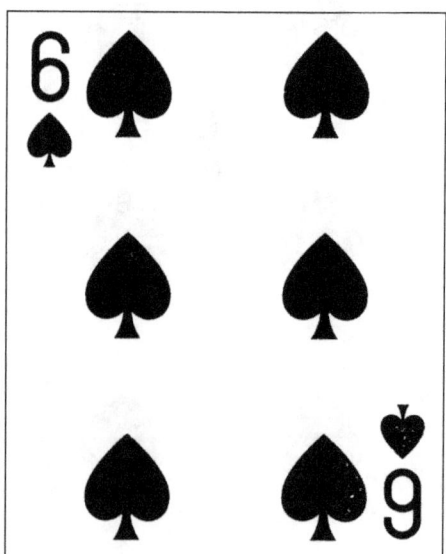

Birthdays: January 8, Capricorn; February 6, Aquarius; March 4, Pisces; April 2, Aries

430

This is a powerful card, and the card of a person who is here to learn the responsibility of such power. These people either align themselves to a higher purpose and vision and achieve great success or have their power turned against them for their own downfall. As a rule, these people are very responsible for their actions but a strong Neptune influence can lead many of them down the road of escapism and time lost in fantasy. They are dreamers to be sure. They must latch on to the highest dream they can and use their power to attain it. Nothing can stop them once this vision is clear. Fulfillment on every level is guaranteed. They must watch a tendency to fall into a comfortable rut. They can also be very stubborn. Through the acquisition of knowledge, they find great fulfillment, life purpose, direction, and many good friends. Some of their greatest challenges come in the area of love and romance. Their own indecision works against them.

Five of Spades: The Card of the Wanderer

Birthdays: January 9, Capricorn; February 7, Aquarius; March 5, Pisces; April 3, Aries; May 1, Taurus

The Five of Spades is the card of changes and travel. These people like to travel and have a certain amount of restlessness and dislike routine. However, their restlessness often applies to their spiritual quest, their striving for truth, and growth of the inner self. With the Jack of Hearts in Mercury, there is a certain amount of sacrifice for loved ones in their lives or for an education, especially in early life. The Ten of Hearts Karma Card gives them much in the way of social success though the Nine of Clubs (Venus Card) speaks of many personal disappointments, especially from friends and loved ones. They may have trouble at work with coworkers and other elements that requires much effort to overcome. They find the most success working with partners and in occupations that allow them to travel and meet new people. One of their challenges is to find success in their business transactions. They don't always make the best deals for themselves. Money often comes in association with love or marriage.

Four of Spades: The Card of Security and Satisfaction

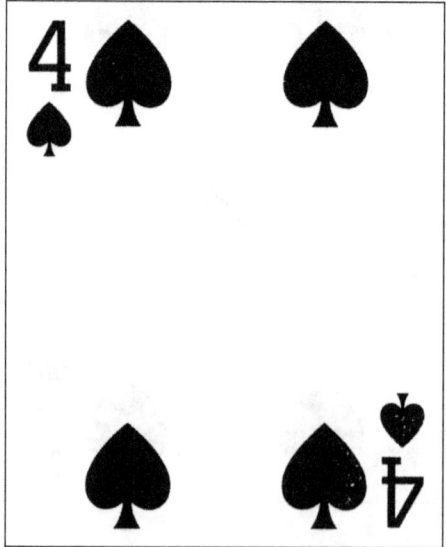

Birthdays: January 10, Capricorn; February 8, Aquarius; March 6, Pisces; April 4, Aries; May 2, Taurus

The Four of Spades is the card of satisfaction and protection through hard work. They have one of the most fortunate life paths in terms of money and success and usually enjoy the work they do. Their Saturn card, the Ace of Diamonds, tells us that even though they are fortunate, they usually worry about money anyway, and this can interfere with their own success if not checked. The Ten of Hearts in Mercury usually gets them instant acceptance at social occasions, and they make good communicators or speakers. Fours can be very stubborn, and the Four of Spades has the right to be, with the Ten of Clubs Karma Card. They know a lot and must live by their truth. The Ten of Diamonds in Venus gives them wealthy friends, but they should not place too much emphasis on money with their choice of friends. They usually have a good constitution, and health is best cared for by natural methods. They are a worker card, and it is in their work that they find true peace and satisfaction. Often, they will align themselves with a humanitarian mission and find great satisfaction there.

Three of Spades: The Artist Card

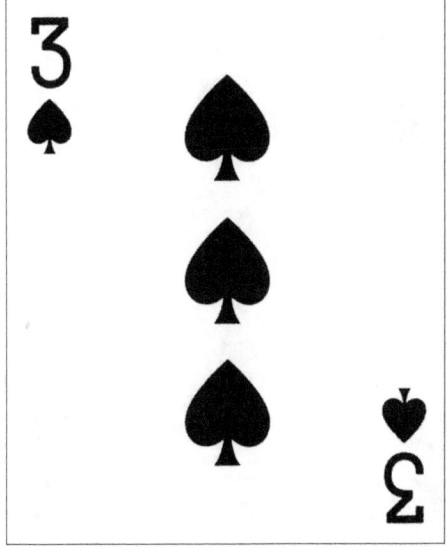

Birthdays: January 11, Capricorn; February 9, Aquarius; March 7, Pisces; April 5, Aries; May 3, Taurus; June 1, Gemini

The Threes of Spades have the opportunity for success in their life if they are willing to work for it. They have a heavier load than most, indicated by their position in the Saturn line. But if they work hard, they will receive the Jupiterian blessings from their column position. The Six of Diamonds Karma Card tells us that there is a karmic debt to pay, and often they are associated with Six of Diamonds persons. The Three in Spades means indecision about work or health, and they should watch their health carefully and stick to sound medical practices and advice. The more they worry about their health, often, the worse their condition gets, so they have a responsibility to watch their thoughts and feelings as they relate to health matters. Having the Queen of Spades with the Ten of Diamonds (underlying influence) in Jupiter gives them the opportunity for great business success through mastery of their values and business lives. However, with the Jack of Clubs in their Saturn position, they will always meet with some disappointment if they stray from honesty. Only the straight path will bring them the success they want.

Two of Spades: The Friendship Card

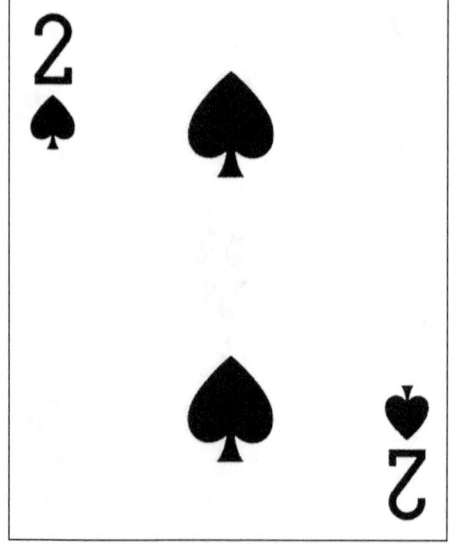

Birthdays: January 12, Capricorn; February 10, Aquarius; March 8, Pisces; April 6, Aries; May 4, Taurus; June 2, Gemini

The Two of Spades is the card of work partnership and friendship. Twos are also fear cards, and it is their own spiritual natures that often scare the Twos of Spades. The displacement and Karma Card, the Six of Spades, speak of karma to be paid in this life time, often in the form of work or health difficulties, while the placement of the Two of Spades in the Natural Spread at the Uranus/Uranus position tells us that they have strong intuitional gifts. The double sixes in the Venus and Mars positions tell us that the Twos of Spades often get into ruts in their family lives and work sphere. When they fight this monotony, there can be frustration. They have strong mental powers and strong intuitive powers, and both of these can make them money. They are very congenial and have success in social situations, but their Three of Hearts Pluto Card speaks of some indecision both romantically and in general that can plague them throughout their life. Overall, they have an easier life path than most and should not let themselves let that ease turn to self-indulgence. Often they marry into money.

Ace of Spades: The Card of Ambition and the Magi Card

Birthdays: January 13, Capricorn; February 11, Aquarius; March 9, Pisces; April 7, Aries; May 5, Taurus; June 3, Gemini; July 1, Cancer

The Ace of Spades is the ancient symbol of the secret mysteries, the most spiritual card in the deck and yet also the most material. These people usually have a lifelong conflict between their material, worldly urges and their deep, past-life spiritual heritage. Their displacement and Karma Card, the Seven of Hearts, suggests trials in the realm of relationships. Their mission is to find the inner peace that comes through a life of service and dedication to higher principles. As their karma from previous births is discharged, they come to realize this and learn to follow the unwritten law of spiritual truth. In many ways, they have put themselves upon the cross. Whenever they deviate from the law or disregard their spiritual nature, they seem to be unjustly punished. Those Aces of Spades who are mostly material-minded seem to have one problem after another. However, whenever they do follow the law, they are protected, finding the inner peace they seek through awareness of their wealth of spirit.

The Fool's Card

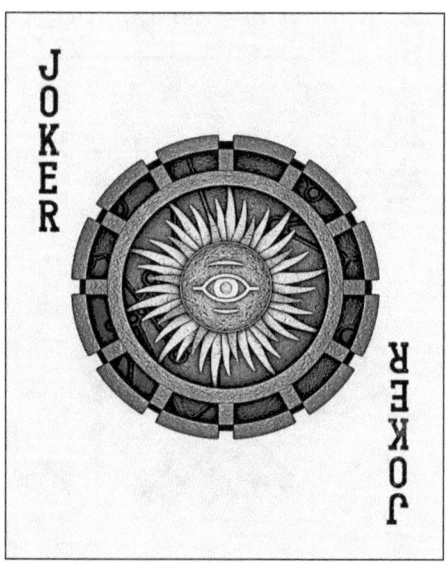

Birthdays: December 31, Capricorn

Little is really known about the Joker. He has no Life Path Cards or Yearly Spreads from which we can make any sort of actions. In truth, the Joker can be any card in the deck that he or she chooses to be. We cannot even make relationship comparisons between the Joker and other cards since it holds no place in any of the spreads that define the Life Paths of the others in the deck. The Joker is no card, and yet it is all the cards in the deck at the same time. The Jokers can assume the personality of any card in the deck at will, and yet they have no personality that is truly their own. Thus, they fall into a unique category in our system of card understanding that separates them from every other card in the deck. Whether this special place is a blessing or a curse is highly dependent upon the individual who possesses this Birth Card. As in the case of the other cards, the very trait we are discussing is either used or abused by the individual, and the choices that the individual makes are what determine the nature of their lives.

The Joker was the court jester in days of old who ascended the throne on "Fool's Day" each year and impersonated the king and all members of the kingdom. His day, December 31, is the time of celebration of the New Year and in ancient times the day to make merry and folly of our serious natures. The Joker would make fun of everyone in the kingdom and in doing so, show them how them how to lighten up a little. He could impersonate anyone with ease. This is still part of the Joker's personality, the ability to take on any role at will. Since we don't know which card Jokers are being, it is difficult to make any definite statements about them.

Jokers might be considered the "Jacks of all Jacks." This would tend to make them very creative, youthful acting, and extremely independent. The Joker is part of the royal family, and so we find that they are proud and not too fond of being told what to do, as is the case with most Jacks, Queens, and Kings. Because of the strong creative urges in the Joker, we find many are attracted to stage or theater. This same creative energy can show up as a dishonest streak in some of them as well. Many are successful musicians or artists. Whatever type of profession they choose, they are independent and must maintain a certain amount of freedom if they are to be happy and satisfied.

They have the potential to be deeply spiritual, being the card that is often associated with God in the Tarot decks (the Fool Card, number Zero). Beyond this, there is little known about them. As Florence Campbell puts it, "They are a mystery unto themselves."